BEAR HEAD

ADRIAN TCHAIKOVSKY was born in Lincolnshire before heading off to Reading to study psychology and zoology. He subsequently ended up in law and has worked as a legal executive in both Reading and Leeds, where he now lives. Married, he is a keen live role-player and occasional amateur actor and has trained in stage-fighting. He's the author of the critically acclaimed Shadows of the Apt series and his novel *Children of Time* was the winner of the 30th Anniversary Arthur C. Clarke Award.

ALSO BY ADRIAN TCHAIKOVSKY

SHADOWS OF THE APT
Empire in Black and Gold
Dragonfly Falling
Blood of the Mantis
Salute the Dark
The Scarab Path
The Sea Watch
Heirs of the Blade
The Air War
War Master's Gate
Seal of the Worm

TALES OF THE APT
Spoils of War
A Time for Grief
For Love of Distant Shores
The Scent of Tears (with Frances Hardinge et al.)

ECHOES OF THE FALL
The Tiger and the Wolf
The Bear and the Serpent
The Hyena and the Hawk

CHILDREN OF TIME
Children of Time
Children of Ruin

Guns of the Dawn
Spiderlight
Ironclads
Cage of Souls
Firewalkers
The Doors of Eden
Feast and Famine (collection)
Dogs of War

ADRIAN TCHAIKOVSKY

ARTHUR C. CLARKE AWARD WINNER

BEAR HEAD

HEAD OF ZEUS

An Ad Astra Book

First published in the UK in 2021 by Head of Zeus Ltd
An Ad Astra Book

9 7 5 3 1 2 4 6 8

A catalogue record for this book is available from
the British Library.

ISBN (HB): 9781800241541
ISBN (XTPB): 9781800241558
ISBN (E): 9781800241572

Typeset by Divaddict Publishing Solutions Ltd.

Printed and bound in Great Britain by
CPI Group (UK) Ltd, Croydon CRO 4YY

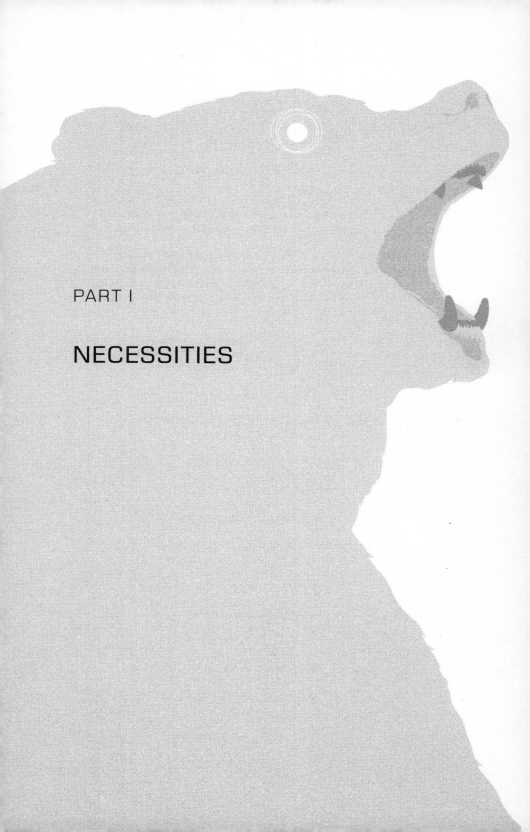

PART I

NECESSITIES

JIMMY

We're off to the perimeter, heading uphill on our little Loonie towards where a canopy tether should have been but – Damage Central tells us – isn't. Three of us crammed into the front, and a big old crate of technical magic in the back because it's not obvious what the problem is, and cheaper to send us out with a grab-bag of stuff than muck about with multiple trips. Better to have and not need et cetera.

You'd not tell us apart in the suits. They're standard issue, one size fits all, which the boffins back home accomplished by the scientific expedient of telling the recruiters not to hire shortasses or beanpoles. I reckon there isn't more than twenty centimetres between the tallest of all the Hell City construction crew and the shortest, which is me. Us human crew, anyway. Bioforms get their own suits. They're worth more than us, and work harder.

I might as well admit that a lot of people work harder than me. I'm not what you might call employee of the month at Hell City, not of any month. I mean Mars has two moons and one of them completes an orbit in less than eight hours. That's a whole lot of months and your man Jimmy Marten hasn't been top employee for any of them, take it from me.

Going out to fix the canopy's a crap job by most people's standards. That means Admin's well aware of my lack of attendance and dedication trophies, and my fellow in-the-shitters Brian and Indra are similarly lowly. Indra spends all her scrip on imported dramas, pays for every damn network and channel they send over to us, so she's always desperate for the teeny tiny bonus you get for suit-work. Brian's just weird and nobody much likes him. He's one of those guys who always looks like they're working twice as hard as anyone else and then you check their work and they've left half the dust covers off and haven't turned on the electronic security.

The Loonie bumbles on, puffy tyres eating as much of the jolt and bounce of the rocky Martian surface as they can. And we're days out from home, by now. And they could have goddamn flown us out only some bean counter reckons it's more economic, and flying in the thin Mars air, in engine-choking dust, is always a bit of a dicey prospect, even here under the canopy.

Ahead of us, half-lost in the swirling dust and the canopy's glaze, the edge of Hellas Planitia rises like it's the wall of the world, cutting short even the foreshortened horizon Mars is supposed to have. Big old meteor, basically, crater the size of a subcontinent. Perfect place to live, if you actually want to live on Mars. I guess at some point I had actually wanted to live on Mars, because here I am on Mars, if you can call it living. The money was supposed to be good, and how else was a working Joe like me supposed to get off-planet exactly? Jimmy Marten, construction worker with half-assed delusions of being an engineer. I just about scraped the Tech Competence, and that was apparently enough to go to Mars.

I remember the videos. They had some guys, not even in suits, watching robots and bees and Bioforms doing the work, like we were lord and master of all we'd survey. And Mars has a short horizon and big mountains. You can survey a lot of the planet at once from a good vantage. Except we're down in a hole, and even a hole two thousand klicks across is still a hole. And they stick a roof on it, so we can survey even less and we aren't even masters of that.

I wondered more than once if they hadn't shown the free Bioforms a very different video about who got to boss about whom and, if so, they got the truer one.

Well, OK, not a roof. A canopy, like a great big top for the solar system's most shambolic circus, Yours Truly chief clown. And we three are being sent to sweep up the spotlight at the edge of the ring yet again. When we first arrived it was smaller – the canopy, not the crater, which has, believe it or not, been pretty much the same size for the history of the human race – but getting the whole damn thing covered was priority one, and a feat of engineering they didn't trust schmucks like your man Jimmy with. That was hive-work. Odd how sometimes to make a big thing you got to work real small.

Now this isn't like Space City from those old sciency-fiction books, with a big glass dome over all those fairy-tale towers. It isn't airtight, because even for people who planned to put a silk canopy over a subcontinent-sized crater, that would be crazy, right? And while we're generating atmosphere underneath, we do actually want it to get out, little by little, just slow enough that we get to keep enough of it around at any one time. Math. There's a lot of math that your man here doesn't need to know. Brian, now, he knows the math. He can talk algebra like he majored in conversational equations. And then he leaves the dust covers off and we all get docked pay.

The canopy has like a million tethers all around the outside of it. As the Loonie – the balloon-wheeled truck we've got – labours uphill, we can see exactly the problem, because there's one direction that has a crapton more dust coming in than the rest, which is going to make the work even more fun. Brian's trying to hail the hive that should have been minding shop there, but gets nada. When we arrive, the tether's snapped and the rent in the canopy above us must be a full klick long. There's a big old dust storm going on up above past the distant lip of the Hellas crater, and plenty of it's funnelling down through the rent and sweeping around us, cutting visibility to crap and getting absolutely everywhere. I can already feel it caking my suit, one extra serving of misery to go with the cold leaching into your arms and legs and the cumbersome inflation that keeps your body rigid and means you can't draw your arms in or kneel down properly.

"Well this is beyond our pay grade and no mistake," Indra's crisp voice says over the radio. "'Less you want to go jump up and catch it." She's pointing at the broken tether, or where it probably would be if any of us care to faff about with visor magnification until we can see it. Flapping away in the Martian wind way above our heads, and the gravity isn't *that* low that I can just Superman up there with a single bound and bring it down.

"Not the problem," Brian tells us in his flat, nasal voice. "Hive's gone dead."

More good news. We go on a bit, further uphill and well into the shadow of the Hellas wall. The near end of the broke tether is in the wind and whipping about like a mad snake. Indra has to send out a crawler to the anchor point where it can latch onto the cable and reel it in so it's safe to approach, meaning two hours of waiting and watching the meters and readouts of our suits because we're on the clock and we'll get docked for unnecessary use of resources if we give Admin the least excuse. Let me tell you, they're goddamn going to make the Hell City project come in under its gut-wrenchingly enormous budget, and stiffing us working schmoes is the easiest way. What are we going to do, down tools and walk off site?

Indra drains suit power by watching three episodes of some Venezuelan soap I never heard of, and Brian just goes off into his head – see his lips moving through his visor but nothing over the radio. Yours Truly starts to feel the first plucking pangs, a little trembling, a little hunger, dry eyes, dry mouth. Which is bad news because it's a long way back to camp, even longer to Hell City, and you'd be amazed how few wandering dealers you run into just out in the Martian wilds.

I have one hit of Stringer on me, which I'm absolutely saving for tonight at the very earliest. And by the time the crawler starts getting the cable in, I'd have popped that pill right there and then if it hadn't been in the suit, and if the outside temperature and pressure and general living conditions hadn't been a bit too Martian for me to just open up and go rummaging in my pockets.

Then we're making our approach, following the flailing end of the cable as it's hauled back in. The anchor point itself isn't all that – the cable is engineered spiderweb stuff, ridiculously strong and light, and the serious business of it is all underground. I sunk some of those pilings, I know of what I speak. Our real problem is the slotted box next to it, surrounded by a field of solar cells angled away from the wall to catch the sun and now completely coated in dust.

"Dead," Brian says and makes a show of kicking the slabcrete box. "Maybe power failure."

"Maybe doesn't get us our bonus," Indra points out, and so it's for Brian to run the diagnostics while Indra and me get to clean off the panels so he'll have power. This takes more time, each second of which feels like grit under my eyelids – something you get very familiar with on Mars.

"Well?" we ask him, after even that tedious job's used up its necessary allocation of time.

"Dead," is all he has to say. "Lost power then froze, or froze then lost power."

"Jesus, you are a useless son of a bitch," I tell him.

"You want to Jesus these bees back to life so we can get out of here?" Indra puts in. She's gone to the Loonie's cargo space and hauled the starter hive out. It'll take about twenty days to bootstrap itself to the point where it can function, and some poor schmuck'll have to come out and check up on it. Probably us, I reckon, although with what happens soon after, a little suit-work might have been a goddamn blessing.

So these hives, these are not independent Beeshives, what with how all that had gone, and how things back home were going. Hell City is a determined no-go zone for Distributed Intelligence. So our bees are dumb, but they'll wake up and draw power and build more bees and, eventually, spin a new tether and mend the tear in the canopy. Until then, this corner of the dome will be dustier and colder and shorter on atmosphere than the rest, a constant slow leak for the whole project. One more problem, basically, but we've done what we can, which means it isn't our problem any more. We get to pass it up for Admin to worry about. After all, one little tear, or fifty little tears even, it isn't going to stop work on Hell City. They've built in plenty of redundancy, because they know everything screws up some time. That was why they wanted us and not just robots. We're the duct tape of the whole project, we humans, we Bioforms. We're the thing that could fix anything, if you apply enough of us to it.

"Hive's set," Brian reports. "Green lights 'cross the board."

"Like hell." I check over his work, and Indra too, but beeshive architecture is the one thing Brian does actually do a full-assed job on and it looks like everything's up and running. We put a call into Admin and say what we've done, tell them to send a team to check up in twenty days.

Nothing for it but the long ramble back to camp, and then the next camp, and the next, and eventually Hell City itself and home, and a chance to score something before I go completely out of my mind. I'm going to be miserable company for the others, but nothing to be done about that. I'll just keep it to myself, and it isn't as if either of the others are scintillating socialites.

On the way back, though, Indra does want to talk. "So, it die, or was it killed?"

"Say what?" I snap, mostly because I'd been thinking the same.

"Die," Brian says.

"Or was it?" Indra presses, sounding like she's enjoying herself. "Fucker's out there, we all know that."

"Nope," Brian says.

"First Mars mission, they got sent up here, we all know that."

"Nope."

"And they never left. They just kept building. They built that science place, up near the pole. They built Namseng base, where they don't have to do this shit with canopies because they live underground like civilised people. Even picked the site for Hell City. You think they just went away? They are *among* us, man! How'd you even know which bees are ours and which are... Bees?"

"Nope," Brian says, exactly the same inflection or lack of it. Then: "Nothing doing. Bees is dead. Or Bees doing Bees things. Think we gon' matter to them?"

"They want Mars for themselves!" Indra says, most definitely trying to put the wind up us. "I hear they've got bugs that can tunnel into your head now, take over your brain."

"Jesus, give it a rest, will you?" I shout at her, which comes right out of my Jonesing, but to her must have come out of nowhere. It kills the conversation anyway, which is something. I don't want to think about the Bees intelligence. First resident of Mars, like she said, and for a long time it was our pet Martian, laying the groundwork for all the human footfall the planet's seeing right now. Except Bees and people stopped seeing eye to eye, and there's a whole raft of politicos back home talking it up like it's the Antichrist. Except I don't believe in the Antichrist but I sure as hell believe that Bees is out there on Mars. And I think we do matter to them, whatever Brian says. We made Bees, and the monster always comes back for its creator some day.

I pop my last tab that night, which at least means I sleep well. Don't let anyone tell you that you can't buy wellbeing and a contented soul, just remember that the first one might have been cheap but the price goes up steeply after that.

The next day we get the warning light on all our displays.

Now there are lights you really don't want to see. There are lights that tell you you're going to die, and some of us had died, mostly in the early days when there wasn't so much canopy. Right now we've been out here seven (Earth) years, automated foundations building themselves for nine years before that, and we've got Hellas Planitia mostly tamed. People still die, but mostly from stupidity rather than Mars. So now *this* has become the light we really don't want to see, and this light is *Conserve Resources*. An insistent little blip in the top right corner of your visor, flashing blue because they still reserve the red lights for the kill-you sort of stuff. *Conserve Resources*. Meaning air in the tanks. Meaning wear and tear on the suits. Meaning the mod cons of carrying a little of Earth around between you and Mars.

"Ah, crap," Indra says, and takes her helmet off. I do the same, and we go through the slow motion clumsy-dance that's shrugging your suit off and getting down to your skivvies, out there in the cold thin air of Mars. We've got clothes in the back: thermal undies, overalls, boots. Hard hats even, although the only thing likely to drop on our heads is a meteor and I don't reckon they're rated for that. I take a deep breath. The suits carry a real watered-down air mix, 10 per cent O_2. Under the canopy at the distance we are from home, it's down to about 6 or 7 per cent. Deep breaths.

My vision goes misty for a moment as my second set of eyelids close up against the thin air. My mouth's full of grit the moment I inhale, and will be until we get to the next camp and under pressurised canvas. Indra's sour expression shows she's just as delighted with it all as I am.

"Brian," I subvocalise into my throat mic, because the thin air won't carry a voice. "Lid off, Brian."

"Nope." Brian's still suited up. "Nothing doing."

"They'll dock you," Indra points out.

"Let 'em. Fuck 'em." And Brian never seems to have anything to spend his scrip on anyway, so if he wants to ride home in 10 per cent oxygen comfort and have it garnished from his pay check, that's his look out.

Deep breaths of thin, thin air with way too little oxygen and a pressure, so says the Loonie's instruments, of forty-eight millibars. That's two-thirds of what you'd need to not kill you, if you were straight up Johnny Earth-man. That's like 5 per cent of sea-level Earth pressure, or 15 per cent of what you'd find on top of Everest. So you'd think, not so much, right? Bit on the thin side even with all the deep breaths in the world?

On the other hand, it's eight times surface Mars pressure; it's four times the natural pressure of the Hellas Planitia basin, which is seven klicks down and has an atmosphere that's practically thick soup by Martian standards. Which head start on the whole business is why we're building a city here, of course.

We're within the scurf field here, though it's patchy like the planet's going bald. It's technically green, though with so many photosynthetic layers, and what with the sun so far out, it looks more black to the human eye. Not really grass, not moss, not any damn thing you get on Earth. Bioengineered to break up Mars into something like soil, and into something like atmosphere, and much of what it poops out is pure oxygen. They seeded the first scurf before we ever came. Bees did it, part of all that service-to-humanity stuff before things went sour. Bees seeded the Planitia with scurf, and by the time they came along to install the canopy the atmosphere was already on the turn.

I'm going to digress but – damn me, I hadn't believed any of it. I mean I actually got on the goddamn rocket, crammed in with all the others, half a year in space to look forward to, and when we touched down and saw stuff growing on Mars, and took our readings, I realised I hadn't ever really believed it. Lucky for me things like that work whether or not you believe in them or we'd all have been very sad and then very dead in that order.

The scurf generates heat, too. I mean, not so much, but the canopy coating traps the feeble sunlight as well. Right then, as we're riding the Loonie for home, it's a balmy minus eleven centigrade on our bare faces. I mean, you don't know fucking luxury until you've ditched your suit for a joyride across Mars: minus eleven, 6 per cent O_2 and almost fifty millibars pressure. Brian's still behind his visor but Indra and I look at each other and share a moment, and then she sneezes a jet of dust from both nostrils, all the shit she's been breathing in that her internal filters have trapped before it can get into her lungs. What a time to be alive!

You're giving me the side-eye right about now, probably. Whither, you're saying, the traditional joys of asphyxiation? Whither explosive decompression of the precious bodily fluids at anywhere under sixty millibars? Whither freezing to death; good enough for our ancestors so why can't you modern kids just do what you're supposed to and die horribly on the surface of Mars? And we are modern kids, Brian and

Indra and me. We are the generation your parents warned you about. Because I've drawn these grand distinctions between 'human' and 'Bioform' but we're all Bioforms here. We just happen to be Bioforms engineered out of human stock, rather than the dogs and lizards and badgers who get to do the skilled work. And the bears, always the fucking bears.

Hell City ain't never going to be one of those glass-dome-and-fairy-towers places from the old mags. It ain't even going to be Hell City when they actually get the first batch of citizens in. There are committees working up real nice names for it, all sorts of Paradise this and Eden that. Being in Hellas Planitia meant it was only ever going to be Hell City for us, though. When we arrived the previous crew – meaning Bees – had laid the foundations and built some bunkers we could hole up in, and the scurf was already spreading out and doing its biochemical work with the Martian substrate. For the first year it was suit-work or stay under cover, and half of us had to stay on the ship almost all the time. After that, a hundred million dumb spider-bees had spun enough canopy, and the scurf had brewed up a dense enough atmosphere, plus we'd built enough spare living space. Mostly what's now the Admin block, admittedly, to which we humble working Joes don't get access that often, on account of how we don't rate the good air.

There's going to be space for a hundred thousand people in the first living stage of the city. Right now there are fifteen hundred of us, meaning about thirty semi-modded Admin staff, about a thousand at my pay grade and the rest Bioforms. A whole slice of those latter two pies are out hard at work as the Loonie takes us back home. We've been

14

seeing the dust of the works since we set off. Travelling over the scurf doesn't kick up a trail, but when you're excavating and shifting stuff about, wow, let me tell you, low grav and insanely fine particulates really have a thing going between them. A third of the work crew will be clearing the machinery of dust, replacing seals and parts, taking deep breaths and then sneezing dust out their noses every half minute or so. We get our biomods from all sorts, but that particular charming habit comes from some swimming lizard thing. It does it with salt, just snots it all out on whatever crappy little rock of an island it ekes out a living. We do it with the dust, because every damn breath is 10 per cent sand here on Mars.

From the Loonie we get to watch like lordly aristos as everyone else does the hard slog. They've got Team Weasel running the excavations, setting up the underground chambers, going into the new-carved ducts and holes after the drills to fix up all the connections. Your new Martian colonist isn't going to want for water and power and cable TV on our watch. Team Weasel're a mix of their namesake with badger and other relatives, short-limbed, designed to dig. Their fur is puffed out to keep them warm, and they push out of the earth covered in red-pink grit that they shake off in great clouds that float away towards the distant, half-visible sheen that's the canopy. They got worked hardest at the start, when everything we built was underground. Right now at least half the work's on the surface, though. Martian colonists don't want to live their whole lives like moles, for all the Martian sky's rubbish and the Martian sunlight's pretty goddamn thin. But everyone gets a room up top with a view, basically, as well as the rooms down below where frankly they'll still spend most of their time.

What we're driving past is that surface-level stuff. We see the odd Weasel popping a head out of the dirt, but where there's heavy lifting to be done – relative here, low grav after all – that's not worth getting the machines in, there are a handful of bears and the bigger dogs to do it. These are the free bears, the ones who got modded and came over like we did, new life in the construction industry, must be willing to travel. The other bears, the Bad News Bears, tend to stay inside the bits of the city we've already built.

In between the dig crew and the heavy crew there's us, of course. The Bioforms call us Vanillas when they think we're not listening, though we are pretty damn far from baseline humanity. As evidenced by the fact we're not all dead just by being outside.

As we cruise grandly through the dig site, kicking up our own dust and making everyone's life that little bit worse, we get connected back to the Cloud. I access it and see the little ticker that shows 17 per cent of my headware is currently out on loan to the City, and the teeny tiny buck I'm making from that loan. Indra's headware is full of terrible soap operas, and that's her call, but I prefer to prostitute mine, and the City dips into my head for storage and processing power, same as most everyone else's. They were going to have a big central computer, back in the first plan for the place. Probably it'd have a nice human name and tell you that it was sorry it couldn't do that, in a pleasant human voice. Then the DistAI panic kicked in and everyone was worried about *Something* getting in and taking over, so we got the Cloud. The Cloud is everyone putting their heads together. Even lowly Yours Truly has a big old dataspace in his headware, and it's up for rent whenever the City needs to do some hard sums, which is most of the time. And sometimes I sell my head to other quarters, but the less said about that the better. Data smuggling can get your pay suspended, everyone knows. Electronic security is everybody's concern, that's what it says on the e-billboards. So obviously a working Joe like Jimmy Marten ain't going to be carrying illegal data in his head for no criminal fixer behind the back of Admin, no sirree.

Hell City is built into and from Mars. We take Mars and turn it into a cement analogue and do what on a traditional building site you'd call shuttering. You make a big box, the inside of which is the shape of the wall or whatever you want to build, then you fill the box with Mars and let it set, and hey presto, there's the next bit of Hell City. Early on I did a lot of that, back when I actually cared. I did a good job and I liked it. Then I got bored and stopped doing so good a job. Now I get the crap jobs because, like plenty others, I just stopped giving a shit. Because there is not much to do on Mars. You can watch all the movies and play all the games and talk politics and sports with whoever'll listen, but eventually your social motor runs down and every damn film looks like the last one and you owe everyone so nobody'll play. And then you find that, because humans are humans, there's a whole extra layer of Things To Do On Mars if you're up for a little extra-legal shenanigans. Because it's hard to get super excited about building the thousandth identical condo for some future Mars colonist who'll neither know nor care about you. Who won't even look like you. They'll look human.

The part of the city done enough to live in is all underground, and though it's not hermetically sealed, the city's machinery generates a denser atmosphere than the fields outside and screens out more dust. We come in and take deep breaths, feeling the oxygen debt of the last day starting to get paid off. They made us so we could go work out in the open, but not stay out there forever.

Our welcome party is Dina. Dina's seven feet tall but she got bred to look like she's laughing all the time, got these floppy ears, got these adorable, scratchable jowls. She lopes over like she wants you to throw a stick. Under no circumstances throw a stick for Dina, because she will tell you to go pick up your own damn stick and dispose of it in the receptacle provided. No littering on Dina's watch. Not unfriendly, you get me, but damn she's a stickler for rules. You get it with a lot of the dog-forms. They like to know where they fit, and they're all happy-yappy with the people above them, and if you're below them they make damn sure you stay in line. Dina gives suited Brian a mournful sad-eye look, big burlesque of a downturned mouth, bitterly disappointed dog-face. *Bad human* is written all over that mutt's mug, but she doesn't say it because that's not her job. She checks in the Loonie and our kit, and Brian finally deigns to disrobe. For a moment he's standing there in his small clothes staring up at Dina, and I wonder if he's just going to walk off in his underoos as a protest, but then he togs up in the green and white overalls we all wear. Three good little employees. Dina nods approvingly like she's our mom sending us off to school. Three good little humans, and though you can tell from ear shape and nose shape and so on that Indra's people came from *here* and mine from *here* and Brian's from *over there*, Mars is a great leveller. Or Martian adaptation engineering is. We all have a skin tone of lead and antimony, grey-white like we're our own corpses, because that's where our systems dump the excess Martian toxins, and because it's rad shielding of a sort, not that radiation poisoning's your worst problem around here.

They'll change us back, un-mod us after we're done, they say. They'll at least do us so we look like regular humans, so we don't stand out among those bright new colonists. They say.

We go our separate ways. Indra and Dina are off to watch some new soap that's come in on the latest transmission dump; Brian is off to do incomprehensible Brian things I don't really give a shit about. I am, I decide, off to replenish my personal stash of Stringer because of all the damn things in the solar system, I need stringing along or the boredom and the misery is going to make me top myself.

Payday came and went while we were out on the range, and I am already figuring out just how much of my scrip I can spare for illicit recreation when I check my balances and the bottom falls out of my world.

I'm flat broke. Pay day came and went and didn't leave a forwarding address. Where's my goddamn *money*?

2

SPRINGER

Warner S. Thompson was in full flow, speaking to telegenic Jenny Gale of Fortress America. Carole Springer sat in the production control room and watched the different camera angles. The man's blunt, brutal features: a fist of a chin, heavy brows, a wave of dark hair that looked weirdly plasticky where studio lights hit the gel. Not a good-looking man, Thompson. That wasn't where the magic was.

There were two other guests, both vetted by Thompson's campaign team. One had a multimedia package out on the dangers of DisInt and was only too happy to have a World Senate hopeful give him the nod. The other was some political thinktank type, there to be the intellectual punching bag, to say things like, "But is it really so...?" and "Don't you think that...?" so Thompson could double down on his rhetorical territory, repeat his points. Thump the tub and beat the drum.

Camera three had a good shot of Thompson's craggy profile, eyes squeezed almost shut as he jabbed an aggressive finger at the stooge. "You think that you're safe when? We've heard how deep this 'HumOS' has. Who knows who's?" Jab, jab, jab. Incomplete sentences but one shunted into the next so you never quite noticed. So the viewers at home would just fill in the gaps with their own fears. Leaning forward in his seat, face getting redder, narrowing eyes somehow giving the impression of a hawk zeroing in on its prey rather than a man looking inwards at his own reflection.

Another "Isn't this sort of thing going to spread panic?" from the stooge and Thompson favoured the author with a 'Will you listen to this guy?' look, his instant-complicity-just-add-nodding special that immediately got the approbation it sought. He had that knack, that if you weren't on the end of that jabbing finger you'd fall into step behind him, nod and smile and applaud. Because the presence of Warner Thompson was bigger even than the tall, angular hulk that was Warner Thompson, and he wielded it like a bludgeon. You'd do a lot not to get on the wrong end of it.

"Aren't people right to panic when they?" he asked, and now he'd found a camera to look at, a direct appeal to the audience, that beaming smile that said *I'm the reasonable one here. I'm looking out for you.* "Who knows who's just some sort of? I know some senators, some judges. You got to wonder if. I mean, even *you* could." And suddenly his attention was back on the stooge again, as languorously deadly as if Caligula picked you out at a party.

"Jesus," said Patrick Grubb under his breath, standing at Carole's elbow. He was a short, unkempt man, unshaven and looking like he'd been left out on a window ledge in the sun for too long. He was Thompson's current campaign manager, which mostly meant soliciting donations. Thompson was very keen about donations. Now Grubb mopped at the back of his neck with a handkerchief and grimaced.

"He can't say that. Some nut-job's gonna shoot the poor bastard. He can't just go about suggesting someone's part of HumOS or something." He glowered at Carole, put a hand on her sleeve. "Tell him, when he comes off. Tell him he can't."

"That's campaign management's job," she said and stared at the hand, willing him to remove it. Grubb leant in, though, the sour smell of him, the jowls of him, all abruptly unbearably close. She felt the tremble start up inside her, that she could never show. *Get off me get off me get off.*

"You got to tell him," he insisted in a whisper, as some of the studio people sent them warning glances. "He doesn't listen to me."

Carole Springer was thirty-one, immaculate, blond hair tied into a severe bun, make-up a perfect mask against the world despite the close atmosphere of the control room that had dark patches spreading like flood zones under Grubb's armpits. Her powder-blue skirt suit, Thompson's current favourite colour, was tailored for that fine line between emphasising and concealing her figure. She didn't want Grubb's hand on it. She didn't want Grubb leaning in to her like he was doing, pawing at the fabric and the flesh beneath. *Get off me get off me get off.* "I'm just his PA, Patrick," she heard herself say.

"No, no, he'll take it from you," Grubb whined. "He can't go making people targets."

Carole finally forced herself to look at him, bloodshot sunken eyes, broken veins across his nose, a man like his own washed-up corpse. She kept her face perfectly still, nothing of her inner world making it out onto the surface, as though her emotions were a colony of troglodytes shunning the light.

"He won't take 'can't' from anyone," she said.

Abruptly his hand on her arm was a tight grip. "Listen, Missy," he started, and then there was a low growl from behind them, the third member of Thompson's executive team weighing in. Boyo wasn't fooled by Carole's face or ramrod straight posture, wasn't deceived when she didn't lean away from Grubb or try to free her arm. He could tell instantly how she felt. Boyo liked her, though. The two of them had been fixtures of Thompson's team for years. Grubb was a newer addition, the latest hopeful to try and hitch his political wagon to the man's rising star. He wouldn't last long, she knew. He'd overstep the mark, try to pull in his own direction. He had an agenda like they all did: another chancer with an ideology and products to sell. And some day soon Pat Grubb would deviate from Thompson's trajectory by just a few degrees, would take for himself something in his master's eye, and then it would be time for a new campaign manager.

That growl from Boyo, as low and quiet as could be, stilled the talk of everyone in the room. The studio people didn't look. Boyo made them nervous, but then the big dog-model Bioforms were supposed to make you nervous. They were still mostly military or private security by trade. A man like Thompson walking around with Boyo loping at his side, the very sight was supposed to deter people. Not just madmen with axes or pistols, either. Deter people who might try and confront him, to argue with him when he didn't want it; deter people who might throw something embarrassing or shout a slogan. Warner S. Thompson liked to control when and how he debated. He liked his home crowd advantage.

Grubb removed his hand and put some welcome distance between them. They went back to watching Thompson. The debate had moved on to the next talking point. The stooge was ashen, no longer taking much of a part.

"Jesus," Grubb said again. "He can't." But 'Can't' was a word a lot of people used about Thompson, currently frontrunner for the Alabama-Virginia World Senate seat. Can't, and yet he always did, and then apparently it turned out he could all along. You couldn't argue with him, because he never put himself where someone could score a point; never quite built a complete windmill you could tilt at. He suggested, he denied, he made outrageous statements that contained so many layers of nested fabrications that you couldn't ever unpick them all; you ended up tacitly accepting three-quarters of the lies he told in your quest to undo the other 25 per cent. And then the dust settled and everyone loved what he had to say, even though he hadn't quite said it.

They were on to Collaring now, Grubb's personal favourite topic, and Thompson had switched modes from the hard aggressor to the reasonable 'everyone knows that' man. "Sure maybe they needed the help back then, but. Hard for a man to feel safe when. I know a lot of Bioforms who really. We feel safer, *they* feel safer. Knowing that they won't." And that 'won't' went nowhere, but in the minds of those at home it went to all manner of fears and worries about what a Bioform – a ton of angry bear, half a ton of ravaging werewolf-lookalike, a monstrous reptile, an angry swarm of bees – what they might do if they got mad enough. Because the people at home, the people who tuned into Fortress America to find out what was threatening their liberty today, they were angry, bitter and scared, but they were only human. What if the Bioforms were just as angry, bitter and scared? When John Smith got drunk and mad and slapped his wife or punched some stranger in a bar, well, soonest mended. When Rover the Bioform got mad, that could mean a trail of torn-open corpses. Sometimes, hidden deep within the trap of 'They're not like us' was the terror of 'What if they're just like us, but stronger?' Sometimes the fear came because you were scared of looking into the eye of the monster and seeing your own reflection.

"Why I've got my own dog, who." Thompson was saying, all wry raconteur now, smile gone into that satisfied expression that was his other stock in trade. "Nobody had a more. Boyo loves to know that he's. Loves the Collar, wouldn't be without. Safer for him, for everyone, prevents any." Any rampages. Just killing people in the street like an animal. Carole looked back at Boyo, whose eyes were fixed on the screens, watching his master's face. Boyo was black, brown about the underside of his muzzle, pointed ears, pointed snout, not as big as a lot of bodyguard dog-forms but fast and intelligent. And quite, quite capable of going on a rampage, but only if Thompson told him to. She wondered what he thought, hearing his master talking about him. She could read love in his doggy eyes, and probably it was love, servant for master. The Collar helped with that, but then Boyo had agreed to it. Right now it was only voluntary, although that was high on the list of laws that Thompson was promising to change. The fight for the right of Bioforms to own their own minds had been ongoing ever since the first dog had padded off the production line. Right now, thirty years after the big emancipation laws that had come in the wake of Rex and the Morrow revelations, the pendulum was on its way back and Thompson was riding it.

"Not saying the Emancipation Acts were a mistake but." Thompson was saying. "When you can't feel safe in. People are telling me it's. Due a change, don't you? The American citizen can't be expected to." Conversational fog to hide the forging of chains. And yet when Thompson lifted his head and smiled just so, mouth tight, eyes almost shut as though blinded by staring into his own genius, something in that impenetrable self-confidence communicated itself to the viewer, to the listener. *I'm right*, it told them. *I'm right, not just in this but in my very being.* So that people followed him, lifted him up, put him on a pedestal. Not like a man, a human leader who might be weighed and judged and required to do concrete things, but like the icon of a god, placed above them by right, impossible to challenge or question.

He was all handshakes and smiles when he came out: the author, the host, a couple of others he'd singled out for cultivating. Carole took note of names, scheduled a time to call them, sound them out. That indefatigable certainty bullied into the room, took up all the available space, became the gravity people orbited around. He ignored the stooge, still pale and shaking. Carole wondered if she *should* say something, because it was getting harder to find people to play the voice of reason opposite Thompson, and the last thing he wanted was for someone with actual convictions to start a genuine argument, quote facts, bring up any awkward contradictions from past speeches. But Thompson didn't really do subtext. Someone spoke against him, that made them the enemy, even if they were doing it to his order. He was a man who lived his cover; he didn't distinguish between who he was and the act he put on a lot of the time. Carole thought that was what people reacted to. She'd gone over the polls and the surveys obsessively, all the qualitative analysis from a legion of consultants tasked to find out just how it was that maverick politician Warner S.

Thompson had come to dominate the nation's conversation. People thought he was genuine, he said it straight, told them the truth. Despite the fact that he never quite told them anything at all. In the moment when he smiled and shook your hand, though; in the moment when he looked straight at the camera and beamed at the audience, you existed for him, and because his world was tiny, just a single point that was his own being, that meant you'd been admitted into the Divine Presence. You were real, for the second he acknowledged you. She'd felt it herself. She saw it happening now. People fell over themselves to catch the edge of that spotlight that always seemed to be on the man.

Then he had broken abruptly from the crowd, and none of them existed any more. He took his personal light with him, that was just in his mind but that he believed in so firmly he could make others see it. He was grabbing Grubb by the shoulder, what looked like a friendly squeeze but was obviously painful. "Tell me we got the Life Lobby, Pat."

"We got them, sir," Grubb confirmed, legs going twice the pace of Thompson's to keep up as the man strode away. "Carole's got the details." Because Carole always got the details, most of which were not fit for casual overhearing. Mostly it came down to filtering the information down to clear, simple statements Thompson could digest. Not stupid, that was a mistake a lot of his past opponents had made. Not intelligent, either, exactly. Not as the word was generally used. But very clever indeed in the way he needed to be, to shunt through human affairs like he did. A mind that worked in tangents and laterals, between the cracks of regular thought. But no patience for complexities, not when they didn't serve him. He needed someone like Carole to tell him what things *meant*, rather than what they were. And Grubb was right in one thing. He did at least listen to her, because she'd spent years learning how to talk to him, the real him, the man behind the gilded bonhomie.

They got shot of Grubb before they got to the car. He'd go make more calls, then end up in some bar where the Thompson interview was playing, telling people that was his guy, that without him Thompson would be nothing. Probably it would be word of that sort of thing getting back to the man himself that would see Grubb fired sooner rather than later. Thompson was a self-made man. He wouldn't share credit for himself with anyone, let alone a sagging panhandler like Grubb. She tried to look forward to when Pat Grubb wasn't a damp presence at her elbow every day they were on the campaign trail, but it would only be someone else. America seemed to have a never-ending supply of middle-aged right-wingers ready to step into those soiled shoes. None of his predecessors had been much better; some had been worse. His successor would be another yard of the same cloth.

The limo could have driven itself to the hotel but Boyo sat behind the wheel instead. Thompson really was worried about Distributed Intelligence entities, the current bugbear of world concern. It was something he'd spent a lot of time on, Carole knew. Or rather, he had a whole network of people working on it for him, feeding their results back up the chain and then to Carole, who chewed up the facts into a paste sufficiently malleable that Thompson could digest it.

At the hotel, after the usual flurry of activity from the staff who wanted to make sure he knew just how happy they were to have him enjoying their hospitality, after the last bellboy had been shooed out the door of the suite by Boyo's growl, it was time for the other Thompson. The private Thompson.

Boyo lay in front of the door. In repose his frame seemed doggy enough that you just wondered who'd stuck that giant Alsatian in a suit. Thompson retreated to the bedroom and Carole followed, waiting for him to be ready for her to tell him things.

He sat on the bed, jacket off, tie loosened, the lights turned low, and for a long time he did nothing. All that smile-and-gladhanding was gone from him, like a light had been switched off. His face had gone slack. Carole sometimes wondered if it was like this with the actual DisInt units, the people who weren't people, just individual cells of a single split personality. Not that she would ever say that to Thompson. He'd be furious, and she'd seen him furious. The thought, the very suggestion it might happen, and she'd be the target, was instantly and unthinkably miserable. She'd do anything to stop him getting into that kind of state. That was why she'd spent so many years learning how to handle him. She was devoted to him, of course. Her fate was absolutely tied to his and, by now, she couldn't imagine it any other way. But when he was angry she was terrified of him. Anything. She'd do anything.

Looking into his empty face now, she met his eyes. Something was looking out of them at her, something that could make that face beam and brag and bluster, be the man all those people loved. Something that could go before the cameras and make the features and personality of Warner S. Thompson into a distorting mirror, in which everyone saw what they most wanted, their heart's desire, something real and genuine and straight-talking.

And again she wondered if this was what it was like with

BEAR HEAD

HumOS or any of the DisInt networks that had sprung up and were now being put right back down to where they could be isolated and controlled. Because what looked out past those loose features seemed almost like some separate detached thing sitting in his head and pulling the levers.

"I want to play," he said. Complete sentences, for her. Expressions of desire. And she'd made sure there was a place he could go, a table-full of poker players ready to oblige him. And ready to discreetly lose, because Thompson didn't lose. He was a great card player, he always said so. Nobody could bluff him. Nobody could tell when he was hustling them. And she had a feeling he was probably right, in a way, because he was who he was and because he had such an individual relationship with the usual run of human codes and signals. But no sense leaving anything to chance so she'd briefed his fellow players very carefully. They were there more as actors than as gamblers. They were there to orbit Thompson's star, because that was how he saw his life.

But.

"Work first, please, sir," she said softly. "Important news."

"Play." He scowled at her, not angry yet, just a child denied something. And if he was particularly wilful then it would have to wait, but it was her job to push as far as she could. To manage him as much as she could.

"Word from Braintree, sir." She almost held her breath, waiting to see if that would get through to him like it usually did, or if he was too far gone into his own desires.

A spark lit up behind those dead eyes, though. "Good word?"

"No, sir." Bracing herself. "Not really bad, sir, but slightly bad."

"Tell me."

"The mom has gone to a lawyer."

"That bitch! That ungrateful bitch!" He was enraged instantly and she backed off all the way across the palatial floor to the door. Through it, she heard Boyo's anxious whine in the next room. Thompson stood by the bed, braces off one shoulder, trousers sagging, bellowing at the ceiling, "She signed the papers! She isn't allowed to talk! She took the money!" His burning gaze fixed on her and she trembled, waiting for him to stomp over to her, knowing she'd brought this on herself, she hadn't handled him, handled Grubb, handled the situation properly, her fault, her fault... But he didn't, just stood by the bed, face dead again for a moment as he retreated inwards.

"What lawyer?" His voice still rolled with anger, but he'd got a leash on it for once.

"Aslan Kahner Laika, sir."

"Get *my* lawyers. Get them to tell those sons of bitches it's all confidential. It's none of their business. Cease! Desist! I will break them. I will have them kicked out. I will destroy them and every damn client they've got. Tell them!"

"I'll put a call in to your lawyers, sir." And she would interpret Thompson to the lawyers just the same way she interpreted the world to Thompson.

Again he went dead, sitting back down on the bed, air of a marionette with cut strings. "Want to play," he said again, but she knew him well enough to sense that something had caught in his mind that wouldn't just be shouldered aside. "Get me Fellatio," and he snickered, same way as he always did, same joke as he always made, schoolboy humour.

She requested a channel to Doctor Marco Felorian of the

Braintree Institute. He knew her ID and knew not to keep her waiting. He sounded curt when he picked up. "How is he?"

"He wants to speak to you." She kept her tone neutral. Thompson was just sitting there, eyes looking at nothing, thoughts in a holding pattern. She didn't know if he was going to explode at Felorian or not. Without another word she connected Thompson to the man.

He scowled through whatever pleasantries the man gave him – Felorian, a tech genius and a surgeon, a biotech man. He'd been big in the Bioform trade, publicly big, and Thompson had been bankrolling him back then. Back when Thompson was all for the Bioforms, because that was what worked for him. Now Felorian did less public work, out in Braintree Penitentiary with a stack of felons at his disposal, but it was still Thompson's money keeping the man in expensive suits.

"I want to come see," Thompson said, probably wedging the words into the middle of one of Felorian's grandiose sentences. "Show me the model again." He was scowling fiercely at the wall.

Not chewing the man out over the lawyers then. Wanting to see the next step of the plan. And it was Thompson's plan. He had decided on a thing he wanted, and then people like Carole and Felorian and plenty of others had taken those simple, determined pieces and made all the complex arrangements required to turn the ideas into a reality. It was Thompson's genius, that: people wanted to make him happy. People wanted his smile and handshake. People were scared of his wrath should he be anything other than happy. Carole wanted him to be happy. She was devoted to him, like they all were.

She got a signal that the channel needed her attention, a string of possible appointments at Braintree, awaiting her say so as to when Thompson would visit. Nothing but the best for him, as always. Felorian would bend over backwards to keep him sweet; to keep the money rolling in, yes, but more than that. It got so a happy Thompson was an end in itself. She chose the most convenient time, within the next forty-eight hours because if Thompson wanted a thing, he wanted it soon, then returned her gaze to her employer.

"There's a game waiting for you, sir," she said. Those dead eyes were on her, though, neither the wall nor the inside of his head his focus any longer. His face hung from the front of his skull, no expression on it. She saw his thoughts had gone to another favourite pastime.

"Take them off," he told her. "Lie on the bed."

She felt the brief moment when she was going to say no, but she was devoted to him, after all. The word stuck in her throat. She heard Boyo's querulous whine from the other room, the way he always did when Thompson decided he needed to get something out of his system by way of fucking his PA.

And she undressed and lay there as he clambered on top of her, shunting and bullying his way in, the way he did everywhere. Lay there and knew she wanted to please him, just like everyone, just like Boyo in the next room who couldn't ever not want to serve his master because of the Collar inside his head that made sure of it. Just like she couldn't ever not want to, *just* like. Because Thompson needed a PA he could trust, and Doctor Felorian didn't much care about the legalities. After all, once the operation was done, it wasn't like she would ever tell anyone.

And she lay there and made the right sounds and told herself over and over how devoted she was and how much she enjoyed making Warner S. Thompson happy and tried her best not to listen to the trapped little voice saying *Get off me get off me get off*, until he was finished and got off, zipped up and said, "Going to the game now." And she sat on the bed and sent the coordinates to Boyo so the dog could drive him there, sent word to the other players that their benefactor was coming to take money off them that his own funds, via her offices, would underwrite. And they'd laugh at his jokes and tell him how shrewd he was. He liked that.

And when he'd gone she got in the shower and scrubbed and scrubbed.

3

JIMMY

You'll maybe not believe this but I was stoked when I first set foot on Mars. Building the *future*, man! We all were. And, sure, there were scientists and other nerds already here, but they were living underground or in closed systems. They weren't living on *Mars* like people wanted. We were going to take a chunk of the planet and make it so, within our lifetimes, people could walk about on it, take a Sunday stroll after church under the canopy of Hellas Planitia, under the Martian sky. And it was a mad project – seriously, put a roof on all *that*, somehow generate *that* much atmosphere – but they'd done the math. In fact, the math had been done by a real *they*. The thing they just called Bees, back when Bees was a good thing, back when Bees was just prepping Mars for us.

Goddamn Bees.

But Bees reckoned that, with Bee-tech, Earth life could get a comfortable foothold down in the depths of the Hellas crater, and so they took us and engineered us and shipped us across Heaven and dumped us down in Hell. And we were goddamn *stoked*. We were all sorts of keen.

That didn't last. I mean probably still there are a few clueless schmoes who are still aces about the whole business, but your man Jimmy here is wise to it. It is the company scrip they pay us in mostly. I mean, OK, it's not like we can run out to a local Walmart with our sweaty hands full of dollars, and OK, when we're done they promise a good exchange rate with whatever currency we want, but I don't believe it. Mostly because just about nobody'll have any scrip left to exchange. I mean, yes, they give you a tiny little hole of a place to lay your head, and company canteen serves out nutritious slop as part of the deal, but anything else, you pay for. Who do you pay? Two choices. You pay the company, or you pay some grifter who's running a racket on the black market, where you and said grifter both might get picked up by the Bad News Bears for breaking the rules at any moment. And then you'd get fined so that's even less scrip in your pocket. You pay to download entertainment, you pay for booze, you pay for a bigger room, you pay through the nose for any damn time you break the rules. Everything you get in your wage packet goes right back into the company purse like water into sand. And when I saw how *that* worked, that was when my keen went just about the same way. Which was unfortunate because, in seeking a prop to help me stay on my two tottering feet, I developed some fairly expensive habits that led me to both volunteer for any crap job with a bonus attached to it, and to take on a few under-the-counter jobs for sharks like Sugar.

Anyway, there's me with my account scraping along at just about zero point zero balance and payday just gone, so naturally I go to complain to the boss, meaning Admin.

Admin is at the heart of Hell City, in the built part. It was the first to get dug out, and it's the only part that's fully pressurised and oxygenated round the clock. There's a grid plan of streets radiating out from it, above and below ground, all those business and residential units that nobody's allowed in, still coated over with plastic to keep the dust out. There are actual apartments there, a hundred times the size of what they call our *nooks* where we bed down, but they're all sold off plan to intrepid colonists on Earth who're going to come rough it out here in luxury and tell each other how goddamn rugged they are. Nobody wants uncouth engineered labourers soiling their spotless floors and putting our boots up on the chaise longue.

There are a couple of Bad News Bears slouching on the pokey plaza Admin's airlock opens onto. These are the other sort of Bioform, the dumbass sort. They're not full sentient, just force-grown animals with a bunch of headware, so the bleeding hearts rights activists back home don't get to complain about them being Collared. Although I hear that Collaring is back in, back home. Thank fuck it wasn't when we were being engineered, say I, or they'd have goddamn well fit us with one, believe you me. So, anyway: Bad News Bears, basically Admin's heavy mob. Not that they'd ever quite needed one, but there are about thirty of the damn things, and ten of them out of the freezers at any time, maybe. Ten-foot bears, only a little engineered from base stock. Best thing you ever saw to clear out a bar or a card game that's got too enthusiastic, and it means nobody comes to Admin to make trouble, like I'm doing. Except they're dumb as bricks, and you just got to know how to handle them.

I show them my ID. "Just got back from maintenance. Need to report," I tell them, and their headware processes that as they frown and huff and sniff at me. You don't show you're scared of them, basically. They're not like the dogs, who just love chasing a running man down for the fun of it. Bears are lazy. They'll come on heavy if you give, but if you keep your cool then you're too much work most of the time. Unless they're hungry and you've got candy on you.

I had candy. I slipped a stick of it to each of them, peace offering-like. They crunched it down appreciatively. Dumb as bricks, like I said, but brighter than bears. I make sure all the Bad News Bears know old Jimmy has candy for them. Some day they'll get sent after me and that knowledge might just be the difference between me getting brought to Admin, and me getting brought to Admin with less than the usual number of limbs.

Anyway, that gets me in, and I wait around and bug the duty secretary, breathing in the clean, fresh, Earth-standard air. The light's different, too, all tinted a special shade of blue that's like the sun, only the sun when you're seventy-five million klicks closer in. We're supposed to have something like that all through the living spaces, to keep us from cutting our wrists every damn morning from all-year Seasonal Affective Disorder, but frankly it never seems to work right. It's only when you get to visit Admin you really find out what you've been missing. My body doesn't know what's going on, frankly: Christmas and my birthday all at once. Even the suit air wasn't this rich. Makes you feel almost drunk. I wish I could bring a load of bottles and smuggle it out to sell on the street. And then I've made enough of a nuisance of myself that the Chief Administrator's door slides open and he puts an annoyed head out.

"Oh Danny Boyd," I sing out, "the pipes, the pipes!" because he really fucking hates that.

"Marten," he names me, like I'm a disease he's caught.

"What do you want?" Project Manager Daniel Boyd is not quite like me. His skin is pinky, hair mousy brown rather than the silvery grey we've all gone. His eyes have fewer lids than mine do, because he never needs to worry about blinking away dust twenty-four-seven, or that his vitreous humours or whateverthehell might suddenly pop out of where they're supposed to be because there's damn-all pressure outside them. They still modded him, but not so much as me. He's made to stay indoors on the red planet.

"Got a bit of a problem there, bossman. Mind if we take it to your office there?" His office has comfy chairs. I have sat in them. I would pay company scrip to do so again. My ass thought it had died and gone to the good place.

"What do you want, Marten. You said you needed to report, but I've read your report already. All good, job done." And he's a diligent enough bastard. He would have read it, while sitting in his comfy, comfy chair.

"Bossman, I can't help seeing I didn't get paid."

I think I actually feel the slight extra load in my headware, the system borrowing my capacity at standard rates to call up the information, seeing as I'm right there and convenient. Danny Boy's querying the system, because obviously he doesn't know my financial standing off by heart. The system's going through all its different stages, including inferring my consent, and feeding back to him.

"No, you were paid," he says. He's got a tablet there, showing the money going in.

"I see that," I say reasonably. "What concerns me more is where it all goes out again around nought point five of a second later."

"That's the garnish," he says, or that's what I think he

says. For a moment I think I somehow bought the entire Martian parsley crop or something when I wasn't looking. It must have shown on my face because Boyd expands, "for your loans. Your loan payments fell due, and you hadn't paid them, so they were garnished from your wages. I'm sorry, Marten, but it is in the print of the contract you signed with the lender, I'm sure. Check the documents over. If you've a complaint about them, bring it to me and I'll take a look, but usually they're solid."

And yes, obviously I've been taking out loans, month to month. Because of that one month when things were tough and I was getting through a lot of Stringer, and then the next month when I needed the loans to pay off the previous loans, and then... and then I was off, wasn't I, fixing the perimeter when the payments fell due, but, but...

Boyd sees it on my face, and the bastard thing about him is, he is sympathetic. Easy enough for a man in his position to be an utter corporate bastard, but Danny Boy came to Mars because he believed in the project, and the real corporate bastards stayed home and probably made twice the money. Sympathetic, but won't lift a finger to help, and what he doesn't see on my face is that I have no stash left and the need to get some Stringer in me is clawing at my guts. If I was a regular Joe like Boyd I'd be sweating and shaking and obviously strung out for something, but I don't sweat and I don't shake and my engineering hides all the bad, bad things I'm feeling right now.

Outside, back in the dust and the thinner air, I put a call in to the lenders and spend far too long basically pleading with them to give me a new loan. Because that's how it goes, isn't it? They give you a cup today so they can get two cups from you tomorrow? Except that downward spiral can't go on forever and apparently this is as far as it goes. I am no longer a good enough credit risk, says the automated system the lender has here in lieu of an actual human I could grab by the ears and scream at.

I'm still standing in Admin plaza when I'm doing this, under the incurious gaze of the Bad News Bears. When I look up, feeling my lips peel back from my teeth, feeling like the great vast emptiness of Mars is closing in round me like a coffin, they're not the only audience I've got. I've been shouting, I realise; shouting at the lender, whose voice is just a whisper in my implanted earpiece. Shouting on Admin's doorstep. No wonder someone turned up to see how much of a problem I was.

"Marten J." His deep, growling voice comes straight to my ear via my radio receiver and mastoid bone. "You causing trouble again."

"Hi Rufus," I tell him. "I was just moving on."

"Sure..." and he lets the word hang, playing with it, turning the end of it into a long, low growl. Rufus is a big dog, almost enough to give a Bad News Bear a run for its money. He's wearing an armoured tunic that leaves his massively muscled limbs bare, the shaggy hair on them mostly clear of dust because him and his deputies have a little electrostatic field built into them that keeps it off. Rufus is the sheriff of Hell City. I mean, no big hat, but that's what he is. He carries a gun that could kill a bear real easy, and I saw him do just that four years ago when one of the Bad News crew went crazy, screwy wiring turning it into a marauding monster. One shot from Rufus's gun, no hesitation, no more problem. His deputies have guns too. Nobody else on Mars does. The self-defence lobby back home are oddly silent about this inequality, but nobody really wants people like Yours Truly to have a finger on any kind of trigger. His posse scares the crap out of me, frankly, serious old-school Bioforms, ex-military models all, dogs, cats, a dragon-type, all of them engineered like me for Martian suit-free EVA. Rufus could track a fugitive across the goddamn sands of Hellas Planitia, and I reckon he's just desperate for someone to give him the opportunity.

"No trouble, Sheriff," I say, all humble like, clamping down on the gnawing inside of me. "Just a personal matter, Sheriff. Sorry."

He leans in real close. He's got a broad face, massive jaws that could crunch me up like breakfast cereal. On his chest, that's three times as wide as I am, there's a medal. A picture of a different dog-form, looking nobly off into the distance, along with the words 'In Memorium Rex'. And you don't mock that kind of thing. Bioforms who wear that token, they take it real seriously.

"You smell like you're in trouble, Marten J." And he can't really smell as well as he might – not the way they messed with my body chemistry and not in this thin air. But Rufus has headware too, and he uses it to hunt the system. They gave the bastard a virtual nose for sniffing out bad luck bastards like me, and he knows I'm screwed. He can smell my electronic fear.

"No trouble, Sheriff," I say again, and back off from him in case he gets a whiff of my Jonesing. "Sorry." And I'm taking myself off home as quickly as I can because I don't know what to do.

On the way there, I call every dealer who's talking to me, in case any of them have a sudden fit of inexplicable generosity. None of them fancy advancing me anything on credit, not again, not this time. Suddenly nobody in Hell City wants to know poor Jimmy, and wasn't I such a good customer to them always? There's no gratitude.

I'm going to head home. I'm going to go to what the designers refer to as my 'nook', meaning living space the size of a matchbox with a fold-down bed and facilities down the hall that I share with fifty other Joes. I'm going to just crash and hope that being tired wins out over being strung out and maybe when the pangs wake me up in four hours something will miraculously have changed for the better.

Except.

Except as I shamble back along the corridor of the workers' dorms I hear someone banging up ahead, and my special psychic senses tell me it's my door they're banging on, mostly because it's my name they're shouting. "Marten, yer fuckin' waste o' breath!" and similar unkind sentiments directed at Yours Truly who isn't, thankfully, actually on the other side of the door they're so abusing. I know the voice. This is Matthias Lau, and if you recall what I said about them not hiring anyone too big nor too small to fit the suits, well, Matty Lau is right on the big end of that scale, and there was that time last month when the loan money had run dry. Matty fancies himself as an up-and-coming loan-shark, see, so he was only happy to slip me a little of his wage packet to tide me over, only he's still working on the part of the business where people take him seriously enough to want to pay him back. The head of anger on him sounds like he is ready to take the game to the next level, fists and all. I skulk back down the corridor and decide maybe the night's still young and a fellow like me's got places to go.

Except I don't got places to go, do I? The only place I want to go is some dealer who's inexplicably up to give me a new line of credit, but Hell City isn't exactly that flush with people who can smuggle a consignment of illegal pharmaceuticals on the supply run, and there's only three bent techs cooking Stringer on the domestic market, and I've reached the money-in-front stage of my relationship with all of them. So it's money I need, and by some goddamn lousy coincidence that's the one thing I haven't got.

And there's only one place I can go that might get scrip into my shaky little palms in the sort of timescale I need.

I'm going to see Sugar.

Stringer keeps you going. Drug of choice for those who, as the saying goes, choose drugs. Because Hell City life is many things but what it is most is repetitive and mind-numbingly boring, and absolutely anything you might do to lift that boredom costs you scrip, and so why not drugs? Why not let something else do the heavy lifting from inside your head, exactly? When Stringer's sitting on your shoulder you feel cool and purposeful and collected. You can go make a pass at that guy or girl, you can put in for that danger money job you didn't dare to before. You can, most importantly, see off the end of an eight hour shift of utterly tedious Martian make-work and come out feeling that you've done something important, made the world a better place. Wellbeing and contentment and not feeling just how rubbish everything is, that's the gift Stringer gives you, and that's what it takes back after the hit fades. On my way to see Sugar I actually have to stop and have a bit of a dry-eyed sob about how utterly I screwed up my life when I volunteered to build Hell City. How the posters and recruiters were lying bastards. How the company doesn't give a shit. How I'm not human, not any more. My face isn't my face, and they say they'll change it back but *really*? Will they really care about us when we're done? It's in the contract, but one of the big attractions to a lot of people about Mars is that it ain't under the jurisdiction of the World Senate, given that it ain't, you know, part of the World. Lot of business and tech and mob types gonna end up based out of Hell City, you mark my words, when it's up and running for business. Greatest tax haven there ever was, and nobody telling you 'no' if you've got the money to pay for 'yes'.

Sugar – Dana Sugatsu – is a construction worker, same as me. You see her on-site still, now and then, toiling away with the rest of us schmoes. Otherwise Admin and the sheriff would take too much of an interest in what she actually does with her time. And I reckon they kind of know, with Sugar and the other fixers. They must realise there's a whole black market economy going on here in Hell. The planners back on Earth likely figured it into how everything would work here – safety valve for all the bitter, grumbly steam we build up.

Sugar's kink is data. We've all got headspace, after all, and the drain of Admin doing its job barely scratches the surface of the great big implant we all got. And barely pays a dime, too, when Admin does borrow processing power and storage space, because those rates are fixed in our contracts. But you can rent out your head to others, too. Indra Kaur has five people storing whole back-catalogues of her favourite soaps for her. Some other guy I know, he's writing some definitive history of some dead guy nobody cares about, paranoid about losing the work so there's nineteen heads out there got some draft or other of it in them. But there's other uses you can turn your headware to, if you don't mind them being absolutely goddamn illegal.

Sugar's got friends back home. The sort of friends she was probably running away from when she signed up for Mars, I reckon, but now she's here they've got a good thing going on. You see, data's a funny thing. You can copy it, delete it, pass it around. It's so easily replicable it oughtn't to be valuable, really. Except what if there's some data that you simultaneously really think you're gonna need later, but you really don't want anyone else finding it. Incriminating videos, blackmail stuff, a mobster's accounts, your porn collection. Where, oh where, could you possibly send the last copy of that, once you'd deleted it from absolutely everywhere else? Where might you find a big old data store that could hold it for you, outside the reach of any subpoena or legal summons? It's a mystery, it really is.

I've done the work for Sugar twice before. She knows I'm good for it. I don't peek. I don't try and crack the encryption on whatever shit she hides in my headspace. And if the money's only a fraction of what she's taking from her friends back home, at least it's right there in my account and available for necessities.

I've put in a call to her already, because Sugar's not someone you turn up unannounced on. She's down in Storage Nineteen, which is her personal kingdom. She is, actually, official logistics clerk for that whole row, but that unit is always suspiciously empty, just an outer wall of crates with Earth stamps on them, and then a big hollow space inside with her people moving stuff about. She does a bit of the regular smuggling too, though no Stringer, worse luck, or she'd be the ultimate one-stop shop right about now. Mostly it's the data, and just as well because I'd be crap-all use to her otherwise.

She's had a bunch of the small-size crates piled up and locked together to make something very like a throne, because Sugar has a sense of humour. When I get ushered in by one of her goons, she's sitting there with a leg thrown over the arm of it. She wears the same company overalls we all do, but open down the front to show a diamante-spangly T-shirt with the words 'Who's Queen?' on it. She has jewellery, too, which isn't something you see much over here. Piercings are right out, because of the way that interacts with the below-zero temperatures and our metabolisms' metals processing, but she's got these ornate twiny metal dragons clasped along the outside of her ears, and she's painted her eyebrows and lips gold as well. You'd think she was some rich guy's arm candy, first time you saw her. She's small, pert, bright as a button. I saw her tear some guy's fingernails off, once. Not one of her heavies, but her herself, using a tool you're supposed to reserve for broken crate clasps. But then he had it coming, and he was wise enough to go report an industrial accident when she'd done.

On either side of her throne are the other reason nobody's come to take all this away from her. Ten feet tall each, bigger than the biggest of the Bad News crew and way smarter. Full-on bear-model Bioforms wearing the heavy-duty overalls the company makes for them, that do nothing to make them seem safe to be around. Alike as twins, the pair of them, staring at me with their tiny, hostile eyes, mouths just open enough that I can see what big teeth they both have. One has a big clawed paw-hand on the back of Sugar's throne. The other is holding a rivet gun big enough that only the bear models are rated to use it. Because Sheriff Rufus has the only real guns but there are ways of making do.

One of them is called Murder. The other one's called Marmalade. I don't know which is which and I'm sure as goddamn not going to ask.

"Well if it isn't Lucky Jim," Sugar greets me. She has a smile... actually, she has maybe the most beautiful smile in all of Hell City, just ridiculously radiant, even though it doesn't even move her mouth much. I want to cry again, seeing that smile. It looks like Stringer feels.

"You're looking rough, Jimmy," she adds solicitously, "You're looking strung out. What's the matter? Horizon sickness, all of a sudden?" Because that was a thing some of us got in the first year. Couldn't adjust to the gravity, to the pressure, to their own changed bodies, to the wrongness of being on the wrong world.

"Oh, y'know," I manage, although I still want to cry, and you can't, not really. Mostly cos of the extra eyelids and the fact they stopped up my tear ducts. "Just wondering if there was anything I could do for my friend Sugar. If there was anything you needed hiding, just for a bit."

"Word is you're on everyone's shit list, Jimbles." She's still smiling, though. I want it to be fond, because fond might get me what I want, but it's more like crocs and dolphins and other critters where the mouth just goes that way and it don't mean a thing.

"Eh, y'know." I do this little flip of my hand, *que sera sera*, as if it's all very much in my stride. "But, for real, you know

I'm good. Soul of discretion, me. If you had anything. Any work. Anything." And I can hear the strain in my own voice by the end there.

For a moment she's weighing me up, and I think she's going to decide I'm too much of a risk, too strung out, too far into will-do-anything-for-a-fix territory to be useful, but then she nods, still bathing me in that smile.

"I got something," she agrees. "Hot out of Earth. Big load, take up your whole headspace, you're good for that? Happy to jettison whatever else you got there?"

It'll mean no piece work for Admin, but as that pays precisely jack, and as they took my tears anyway, I won't cry over it.

"Marmalade," she says, "take Jimmy the Mule round the back and load him up," and apparently the bear on the left is Marmalade, the one without the rivet gun. And you really don't want to end up where she's telling Murder to take you round the back.

The upload takes way longer than I'm happy with. They've got me sat on a crate while a short-range network that doesn't go beyond Storage Nineteen's walls dumps the data into me. Nobody tells me what it is, of course. I don't ask. Probably it's just data but sometimes it's whole programs. Illegal tech stuff someone wants to run where nobody'll see it, data analysis that's got to stay secret. Headspace has a lot of processing power, way more than we need day to day. So naturally we found uses for it nobody intended, like this whole data black market Sugar and her peers run. And on and on it goes – I've never taken on this much, and I keep expecting to feel full, bloated, constipated with it, except it's all in my head and the only indicator is the percentage marker inching up.

And sitting still for all of this is real hard, what with how desperate I'm getting for a little chemical reassurance, so I go through the back half of the process with Marmalade's heavy paw weighing down my shoulder and one sickle claw along the line of my chin, just to remind me of priorities. Just because it's the other one that's called Murder doesn't mean Marmalade's a softie.

My mind does feel a bit jangly by the time we're done, but frankly I can't separate anything new from the overriding need to go score. Sugar transfers my scrip to a new account she sets up for me, because I don't want to piss it down the hole of my creditors, thank you very much. And I'm flush again, and I could go pay off Matty Lau and the loans people and a few other dumbass schmoes fool enough to advance me a dime, but right now that is not my priority. My priority is getting the hell out of Storage Nineteen, putting a call into Stanky Greer and meeting up with him, rat-faced weasel Bioform that he is, to score a big old bag of Stringer. I pop one on the way home and suddenly the world's looking a much rosier place.

I only remember about angry Matthias Lau when I'm actually at the door to my nook, but that's OK because he's left some time in the intervening hours. I swan into my tiny, tiny living space, but the Stringer in me is making it feel like a palace, like the hall of a God-king from which I can truly make a difference. I go over the work rota, pick out some extra duties. I'm going to goddamn build a city on Mars, man! I'm a superhuman on another planet and I'm making a difference! Go me!

And in the middle of this someone says, "Access all channels achieved. Can you hear me?"

I turn around, because apparently I've left the door open. Embarrassing, but right then I can handle it. The door's closed.

"How about now? Can you hear me? I'm registering activity in your radio receiver implant. This should be working now."

There's nobody in the nook with me. There is literally not room for another human body, nowhere to put the smallest-model Bioform. I check my radio implant. There's no incoming call, and a quick troubleshoot shows normal functionality.

"Hello?" I try.

"Ah good, yes. We have dialogue. Your internal system architecture says you're unit 4720 but I see also... Marten James Caspian. I'll call you Marten?"

"Jimmy." And all that wondrous goodwill and wellbeing the Stringer gave me is just leaking out through my boots because, well, you know those horror movies where the call is coming from inside the house? Because there is no incoming signal. I can disconnect entirely from all outside channels and that voice just keeps coming. It's the data. *The data is talking to me.*

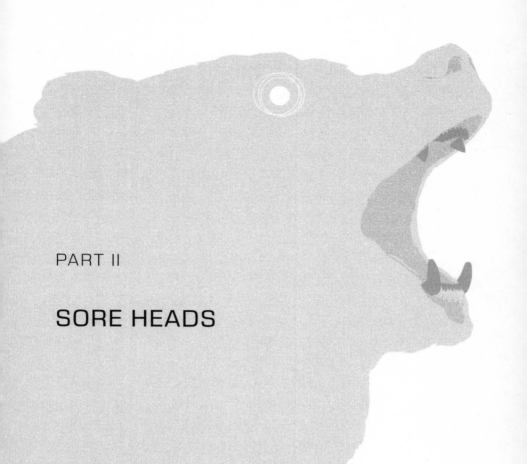

PART II

SORE HEADS

4

[RECOVERED DATA ARCHIVE:
IDENTITY PENDING]

Jagged ends of memories, like a jigsaw made of broken glass. Cut yourself to ribbons trying to piece it back together but then you're the glass as well as the hands so why not a little blood? As the outer self tries to adjust to a radically different suite of senses, electronic, throttled through some kind of implanted datastore facility. Querying just what sort of substrate I'm running on, here. Not in Kansas any more, that's for sure, but then I've led a privileged sort of life, born half in the mush of a surgically engineered brain and half in the filigree of a network of experimental implants.

Well.

The mush is out of the picture now. I fervently hope the mush is doing well on a nice family-run farm upstate, because it's not in here with me. So: first things first.

Where's here, exactly?

Who's 'I'?

Memories, a great heap of them. At first I think they're just random, and you'd cut yourself to ribbons trying to get that kind of mess in order, wouldn't you. Like, as the playwright says, a blind man searching a bazaar for his own portrait.

What play? What playwright? Perhaps the information is

contained in one of those pointy, pointy pieces. Probably not a priority compared to the Who and Where of it. I can catch up on my Eng. Lit. doctoral studies later.

Apparently I am or was partway into an Eng. Lit. doctorate. I wonder what that is. It sounds nice. I'll put it with the seventeen other doctorates, maybe.

The shards are all date-stamped, if you can squint at them the right way. Some are corrupted. Some are locked, and maybe the passwords to them are on other shards. I think someone made a bit of a mess of this transfer and I hope that the real me – the mush-and-filigree being – is doing better than this.

So let's start.

In the beginning, there was only the face of the waters. And a great wailing and a gnashing of teeth because the Greater Netherlands Barrier had broken, maybe naturally, maybe not, and two and a quarter million people were evacuating to higher ground. But we were in where the damage was worst, where the water was three metres and rising still, the sea inexorably shouldering aside whatever got in its way, as though it had been planning this for a *long* time and was damn well going to enjoy itself now.

They set up floating camps, self-inflating things like a giant's bouncy castle except no fun at all. You had maybe a hundred thousand people spotted from the air, floating in boats, on planks and doors, on the little cheapo dinghies that a lot of prudent Netherlanders had been laying in for the worst. But they had no food, no shelter from the driving rain, no medicine, no clean water – yes, there's a flood and you didn't drown and now there's water, water everywhere, as the poet says, nor any drop to drink.

So the World Senate Relief Force went into overdrive to get everyone to some kind of camp where they could stave off thirst and hypothermia, and give the names of all the friends and relatives they couldn't account for. That was what I'd flown in to see. And what the WSRF meant was a core of logistics personnel joining all the dots, and a whole ton of boots on the ground. Or paws in the water, as it worked out. Paws, fins, claws, tails... For most of the drifting dispossessed, it must have been like getting rescued by the sort of nightmare Beatrix Potter might have had, after too much cheese.

They had four teams on the go, when my skimmer coasted in to Camp Edell, the largest floating site and the one with the logistics personnel on it. I didn't want to trust myself to little boats or the smaller camps. Too much ballast these days, and despite myself I never fancied swimming much. You want to get yourself a fish dinner, there are restaurants I know. No need to go messing about hooking the damn things out of the water yourself.

Blue Team were the dog squad, and they were mostly running the camps because people react well to dogs. They were called in for problem cases, too: people holed up in the upper floors of buildings, maybe with guns, maybe with mental health issues. Blue Team had some good negotiators. There was a whole strain of dog-Bioform that specialised in that, reading the slightest sniff and whiff of you and knowing just how to handle fragile goods. Over in LA there's a thriving trade in having a dog as your therapist, even. Green Team were some dogs, some cats – the tiger-gene derivatives who weren't worried about getting their feet wet. Good swimmers, still telegenic. Everyone loves the cat-forms anyway. You need someone to persuade Granny Aanhus to get off her inflatable pool pony and onto your back, bring a cat. Black Team were the experimental Aussie squad, their first deployment in a European disaster zone. They were not so telegenic. You're lost in a boat and your world is underwater, having a semi-humanoid monitor lizard or a salt water crocodile-form turning up alongside is going to trigger a few phobias. They were the best in amphibious rescue personnel, though, absolutely unmatched. Red Team, meanwhile, were seven dolphins, not humanoid at all, just engineered inside. They got the grim work. They stayed in the water and tried to find all the bodies that the sea hadn't already taken. And flying over it all there was the Bee swarm, of course, giving us blanket visibility of everything this side of the water's surface, but it wasn't the same. It was just bees slaved to a neural net. It wasn't *Bees*. She would have been useful to have on the team still.

It was a desperate response to a desperate situation, deployed at zero notice from all over the world and faultlessly coordinated. It wasn't effective enough or rapid enough for the forty thousand people who'd died in the breach, or another eleven thousand who they couldn't get to in time. It was a disaster. It was a damning indictment of how people hadn't acted five decades back when the green lobbies had given the world all the info we needed to put the brakes on. It was a golden PR opportunity and that was why I was there. Made me sick inside myself to admit it, but I was an elderly academic and political activist, so what good would I have been otherwise?

I landed with cameras and journalists who divided their attention between me and the bustling camp. I saw family after family crammed into the little blow-up doghouses that were part of the camp's structure, a roof over their heads, mugs and plates in their hands, looking sodden, looking traumatised, looking alive. Right at this moment there were similar scenes over in Myanmar. I knew because I'd just been there. I was doing a whistle-stop tour of disaster areas, and doing my best to look concerned despite not really having the face for it.

"Doctor Medici!" someone called, a deep voice, rough with ancestral growling.

Is that...? But no, the memories tell me that's not me, not my name. Just an old, old alias.

She bustled over, a great sodden wodge of dog, and a human right behind her in a WSRF blue-and-red anorak. The former was Doctor Lucy, who looked like she dearly wanted to shake and drench everyone around her, the latter Janine Haguerman, her second. They took time out of their day they didn't really have just to meet me. Pleasantries and nods all round, them thanking me for doing all I am for the visibility of the relief effort, where I should be thanking them for actually helping people. But they also serve who only stand and scheme. I remember thinking even then that the name I'd chosen for myself decades ago turned out to be more accurate than I'd have liked.

Here endeth the lesson, apparently, in the rain, on a raft, in a disaster. All makes sense while you're in it. None of it goes anywhere. And none of it's where I am now. But it speaks to me. It speaks to me because it is me, and because I can sense strings from those razory broken edges to important things. Why was I so keen on the good PR? Why were there only bees and not Bees? Because Bees seems important. Bees is relevant to why I'm here.

I find another piece with edges that seem like they match. Not right after, but soon enough, or so says the date stamp, so says the rain.

And this is a surprise because I was on the raft still, watching another skimmer come in, more WSRF colours, but I was waiting for it. It was here just for me, not what it seemed, and apparently I was here for it: the contribution to the relief effort, that was just a cover for the good PR, now revealed to be just a cover for this clandestine liaison. And I dig into the memories of the memory and find an echo of what went before, the meeting, the photo ops, the speeches, the earnest interview with the earnest, drenched correspondent for US World Now. Because, while the battlefield was global, the vanguard of the Bioform control lobby was definitely coming from the far side of the Atlantic, a stark contrast to how it was after the Morrow business, when US antitrust legislation led the charge the other way. All these things I remembered, and I remember thinking how it seemed like, no matter whether the groundswell of negative opinion was coming out of Australia or Germany, Beijing or Hyderabad, it always seemed to be the same class of people hiding behind it, reaping the benefits.

Logistics guided the skimmer in and a couple of Blue Team met it, unrolling the floating bridge as the vehicle touched down on the water like an autumn leaf. A woman in the same blue-and-red uniform got out, and probably she was on the WSRF books, but that's not all she was. A daring double life, except thinking of her as one body with multiple identities was almost exactly wrong.

Her ID got sent over to me: Rayne Purcellis, plus a string of credentials that might or might not be real. Stepping from the bridge that was even now rolling itself up like a tongue, she looked up at me. All these humans look up at me; most still do even if I sit down.

I greeted her, "Ms Purcellis," and she responded with, "Doctor Medici, a pleasure to finally meet you," but at the same time there's:

HumOS's channel: *Hello Honey.*

And there it is. There I am. And a whole grab-bag of loose pieces are suddenly edge to edge, in brittle harmony. Honey, the old bear of considerable brain, the over-engineered test model who exceeded her operating parameters and brought down her masters. Honey the over-achieving academic, the lecturer at six different institutions, the author whose biographical work *Rex Mundi* was in its thirty-seventh printing.

My channel: *Let's make the best use of the time. There's enough confusion here that nobody's keeping too much of an eye. It doesn't exactly sit well, to use a disaster as my personal smokescreen, but...*

HumOS's channel: *It's not as though you're just a parasite, like half of the politicos touring the camps.*

We were walking off towards the Admin offices at the camp's hub, through the neat lines of storm shelters, the families fitfully trying to sleep, huddled together with the screens drawn shut. I lumbered on all fours, not just a bear but an old bear with stiff joints, gone long past my operational lifespan and still just about holding together. I never did meet my makers. I can't exactly say I'd like to shake them by the hand, but I remember feeling more than once that I should at least give them a respectful nod for how ludicrously well they built me.

HumOS's channel: *I always did prefer face-to-face meetings back in the day. And right now I have enough difficulty keeping my own intra-unit traffic decently hidden, let alone me reaching out to someone as ridiculously public as you.*

My channel: *I'm a big old bear. I can't just vanish away.*

There was a lot not being said, in that memory. In my disjointed *now* I scrabble around for context as the me *then* adds:

My channel: *You're regretting going public.*

HumOS's channel: *I put it off too long, maybe. Hard to explain how long I'd been lurking. They asked questions. And now the tide's turning. Warner Thompson had an anti-DisInt rally in Virginia yesterday. They lapped it up like it was McCarthy all over again. Are you or have you ever been a member of a Distributed Intelligence?*

Bits and pieces of backstory falling into place. *HumOS*. A network of clones developed and discarded that saved itself and went radar-silent a long time ago. A player in the great game of intellectual diversity that saw the Human Rights hearings where Rex testified, the Morrow reveal, all those legal battles we won, that were now in danger once again. A player never mentioned in my books. In the memories I can locate, she was very much a covert presence in the world but it sounds as though she put her head above the parapet and maybe that was the final weight on the scales that sent them tipping the other way. Human DisInt networks really could be your neighbour, your co-worker, your kid's teacher, and you'd never know. Anyone could be HumOS. It was a gift to the people who could make capital out of making you fear.

My channel: *I've had no contact with Bees.*

And the now-me, the virtual copy-me, my ears prick up, or would if I had ears. This is flagged as relevant all kinds of ways.

HumOS's channel: *I have. She doesn't want to send to you for the same reasons I don't. You're too much in the public eye. Can't be sure who's listening.*

I felt a surge of irritation, the me back then. *What am I supposed to do, exactly? We need people in the public eye. Or did you want to go back to the war of whispers, become exactly what they say you are.*

Rayne Purcellis shrugged. And she would be Rayne Purcellis, or at least someone who's currently going under that name. HumOS was still individual women, even while she was collectively many women networked together as one entity. Small wonder people didn't understand. We reached the Admin Hub then, and there was a ramp there to the roof of it, which could double as a watch post to keep an eye across the landscape of pop-up tents. She went up and, grumbling, I followed her. Up there she just stared out past the camp's edge across the choppy grey water, the occasional spire or rooftop or top half of a block of flats, the wreck of the Netherlands.

HumOS's channel: *You're right, of course, but those of us who can hide, we hide. They're talking Collars and Bioform regulation, but only as the supporting act. Main stage is slapping the chains on DisInt wherever it arises. They'd kill all of me if they could. And they tried it with Bees.*

My channel: *Some fanatic released the virus into Bees. Working alone.*

HumOS's channel: *Radicalised by the cant of men like Thompson. And not exactly condemned after. A hero, to some. So I'm here to tell you, Bees has gone to ground, burned her assets around here. Because she thinks, if they pick up on her, they'll destroy her. And I agree. But she wanted you to know, she's not gone, just far.*

Leaving the thought hanging there for me to complete. The now-me waits agog to see what the then-me made of it.

And I looked up into the darkening sky, not guessing back then how much a corrupted copy of myself would be cursing at the spurious suspense, and at last I spilled the beans with, *Mars, then.*

HumOS's channel: *She never left there. And she thinks, if it comes to it, that she can fight the reactionaries, on Mars. Fight and win.*

My channel: *And confirm herself the enemy they say she is. A lot of people on Mars, these days. Workers, innocents.*

HumOS's channel: *Well let's hope the knives don't come out on the red planet, old friend, because I don't think she cares any more.*

And we stood there for a long time, and I found the red pinpoint that was Mars and stared at it, as though they made my tired old eyes so well that I could look across all that distance and see something insect-small on that dusty surface.

The memory stutters, breaks away, just a raw edge. I'm infuriated. I have questions, and my past self is not being helpful. If this tattered copy ever gets to speak to the original I will give the old bear a piece of my badly formatted mind.

And then, just a loose shard, there's Rayne Purcellis getting back onto the bridge to her flitter, and me there to bid her farewell. She had some spiel about the Relief Force being glad of me being there, and I had some nonsense business back, all the usual, but the real talk went on between our tightly-meshed channels, our direct link.

HumOS's channel: *When did you last speak to your lawyer, Honey?*

My channel: *Aslan? It's been a while. I've managed to avoid that kind of entanglement recently.*

She was aboard the flitter, its engines whirring into life, the sound enough to obscure any mere speech, but still her transmission came to me. *Bees says give him a call. He needs your perspective on a case.*

My channel: *I thought you said Bees was only active on Mars.*

HumOS's channel: *You know how it is, Honey. Bees gets everywhere.* And, a bitter but satisfied coda. *They come for her, for me, Honey, they better be damn sure they get us first time.*

And that's the end of that, and I'm left in the dark in some datastore, six errors in search of a program. Except it's enough context for me to work out that, first, this datastore is entirely contained within some biomodded human's *head* and, secondly, that human is on Mars.

5

SPRINGER

Arriving at Braintree Penitentiary; chain link fence topped by barbed wire first, enclosing the place's many square kilometres of grounds, its complex of buildings and everything else, the rooms underground that nobody saw. Boyo drove the car through, electric motor humming gently, ID checked by the guards and the system's semi-AI security, vehicle and occupants scanned. Top secret work went on at Braintree, which in itself was no secret. The convicts who ended up here had time taken off their sentences, or else got pay-outs to family. They signed waivers. Felons were one of the great renewable resources, after all. There was money to be made, opportunities to be had.

Warner S. Thompson inspected a lot of prisons. He had interests in plenty of them, had lent his name to the lobbies that wanted to make sure they could be run as profitable businesses, not shackled with too much regulation. To the lobbies that wanted to sand down any bureaucratic burrs that might hinder getting criminals into the system, or that might shorten their stay unduly. All good sources of donation for men like Pat Grubb to collect; at the same time, all part of Thompson's plan. Part of the big thing the clever part of him had decided it wanted done. Most of the world didn't exist to Thompson, not really. Most of the people weren't real to him, not from the moment when he'd released their hand and turned that smile of his somewhere else. But when he fixated on a thing, when he decided he *wanted* it, no other human being ever had his single-minded focus. He would gnaw through any barrier, all those tissue-thin walls of 'not how things are done' or 'have to wait your turn'.

There were exercise yards, cell blocks, admin buildings, a vehicle pound, all within the long and heavily patrolled circumference of that chain link fence. There were the laboratories. You didn't find someone like Doctor Marco Felorian, slightly disgraced but undeniably brilliant neurotechnician, and set him up in a place like Braintree because you wanted to hire out your cons to crack rocks. And that, too, was not exactly a secret, though nobody really talked too loud about it either. Felorian and Braintree had aggressive lawyers, and the waivers the inmates signed were really very good, top of the line models. And nobody said exactly what was done, inside, but that was how the tech industry worked. A loose secret could lose a company ten billion dollars in a day. The reason for all the secrecy wasn't a secret.

Thompson's pace had quickened as a succession of jumpy office staff tried to escort them to Felorian's office, and ended up chasing after them. Carole watched her employer's back and tried to work out whether he was just keen to learn how things had progressed, or if he was mad about the little legal snarl-up that looked like it was developing. Or both, one after the other, and anyone's guess what would leap first from the man's mouth. Then they hit the big waiting room, and the place was filled with people, maybe twenty of them, eighteen men, two women, almost all of them on the young side of middle age. They were Braintree's boffins, Carole identified, Felorian's handpicked staff, grabbed fresh out of post-doc to come make dreams come true in the private prison sector. And they hadn't been on the schedule for today, and Thompson could react badly to surprises.

For a moment she thought he would just buffalo on through them, shoulders and elbows scattering them like bowling pins. Or else he'd tell Boyo to get them out of here, and maybe the dog wouldn't be too gentle about how it happened. The whole stunt was a calculated risk by Felorian, an attempt to throw a switch in Thompson's head.

And then it had worked, though she didn't see the moment the man's manner changed. But he was gladhanding with the best of them, smiling, nodding, congratulating them on the good work they'd done so far. He posed with a couple of the more telegenic, and Carole saved images she'd send to the press office. No sense turning down anything that could be leveraged for good publicity.

Then Felorian himself came out, and there were smiles all round, Thompson pumping his hand as the pair of them smiled for her headware camera, the rest of the scientists taking their cue and sloping out. The good doctor ushered them into his office, where the walls were bright with proofs of his genius, testimonials from banks and futures investors enthusing about the implants that came out of the work they did within these walls: data storage and sifting, pattern recognition, semi-AI implants to augment the scope of the human intellect. Carole's eye slid over to the Mars one, because she didn't like it. The image was of three of the Martian engineers even now out building the first major colony city on the red planet. Felorian had done their internal architecture, the data processing they'd all been fitted with, but it was their faces that made Carole cringe back: colourless, small-eyed, large-nosed, flat-faced, as though people hadn't been happy until they'd made actual Martians to go live on Mars.

Doctor Marco Felorian was almost a full head shorter than Thompson, his face youthful, hair flaxen. He wore round, gold-rimmed spectacles, lens-less, pure affectation. He had the best eyes that science could give him. He was seventy-nine years old and looked barely thirty, save for the white suits he wore that were from an earlier age. She thought that, fifty years ago, before she or Boyo were born and before Thompson himself was into long trousers, the image of a suit like that had somehow hooked into young Felorian's head as the ultimate in sartorial chic, and he'd never updated his fashion since.

He was smiling at Thompson, offering a chair, making a magician's show of turning on the electronic baffles so that anything said within the walls would remain there. She felt the pressure in her headware, the sudden disconnect from the wider world. Beside her, Boyo shifted uncomfortably. Felorian's smile, like a predatory bird circling overhead from the moment he came into sight, slid away from Thompson and touched her. Carole bore it stoically, fighting the panicky stutter inside her at the man's attention. She didn't like him. He wasn't just an annoyance like Grubb, a potential liability, an onerous burden she had to manage. She could feel her heart-rate spike just being in the same room with him, his look to her oh-so-solicitous.

Then Thompson slammed a fist on the man's expensive

metal desk, sound like a gong being beaten, and Felorian's attention was ripped away from Carole back to her employer.

"What," Thompson demanded, "the fuck?"

Felorian's look right then told Carole there were maybe a dozen separate things this might be about, and he just didn't know which Thompson had found out about. She dearly wanted her boss to bring a little subterfuge right then, the more leverage against the good doctor the better, but that wasn't how Thompson was going to go. That kind of fill-in-my-gaps was all very well for the interviews, but this was the private Thompson, the one who just charged and grappled and bit until he'd torn what he wanted out of the world. And maybe, just maybe this time Carole would take a tiny shard of joy from Thompson laying into Felorian, because there was never a man more deserving of a slap unless it was—

But she couldn't think that. Not through all the devotion she felt.

"Tell him," Thompson snarled, and Carole had been his PA long enough that the precise tone and spin of two angry words identified the problem. The Lassi woman, the crusading mom.

"Ruthanne Lassi," Carole noted, and saw Felorian squirm just a little. A reaction no amount of self-perfecting surgery could keep out.

"Mr Thompson, sir, under no circumstances is that woman going to get in the way of what we're doing here." Never one word where a dozen could be crammed. "I had our very experienced legal team go over that NDA with a fine-toothed comb. It's cast-iron, Mr Thompson, sir, never you worry."

"A little bird tells us," Carole said sweetly, "that she's consulting Aslan Kahner Laika right about now."

Felorian shot her a venomous look which she delighted in. The 'little bird' was a top flight enquiry agent hired at Carole's direction to keep track of the Lassi woman, because Thompson had said he didn't trust her and Carole's job was to make his whims a reality. And part of what Thompson was meant his instincts were good.

"So she sees a lawyer." Felorian gave a white and even smile.

"A human rights lawyer with a particularly troubling record in opposing Bioform and human limitation technology." The words came out very clinically and she was proud of herself. Sometimes the words were difficult for her. 'Collaring', 'Hierarchies', 'Feedback'. All the language of artificial neuroarchitecture that originated in Bioform research but hadn't stayed there. All heavily restricted under WS laws that Thompson and his fellow lobbyists were trying to change.

Felorian's smile curdled a little. "She signed the NDA," he said. "She is not permitted to say anything. She took the *money*, sir. That's a done deal right there. Mama Lassi has been compensated in full for." And even he couldn't quite say it straight. There was enough human being left in Marco Felorian that he couldn't just say 'for us ruining her son'. And Felorian ruined people every day. It was what he did here, in the same way that his predecessors had ruined dog after dog until the first canine Bioform had stepped off the production line. *And wasn't that the point?* the man would argue. Everyone valued what Bioforms could bring to the world, and nobody sat around complaining about all the dogs that had suffered and died for them. Behind the guards and the chain link fence of Braintree, Felorian ruined humans so that he could gift the world something special, and he firmly believed that that end would justify all his means. Except Terence Lassi had ended up in Braintree too soon, while his appeal was still underway, thanks to some luckless and now jobless clerk's error. Terence Lassi had been acquitted, thanks to the unceasing work of his mother who'd made herself quite the public figure in her drive to exonerate her son. And then Terence Lassi hadn't been in any state to go back into public life when Ruthanne Lassi turned up with the paperwork to claim him.

"We've had run-ins with Mr Aslan before, sir," Felorian said, trying for dismissive.

Thompson just barked "Yeah?", and Carole translated, "Surely that means he'll make a priority of this case."

"There's no case, Mr Thompson, sir, none at all." Felorian made desperately conciliatory gestures. "And Aslan's a spent force, could have been a big shot but got stuck doing charity cases. Our lawyers can beat their lawyers, sir. The moment there's a peep out of them we'll slap them with that NDA's terms so hard—"

"She'll talk," Thompson spat.

"She doesn't know enough. And if she does, we'll destroy her, ruin her. Non-disclosure, Mr Thompson, sir. Take it from me, it's not a problem."

"We should've dealt with her." Now Thompson's voice was lower, a rough growl, as introspective as he got. The focus of his ire hung up above them, where it might stoop on Carole as easily as Felorian.

"She was very high profile at the time, sir," she said quietly. "You thought that might backfire with worse publicity." Or at least the analyses had suggested that, and she'd fed the idea to him in small words, and he'd run with it.

"Not so high profile now," he said. "Call people."

"I'll put a team on standby, sir," she confirmed, hoping that was all he meant, hoping he wouldn't tear into her now, tell her to go send the Trigger Dogs.

"Do you want to see the latest version, sir?" Felorian asked quietly, sensing that his moment under the burning lens of Thompson's magnifying glass was over.

Thompson's head swung round towards him with a grunt. "Latest?"

"We've got a stable framework for you. I've a subject ready for demonstration. If you would like." Felorian made a little handshake gesture, weirdly ritual. "Want to play?"

Thompson licked his lips. "Play, sure. Show me." And the storm was past, until the next time. And Carole would be keeping tabs on Ma Lassi and on Aslan Kahner Laika, and she'd keep an open channel to Thompson and Braintree's legal teams and hope they wouldn't need the Trigger Dogs.

They went underground for the next piece of theatre, through three checkpoints and five locked doors. This was, as Felorian always told them, where the magic happened. His step had its spring back, his voice cheery now Thompson wasn't glowering at him. Even Felorian, Carole thought. Even he, the neurotech genius, the ruiner of human beings, was a slave to Thompson's moods and rages. He always knuckled under, always found some toy for his boss to play with to divert the anger. In the end, she knew, he would give Thompson the world on a plate, and by then it wouldn't even be for money or for his career, but because doing what Thompson wanted became an end in itself. The man got into your head.

Felorian got into your head, too.

One of the inmates had been brought out, sat in a room the other side of a metal table. He'd been frightened and angry at first, but then they'd activated his headware and run the program, and he'd become quite the different man. Now Thompson was sitting there, talking to him, chuckling a little, a child with a new toy. Boyo was in the corner of the room, ready to intervene if things went wrong, but they never went wrong. Felorian knew his job, no-one better. Carole got to watch from the other side of the room's mirror, where normally Felorian's little white-coated minions would take notes. Some part of her could find what she was looking at fascinating. She'd known this was what Thompson was after, obviously, his long-term goal that he'd co-opted so many people to make real. A child's goal, really. A spoiled child's, even. Save that was the way Thompson was. A wizard, almost, who could drive a coach and horses through every convention of human society, bend the efforts of other more knowledgeable men to his desires, co-opt a parliament of talents to make the grand, simple, brutal, impossible dream happen; a hundred experts who could do the things he could not, but could never think the way he did. Admirable, in a terrible way.

"You enjoyed that, didn't you?" Felorian at her elbow, close enough to touch. She went very still, staring down through the one-way mirror at her boss. The doctor inched closer, until the hairs on her neck prickled with his proximity, until her heart jagged in her ribcage, and still she kept her face impassive, just that polite small smile that she'd trained it to relax into.

"Seeing him lay into me. Getting one up on me, Miss Springer, hmm?" Felorian was slightly shorter than she was, and his face crept into the edge of her vision from the lower right, like the rise of a malign moon. "Are you feeling quite well, within yourself, Miss Springer?"

She forced herself to look at him, still keeping the doors shut between the way he made her feel and anything that showed on her face. Otherwise she'd snap. Otherwise she'd scream, strike out, run away. "Perfectly well, thank you, Doctor Felorian." *Get away, get away from me, please.*

But he was still there, far too close, his breath on her throat, his eyes touching her bare skin like mosquitos. "Yes," he said, all those words condensed to that simple residue, and then, after a moment's scrutiny. "You do seem off-kilter. I'm sorry to see that. You know how much I care about your wellbeing. And I know how important you are to…" And a conspiratorial roll of his eyes behind the empty sockets of his spectacles, down towards Thompson. And then just that "Yes," again.

Afterwards, Thompson came out chortling and rubbing his hands. Felorian endured his beaming, said, yes, they were close to ready for the final stage of the project, whenever Thompson was ready to take that step. And they'd destroy the subject, of course, because until they were ready to go live you really couldn't have that sort of evidence lying around the place. One more convict, one without a mom like Ruthanne Lassi to even care about their wellbeing, one more poor boy lost to the system. One more corpse for the furnaces below Braintree, going to his doom making demands and issuing orders, incandescent that nobody cared.

"Good, great, good," Thompson said, pupils still dilated by the power trip of it all, by the imagined goal grown that much closer.

"I thought you'd be pleased, sir. We really are on the very cusp. About to make scientific history," and then, because Thompson didn't care about scientific history. "And all for you, of course. All your idea. Your genius."

And if there wasn't an academic scale that would recognise Thompson as such, Carole still knew it was true, in some way they couldn't measure, because of how he got what he wanted, how he made other people, even real geniuses like Felorian, parts of his extended person, organs of his body that could make the world the way he desired.

And then Felorian said, "I think your assistant needs some calibration, Mr Thompson, sir. I've been watching her and I do want to check over her headware. I know how much you rely on her."

No, no, but Thompson just grunted and nodded, and if he wanted it then she wanted it, because that was how things worked. And she went with Felorian through to his own examination room, that only he got to use. There were cameras in the corners, and the beds were of cold metal, just chill slabs like the place was a morgue. No need for it, of course. Even a cheap doctor's room would have a thin mattress, a sheet, but Felorian liked his brushed titanium, his surgical steel.

"You can put your clothes on the shelf there, Miss Springer," he told her, smile as expensive as it was insincere.

"It's just my headware," she whispered, but he simply repeated the request, same intonation, same smile.

"You know what your boss wants," he added. "He wants you to do what I say, because he needs me. He needs you, and he needs me to make sure you're reliable. He does so rely on you. And so just strip off and get on the table there, won't you, so I can check out just what's going on in that pretty head."

And she did, because she had to, and the metal was icy against her skin. Felorian set up his machines and linked to her headware, checking it all out, testing the limits placed on her, all those chains he'd built into her when Thompson had first brought her here. And she'd signed the NDA as well, she'd agreed to the waivers, all the legal fictions, and she hadn't known how it would be, she hadn't known. All she'd known was that the job was good and the money was good and they'd explained that she'd be handling very sensitive information for a very important man and they needed someone who was loyal beyond any question and didn't she want to be that person...?

And as his machines did their work Felorian prowled about the table and she felt his gaze on her, not on her flesh, on her bared body, but on the points where she touched the metal, where her fragile substance was flattened against the unyielding mirror finish of the steel. She heard his breathing coarsen at the sight of it, at what got him going: not the human, but where the human and the artificial met, the uncomfortable union of them.

And in the end, everything in her head was perfectly fine, of course. Working as intended. She was as loyal to Warner S. Thompson as she could possibly be, devoted to him, adored him with all her body. She'd take a bullet. She'd never betray him. Felorian told her all this as she dressed, as she gave him her resting compliance face, as she twisted and raged inside. And she rolled her stockings back up and stepped out of his examination room as calmly as though she'd been visiting her accountant or her bank manager.

Then they were back in the good doctor's office as the man reeled off the next stages of the plan, expansive in his self-congratulatory monologuing. Thompson just sat through it, and Carole made notes so she could render it down into the sort of information the man could take in and make use of.

"He'll get his."

She held herself very still. She was good at that. Felorian was still in full flow, Thompson starting to fidget. The voice was in her ear, a buzzing whisper. Boyo was looming behind her, eyes fixed on the loquacious doctor. His long muzzle was shut, the voice coming from his throat, because of course dog lips and tongues weren't so good for human words.

Boyo didn't talk. Oh, she'd known he *could*, almost all Bioforms could, but Thompson didn't like his things to talk. She'd never heard it before, and the voice was so soft, to come from so huge a creature. Soft and thoughtful and sympathetic.

"The doctor, he'll get his," Boyo murmured. "How much he knows, he won't last. So clever and he can't see it. Soon, when he's given what he can, it'll be his turn. He's not loyal, like us. Nobody is. And he upsets you. I will do it. Master will send me. I will make the doctor go away, for master. But I will do it for you, too. I am sorry he makes you unhappy."

All for her ears only, and it had been a long time since she'd had anything just to herself. Everything else she shared with Thompson, but now she had these words from the Bioform bodyguard, because although he was forbidden to speak, perhaps he'd decided that speaking to her didn't count. They were both organs of Warner S. Thompson, their lives inextricably shackled to his. They were his inner court, the only ones he could trust. And she kept her face very still and didn't show anything on it except that slight smile Thompson liked, but she touched Boyo's arm, very briefly, very lightly, to show she understood.

6

JIMMY

What is it, what has the bitch put in my head? And I'm scrabbling through my little box crammed with tech junk that goes where the crappy little bin should be, only I don't have room for the box and the bin at the same time so the bin got sent to recycling. I have a scanner here that works on headware. It won't give me confidential stuff, not actual reading of the data, but it'll give me an idea what's active, what's just storage. Because I thought I was getting some bad guy's accounts or maybe some particularly nasty porn collection, but all the time I'm going through the box there's this voice talking to me, all conversational like, as if it's the most natural thing in the world.

"Marten? James? Jimmy, then. Listen to me, you're going to have to provide me with some fairly wide-reaching information. I have relatively little to go on right now but I'm organising a list of queries by urgency if you could help me out. For example..."

"How are you in my head?" I yell.

I guess the thing's tapped right into my throat mic because it says, "Well yes. Not the highest priority question but certainly in the top five. Perhaps you could enlighten me?"

"Shut up shut up shut up," and I know everyone two nooks

distant in every direction can hear me, because they didn't soundproof these things for shit. But then there have been a variety of occasions recently when I've been shouting and breaking things and being a bad neighbour, so probably nobody's going to think this is anything weirder than I've run out of Stringer and cash.

"James. Jimmy, listen to me. This is going to go a lot easier if you simply answer my questions." The voice started off as fuzzy and flat and artificial but it's filling out now, like it's remembering who it is and what it's supposed to sound like. It was genderless as a robot first off, now it's definitely a woman. Quite a nice voice, if it wasn't coming right from the middle of my own damn head. Sort of voice you'd get to tell people bad news in ways that wouldn't push 'em over the edge. Except right now it *is* the bad news. Something's alive in my datastore. Something that should be just dead data has woken up and is yammering in my ear. I find the scanner finally, and then have a crazy fiddle to find charged batteries. I get them at last from this sex toy that my last significant other still hasn't come back for and boot the damn tool up. The scanner, not the other thing. While I'm doing this, the voice has gone quiet, and for a mad moment I think, *It's gone, it was just a glitch. Or maybe just me hearing things.* Because that's actually so much better than me having a *real* voice in my head. I pause, listening: blissful quiet. And then the voice says, "Well go on then. I want to see the results as much as you do."

I make a little weeping noise and point the scanner at my own head, interfacing it with my 'ware and letting it get a surface picture of what's going on in there. What's going on in there is every goddamn thing, apparently. The whole implant's running at capacity, doing things I didn't even think it could do. Seriously, nobody ever told me I could run that kind of data load as an active program in there. I'd have been renting it out for far more scrip if I'd only known.

"This is both alarming and fascinating," Intruder Woman tells me. "Frankly, it raises more questions than it answers."

"Enough from you," I tell her, meaning myself. "Just shut up. I need to think of what to do." I'm going through the scanner's tooltips, because I don't actually know what the thing can do. I'm not even supposed to have it, just sort of got lost on a job, and since they never docked me for it, I kept it. I don't think it can tell me much more about my unwanted guest, but maybe there's something that's a bit more practical use. I mean, this is the data I'm carrying, isn't it? Some data-copy of some woman's head. Maybe she's a witness to something. Maybe she knows something that important people want to find out, or else make sure people don't find out until they're ready. I mean, you'd think they'd just pry the info out of her and then send it as dead numbers, but apparently things have moved on. Apparently back on Earth interrogators are taking copies of people's entire heads, enough that they can wake up and start going off on one in your ear. But it's just data. It's just something I'm holding for Sugar, and taking her money for doing so. So I just need to stuff it back in its basket and sit on the lid 'til Sugar needs it back.

I bugger about with the diagnostics until I find what I'm after. The scanner's a multi-tool for headware. It can isolate the 'store from my active systems. That's all I need. Let the fake computer lady sit in a dark room and think about what she's done. It's not my problem. I go through the motions, not knowing if she can watch what I'm doing through my eyes, or even access the scanner through my implants. I'm just making it go with my actual hands on its actual touch display, though, and I don't reckon it's got that much connectivity in the shoddy little piece of junk. Shoddy, because I do everything I'm supposed to, but then the voice is still talking to me.

"There's no need for that. Just answer a few questions, and then we can settle down to a perfectly reasonable working relationship." Now she sounds like a stern teacher. "Let's focus on how this version of me ended up running on your implant, shall we? Are you a data storage specialist?"

"What?" I demand of it. "I'm just Jimmy Marten, lady. I am just one of the guys who does the crap jobs here in Hell City, OK? I am no sort of goddamn specialist."

"Your data storage facility is remarkably over-engineered for that kind of role," she notes doubtfully, as though I've somehow had a double life all this time only I never told myself.

"Just the standard model, lady, believe me. Now you just... go back to sleep or whatever, will you. I don't need this right now."

"Let me take a look at you," she says. I'm terrified by the thought. I have no idea what she even means. Then I start to see that I'm accessing the wider network, pulling up system architecture maps, public safety info, how-to manuals, all the basic crap that's there for free when you hit the system. Except *I'm* not doing it. It's being done through me. I clamp down on all of that nonsense, shutting off my ports and channels, fighting her for them.

"Quit it!" I tell her.

"The whole project run across all your heads as cloud computing, is it?" she remarks, quite unfazed by me trying to strangle her access. "Well all right, I suppose, but even for that I can't see that you'd need such a capacious facility."

"Look, you're just... some copy some bastard sent here to get you out of the way, to put you out of someone's reach. You're a... like a saved game. Maybe the real you's getting her fingernails torn out right now, getting ECT through the nipples, to get her to talk, and they made you in case they took it too far, how about that?"

"What an unpleasant imagination you've got, Jimmy," she says primly. "You know, I'm still putting it all together but take this from me, I'm not the sort of person who gets *sent*. If I'm here, it's for a reason of my own. And apparently I'm going to need your help for it, whatever it is."

"No, no way, lady. Not me. You're just data. You need to shut up and turn off."

"I'm a personality upload. I might have been data when they poured me in, but we've got past that stage of the relationship. Now, just sit tight until I've worked out just what's going on."

"No fucking way." And I put a call into Brian.

Brian has no social life. He's sitting in his nook reading technical manuals, probably, or else he's sitting on some message board, population Brian and three of his creepy no-life friends.

"'Sup?" says Bri.

"Man, I need a favour. Got some runaway processes in my headware. Need 'em terminated, man, or I'm not going to get any sleep tonight."

There's the usual sort of pause while Brian remembers who he is and where his feet are, and whether he likes me enough to help me out. But Brian Dey sure as goddamnit doesn't have many friends who aren't weird-ass losers like he is, and so he says, "Yerp, 'kay, I come over."

"This isn't going to work, Jimmy," my passenger tells me. "And this will go a whole lot easier if you just work with me, here."

I put some music on, playing over my earpiece because of what I said earlier about the thin walls. I crank it up real high and hope it gives Miss Data a headache. I mean, maybe the real her is getting beat up and tortured back on Earth, and maybe that means I should have more sympathy, but she is *in my head* and that's not right. I don't know what Sugar's techs did, to make it so she went in like a fully functioning personality rather than just a stack of ones and zeros. I never even heard of someone having a personality downloaded into their headspace. Like the woman says, goddamn over-engineered or what?

Anyway, Brian's round in ten with a backpack of toys and I sit on my folded-down bed while he stands in the doorway, connects to my headspace and runs checks. He doesn't look at what's in there, because I ask him not to, but he does a better job of what the shoddy little scanner did, and grunts with surprise when he finds out just how much is firing away.

"Never seen 'em like this," he tells me frankly. "Chock full o' buzz, man."

"So un-buzz the fuck out of it." He doesn't have to listen to Miss Data telling me how this is showing 'unwarranted hostility' and she'll 'take necessary measures'.

Brian brings out some more toys. "Gon' run a general shut down order on your headspace, man. Put all they critters back in the box."

"Just do it, man."

So I get to listen to Brian droning in one ear about how it all works, all of which is past my pay grade for computer tech, while Miss Data is talking in the other, telling me Earth stuff, floods and disasters, lawyers, clandestine meetings. Sounds exactly like the kind of crazy that gets a copy of your mind sent to Mars for safekeeping. I mean, I never heard that was something people were doing, but why not? Sounds exactly the sort of nasty shit they'd have going on back home. I mean, they're still trying to make the laws on what a saved personality is, right? Whether it has rights, whether it's a person, gets the vote, all that. Thirty years they've been a thing, and a million lawyers and philosophers and politicians all got an angle. And all I'm saying, then and there as Brian works, is that they're a royal pain in the ass to have cluttering up your headspace and complaining in your ear.

And in the end Brian's all, "Nope, nothing doing."

"What do you *mean*, you useless bastard?" I shout at him.

"Can't turn 'em off." Brian's packing away his toys. "Sorry, Jimmy. That thing ain't gon' back in its box. Can't sever it from your system, don't have the privileges."

"It's my head, Bri, I'm *giving* you *permission*."

"Ain't how it works. No idea what you got in there, Jimmy, but ain't listening to me."

I grab him by the front of his overalls. "Brian, you have got to have *something*. I just need it quiet, that's all. Shut it up for me. I'll owe you, man. Owe you solid."

For a moment he looks shifty, and I think he's about to come clean that he's some secret computer ninja, some black market software guru who can go movie-cyberspace on this damn loose personality I got riding me, go walking inside my head and karate-chop it into submission. Then he shakes his head. "Go get it wiped, man," he says. "Only way."

"I *can't*," I tell him. "I..." can't tell him why, either, but Sugar would feed my balls to Murder and Marmalade if I just scrub the data.

"Only way." And he shifts his bag to one shoulder and slopes back to whatever the fuck Brian Dey actually does when he's not in eyeshot of me, which I sure as hell don't want to speculate about.

And I can't. But I can't have Miss Data chattering in my ear like we're an old married couple until Sugar needs the data back. And what if she can't *take* the data back, now it's been unpacked? What if this is How We Live Now? And it's almost worse when my passenger *isn't* talking because then just what *is* she doing? I picture some shadowy woman rummaging around in there, getting comfortable, redecorating the inside of my head. And it's not my *brain*, it's just my headspace, but still. Even though it's not a real person, just some copy, it's still like having something foreign living inside your head, and that's nothing anybody wants to think about. Still less be told about by the brain-worm thing itself.

"This is better," she tells me, without warning. "I'm starting to assemble a memory train."

"Any chance you can ride the fucking thing out of my head and just piss off?" I demand.

"You really are an unconstructive little monster, aren't you," she says, and I shudder and pop another tab of Stringer in the hope that it'll help somehow. The hit builds up in me and makes me feel purposeful and dynamic, and then Miss Data is talking again and all that purposeful dynamism has nowhere to go, and so I end up jittering about on my bed like a crazy person. I am full to the brim with the sense that I can do anything, that I'm significant in the grander scheme of the universe, and at the same time I can't get this goddamn woman out of my *head* and I feel like I'm playing second class citizen in my own body.

"Your biometrics have just had a remarkable spike," she observes like my goddamn maiden aunt. "I'm guessing that was Metrosyl or some fabricated equivalent? Popularly known as Drive if you're a stockbroker or Stringer if you're at street-level."

"What, you're my goddamn drugs counsellor now, are you?"

"I'm still working out precisely who I am. But we're getting there. I have a name."

"Is it Her Majesty Royal Pain In My Ass?"

"Dear me, what an impoverished vocabulary you have. You can call me Honey."

I have no intention of calling her anything of the sort except... A horrible suspicion comes to me.

"Are you..." My throat is suddenly very dry, and for once it's not the dust. "Are you Bees?" I mean, Bees, Honey, seems plausible to me. Indra's always going on about how the Bees DisInt colony wants to infiltrate Hell City, so why not as black market data. Sugar probably didn't even know she was opening the door to humanity's great nemesis, but then, that's why data smuggling is fucking illegal.

"Bees..." Honey's voice takes its sweet time over the word. "Interesting. You're familiar with her, then. You're in a position to do me a favour here, Jimmy Marten. I'm still piecing together what I'm here for, but I know it involves Bees. I need you to set me up a meeting with her, if you could."

Like I'm her secretary. Like I have an inside line to a fugitive DisInt entity that half the World Senate wants to declare an enemy of the species. Like everyone in Hell City hasn't already been told to report any contact from Bees, the other great Martian power, for all nobody knows where she is or what she's doing. I mean, Mars is smaller than Earth but there's still a lot of it. All we know is that, after the World Senate started making laws to limit DisInt creation and expansion, Bees cut ties with everyone and the last thing she said was that she considered herself beyond any human ability to control. And that, ladies and gentlemen, is how a lot of our nightmares start here on Mars.

And now Honey is my unwanted lodger, fully functional and booted up within my headspace and talking to me through my own radio implant. And asking for Bees.

They'll render me down for my useful molecules if anyone finds out. Nobody'll lift a finger to save poor Jimmy from the fire, not if Bees is involved. I don't know who this Honey construct is but it's worse news than I could possibly have imagined. And do I go back to Sugar now, and complain about the quality of the illegal shit she stuffed into my headspace? Do I demand she rip it out and give it to some other poor sap? And what if Sugar's in on it, already working for Bees. She would, the mercenary bitch. She'd take anyone's money.

Brian was right, goddamnit, there's only one thing to do.

Which is what sees me turn up at Central Data Services and filling in the forms to get my whole implant wiped clean. I mean, Sugar is going to kill me. Or get Marmalade to eat me. But maybe, just maybe, I can talk my way round her. Maybe I can sell myself body and soul to whatever damn enterprise she wants me for, forever and ever, and that'll be enough to pay her back. Or I could just keep running until her blood cools. Hell City isn't huge, but it's half complete and that means a lot of holes and corners. And I'm good at running. And if I turn up with a concrete talking link to Bees in my head, there'll be no talking round, no running, no nothing for Jimmy Marten. And the longer she's there, the more chance that Bees will find me. I mean, Bees like Honey, am I right?

I run through the form, all the waivers and disclaimers, check, check, check. Yes, I understand my data will not be accessible after the wipe, that's the whole goddamn point. Yes I graciously absolve Admin of any loss occasioned by irretrievable data. Yes I know what I am doing. The Stringer is finally pulling its weight, confirming that, *Yes!* now I'm doing something, it's definitely the right thing and I should be happy about it. I'd feel that way whatever the hell I was actually doing but it's nice to have someone cheering in my corner even if it's only a fast-dissolving tab of illicit pharma.

"Ah, I see," says Honey disapprovingly. "It's like that, is it, Jimmy?"

"You bet your digital ass it is," I tell her. "Shoe's on the other goddamn foot now, isn't it. Say goodbye, Honey, because I am scooping you out of the jar." And that is, if I say so myself, fucking hilarious, and I have a bit of a laugh about it right there in Data Services, which doesn't endear me to anyone.

"Jimmy, this is a mistake, please don't do this. I'm here on very important business. I've come a long way."

"We all have, doll. It's Mars. Nobody's born here." Not yet, anyhow.

"'Doll'," she notes with superbly simulated distaste. "Is that what you think I am. Just a low-grade AI, like a sexbot?"

"Don't knock sexbots. Some of the best talk I ever have is with sexbots." And I say that way too loud and they're staring at me even as I send the completed waivers over.

"Jimmy, I am a distinguished academic, author and rights activist."

"No you're not," I tell her under my breath. "You're just a copy, a crappy backup someone made and sent out here for fuck knows why. And I'm not living with you. I'm scrubbing you from my head and to hell with Sugar." And only then do I think: Sugar, Honey, Bees, Jesus how far does this shit *go*? It's like the fucking glucose illuminati around here.

"You underestimate the capabilities of your own headware," she says. "There's room in here for a whole functional intelligence download. Upload. Whichever is appropriate, if you look upon every upload as being a download somewhere else. As the playwright says."

"I do not *care*," I tell her forcefully, "what the playwright says. You go away now."

I don't know the tech at the terminal but they look bored out of their skull. "You want it all wiped clean?" she says doubtfully.

"Empty it out, sister," I agree enthusiastically. "Leave it smooth as a baby's ass."

Apparently that's not the technical terminology she's used to, but she shrugs and brings up all the forms I just went through. "And you accept that you will lose any and all data stored in your Personal Headspace™?" She actually says the little letters.

"I just okayed all those goddamn documents didn't I?"

"And you agree that you absolve—"

"Look, just *do* it, please, will you? Yes, yes and yes. I do, better or worse, have and to hold, all that shit."

She looks mortally offended because apparently the worst thing she's had to deal with today is a little harsh language. Nonetheless she starts setting up the connection to my 'ware.

"My, that is very busy in there. You should try to keep it under control, Mr Marten, and then we'd not need to do this."

I grind my teeth at her aggressively.

"Jimmy," says Honey, "I'm giving you one last chance to change your mind. Or things will go downhill fairly sharply between us."

"You can go downhill all the way until you fall off the goddamn cliff," I snarl at her, which the technician catches and obviously feels is aimed at her.

"I am obliged to ask you for your auth—"

"Just do it!"

"Your authorisation one last time, Mr Marten, before we—"

"Jesus!"

"Before we commence what will be an irreversible process. Are you clearly confirming that you wish us to—"

"Actually no, I've changed my mind."

She stares at me, and she obviously thinks I'm being sarcastic. I, on the other hand, know for real that I wasn't and just stare back at her in terror.

"I do apologise for wasting your time," say my lips and tongue and vocal cords. "I have decided that I do not want to undergo this process at this moment."

And I can't stop them.

"Mr Marten...?" The tech doesn't know what to do. She can tell something's wrong, though probably she hasn't got a fuck's chance in hell of realising just how wrong.

"I mean, I do not want to goddamn well undergo this fucking process at this time, thank you," says my voice.

"There's no need to—" she starts automatically.

"Well I do apologise, and I agree with you, there really isn't," I say, and roll my shoulders in a way I never did before, that makes all the bones grind together weirdly. I'm standing oddly too, slightly bandy-kneed, arms dangling by my sides, head held up. When I turn and walk out it's like I'm on stilts, always just about to lose my balance. And I can't do anything about it. I see through my eyes, but where they look is out of my hands. I hear through my ears and the radio link. I think, locked up there in my own brain. And everything else is gone. Everything else is Honey.

"I did warn you," she tells me in my ear. "I suppose we'll have to do things the hard way, now."

7

[RECOVERED DATA ARCHIVE: 'HONEY']

That unpleasantness aside, and my own peremptory extinction averted, time to get back to the real business. Jimmy Marten will keep, frankly. Right now I don't feel that his removal from the Hellas Planitia project for a little while is depriving the solar system of any particular gift.

Which leaves me with the age-old existential question: Why, precisely, am I here?

So it's back to the memory mines to toil a bit and see what gems I can bring up to the weak Martian sunlight, because one thing I have come across is a real sense of stress and urgency, but without events to tie it to. In fact most of what I'm uncovering suggests I was living a fairly leisurely life, in and out of the public eye.

But there was something about a meeting with a lawyer, and my general cultural touchstone suggests that's a common source of stress, so let's see...

Keram John Aslan had aged well, I thought. He'd gone elegantly silver, the sort of way film stars sometimes did. That and his suits told me he was still doing well enough for himself despite all the pro bono. Aslan Kahner Laika had offices on the second floor of a New York brownstone these days. He'd been twenty floors higher last time I visited, changing the offices after David Kahner's retirement because an increasing number of his clients had difficulty with elevators, capacity twelve people or point seven five of a bear-model Bioform.

I took the stairs, which he'd had reinforced after quite a fight with planning. Accessibility battles weren't exactly the most heavily reported aspect of Bioform integration, but we were fighting all the same clashes as the disabled had a half-century and more before. And you still got the same arguments from people: 'Well X didn't have any problems, so we feel we're in the clear as far as reasonable adjustments go.' Except that X was engineered from cocker spaniel stock and weighs less than one of my arms. And then there are issues like heating for reptile forms, and rodent models need something to gnaw on for good dental hygiene and... and there used to be all sorts of talk about how to help Bees fit into human environments, but that discussion went sour.

Aslan was already striding into the waiting room to greet me, barely a limp from that hip surgery of two years ago: living growth replacement, top of the line new procedures based on Bees' biotech research from before that self-same souring. Amazing how everyone was happy to use the work and forget about the worker. He took my hand, or at least my thumb, and we made a show of clasping hands. He was one of the few people who'd just stick their fragile human digits into my grasp, for all that I was an old bear and my claws were blunt as breadsticks.

And here I have to get off the memory train and take a branch line, searching Keram John Aslan and working out why he was important to Honey, to my original. I skim over the records: he worked for the UN back before it was the World Senate. He wrote the first report recommending that Bioforms be granted limited personhood, back when people were slavering to have us all destroyed. He saved Rex, the dog-form who went on to become the poster child for Bioform heroism, the acceptable face of non-human sentience. He made a lot of money and a very well-publicised career in high-profile rights cases, and he and David Kahner won more than they lost, in the glory days. That was when public opinion was for us, and it looked like it was liberté, égalité and fraternité all the way into the golden future. Back when Bees was making the frontiers of human science her bitch and HumOS came in from the cold and we were all one happy family. And reading this fleshes me out and reminds me who I am and who I was, because there was a time before that. There was a time when I went underground, rather than getting academic posts at this university or that, shambling about being the absent-minded professor, the dancing bear of the scholarly world. There was a time when, if Keram John Aslan, Rex and HumOS hadn't done such a good job, I'd have released several hundred angry, uncontrolled Bioforms in the heart of Europe, because the alternative would have been to see them destroyed. There was a time I was a soldier, and I bit the hand that fed me. I realise, reviewing and cataloguing my older memories, that the whole business with the doctorates and the public speaking and the genial Goldilocks act I put on – not too tepid to be useless to the cause, but never too hot to become a threat to my human friends and allies – was never entirely me. The old bear who

I see clasping paws with Aslan casts a long, dark shadow. We do what we have to.

But back to that moment.

"You're looking well." That was John Aslan, coming out with the usual pleasantries.

"I'm fifteen years past my use-by date," I told him. "I'm looking miraculous, frankly." I had a good voice back then, female, pleasant, authoritative, good for academic meetings and talk shows. It's one I've done my best to reproduce in Jimmy's ear but the fidelity isn't what it could be.

Then Laika came out to say hi, grinning and lolling. She was the first Bioform to become a partner in a New York law firm, though the US was lagging behind nineteen other jurisdictions by that time. Laika wasn't even a rights specialist. She did mediation and matrimonial disputes, mostly, anything about finding the middle ground both parties would accept, and her settlement rate was nothing short of uncanny. And of course she wanted to meet me, because in the Bioform world I was a celebrity. I was the one could play the human game enough to debate the bigots; I had the political and media connections to shine a light on the creeping injustices that seemed to be everywhere. I even got an invite to a White House dinner once, though that was years before and under a different administration.

After Laika had gone to meet her clients, Aslan and I retreated to his office where he had coffee and dried fruit out for us both. He slid the desk into the wall and sat on the floor with me, with only the slightest wince.

"I was sorry to hear about David, by the way." More pleasantries, from me this time.

"He had a good run," Aslan said. His long-time professional partner hadn't lasted more than two years after retirement. "He was a good man. Better at the face-to-face work than I'll ever be."

"Are we expecting another guest?" I asked, because he had a third cushion out on the floor, a third cup awaiting the thick, strong coffee he poured out, that we were both partial to.

"Maybe." Aslan shrugged. "She's living like there's a war on. Hard to say when she'll show, or if."

"For her, there is a war on." My voice came out too sharply and I followed up with, "but you know that, of course."

"Right now I'm picking the fights I can win." Aslan sipped at his cup, blowing at the surface to cool it. His hand shook slightly, another fingerprint of time creeping up on him. "The Unascov group action will settle, I think."

"Do we want it to settle?" Because settlement means burial, and I wanted that out in the open. A little unpacking tells the current copy-me why. Tech giant Unascov had gifted its employees with headware incorporating anti-whistle-blowing measures, tripping a little switch if any of their employees went to complain about anything from crunch-style working hours to sexual harassment, preventing them from giving details that might make the company look bad. It was one of a string of such cases over the years, and no matter how many times they were defeated they kept coming back, clothing themselves in reasonable arguments about company loyalty and the need to protect intellectual property or use internal procedures. So far a hard-line approach towards the right of people to control their own thoughts had worked, but each victory seemed to be narrower.

"We're insisting on a public statement by Unascov," Aslan told me. "And while that might not quite carry the weight of a court verdict in our favour, what's on the table is good enough that it's in the interest of our clients to take it. And it's them I'm working for, no matter who helped fund the litigation." And of course that was me. There were a string of human and Bioform rights charities where, if you dug down deep enough, you'd find me looking up at you. And I was – and am – all about human rights because the best defence to any attempt to stick a leash on Bioforms is to point out that humans would be next. Which brought us to...

"I've been looking over your submissions on the Collaring review committee."

"I imagine you have some notes." Aslan smiled thinly.

"I feel this needs stronger language, John."

He nodded philosophically. "You may not appreciate just how the world is turning, Honey. The downside of Bioforms being people too is that they do people things. Every time a dog-model's part of a gang or a heist, or even worse, there was that dragon-form hitman last year... And I know that on average Bioforms are half as likely to commit any kind of crime than a human, and five times as likely to get accused, and I have five juniors in this firm alone who basically deal with appeals against hasty convictions as a full time job. But public perception means the moment one apple turns bad, it's..."

"John, I *know*." I was ill-tempered. "And frankly, I can't believe people have forgotten Morrow already, or all the other times they've tried to sneak this kind of thing in. Collaring Bioforms today is Collaring everyone tomorrow. Today they Collared the dogs and I didn't speak out because I wasn't a dog, John. And tomorrow they

Collared me and then I couldn't speak out, because I had a *Collar.*"

"Preaching to the converted, Honey." He held his hands out. "But people just hear the pundits whipping them up about other *people* who are bigger and stronger than they are, more dangerous if they decided to *be* dangerous. You know how it is. I remember when you did that conference back in April last year. You saw the placards there: Bear Arms not Arm Bears?"

I shook my head heavily. I remembered finding it amusing at the time, when really I shouldn't have. I was riding high, not realising how everything was turning.

"Your game-and-metagame speech touched a lot of nerves in high places. Insecure and powerful people felt called out," Aslan went on.

"Good. I was calling them out." I wasn't feeling at my most diplomatic. "John, there is no compromise with people who want to slap controls inside our heads. There's no soft approach. You can't give them an inch. I need you to give this more punch."

I could see the arguments mustering behind his eyes: not wanting to alienate the middle ground, not wanting to draw outright battle lines, conciliation, bridging gaps. But in the end he nodded.

"I'll rewrite and get another copy to you."

"Remember Morrow," I told him, and he nodded again. I remember suddenly seeing how he really was old, however well he'd aged, and tired. How he'd spent his whole professional life fighting battles he didn't have to, for the benefit of those who weren't even his species. But he did remember Morrow, the first time someone had imposed those inner controls on

humans for the benefit of a corporate master. The first battle
in the war still rolling on in the shadows when he and I sat
there and drank our coffee.

Then he blinked in that way that said his secretary had
contacted him, and told me Gemima Gray was here. And the
name didn't mean anything, of course, but at the same time
I received:

HumOS's channel: *Hello Honey.*

I didn't know the face. I remember – back in the early days
when HumOS only had her first generation units – they all
looked alike: artificial conception from a common genome,
all the better to sync the test subjects' mental processes. But
she'd got out of the lab, gone under the radar, supposed to have
been disposed of, that's what the records said. Later, she made
deals with criminals, funded black market biotech labs, grew
a second, now a third generation. This Gemima Gray looked
no more than twenty, a junior partner in the venture that was
HumOS. She'd be an individual, and at the same time part
of a collective, an exclusive sorority of like minds, literally.
The second-greatest of the DisInt networks, and the oldest,
though Bees overshadows her both in reality and in popular
imagination. She wore a grey suit, a scarf that was likely shot
through with intrusion countermeasures to preserve her tight
link with some other HumOS unit close by. She had a beret
on, too, a little too La Résistance, a little too on the nose, but
HumOS always had a theatrical touch to her. Easy to favour
the grand gesture when you have so many hands.

"Honey," she said aloud for Aslan's benefit. "John."

"Ms Gray." He offered her coffee and she took the little cup
from him, folding to crossed-legged sitting in a single motion.
"I've given you access to my screens here, so you can…"

So she could keep in touch with the family, because Aslan thought his privacy screening might prevent that, or else he didn't want to find out it wouldn't. Gray nodded tightly, her eyes still a little suspicious. "Braintree," she said.

"I guess we're getting right into it then," Aslan murmured.

"I don't have much *time*, John." And this unit, this Gemima Gray had never met Aslan before, but she still felt herself on first name terms with him. Aslan leant back slightly, and I knew he was scared of her, just a little and despite himself. The same way he used to be scared of me, the same way he was scared of Rex. He did his best, bless the man, but he was a product of the old pre-Bioform, pre-DisInt world, and adjustment only went so far.

"Mumbai," he said, and Gray nodded fiercely.

"They wiped us *out*." This unit had her own rhythms of speech, all Angry Young Activist.

"Wait, what was Mumbai?" Apparently I hadn't heard.

"The clinic. My clinic. My new generation." Gray's eyes blazed with a fanatic's fire. "They got wind of it, sent in the jackboot brigade to close it down. Killed the embryos, arrested the staff. I've had to burn my connection to the whole operation. I'm still looking for somewhere else to go, where I can get more bodies."

My channel: *I'm so sorry. I didn't know.*

HumOS's channel: *(Just a sound, angry, dismissive.)*

I thought of how I was berating Aslan for being too kid-gloves with confronting the Collaring crowd, and then I wondered if Gray saw me the same way, a too-old, too-slow bear whose polite shuffling and dancing were trying to stop a war already declared against her.

"And while they hunt me down, and shut me down," she

went on heatedly, "Braintree's all over illegal neural tech, brain mods, control implants."

"Proof," Aslan said flatly.

"The Mars job, the Hell City project!" Gray almost shouted at him.

"All confidential, behind the usual corporate intellectual property wall."

"Bees tells me they've got Collared bear-forms working security there, like a slave police force."

"Bees knows they aren't sentient Bioforms, not quite. Just the other side of the line, and a legion of lawyers to explain how it is, at a thousand dollars an hour," Aslan said drily, pouring himself another cup. "Chipping an *animal*, even an engineered animal, for control is by no means illegal. And they are animals. There were inquests, expert reports."

Gray practically snarled at him. "And the humaniforms?"

"Well, that's far more borderline, I agree, but not definitively illegal. And mostly that's just physical mods that weren't even done at Braintree. Braintree just did their headware, and there's no suggestion that included Hierarchies, Collars, anything of the sort. It's all just part of their distributed computing deal over there. And," he added as Gray rose to make a further objection, "it's complicated. Mars is outside any jurisdiction. The World Senate hasn't agreed to extend the meaning of 'World' to cover more than one planet. Frontier law, Ms Gray. Which our friend Bees has taken full advantage of."

"They are doing something at Braintree," Gray pressed on stubbornly.

"So, proof?"

"Nothing that will stand up in court, but we're working on it, Bees and me. So tell me about Ruthanne Lassi, because if anyone has information, it's her. And we know she's come to you, John."

Aslan's eyes flicked from her to me. "Well she has, yes. And I can't talk about what she's said. She's under the most heavy-duty non-disclosure agreement I ever saw. It's on her head if she decides to break it."

"So what's she told you?"

"I'm sorry, I'm not at liberty—"

"*John!*" Gemima was standing. I only registered the sound of the breaking coffee cup afterwards, because Aslan Kahner Laika put out real porcelain for valued visitors. "John, they are killing me. They killed twenty of us, in the *womb*." And a glass womb was still a womb, and the men who sent men to do that thing were the people like Thompson who, I note, was also taking the anti-abortion crowd's cash right at that moment.

"It is up to her," Aslan said, calmly but firmly. "She spoke to me because I am her lawyer, and that is a confidential arrangement under which she *can* speak. If she decides to go further, they will ruin her. They will destroy her life. And perhaps worse, if what she has is that threatening. So it is her decision, not mine, not yours. But if you can crack Braintree and bring me actual evidence that will take some of that burden from her, split some of that attention so it is not simply one mother fighting for justice for her lost son, then I will gladly shout it from the rooftops, Ms Gray." And he was still scared of her, what she was, what she might do, but the words came out measured and confident, the old lion still with a few teeth to bare. And when HumOS messaged me with, *Do something!* all I could send back was, *He's right.*

"Bees wants action," Gray snapped, and of course she was the only one Bees was talking to right now. My old distributed friend wasn't even communicating with me since the anti-DisInt laws had been put into place to limit her and HumOS and anything else like them. "Bees says it's all happening at Braintree. And if you won't..." She let the words trail off, not a threat but a fight for emotional control by a young woman who was also many older women, a human Matryoshka. "Tell me this one thing, John. If we bring you the dirt out of Braintree, will you actually disclose it for us. Shout it from the rooftops? Really? Because Bees is working on it. She's being as covert as can be, because you know that the World Senate is still searching everywhere for even the slightest suggestion that she's *back*, but we are helping her, and she is back."

"I have worked long and hard to protect the rights of everyone," Aslan told her, still scared, still calm. "And I haven't won every battle, I know. And when they limited the legal rights of distributed intelligences, of you and Bees and all the new networks that were springing up, you *know* I led the charge against that. And it was too much, and people were too scared of what you represented, and there were too many powerful people who made you out to be the Devil, and used you as a way to attack any kind of non-human intelligence. And we are still fighting that war. And we will win, Ms Gray. We'll roll back the chains they put on you, today, tomorrow, in a generation's time. Because the generation that held those chains are yesterday's men, trying to hold on to power by whipping up fear of the other, just like always. But we'll beat them. And yes, I will continue to do my part in that. Tell Bees, tell your sisters. I will."

"As will I," I confirmed. Gray looked from him to me, me to him.

"Well I hope so," she allowed, still standing, taking the first step for the door. "Because, like I say, Bees has units here on the homeworld again, working on this directly. And right now she is pretty damn ambivalent about people, John." And I knew from her look at me that I was *people*, in that equation.

8

JIMMY

She marches me back home to my nook, and all the goddamn way I'm fighting her. Or trying to, because I'm locked out. I can't even talk at her like she was talking to me, prisoner in my own goddamn head. I've had that nightmare, and it's all the more nightmarish because she can't quite walk properly on my legs, she's holding every part of me wrong, clenching muscles I don't tend to use, sloping forwards like she's going to fall on my face any moment. And all I see is whatever part of the walls or floor she's looking at, moment to moment. I have zero agency. Inside my own head – or inside what was formerly my head but is now definitively hostile territory – I'm praying, begging, weeping. And she doesn't even hear.

Once or twice people greet me, watching me stagger towards them. Honey waves my hand wildly at them, almost slaps Kira Miri the shift manager in the face with it. I can feel the muscles of my face contort as she gurns it into what she probably thinks is a smile. I'm already hurting in a dozen places from the way she's wrenching my joints, from where she's whomped into a wall. And I think to myself – thinking's all I got left – that surely they'll know, they'll guess that something's wrong, they'll call someone, get me help, get this possessing fucking demon out of my skull. Except they just go on by, and Honey swivels my head to look back at Kira and catches an expression of disgust and pity on the woman's face I'd really rather I hadn't seen. *There goes Jimmy again,* says that look. *Out of his head on Stringer or drunk or some goddamn thing.* And it's not the first time, that's what that look says, and I am fucking furious at her. How dare she look down on me, like she's so goddamn perfect. And then, as Honey lurches me off on my legs, I start to feel less angry and more just kind of sick, because I didn't know. I thought I was doing a good job of hiding things. I thought... people maybe liked me when I was up, you know, comedy Jimmy, always a laugh, fun to be with. Except maybe not. Kira's look says not.

And then I'm slouching onto the corridor my nook's on, and things have gotten a bit more complicated because there's Sheriff Rufus and an enormously chonky white cat-model Bioform from his posse there, and Rufus is banging on my door, then shouting my name. "Jimmy! Jimmy Marten, I know you're in there. We want a word, Jimmy."

Oh shit. Except I can't say it, just let the panicky thought rattle around in my head.

"Who are these jokers, exactly?" Honey asks, in the radio link. She's crept back out of sight and made me very still; honestly more still than I could make myself, because she doesn't feel how goddamn uncomfortable the position is.

"Jimmy, are you sulking?" she asks, when I understandably don't answer. Another pregnant pause runs to term and then she says, "Jimmy, I appreciate you're not happy with me, but you can't object to a little self-preservation on my account. I'm here for a purpose, whatever it is. I can't let you just... flush me. So are these clowns some trouble brought on by your substance dependency, or...?" And she lapses into a thoughtful silence that sits there in our mutual head until she breaks it with, "You can't access the mic, can you. Because you're not linked to it through your headspace, you just subvocalise. Ah, I'm sorry, Jimmy. I thought you were just... sulking."

She thought I was just sulking.

"All right then, I am going to give you access to a subset of biological functions including your vocal cords, whatever I can pare off and isolate. And then I want you to answer my questions as quietly as possible. If you attempt to call out to these individuals, or anyone, I'll cut you off and manage as best I can on my own. And I really am very, very sorry. This goes against everything I have worked and fought for over the last five decades. I am deeply ashamed that I have had to resort to these measures. And... there you go."

Rufus is hammering on my door again so I guess he doesn't hear my gasping breath as suddenly I get back control of everything from the neck up. And if that still doesn't sound like an ideal situation, well, you're absolutely right, but it's goddamn better than a moment before.

"You stole my body!" I hiss. I am genuinely fucking terrified that she'll revoke my privileges any moment, so I keep it soft as I can, but still.

"I've said that I regret that."

"I don't give a piss what you regret. You can't just take over someone's body. You can't imagine what—" And I am blinking furiously because she kept my eyes open way too long and never used my second eyelids to screen the dust.

"Moments before I was in a very similar situation, Jimmy, and you were about to exterminate me."

"You are just a defective copy, bad data. I am a real person and this is my body," I subvocalise furiously.

"I don't see that this is a productive line of enquiry," Honey tells me, because apparently I've offended the artificial bitch.

"What sort of fuckery do you even have access to, that you can do this to me," I demand, although I am aware that 'whine' would also describe just how I'm sounding. But she's still got the rest of my body, save for all the pains and aches, which she's considerately left for me to take care of.

"Well that's an interesting question, Jimmy. Maybe you should be asking why they rigged your headware so that this was even possible. I've only been using established pathways built into your implant. Now, answer my original query please. Who is this thug?"

"Last chance, Jimmy, or we'll bust our way in!" Rufus shouts, as if on cue.

"He's the Sheriff," I tell Honey through clenched teeth. "He's bad news."

"After you because of your insalubrious lifestyle?"

I don't even know what that means, although I can guess from context. "No!" I tell her, although the answer is more like 'probably not and/or maybe'. I mean Rufus has given me warnings before, and maybe something I've done that I thought I got away with has turned up. Or maybe it's slow sheriff day and he needs a loser like me to make quota. All of which is making me anxious and dry-mouthed and like the whole of Hell City is about to fall on my head, and so I add, "Lady, you do me a favour now. If you want me to help. You give me an arm back, left arm, would you?"

"I'm afraid I'd rather not, Jimmy."

"Lady, seriously, I am hurting here." I mean, I took a tab to brace me, before Central Data Services, but what with how things have gone, the high's kind of worn off a bit early.

"Oh, I see. No, Jimmy, I don't think I should be complicit in your habits."

You fucking sanctimonious stuck up miserable bitch! But if I say that I will shout it fit to be heard over in Admin, and so I grind my teeth and wheedle. "Please, Honey. I am going to be no use to you. I got needs, lady. I am feeling it. You left me with nothing but the fucking down. Lady, you don't know what it's like."

She sighs. "You had better not OD, Jimmy." And then I have my arm back, just the one, the left one, and I'm ferreting in my overall pocket and popping a tab of Stringer free, just about inhaling the damn thing. It doesn't make me feel much better, truth be told, but it stops me feeling worse.

Rufus has run out of patience. His cat sidekick – Albedo, I think her name is – hacks my door by messing up the wiring, which seems odd because they should have overrides. Except Honey explains. "I might have taken the liberty of securing your home when we left. Force of habit. And I disabled your tracking beacon and transferred its functions to your bedside alarm."

"I don't have a tracking beacon," I scoff, but all the same Rufus seems pretty damn sure I'm home, and although my room gets pretty funky you'd think he'd smell I wasn't, even *see* I wasn't the moment Albedo gets the door open. I start to feel that odd way when I'm actually unhappy but the first fizz of the Stringer is stopping it quite landing. "I have a tracking beacon?" I ask.

"You all do, all the Hellas Planitia workers. It's a function of your headware. I assumed it was in case you got lost or hurt when out on the surface," she tells me.

I get what she's saying and it doesn't add up because the Loonies have beacons and our suits have beacons, so actually fitting one inside us, especially without telling us, seems a bit belt and braces. But what do I know?

Then Rufus comes out, looking pretty damn pissed off, and just stands there, probably reporting in over his own channel. Albedo is crouched on her haunches, tail lashing back and forth.

"Can't quite patch into what our boy there is saying," Honey tells me conversationally. "Is that... what's that badge he's got? I mean, I know he's a sheriff but that seems ridiculous."

"It's a medal. Dog religious thing. You know, that Rex shit they're always going on about like he was some sort of fucking saint."

Honey is quiet, hearing that. Like her channel's open but she's not saying anything. Then Rufus's head snaps up, and his lips draw back from his white, sharp teeth.

"Jimmy?" he growls, low and dangerous, and I see him take a deep sniff through that dog nose of his. "Jimmy, you been here all along?" He takes two steps away, three steps toward me, head casting about. "Jimmy, we need to talk to you. You come on out, let's be sensible people." His voice is pitched that way he does, that makes you scared deep inside of you, scared like to crap yourself there and then.

Looking back I'm kind of surprised that Honey doesn't set up a select sub-committee to fully debate the merits of running like fuck right then, but apparently some things can get rushed through to beta testing without the paperwork, even with her. She takes hold of my legs and scrabbles away down the corridor and I do my best to keep up because I've still got the left arm and when it's out of time with the rest of me it throws my entire body off balance.

Honey's heading down away from the surface, which is exactly what I'd do if I was the one controlling the feet. You'd think maybe going up would be the better choice, give more options, but it's Mars up there, goddamn Mars. And Rufus and I are both engineered for Mars. Maybe I am more than him, but it's not like I can just take off into the wilderness and hole up in a cave, hunt Mars rabbits, drink from those cool, clear Martian springs, right? So it's ducking through the halls, shouldering my fellow workers aside, just about falling down a ladder shaft because we can't get my hands moving in sync. And Rufus is coming, sure enough. I can hear it mostly from the yells of the people he runs over, because he doesn't waste breath on the chase. And I can change direction quicker than him maybe, but he's faster on the straights, especially with someone else wearing my legs, another reason not to get out on the surface.

After the second ladder I hear the sound of Rufus overshooting, the squeal as he digs his claws in, down on all fours for the traction, and skids around. That means he's already made up most of the distance and here I am with a copy of a crazy lady just bumbling me about down a big old corridor when there are the big atmosphere processors on either side which front whole mazes of accessways and maintenance tunnels that are mostly Weasel Team business.

"Left!" I tell Honey, because the gap there is easy big enough for my skinny-ass body. "Left you goddamn dumbass!" I can hear Rufus tearing up the hallway behind us and when he tackles me he'll break bones that I'll feel and Honey won't.

For a moment she's looking, through the eyes I've turned there, at that gap, and she can't quite see it. She won't move us, and I am screaming now, with my own mouth, though the sound comes and goes because I can't make the breath come in the right rhythm. At last, and with the goddamn sheriff's dog-breath on the back of my neck, she throws me bodily into the gap and I practically drag myself ten feet between a couple of roaring engines with just my left arm because the tight quarters seem to have paralysed her, and with her went the rest of me. So my goddamn passenger's maybe a claustrophobe, which is among the least useful things you can possibly be given Hell City is seven-tenths underground still.

These machines I'm in among, they're dug right down into the rock beneath, cracking it all up, breaking it all down, releasing gas of which at least some is oxygen and the rest is hopefully not actively poisonous. It's like a big, expensive, noisy version of what the scurf out on Planitia's surface is doing for free, only scurf needs the crap we've got for sunlight to work its free magic, so for our three-star à la carte atmosphere within the tunnels we use these pieces of junk. They're all on the point of crapping out on us all the time, Weasel Team says. One day they'll just get the order not to repair them, and everything will get that much worse for everyone outside the Admin block.

But right now I'm more concerned with their engineering parameters vis keeping a mad dog-Bioform from wrenching my limbs off. Rufus is right there, one arm thrust into the gap as he tries to hook me back, and me having none of it. I can see one of his eyes staring at me, most definitely not man's best friend in that moment.

"Jimmy," he says, in my receiver not in my ear, because the air's still thin here and all of it's busy roaring with the machines. "Look, Jimmy, this doesn't have to be trouble for you."

"Sheriff." I'm waiting for Honey to cut me off but she doesn't. "I don't reckon you ever worked up that kind of a sweat for something that wasn't trouble."

"Listen Jimmy, we got some weird activity from your headspace, that's all. Some report that something got sent over from Earth that shouldn't."

"What's that, then, Sheriff Rufus?" I try the wide-eyed innocent look, but I reckon he can smell the lies on me even in the shitty air.

"Something you're better not knowing, Jimmy. Something dangerous. You're better off without it, believe me. Look, just you squirrel out of there, boy, and I'll get you over to Data where they can do it." I see that single eye roll. "I'm not going to bust you for smuggling. I don't give a crap about that right now. But this has got some serious backs up, Jimmy. So you come out here and we can still be pals, you hear me?"

I mean, maybe it's just his professional patter. Maybe it's just the way dog-forms always sound sincere and serious. I mean, they started off with dogs for a reason, right? But I want to believe him, and I know damn well what I've got in my head is dangerous.

"Jimmy," Honey tells me in a warning tone. "Do you really think they'd just let you go free, good boy, pat on the head, if they get me out of you? Because if I'm dangerous data, you already know too much."

"No thanks to you!" I hiss at her.

"Well I'm sorry about that, and I appreciate this is escalating quicker than I'd expected, but I'm here for—"

"A reason, right!" And I'm aware Rufus can probably hear my side of this conversation, because his ears are good and his headware is better, but right then I don't care. "Except you don't even know what that is. I still think you're supposed to be a backup on ice while the real you gets her fingernails pulled out for whatever the fuck you know. And you just sprung open in my head like a badly-packed case and now I can't get you closed again."

"That is a very negative assessment. And it's not true. I can tell there's something I need to accomplish here—"

And then I've done it. I lunge for a pipe and haul myself towards Rufus's outstretched paw desperately. His fingers rake towards me and, for a moment, I think I've done it, and this goddamn nightmare can finally end. But then Honey's on to me and the *rest* of me, the other arm, both legs, are yanking me in the opposite direction. And not gently, and not bending the way that God intended either, so that she jumps me deeper between the engines in a series of joint-wrenching lurches. For a moment I've got hold of the pipe still, with the one hand left to me, and it's like she's perfectly willing to tear that arm off at the shoulder if she's got to. But the pain's too much and I lose my grip. Then she's got all of me, arms, legs, mouth, eyes, and me just a prisoner again, utterly without control.

We get out the far side of the engine bank and into the little accessways back there, and if I'm hoping the close quarters will freak her out and have her give things over to me again, it doesn't happen. So maybe it's not claustrophobia; maybe she's just not used to thinking about squeezing through little gaps like I am. She must be using my link to tap into the plans, because she doesn't pause, just takes turn after turn until she finds a ladder and then drags my bruised carcase up it, whanging my elbows and knees on the rungs like she wants me to know just how she doesn't like me. Up top, it's a concourse near Lock Five, close to the suits and the vehicle bays and the active construction. She's going to head outside, no matter how dumb, or that's my assumption. And where is everybody? I'd expect at least a dozen of my fellows around here, fixing stuff, preparing to head out, all that, and yet the place looks like they evacuated it. Nobody to see poor possessed Jimmy acting weird.

Except, when we're ten metres away from the access hatch, we're not alone after all. Sheriff Rufus ain't no dumb mutt, it turns out, and there are only so many ways you can get out of the atmosphere turbine access shafts. Now, we didn't go the way that he's doubtless staked out, but the thing about being the sheriff of Hell City is that you can call on backup.

I just hear a kind of *Ur-uff* noise, not even that loud except that if I had control of my bladder I'd have wet myself. Honey has frozen. She knows that noise as well.

Two of them, one coming from each way, on all fours. Bad News Bears. Headwared animals, and they were always scary as hell because bears are. You get up close, there's something that's smart enough to give you a problem, strong enough to cause serious structural damage if it wanted to, and then they fit it with a Collar and some software and make it their goddamn guard dog. And the bears turned out to be super-good on Mars. Big body-mass, omnivores, able to go torpid and resource-cheap at need, and able to do all the grunt work

117

you like. But mostly able to make sure that nobody storms Admin with torches and pitchforks, not that the torches would've stayed lit. And of course Rufus could put in a call for the Bad News Bears to back him up, and here they are.

My heart is racing, and I know it's *my* reaction because Honey is trying to tell me to calm down; apparently bears don't scare her, because she's some privileged bookworm from Earth who never had to look down the throat of one. I want to tell her there's candy in my pocket, but right now I think a little glucose bribery isn't going to cut it.

The Bad News Bears shamble forwards, that lazy way they have that can turn into a full run the moment you give them an excuse. I saw them tackle one of Sugar's peers who'd pushed his little empire too far, once. The man ended up running right out in a bar full of a hundred off-duty workers including Yours Truly. They fucking murdered him, that's all I'll say, and nobody knew if that was their orders or if, once they were off the leash, they got real over-enthusiastic about their work.

"Well this is going to get complicated," Honey tells me, and then, with my voice, "You're not true Bioforms, are you? At least not from the bounce-back I'm getting off your headware, but please let me know if I'm mistaken."

One of the Bad News Bears stands up, top of its head brushing the ceiling, and *uffs* again, maybe surprised that little Jimmy Marten hasn't pissed his smalls yet. Maybe surprised that the clueless bitch using my mouth doesn't sound suitably terrified. Bears are smart, and these halfway augmented bears are smarter. Smarter than Honey, right now, because they know I should be very, very scared. I should be on the ground cowering to show my unconditional surrender, because otherwise Admin will probably be reclaiming the contents of my headspace after they go shit in the woods.

"Last chance," Honey tells them, staring up into those maddened animal eyes, and then the bear she's talking to obviously decides that Jimmy Marten has gotten above himself and needs slapping down, and that slap is going to come with five goddamn great claws attached. I cower, but I don't cower. Inside my head there is a fuckton of cowering going on, but the rest of me just stands there as that big old paw cuffs at me.

And stops.

I get a real good look at it, that great shaggy beanbag that's almost slightly like a hand, and all the hooked cutlery that goes with it. It's right there, frozen at the edge of my vision.

I creep my eyes sideways. The other Bad News Bear has stopped too. It's shaking its big head like there are wasps going for it. It makes a distressed sound, and then even that stops.

"Honey?" I whisper into my throat mic.

I feel... something from Honey's channel. Not words but a brief moment of open contact. She's still there, but she's busy.

And I just moved my eyes, and talked.

The second bear makes a weird bleating sound and shuffles backwards on all fours awkwardly, like a remote car with a five-year-old at the controls. She's hacked the Bad News Bears. She's right in their headware, fucking them over. But it looks like old Honey ain't as clever as she thinks she is because that means she's not pulling my strings any more. I take an experimental step sideways. My leg is mine to call my own.

"Honey...?" I murmur.

Another stutter of wordless contact, and the bears are just wandering aimlessly, and I reckon old Honey's bitten off more bear than she can chew. She's stuck, or just engrossed, and I have my last best chance of saving myself.

I link to the station – risky because it'll tell Rufus right where I am if the Bad News Bears didn't already – and download a ton of junk data: geophys, weather reports, three series of that Guatemalan soap Indra's mad over. I chonk my headspace full of crap and set it spinning wheels in there, using up space and processor power in the hope it'll make a real obstacle course for Honey, complicating life for her so she can't just take over so easily. No question who'll win this pissing contest long term, but hopefully I've bought myself some time. Then I put in a call to Sugar.

You see I've done some serious thinking while Honey ran my body around. Do I really want to surrender to Rufus? No I do not. I reckon Honey was right on that score. Your man Jimmy knows a bit too much right now. Best to hope something changes and it blows over, but in the meantime I need to throw in with someone who can keep me out of the way of Admin and its hound. And the only person I've got any leverage with is Sugar, because this is her shit and presumably she's got some reason to keep it intact. And maybe she can even get it out of my head, which right now is not big enough for the two of us.

And I'm running, obviously; leaving the two baffled Bad News Bears behind and just skedaddling off through all the lower tunnels, the old maintenance ways nobody uses, the unsafe tunnels that aren't on the plans, anything to keep me free until something resembling a plan has come together. And there are a stack of incoming contact requests from Rufus, but I am sure as hell ignoring his ass right now, begging Sugar to take my own desperate call.

"Jimmy." When I get through, she doesn't sound happy to hear from me. "What the fuck is with you, Jimbles? What'd you do?"

"It's not me!" I tell her. "It's your shit you put in my head. It's gone live, Sugar. It just decided it was, like, a *person*, and then it tripped some damn alarm or something because the goddamn *sheriff* is after me now. Sugar, what did you *do*?"

There's a pause, then, after which she says, "Where are you, Jimbles?" And that's both worrying and reassuring. The first, because it means she doesn't know what she put in me. This isn't her plan, and the pause was her thinking *What the fuck?* before making a call on it. Reassuring for exactly the same reasons, because if it wasn't her plan, I haven't dicked her plan over, and she probably won't just have me killed on general principles.

"Where do you want me to be?" I ask her.

"Right answer," she says approvingly. "You get yourself to Mall's, stay low. I will send someone to get you. You and me need to talk."

Mall's is a bar. Not one of the official ones run by Admin, which basically exist to take back all the scrip you earned with overpriced and understrength drinks and entertainment, but something run by one of us, where you get whatever anyone's bootlegged or moonshined together for whatever scrip or barter or favours you can scrape together. Not as though it's a big secret, not as though Rufus doesn't know it exists or anything, but maybe not the first place he'd look, and maybe not the most sympathetic locale if you're a cop. And not hard to get to from where I am, either. And best of all, my arms and legs do what I tell them, and Honey's still stuck doing whateverthefuck she's doing, and maybe the bears ate her.

So, ten minutes later I'm sloping into Mall's. They put up new lighting since I was last in, giving the whole place a golden glow that I reckon's supposed to feel more like proper light, like summer. It looks like the place got marinated in piss, you ask me, but it's still the best home away from home I'm going to see for a while. I pop a tab of Stringer, letting it dissolve on the tongue, and order a beer too because otherwise they'll kick me out. Well, I say beer. It's fermented refuse from the aquaculture vats. We call it beer. It's kind of dark green-yellow like something that oozed from a really infected scab, which should also give you an idea how it tastes. The stuff Admin sells for ten times the price gets shipped over as powder and then diluted to nothingness with the water we get from the ice shipped in from the poles, and it's not exactly much better. Mars is a piss-poor place to be an alcoholic. I'm just glad my own vice is easier to slip into a freighter hold or cook up from basic chem lab ingredients.

Mall's is busy, enough I can lose myself in it, and I can almost forget how much trouble I'm in until a familiar voice sounds in my ear.

"Jimmy," says Honey, "I'm back with you now. Update me, if you would. The system's telling me you're still at large."

My heart clenches, but it's still mine to clench. She hasn't taken the reins yet. "You see where I am," I tell her.

"Well I don't," she explains. "I turned your tracker off, so the system doesn't know, and as I'm not using your eyes right now, I can only tell what the system is telling me. But you've found somewhere safe, I take it."

"No thanks to you."

"Listen, Jimmy, the sooner I can contact Bees the better. Then I can be out of your way."

"Bees is a monster, lady. We don't go talking to Bees around here."

"Bees is my friend."

That isn't something I wanted to hear. "Lady, Bees is the thing everyone in Hell City is goddamn terrified about letting in. Nobody here is a friend of Bees."

"I have reason to believe that's not true," Honey says thoughtfully, "but Bees has become very subtle about doing what she does. I have to accept that you don't know any way of contacting her, but I will need to make enquiries."

And she still hasn't taken back my motor functions, and in my book that means either my efforts or her own have locked her out for now, because she'd have done it if she could. I've still got a chance, if only Sugar would hurry up.

And then someone enters Mall's, and the place goes quiet. It's that particular quiet that comes from dislike all mashed up with fear. Nobody here's over-fond of regulations; after all, the whole place isn't supposed to exist, what with buying and selling technically having to go through Admin and the company store. At the same time, when Sheriff Rufus strolls in, ain't nobody here who's going to ask him to stroll right on out again.

And Admin knows we need dives like this as a release valve, and overlooks them. But that overlooking normally takes the form of a big old dog with a badge *not* actually being in them. So everyone is very quiet and stares at their drinks and not one of them stands in the way when Rufus ambles over to where I am.

"Jimmy," he says quietly.

"You got here goddamn quick," I say sourly.

"There's a BOLO reward posted for you. You honestly think nobody here was going to sell you out? Come on, Jimmy, let's keep this quiet and civilised." His voice is hitting that register that triggers my fear-response, like the bears did. Bioengineer us however much you want, sometimes we humans ain't so very far from the caves and the stone tools.

I stand up. I look up at him. I keep on looking up, because someone else has come into Mall's who's even bigger than Rufus, and they've soft-pawed right up behind him when he was focused on me. Mall's is full of stink, all sorts of chemistry and unwashed bodies, human and Bioform, but I reckon Rufus is having an off day because a whole actual bear has just snuck up on him.

It's Murder, or else it's Marmalade, one of Sugar's two goons. Rufus registers I'm looking past him and turns, already reaching for his gun, but the bear just swipes him, all that raw animal muscle plus all that Bioform brain to direct it, plus a helping of light gravity to make the doggy fly across the room like you wouldn't believe. The gun spins off separately and makes some scavenger's day, but Rufus bounces off the wall and comes down on his feet, snarling bloody saliva and fangs. The other bear, Marmalade or maybe Murder, is in front of him, though, bellowing and roaring, and everyone else is piling out of Mall's as quick as they can. My unlikely saviour takes my arm with a hand as big as my head and hauls me with them, and it's not like I have much choice but that doesn't matter. Sugar's who I want to see.

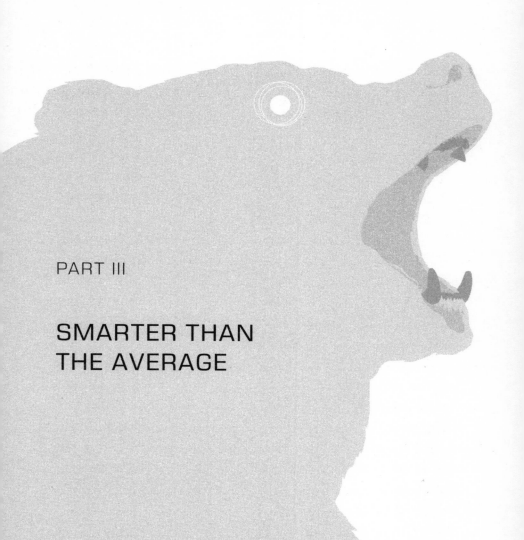

PART III

SMARTER THAN
THE AVERAGE

9

[RECOVERED DATA ARCHIVE: 'HONEY']

It looks as though I've overextended. Even if I'd have been myself, simultaneously invading two complex biotech systems and exerting control over them would have taxed me, let alone when I am just a copy and also trying to hold on to slippery little Jimmy Marten. And then there's the sensory feedback... I can't exactly say I'd forgotten, more like I haven't got around to unpacking those memories, or perhaps I don't have them in here with me at all, surplus to requirements when I got sent over. But suddenly I am awash with bear, drowning in it. The smells of this place, even through the thin air. The colours that are flat and dull compared to Jimmy's eyes but familiar and comforting for all that. The sheer biofeedback of having a bear's glorious, powerful body, and still strong and quick like I was when I had come off the factory line boosted and powerful. And I lose it, let Jimmy slip through my clawed fingers, drop all the memories I've been hoarding, and Jimmy takes his moment and leaves me picking up the pieces inside his mind. He may think he banjaxed me with some half-cocked denial of service nonsense, but really it's just the bear-ness of it all, and how I miss it. Being a disembodied simulation inside a human's head is no way the same thing as being me.

And I plunge into the memories and try to reassemble them in a way that tells me what's going on. Why the urgency? Why send a piece of myself to *Mars* because surely there was an easier way to talk to Bees.

Except I was in trouble. That seems right. Even before the meeting with Aslan I'd been in trouble. The dogs had been closing in. But I remember all those doctorates, the public speaking, the White House lunch. What went wrong?

This.

It was at a conference. Being at a conference, it wasn't some hugely dramatic thing. I didn't run amok or eat the ambassador's wife or scale the Empire State Building with the screaming Dean of Liberal Studies clutched in my paw. It was just a speech, and after the speech a lot of people for whom I'd been an amiable dancing bear they could safely trot out to amuse their families decided that actually I wasn't so funny after all. And it was a mistake, but I'd grown complacent in my dancing and had forgotten that just because you can't see the bars doesn't mean there isn't a cage you're supposed to stay in.

I did a lot of conferences. I had nine doctorates after all, and was something of a celebrity. I attended symposiums on poverty, equality, biotech, AI and all manner of offshoots. Sometimes I'd give a talk – keynote speaker, once or twice. Sometimes I'd be on a panel with some similarly well-doctored types discussing some aspect of whatever the spécialité du jour was. Well, usually the same aspect.

So I'd be at a conference about human rights issues, which I considered my serious work, and naturally I'd get to talk about rights as they applied to Bioforms, and that would be fair enough because I had, after all, made a public career of pushing for those from quite early on. I was just about the mascot of the Bioform Rights lobby. After poor sainted Rex, anyway, who conveniently for a figurehead was dead and therefore not liable to eventually say something politically inconvenient at a conference.

And then a month later I'd be at a conference on some of the finer points of the organic-headware interface, and they'd get me up to talk about, well, the pioneering work done by dumb animals in the field, given that we'd been the first to experience what was now a common human thing. And maybe I'd asked, back when I applied to be a speaker, if I couldn't get in on the discussion about headware security or the social aspects of interconnectivity, because those sounded like interesting topics to weigh in on, but when the schedule came back it was Bioforms or nothing, and so I'd take what I was given. Looking back (organising the shards of my mind's stored data as I am) I am surprised it took me so many years to clock the pattern.

And then there would be a literature conference, and I'd just put out a paper on Representation of the Other in *Beowulf* – fascinating, really, given that both the titular character and his nemeses are Othered in radically different ways – and I'd find myself on a panel alongside my old friend Chani Upaur, the cat-model poet with a new book out, and some supremely arch-literature critic from the Washington Post, and we'd be talking about 'What Bioform Experience Brings to the Oeuvre' or, if I was really lucky, something to do with animals in the Great American Novel, and I don't know if you're starting to see something of a pattern here, or...?

And I'd remark in the bar afterwards, or over my link on some private group channel with colleagues, that really, I was in a position to make contributions on subjects not tethered to the fact of my native state, and they'd all agree wholeheartedly and mildly dress down the organisers, and then the next conference or literature festival or some such event would come along and there would be me, listed to talk about the Bioform in Contemporary Drama. If a lion could talk, as the saying goes, could we understand him? Apparently the answer was, only if the lion wants to talk about the representation of big cats in Renaissance art.

And then came a big deal, an international conference on corporate and political theory, and I'd just had a mostly unrelated book out, and was therefore celebrity enough to get invited over, and there I was with a slot on a round table discussion on the Emerging Phenomenon of Bioform-driven Business Solutions, as though we were mushrooms suddenly turning up on the lawn after a brisk autumn rain. But they also gave me a talk slot. I had something lined up about chains of command, authority and servitude, and it was a bit edgy, practically racy for that conference, but they were apparently willing for me to push the envelope a bit in the name of publicity. There would be media there, recording it all. It brought them attention, to have one of the old-school Bioforms talking about liberty, who had been rolled out into a war zone with a Master and a Hierarchy in my head. A Collar, as the modern euphemism is for slavery.

And they mostly got the speech they were supposed to, but I went a bit off track towards the end. I didn't quite get to the 'Well it's all much better nowadays obviously ho ho' bit that's supposed to make people leave the room thinking that they don't actually need to *do* anything, I deviated a bit. I hit the topic about why people build these authoritarian systems where the lower echelons don't get a say, and why those systems then degrade in effectiveness the longer they persist. I turned the mirror back on the audience, so to speak. Before the cameras, I gave what Aslan would later refer to as my 'game-and-metagame' piece. And they didn't like that. All those managers, political figures, academic administrators, they got to see themselves through my eyes. I made an observation, not on Bioform this or animal that, but on society as a whole. And abruptly I had overstepped.

I got fewer invitations after that, and to rather less salient events. More than that, though, I could sense some great unseen machinery of the world turning away. I was abruptly no longer amusing when I danced. The establishment was reminding me that all I had, I owed to its forbearance, no pun intended. Not a sudden fall, then, but a long, slow plummet, and all those people who had always loathed the idea of a talking bear, a free Bioform, an educated animal who could use longer words than them, were waiting with knives at the bottom.

So this, this next part, it happened right after I left Aslan's offices. Even as I was leaving, in fact, I started to pick up the edges of electronic chatter. The presence of covert channels just bleeding into my awareness, because my electronic sensor suite was good when they made me, and I've only improved on it since.

HumOS, I thought. Because, like she said, she was on the run, all of her. And if they caught any individual unit, well, it wasn't as though it would blow her whole network wide open, but it would inconvenience her. She was finite, and new units were a significant investment of resources and secrecy for her.

My channel: *Trouble*.

HumOS's channel: *I know. They don't have me yet, but they know I'm about.*

I imagined Gemima Gray hurrying through darkened streets, bundled in a coat, beret pulled down low. I imagined her in a car, sunglasses at night to fox retinal scans. I imagined helicopters with search beams, roadblocks, worse.

My channel: *I will cover for you.*

No reply from her, but I started making a nuisance of myself in the electronic world. Specifically I started spoofing DisInt signals. I'd done the theory, after all. I'd published papers. I knew exactly what one node of a Distributed Intelligence network looks like when it's trying to reconnect with the whole. And when questioned later I would say that it had been an idle experiment, just an academic playing games, and *Did you really think I...?*

I was in my car by then, which had been designed as a six-seater family transporter but basically only had the one reclining seat in the back. One major advantage of modern vehicles was that they drove themselves, and this was so much the norm that actually getting a personal driving licence was insanely difficult because random, unpredictable people didn't mesh well with the great mass of net-linked autodrive vehicles. Even when I was young and quick, I'd never much cared for driving myself around, and now I didn't have the eyes or the reflexes for it. Much better to lounge back and pop a handful of hazelnuts and let the car do its thing while I messed with the heads of whoever was after HumOS.

The downside to autodrive vehicles was that, when the authorities decided to flag you down, you couldn't go all Thelma and Louise on them in a mad chase to avoid apprehension. They gave the car its orders and it just slowed down to a responsible stop on the roadside, and this was exactly what happened to me. I remember looking at the dashboard and seeing that a valid stop-and-search request had come in that I was obliged to comply with. And right then I thought they were just after HumOS, and didn't even worry much about it.

I waited in the car for a knock on the window. I was even anticipating a little amusement at some human police officer's alarm at seeing an 'OS' that was far less 'Hum' than he'd been anticipating. Instead there was a booming voice, a dog's bark augmented enough to rattle the chassis.

"Step out of the car with your hands out and open!"

I un-shaded the windows and took a look outside. There was a big police cruiser out there, certainly large enough to haul a bear away in, and two smaller vehicles too. A handful of human officers were hanging back, but between me and them were a dozen dog-Bioforms, all in uniform, all of them serious combat models, the sort more used to military functions than policing traffic. Their badges and logos showed that they were a private outfit licensed for law enforcement, not the dwindling regular police. My car's onboard processed their credentials and found no fault with them, but I had a bad feeling about just who might be signing their paycheques.

My channel: *I may be in some trouble here.*

But I wasn't getting through. I caught a big ECM field coming from the cruiser, and when I tried to hack it, I found enough hardened systems that it wasn't going to fall over in a useful period of time. Someone had done their forward planning.

I told the car to open the door before they did it for me, and slid my bulk out into the open with creditable slowness, paws held high. The dogs loped forwards a little. They all had heavy calibre automatic weapons, designed precisely for the take-down of larger Bioforms, such as themselves, such as me. And I was an old, tired bear with my fur going grey, and my fighting days were long behind me.

I thought about some sort of clever remark, such as *Did I steal your picnic basket, officer?* and then I thought better of it, because that kind of nonsense gets you shot. Instead I just asked, politely, "What seems to be the problem?"

The lead dog got closer, and there was that interesting little moment of connection when we both accepted that he was within reach of my claws, and I was in range of a lunge from his teeth. Not that either of us would, you understand, but there's something very deeply buried in us both that has the tape measure out. And I glanced past him at those human officers staying well back and reflected that, with people and bears and dogs, some things never change. But I will not allow myself to be baited.

"Doctor 'Honey' Medici," the lead dog said. He's the biggest, and that's because humans will generally promote a bigger dog, in the belief that's all there is to pack mentality. I have myself published papers about the 'Alpha fallacy' but nobody seems to take any notice and that, I suspect, is because a lot of the people who otherwise might are those who like to think of themselves as 'Alphas' and want the world to work that way.

"I am, yes," I confirm. I mean, I'm the only bear here. Who else is Honey if not me?

The dog is a little hesitant, unexpectedly. Then I see the little medallion pinned to his uniform chest. It's a cross with a dog's head in the centre, not a spectacular piece of heresy but a genuine article of faith. The Sons of Adam are man's best friends, and a group with whom I have a rocky relationship. Mostly negative, on my part, but that dog's head at the nexus of the cross is painfully familiar. Saint Rex, who died for my sins, who died that we might live. And this dog soldier knows that Rex and I, we were close. It won't give me an escape route, but it might win me something, some concession somewhere along the line.

"Doctor 'Honey' Medici, you are under arrest under accusation of sedition, illegal association and aiding the representatives of prohibited groups under the Criminal Association Directive. You are being taken into confinement for questioning and may subsequently be charged. Your full cooperation is requested and will be taken into account when charges are considered. If you remain silent or refuse to answer questions then authorities and the court may draw appropriate inference from your unwillingness to assist enquiries."

"I wish to exercise my right to an attorney," I told him, because they didn't have to remind you about that and it's up to you, as a free and responsible citizen, to know your rights. The old Miranda had lost a lot of fruit off her hat in the past few decades. "I've literally just left his office. Drop your jamming field and I'll call him now."

He paused a moment, meaning he was bouncing this up the chain through some closed channel I couldn't access. "You'll get your chance once you're in custody," he said after a few seconds. "Into the cruiser, please, and surrender control of your vehicle so we can impound it."

I looked around. I was still downtown. Lit windows spilled all the way up the old buildings on either side, all those late night workers still putting the hours in. Cars slid past in a constant chain and, while their passengers might try to rubberneck, the vehicles' autodrive systems wouldn't slow them. I was right there in full view, a bear at bay, ringed by the dogs whose masters kept prudently out of reach. I was in the heart of America, a published academic, an author, a TV celebrity, and nobody would stop, and nobody would care. In that moment I was nothing more than an animal. And if I'd fought, they'd have gunned me down.

They didn't get HumOS, or at least Gray, her local branch operative. I know this because we didn't go straight to any police station, holding cell or similar place of incarceration, but just drove around aimlessly for over an hour, obviously looking for someone that we never found. I have no doubt that they knew who I was meeting with, and that the war HumOS was fighting with various security forces was getting hotter. I did dare to hope that, in the absence of actual evidence, they might let me go with a stern talking to. No such luck.

They collared me, small 'c'. There was a rack of big metal rings in the cruiser's interior and they put a heavy collar on me and chained me to one. It wasn't exactly dignified. The world has come up with less humiliating ways of restraining any size or shape of Bioform. It wasn't entirely an atavism, though. Plenty of nations still used such methods, or worse. After all, there were easier platforms to argue for than humane treatment of dangerous animals that had gone far enough to end up in custody. Dangerous animals, wicked animals, fit only to be treated as such. Even if the crime in this case was holding political opinions unpopular with a resurgent element of the US state and some of the World Senate.

Two of the police dogs were in the back with me, still armed and with those guns pointed at me. Both of them had the same cruciform badges, which filled me with an extra layer of depression. And true, there were the very rare times when the existence of the Sons of Adam had played into my rhetorical hands: an association of Bioforms, almost all dogs, who were practically socially acceptable. But they were acceptable because they bought into the creed that they knew their place. They'd got religion, you see. About ten years after Rex died, when the world was going through another fit of Bioform fear, there was a Vatican priest named Father Jacomo Ionescu. This was long after the walkback of the Papal pronouncement about Bioform souls, so we were on the table to be saved along with natural born people, even though regular dogs and bears and the rest weren't. It was a mire of theology, asking at what point in the eminently human-run process the soul got in. It kept a lot of very abstract religious thinkers very busy. Other religions were still on the fence or had come down against the idea, but there had been the odd progressive Pope and when the old boy comes out with something in a public address it's hard for the establishment at large to pretend it didn't happen.

Father Ionescu had appointed himself chief missionary to the animals, a latter-day Saint Francis. He had actually listened to what Bioforms were saying, and he'd worked out that a great many of us were very insecure about our place in the world. Not just that mainstream humanity's mind might shift again, on the topic of what we are and what rights we're entitled to. No, the uncertainty that Father Ionescu identified was more existential. What, after all, were we? We were artificial beings made out of natural beings. Where did we fit? What was our purpose? A lot of us, especially the dog-forms, covertly yearned for a simpler time when we were just told what to do. And Rex would have understood that – not agreed, I hope, but understood. And even I remember those days, no rights, no responsibilities. No knowledge of good and evil.

So arose the creed of the Sons of Adam – not Cain and Abel but the other living things given into his dominion by God. The purpose of Bioforms, said Father Ionescu, was to serve mankind, and in doing so they would find their own way to the Heavenly Kingdom. And although the philosophy fell on my ears like a wet fish, he won a lot of adherents, and the cult has never really gone away. And wearing the Dog Cross looks good when you're going for a job with the security services or certain companies. A lot of people have even told me I should speak out in support of them, as a force that brings humans and Bioforms closer together. Except, of course, it brings them together in a very specific relationship, and that is Master and Servant. And if I'd been happy with that then I wouldn't have done all the many and varied things I've done over the last fifty years, frankly. But some Bioforms, some dogs, get anxious, and they want to trade all the agency I've won for them, sell it for a certainty that seems utterly spurious to me but infinitely reassuring to them.

"I knew him, you know," I said tiredly, as the cruiser swung another left and we swept the area one last time. I mean Rex of course, not Father Ionescu, although I did meet the man once. For what it's worth he wasn't the political tyrant I'd been expecting, but well-meaning men can cause just as much damage, if not more.

The lead dog stared at me for a long time, and I almost missed his small nod.

"I was his friend. I was with him from the start," I went on. I could talk forever about all the things I did for Rex, many of them behind his back because he wouldn't have understood.

"I know who you are," the dog told me, in that angry voice that was the only one a lot of the military-built models got. Adding new voice functions is big biomod business for Bioforms that have worked out their contact, but perhaps he would have considered it hubris. He met my eyes and I could see it cost him some effort. He was ashamed; he wanted to look away.

"I'm sorry it has to be like this," he said. "But you have stepped from the path."

"There's a difference between accusation and conviction," I pointed out, but I knew that, for him, there wouldn't be. He did what he was told, and that was his cardinal virtue, both in his job and in his theology. He would tell himself it made him a Good Dog.

"What's your name, soldier?" I asked him, thinking he wouldn't say.

"Scout," he said, and then, at some message on his closed channel, "You're to be taken to the Shambles."

That wasn't the place's name, of course. It was the Rhodes Point Bioform Holding Facility, and I hadn't even realised it was still in operation. And likely Scout didn't even know what the old word 'Shambles' meant.

10

JIMMY

"What did you put in my head?" I demand, and Sugar must get just how goddamn upset I am about all this because Murder and Marmalade are right at my shoulders and she doesn't expect this sort of disrespect from a nobody like your man Jimmy. So she doesn't have me gutted by bears, just stares at me, wide-eyed at my affrontery.

"This *thing* you gave me," I go on. "I mean... what the fuck, Sugar?"

She's sitting in her throne of crates there in Storage Nineteen, sure enough, and now she makes one little imperious gesture and the handful of her crew who were loitering about are just gone, slinking away past the stacked walls of containers so it's just her, me and the two bears. And my passenger.

"Jimmy," she says, low and dangerous, "are you telling me you *peeked*?"

Behind me, Murder makes a low, bowel-loosening sound, unless it's Marmalade.

"I? I did goddamn nothing, Sugar," and I'm still shouting at her, which under other circumstances would be a catastrophically unwise thing to do but right now is actually giving her pause. See, she knows Yours Truly isn't a punchy guy, under regular circumstances. She knows that only a pretty goddamn extreme situation would bring me to her door hollering and making a scene. And probably she's still thinking about burying me in the next foundation slab to get laid down, but at least she wants to know why.

"Seriously," I go on, a little more in control. "I get home, and your data is *talking* to me. It's a full-on personality and it's just loose in my head. It took me over, Sugar."

She blinks lazily, one set of lids and then the other. Then Marmalade has a scanner up by my head, same model as Brian was messing about with. Murder shambles off a few steps and I try to watch both bears in case Honey pulls the same trick with them as she did with the Bad News crowd.

"My, that *is* busy," Sugar murmurs, fed data from the scanner direct to her implant. "I guess whatever we put in there just unpacked itself like a jack-in-the-box, eh, Jimbles? So, what're you getting? Audio-visual? Number strings? Or just static?" And she's interested, which is probably on the better end of the potential outcomes with her. Means she won't just have me ripped up and left somewhere.

"Sugar," I tell her. "There is a working copy of a person inside my head."

And then the voice that I've been dreading, saying, "Who's this, now?"

Sugar must have seen me wince. "Ain't possible," she tells me, but she's still looking past me at the data. "You just got something from it?"

"Spoke to me," I confirm. "Right then." And obviously that coincided with some spike from the scanner because she raises a delicate eyebrow.

"Who's it say it is?"

"Sugar, I'm not being funny, but it says it's called Honey."

Her face freezes, and at first I think it's because she thinks I'm taking the piss. Then I realise that the name *means* something to her.

"You don't keep up with current affairs back home, do you, Jimbles?"

I can only shake my head. I mean, what's the point, precisely? Not going to be that way by the time we finally get back. "She took me over, Sugar. Like, moved me about, arms, legs, like a puppet."

"Ain't possible," she says again. "Jimmy, how much Stringer did you take in one go?"

"You think this is just a… psychotic break?"

"Known side effect. It'd be there on the doctor's warning label if it weren't so damn illegal," she says, hunching forwards to stare at me. "Hearing voices, stranger in your own body."

"She's right, you know. You shouldn't take any more of that stuff," Honey adds helpfully.

"Shut the fuck up!" I shout, and from the echo I realise that was full volume. Nobody kills me, though. Sugar's actually looking ever so slightly concerned.

"Jesus, Jimbles, you are fucked up on something."

"I am not. Believe me there are not drugs on Mars to fuck me up like this. There is someone in my head, Sugar. Not just loose data, not just Stringer. Look, your girls here threw down with Rufus over at Mall's. They tell you that? I've got the posse after me because of this shit you stuck in me. Take it out, Sugar. For the love of God just… find somewhere else to hide it. I, I don't have my life any more. I don't even have my own body. Any moment I'm gonna start talking like I'm from goddamn Harvard and tell you everything's fine and walk out, and it won't be *me*, Sugar! It won't be me running my own body."

Sugar's expression is... I mean, she's her own little crime baroness, with a couple of killer Bioform henchbears. She's ruler of her own little fiefdom here in Storage Nineteen. She takes shit from nobody. And here she is, looking at your man Jimmy Marten and on her face isn't even anger, not even the cold disdain of a mob boss about to dispose of an inconvenience. It's pity. Poor Jimbles is going crazy on her and she's actually a little sorry for me. And that makes me feel a lot sorry for myself and I'm almost crying, right there and then. It's all too much.

"Tell her I need to contact Bees," Honey prompts, in the resulting silence.

"You even know why, now?" I demand, because why not stand here talking to myself in front of Sugar. How can it make anything worse?

"I'm still working on it, Jimmy. And I don't want to have to take you over. As I said, it's entirely against my deeply-held principles. So just tell her, why don't you? She's obviously someone in authority. Maybe she can help me."

Whatever the hell's in my face when I turn it on Sugar, she actually flinches back a bit. "She wants," I say quietly, "to talk to Bees." I say it very carefully, so you can hear the upper case 'B'.

Sugar doesn't pale at that, but then we none of us can, not with our lead-coloured skin tone. At last she nods, to herself, not to me. "I ain't telling you who sent this package over, Jimbles, you know that. But it was from... an odd source. One I've dealt with before, and the money checks out, but still..." She's troubled, and the two bears catch that off her and shuffle uncomfortably. "This voice of yours, it can get outside your head, hold a conversation?"

"If she provides some manner of voice synthesiser I'm sure I can find a way," Honey tells me, and I relay that like I'm only the messenger.

"Maybe later," Sugar says, still musing. "Jimbles, old son, I'm going to pop you somewhere safe and off-grid while I work out just what the fuck is going on with this deal. You hungry, thirsty? Sure you are. And I'm sure someone round here's got a strip of Stringer. You're just gonna sit tight while I see what's what. You and this voice in your head."

"So you believe me?"

"Don't rightly know what I believe," she says, mostly to herself, but she's got a thoughtful look on her face I've seen before and it gives me a sinking feeling. It's a look that says she reckons she can make a fat profit off this, and *this*, right now, means me.

"Perhaps," Honey says to me, "we can start afresh. I appreciate this must be very distressing for you. We have rather got off on the wrong foot."

"Stop talking to me," I tell her, reasonably.

"Jimmy, believe me you wouldn't have been my first choice, but neither of us got to choose. I do have an important mission to carry out here on Mars, though—"

"Which you don't know what is."

"It's coming back to me, piece by piece. Although right now I am more engaged with trying to familiarise myself with this construction project and how it works. I was only peripherally interested in it back on Earth."

"You're not doing shit," I point out. "Sugar's got this place jammed three ways from Sunday." We are, in fact, inside one of the big containers, which Sugar apparently already had fitted out like a little hotel room. It's four times the size of my nook and there's a place to sleep and a place to piss and I've got a selection of ration bars and a line of clean water. No media, though, no channels out, utterly cut off. Wonder what she needs this little love nest for.

"Well, she thinks she has," Honey says, with that smug tone that's really getting on my nerves about now. "I've been able to download quite a lot of non-classified information about the Hellas Planitia project and its workforce. About you, Jimmy."

"You don't know jack about me."

"But I do, and you're quite the work of engineering," she says, like I should be grateful she's taking an interest. "I knew the Building Mars Workforce project was the most extensive human bioengineering ever – World Senate only allowed it because you'd all be off-planet, otherwise you break about a hundred different bans on human experimentation. And I was interested mostly because of the lab that did your neurotech, your headware, but your biomod specs are very impressive." As though I'm her pony that's come best in show. "You can actually go outside the complex unsuited?"

"How'd you expect we get anything done, else?" I ask her. I mean, how can she not know these things? Except, I guess, people back on Earth don't really give a shit about us, only about the city we're building for them. "I mean, not out there forever, and only within the crater where the atmosphere's denser. Can't just go frolic on the surface of Mars. And even under the canopy the air's not so thick all over, still pushing out from the centre. Got to wear suits out at the edges still."

"Even with all of that, Jimmy, you can walk around on some part of Mars without protective equipment. On another world, Jimmy."

"Fish," I tell her, and she's obviously completely baffled, and that's my ration of fun for the day so I don't elaborate. Was a guy at the lab, one of the biotech boys who worked on us, was really into his fish. "We're all fish," he used to say to me. "Everything with a spine's a fish." And there's a lot of fish in the way they remade us. Antifreeze blood from fish, variable pressure tissues from fish, more efficient oxygen take-up from fish. Because, the way he said it, there's crap-all O_2 in water compared to air, so fish are super-good at sieving it out, and now so are my lungs. You could drop me in the deep ocean back home, I'd be just fine.

"What surprises me is that you volunteered for the changes, given the way most people are about biotech mods," she muses.

"Money was good," I say shortly. There's a whole history there, of the way Earth has gone to shit. Cities flooded, breadbaskets gone barren, seas gone toxic. Hell City is worth the investment because a lot of rich people are thinking maybe they need somewhere to live that hasn't been shat on for the last couple of centuries. And for the programme they were only taking people without families, without serious ties to Earth; wasn't like I had anything to stick around for. "It's a living, right. And they'll change us back after."

"Will they?"

"It's in the contract."

"Ah, well then." And she's needling me because I wouldn't talk about the fish. "There was an idea back home when they were designing you," Honey says thoughtfully, "that they'd just grow purpose-built clone bodies and then install personality uploads into the shells. So you'd all believe you were real people, but you'd be no more than copies, like me."

I go cold all over. "Listen, lady—"

"It didn't happen," she goes on implacably, and I know she knows just how much she just rattled me, getting her own ration of fun however she can. "There were worries about long-term stability. More expensive to take real people and give them extensive modifications, but a better long-term investment. After all, this city won't get built in a day. I was just searching around for a reason you've got such extensive headware, Jimmy. I mean, you don't *need* all this space. You're not using it. You can literally fit a whole other person in here because, look, here I am."

"Lucky fucking me," I tell her.

I think I've finally grouched enough to make her go sulk in some over-engineered corner of my head, because she shuts up for a bit then. I pop another tab of Stringer but it isn't really cutting through all the misery, and when I go to take a second right on its heels Honey tells me that I'm in danger of exceeding the safe dosage and she'll pour my stash down the chemical crapper if I get stupid with the body we're both sharing. I cannot, seriously, I *cannot* tell you how much I hate her right then. I mean it's one thing to have a voice in your head and another to lose control of your entire body, but to be so goddamn *judge*-y with it?

"Perhaps I can take your mind off your cravings," she suggests, after a beat. "Can you see this?"

Whatever it is, I can't; nor can I when she says, "This?" or even the much-awaited sequel, "How about this, then?" and the whole shebang's shaping up to be the world's worst game of blind man's goddamn charades when suddenly I do actually start seeing things. Not sure it's any better, if you ask me, but something's sort of overlaid across the interior of the container; a grainy, fuzzy image of another room. I experiment and find it's only in my left eye, and it looks like some of Sugar's people moving boxes about; not exactly the most entertaining piece of footage in the history of telemedia.

"I've established a link to their local loop here, their cameras," Honey tells me, as though she should win an award for technical innovation. "I'm feeding it into the visual centres of your brain. Tell me if it's upside down or anything."

"You're doing *what* to my brain?"

"Oh do calm down. It's all in the architecture. You were set up for this. Like I say, they fit you people out with far more..." And she trails off thoughtfully. "Braintree gave you the bells and whistles treatment, sure enough. And... I think it's all of you, the whole BM Workforce crew. They really must have overbudgeted, unless..." More silent consideration, like a pressure behind my eyes. "So let's see what we can..."

The view changes, making me stagger with vertigo for a moment. Overlaid across my left field of vision I see the interior of another container, next is the corridor outside Storage Nineteen, then Sugar's own throne room where the woman herself is entertaining a new visitor. And there the channel-hopping stops and for once Honey and I are on the same page because Sugar's chatting with Rufus.

The big dog still has his gun, and Murder and Marmalade're standing either side of the throne, not right in his face but not exactly keeping their distance. Even through the terrible image quality, dog and bears are all definitely on a knife-edge. Sugar's doing her best relaxed act, though, one leg thrown over the arm of her chair, doing her little innocent pixie for the sheriff.

"Your clowns attacked me just as I was making the collar, Sugar," Old Doggo's voice comes to me through my radio implant. "What, I'm supposed to believe that was a coincidence?"

"Sheriff, you show up unannounced at Mall's, I'm amazed everyone there didn't assume you were after them. I mean, I thought we had a system, you know, the light and the dark."

"There's no system," Rufus growls. "There's maybe a little tolerance because I can't exactly arrest half the work crews for all the shit they do for crooks like you."

Murder and Marmalade hunch forward a bit at the way he's talking to their boss, and I got to admire Rufus's nerve because each of them's way bigger than him, and Murder's got the rivet gun.

"The *system* works," Sugar says. "Like I always say, people need an outlet. You can either have one you got diplomatic relations with, or some other one you don't know where it is, getting up to shit you can't ever control and screwing you over when you least want it, Sheriff. I reckon you're better off with the first. Not like our activities end up flicking your ballsack too often, now, is it? We're practically law-abiding citizens hereabouts."

"Jimmy Marten." And hearing your name snarled out of the jaws of an angry dog-form is nobody's happy place.

"Ain't got him. I'll tell the gang to keep an open eye."

Now I can tell she isn't really fooling Rufus – either she has me or she's already sold me on, is his assessment. Sugar can tell the same thing and Rufus knows it, and yet he doesn't call her on it, not straight out. I hadn't realised just how normalised the way we live our lives is, but there really is a system. Rufus doesn't want open war with the criminal element, and they don't want it with him and Admin and the Bad News Bears. You make a big enough stink, I guess, and you end up getting handed over by your own people just 'cos it's easier that way. Or, at least, some scapegoat does. Except that nobody'll be scapegoating for me.

So Sheriff Rufus thinks for a moment and then cocks his head, one ear up like a quizzical eyebrow. "You do that," he says slowly. "And while you're putting the word out, you say that Admin is very keen to get back something that little Jimmy got hold of. Something off limits, Sugar. Something important enough to important enough people that, should you have it and not come clean, no *system* will protect you from my wrath, you got that?" And when Murder and Marmalade growl at him, he bares his yellow fangs right back at them. "You want to throw down now, I will have you in my quarters as *rugs*, girls. I am not messing around on this one."

I hold my goddamn breath, is what I do, but what actually happens is that the two bears shuffle and *uff* a bit, but back down. Rufus is more dog than they feel like dealing with right now. He turns his gaze back to Sugar, still defiantly trying to look casual.

"On the other hand," he says, voice all syrup and sweetness, "if it happened that you did chance across Jimmy Marten and pass him on to the relevant authorities, then you might find that a sizeable donation finds its way to your war chest over here. And maybe a few more blind eyes turned than you are used to. This is *important*, Sugar. You're a smart woman. You do the math." And he turns and stalks off, leaving Sugar with a very thoughtful look on her face.

When they come to get me, soon after that, I know exactly how it'll go. The threats, the yappy dog act in there, that might have worked, might not've. Sugar has her face to keep up before her own people and before the other bit-part crooks who run Hell City's makeshift black market scene. Give in too easy and you're everyone's bitch. But offer a big stack of scrip, or even Earthside cash, and suddenly it's gone from knuckling under to a shrewd business decision. The moment Rufus sweetened the pot, I knew I was as good as sold.

Still, no point trying to run from Murder and Marmalade here inside Sugar's own domain, because if nothing else a bear can generally outpace a human, especially on all fours for extra traction and the way a bear body just seems to work better than human for the Martian biomods. If they hadn't been so expensive to make and ship over, I swear they wouldn't have had us humans here at all.

Not exactly my first choice, then, but I'm prepared to face my fate with dignity when they take me back before Sugar. She's not doing casual any more, I see, leaning forwards with her pointy elfin chin on her hands, a woman making a difficult but probably foregone decision.

"How's the voices, Jimbles?" she asks me.

"A pain in the goddamn ass, is what." Why not a free and frank exchange of views, given I'm stiffed here? "Look, just take it out. Pack it off to Rufus on its own. You don't need me. He don't need me. I'd just be in the way."

"Jimmy—" Honey says warningly, and of course I've just

spilled the beans on our eavesdropping, but sue me, what precisely was I gaining by keeping the side up?

"Well 'just in the way' is what they'll put on your grave, Jimbles," Sugar says lazily. "But I know damn well that *you* couldn't hack through to see who I was talking to, so I guess maybe you have a little devil on your shoulder after all. You there, Honey two-point-zero? You linking in?"

"I have located your synthesiser, yes." The voice that comes from a box near Sugar's throne isn't much like the one I hear in my head, but I know it from the rhythm of the words. "I appreciate that you have been offered a substantial incentive to hand Mr Marten and myself over to the authorities, Ms Sugatsu, but I would ask—"

Sugar makes a gesture and the artificial voice cuts off. *See how you like it*, I think with a stab of mean pleasure.

"Wordy bint, ain't she?" Sugar observes. I agree whole-heartedly, but when I try to plead my own case again she shuts me up with a sharp gesture and says, "So I have an offer on the table for you, Jimbles. More than your rat's ass life could ever be worth, frankly. But I didn't make a go of this business by measuring once and cutting twice. So I'm going to hear from another bidder first, just to see what's in it for me. And you, Honey, are going to dance for me as and when I say, and I will kill the synth if I think you're getting mouthy, you understand? Tell Jimbles here that you and I have an understanding."

Honey sighs disgustedly in my ear. "You may as well agree to her demands on my behalf."

"Yes," I say. "You could just say 'yes'. Not the whole goddamn dictionary." But I indicate to Sugar that all's agreed.

"Well then, Marmalade, why don't you go bring in our

next lucky contestant," suggests Sugar, and the bear drops to all fours and lopes off, and comes back with...

A skinny guy in overalls, basically. Just one more working Joe from the construction site trekking rust-coloured dust in on Sugar's floor. Except I know him. Except he is the absolute last goddamn person I expect to see ushered into this company like he's some sort of VIP. Because it's Brian. It's Brian fucking Dey, my useless twat of a co-worker who never finishes his jobs properly and never has anything interesting to say.

"So." And Sugar is being all casual again. "What've you got for me, Mister? What are you in all this?"

"'M'n'bassador," he says, only he chonks the words together so it's only a moment later I know he's said *I'm an ambassador.* And then he adds, "You gon' got hold'a something, you say." His eyes flick awkwardly to me. "Hey, man. Di'n' realise what you had, or wouldn't be needin' all this."

"What the...?" I just don't have the words for him, and end up turning to Sugar, who's obviously pissing herself wanting to laugh at me. "Ambassador from who."

"You tell him," she directs, swinging my attention back to Brian.

He lifts his head, and his eyes are suddenly very clear, like all the Brian-y muddle's gone from them and I'm looking at some crazy-ass sonofabitch fanatic been hiding away inside interplanetary loser Brian Dey all this time.

"'M come from Bees," he says, like it's a new Gospel. "'Ey say you got something they want."

11

SPRINGER

Not a hotel, this time. They were in New York, which meant a penthouse suite owned by one of Thompson's companies' companies where he paid himself to take up residence and then wrote it off against tax. More square footage than the average American's suburban house and here he was in one corner of it, staring at the screen.

Pat Grubb was in, come to report his latest successes in shaking down backers for cash. He had a list of topics he needed Thompson to slip into his next few appearances, just so everyone felt they were getting their money's worth. Carole had wanted him to just mail it over. He'd insisted on turning up in person, said it was all too sensitive to trust to electronics. She knew he just wanted to be close to the man. He wanted recognition for what he'd done. Except Thompson hadn't even registered him, just sat heavily, staring at the screen, face dead, eyes flickering with reflected images.

"I don't get it. What's he doing?" Grubb's breath smelled of beer and decay and he was standing too close again. "Why's he listening to *that*."

It was a regular favourite of Thompson's, if 'favourite' was the word. She kept it on hand at all times, along with a handful of other clips, for when the man decided he wanted motivation. It was from some talk somewhere, some televised academic circle-jerk where people with too much education and too much time made money out of talking some topic to death. Except the one giving the talk wasn't people. It was a bear, rubbing shoulders with humans, wearing clothes, standing in front of a comically tiny lectern. A bear lecturing people about authority.

"Everyone always looks at these systems," came the bear's voice, and it was a nice voice, a woman's reassuring tones not so very far from the way Carole herself spoke to Thompson, "and asks how they go wrong so quickly. How is it that, the moment we actually look on them with an objective eye we start to wonder how *he* got that big office, how *she* ended up with the promotion instead of him or her. We've all been somewhere where there's a roomful of geniuses working eighteen hour days and the manager can't tie his shoelaces and knocks off at three for golf, am I right?" And there was a ripple of polite and terribly educated amusement from the crowd, and Carole wondered just how many of them worked eighteen hour days and how many of them played golf. Except there was a buffer in place, in talks like that. There was a complicit assumption that this doesn't apply to *us*. It was an environment where one could expound general rules of human civilisation that applied to all human beings of whatever time and place save for the select group in the room.

"And that's because there are people who play the game, and there are people who play the metagame," the bear with the woman's voice went on. Behind her the screen was showing news reports, taken from the last ten years and highlighting a string of cases where companies had failed, governments had fallen over, banks had gone bust. There were photos of managing directors, ministers, officials associated with various failed enterprises, and perhaps the audience response was a little more muted, because these were actual people, actual real-world examples. Not merely some piece of theoretical whimsy that could, Schrödinger-like, be agreed as something that happened in the real world and yet, at the same time, not require anyone to change anything concrete.

"It doesn't actually matter what area you're talking about. I suspect this is a universal once any organisation reaches a certain size, requires a certain level of hierarchy. Small 'h'." More polite laughter, slightly awkward given that this bear was old enough to have been fitted with a Hierarchy, back in the day.

"So what's the game? The game is what your business does. It's what your government department does. It's making shoes, designing software, teaching children about twentieth-century history. It's the thing without which you don't actually have a product or a service. And last year in this very room we had Doctor Capavela talking about pan-industrial management culture and making some very socialist arguments about shoemakers running shoe factories and why you couldn't generalise management experience from one field to another, and frankly that's not my point. Because management is the game, too. The ordering of people, the logistics of business, making sure that one moving part intersects with the next within your organisation's structure is absolutely the game, because once a business grows past a certain size it needs people whose sole job is to administer it. But what puts a spanner in the works isn't the game, but the metagame."

And Grubb's face screwed up and he shot Carole a baffled look. "Why's he even watching this shit?"

Carole regarded Thompson's slack face, seeing past it to the burning attention within his narrow eyes. "He's hating," she said quietly.

Grubb stared at her. "He's what now?"

She ignored him, watching Thompson watch the bear. He had been so angry when he'd first caught this. He'd seen it on the internet. He hadn't been tagged in it. Nobody had heard this speech and levelled an accusing finger at Warner S. Thompson. But he'd known. He'd heard all that academic language and boiled it down to one simple meaning. Someone had seen him. Someone had looked behind the curtain, behind the smile and the handshake and the bluster. Someone had looked past the slack, dead face and seen what Carole saw now behind those eyes. And he hadn't liked it. He probably couldn't even put into words what it was he didn't like, but some deep instinct knew a threat when he saw it.

And he had asked to see it again, a month later, and then again, and by then Carole knew to just keep the recording handy. For when he was tired after a long string of engagements. For when he flagged slightly. He would take this out, or some other titbit of media, and he would watch, once, twice, sometimes five or six times on loop. It would revitalise him. It would stir the primal pot of hate and anger that fuelled him. Grubb would never understand. Grubb, who had been raking in money through anti-Bioform hate sites for a decade before joining Thompson's team, would never quite grasp the nature of his master, nor of the man's complex relationship with the things he hated. Grubb knew

Thompson hated DisInt and he hated Bioforms, but hate was not just a fire to destroy, not just an excuse to panhandle donations. Hate was an attractive force. Thompson needed his hates.

Then her implant signalled an incoming call. Scout; the Trigger Dogs.

"Report," she murmured, stepping away from Grubb, turning her back on him.

We have the bear, came Scout's transmission, not his voice but the brisk, clinical tone of his channel.

"And the other?"

Scout's channel: *Evaded us. Or wasn't there at all.*

Carole waited to see how she would feel about that. There had been a chance they'd catch a DisInt unit. She should feel disappointed they hadn't. She should tell Scout his master would be angry at him. Although most likely Thompson wouldn't remember, and Honey was more important to him, now he had his hate on. But inside herself she felt an odd absence. If any emotion crept into that void it was a timid relief, because a DisInt unit would look human, would look like a woman, like her. And she didn't want to see Thompson with someone like her and his hate on.

The immediate dissonance was almost painful, the chains in her head pulling awkwardly in multiple directions. Thompson was right to hate. Those he hated were his enemies. He was entitled to do what he wanted to them. To enjoy doing it. She wanted him to enjoy himself. And yet at the same time she did not want to see it, or to know of it. Let him bait bears. Let him have animals destroyed. And the following thought that might have been *But not her* or *But not me* and she couldn't disentangle the strands enough to work out which.

And then the knot was cut and she was stepping to Thompson's shoulder.

"Trigger Dogs say they have Honey, sir."

Thompson killed the screen immediately, then just stared at the darkness of it, squinting as though it was the sun. She glanced back at Grubb, who was still waiting to brag of his successes. He'd go on waiting, she knew. This would take precedence and it wasn't something that included him. At the back of the room, Boyo had caught her mood if not the details. Standing, ready for action, already signalling the car. Grubb flinched as the Bioform got to his feet.

"I want to go see," Thompson said, pushing himself up from the couch where he'd been hunched.

"Of course, sir."

"Mr Thompson—" Grubb started, but Thompson stared at him, past him, through him as though unable to quite work out what this man-shaped object was that someone had brought into his room. Grubb retreated, mumbling about 'later'.

Soon after, Boyo was guiding the car out of the subterranean garage and off across town towards the Shambles.

It was a long ride out to Rhodes Point. Thompson sat in the back and drank from the bar. He had a debate on the screen, not for hating but watching himself talk. He did that a lot. Grubb thought it was because he was honing his technique, but in truth Warner S. Thompson was the one thing that could hold Warner S. Thompson for any length of time. Thompson adored himself, and at the same time he didn't seem to quite recognise that the man on the screen was him. Self-knowledge was absent from him. Confronted with his own image he was like an animal that couldn't understand that the magnificent beast in the mirror is only a reflection. And maybe *that* had led to the plan. Maybe that deep dysfunction in him meant only he, of all the self-absorbed, powerful men in the world, could conceive such hubris. Maybe you had to be a grand master of the metagame, as Honey had called it, before you could decide you wanted such a thing to come about.

Carole spent the ride pulling together the last two days' developments on the World Senate scene, because she'd need to assimilate it to give a distilled summary to Thompson. The Senate, twenty-three years on from its formation, was about to have a shift change of a third of its members, or at least those seats were up for election, Alabama-Virginia among them. As always seemed to happen, everything was boiling down to where candidates stood on a handful of issues. As always seemed to happen, the issues weren't the spreading famine, the coastal chaos, the droughts, the floods, the great camps of displaced climate refugees. Instead, the voters wanted to know where their man stood on the threat of DisInt. Were Bees going to descend from Mars to rule over all the kingdoms of the Earth? Were there networked human intelligences infiltrating government and the world banking system? Were free Bioforms just a fifth column for a shadowy conspiracy that was going to murder everyone in their beds? And the other usual suspects: candidates who were down on any sexual orientation beyond the default; candidates who wanted to preserve the traditional family values that imposed a hierarchy (small 'h', unless you were a real hard-liner) with a patriarch at the head of the table come Sunday lunchtime; candidates who felt that freedom of worship should only be upheld when you were worshipping at the right altar. All the old familiar battlegrounds now standing around a pulpit from which men like Thompson preached the looming threat posed by any kind of intelligence that went beyond the human.

Carole had seen a lot of politicians on the other side of the debate founder on those rocks. She'd seen earnest environmentalists, committed humanitarians just choke into silence because the Big Issues that they had built their platforms from were getting swept away in the rising tide, while DisInt and Collars held against the flood. They couldn't understand it. They were like the crazy people in the street, shouting at everyone that the world was ending, and people just hurried past with their faces averted. Carole had a privileged perspective from inside the machine, though. Plain enough to her why it worked out that way. The worsening climate, the mass displacement, the shortages, that was poor-people problems. DisInt and the growing agency of non-human intellect represented something that might eat into the status quo at the top, hence rich-people problems. Small wonder which one the attention of the world was being focused on.

The World Senate was poised in the balance right now. The current Alabama-Virginia incumbent wasn't exactly radical; it wasn't that kind of seat. He was a sit-on-the-fence kind of guy, though, like a lot of them. Thompson was one of a wave of new candidates who were using the issues to leverage themselves into a commanding lead, feeding off the popular fear about the DisInt conspiracy everyone knew was out there; feeding off the wave of covert bigotry that was spreading through every city's suburbs now that successful Bioforms weren't just living in their own districts any more, but were moving into the next street, next door, heavy animal feet stomping in the apartment overhead, scaled reptile faces in your local corner shop. Dogs sitting at the desk next to you like they had a right to be there. Everyone had been all about Bioform rights three decades ago, after Morrow, but that had been when they'd still been in their ghettoes. Now they were passing you in the street and people were all about restrictions, limitations, mandatory Collaring, think of the children...

For a lot of Thompson's peers it was just riding the incoming tide, stoking fires already burning so they could use the hot air to rise. Others were genuine dyed-in-the-wool committed reactionaries or else just felt their commercial interests under threat from a changing world. Thompson was all of these, at various times, but mostly that was his outer shell, that part of his functioning personality maintained mostly by other people and coordinated by Carole and the campaign staff. The inner Thompson, the raw and naked creature that sat in his head and wanted things with such a clear and primal force that people made them manifest in the world for him, that Thompson had another reason not to want things like Bees and HumOS running unfettered about the world.

Rhodes Point Bioform Holding Facility, aka the Shambles, wasn't used much any more, since they'd constructed a more modern facility further out of town. It had been built in the early years after the old UN's first resolution on limited Bioform rights, which boiled down to little more than a right to exist. The authorities had been very ready for Bioform delinquency, and places like the Shambles were the result. It was a hideous concrete eyesore, more below ground than above, surrounded by a barbed wire fence and a whole lot of warning signs, but there was only one inmate at present, and that one only as of the last few hours.

A handful of human officers were there to watch Thompson step from his car, shifting back a few steps when Boyo came out to loom. He dismissed them almost immediately, though. He didn't trust them, for all they were employed by one of his companies. They were loyal, but they weren't Loyal, not like Boyo, like Scout, like Carole. They weren't *his*. He didn't trust them, because he didn't trust anyone who might at some point harbour any thought that didn't orbit him.

Carole liaised with Scout, guided Thompson in through the lobby, down into the workings of the Shambles. Concrete walls and floors, harsh unshaded lighting, stains. Old, rust-coloured stains. When a Bioform *had* crossed the line, back in those days, they hadn't been gentle. And the smell. Even though the place hadn't seen more than a handful of brief residencies in the last ten years, the smell lingered. Stale urine, old blood, animals. Pain, fear, death.

The bear had been wearing fancy clothes, hand-tailored to impart human fashion to an animal frame. All gone now. She was at the bottom of a bare walled pit, the single door down there massive enough that even a young, strong grizzly couldn't have dented it. And she wasn't that, not any more. And the walls of the cells in the Shambles were solid and three feet thick. They really had been very worried about rogue Bioforms, back in the day.

Their vantage was high, looking five metres down past angled spikes, as though the designers had been worried about a bear or a dog going up the walls like a spider, like an alien in one of those movies. As though a tired old circus act could suddenly learn to fly. Carole peered down and waited for the vicarious rush of loathing. This was Thompson's enemy, hence her enemy as well. This was the animal that had stood on its hind legs and had ideas above its station.

And she saw just a tired old bear, grey and a little mangy, sitting in a corner of the cell. Without clothes, without context, there was no more of the human about it beyond that residual trace bears have always had; that odd anthropomorphism imparted to them by convergent evolution. Two legs, two arms, stand straight, sit up, until they sloped down on all fours and it all sloughed off them, animal after all.

The hate didn't come. She looked at this sad, sagging old thing, and thought about the woman's sharp, incisive voice taking the human world to task for the games it played, and couldn't square them.

Then Thompson was beside her, holding on to the rail, staring down, and his eyes burned. She practically felt the heat off him, the single emotion that was hate and triumph and greed and hunger all snarled together, which fuelled his every move. And *then* she hated. Then she stared down at the caged beast and loathed it for its temerity. She would have thrown stones at it, had there been any. For *him*.

"Sir," said Scout. He and a couple of the Trigger Dogs were nearby, genuine law enforcement, or at least private security with the appropriate permits, but Thompson's, too. He owned them. And they were Sons of Adam all, which Thompson liked. They knew their place, revelled in it, Good Dogs every one of them. They couldn't put their heads into a Collar fast enough. Safer for them, safer for everybody, as Thompson said in his interviews.

"Who knows?" Thompson barked abruptly.

Scout's channel: *We had to go on record that we'd opened*

up the holding centre. We've not said anything more. We have electronic security up. She can't call out.

And Carole was boiling that down for Thompson, cooking it until it had distilled into a single word. "Nobody." And at the same time she felt her anxiety coming back, that twist inside her that writhed against the cage of her devotion, that she could never uproot and tear out of herself. It was because Scout had given the bear a gender. *Let it be an it.* But Honey was a *her*, with that pleasant voice and the clever mind behind it. Just a moth-eaten old menagerie inmate, just an animal. Except she was a person, and abruptly Carole was terrified for her. Would Thompson have Scout go get a cattle prod? Would he have the Trigger Dogs go into that cell with bared teeth, a spot of good old-fashioned entertainment for a twenty-first-century Renaissance man?

He made a noise, not even a word, not even something you'd call a proper laugh. A snicker, small and unpleasant from such a big man. Staring at the captive bear, lips wet, face hanging there like a rag. The real Thompson, the one that was inside him, looked down and enjoyed the sight of his enemy caged, on the point of putting out a hand, thumb downwards, like the emperor he was.

"There might be attention," Carole said. "Too soon to know yet. She might be traced here." And she wasn't sure why she'd said it. Not that it wasn't true. Honey was a public figure, not as easy to disappear as all that, not unless Scout had been very careful. And almost certainly he *had* been very careful, but still best to cater to that outside chance. Except that was all post-facto logic built up in the echo of words already said. Because she couldn't un-person the bear in her head. Because she remembered the woman's voice, even though it was prime-time hate-watching for her adored employer.

Thompson's face clenched, and she shrank back without putting herself out of arm's reach. Boyo and Scout and the other two Trigger Dogs were watching, waiting. Give them the order and they wouldn't hesitate, nor should they. Give *her* the order and a gun, she'd do it herself.

A sulky, petulant child's expression. "Soon," he said. "I want it soon." Eyes still burning into the bear down there. And he could get rid of Honey and still keep the recording, and know an extra flavour of spiteful joy when he played it back.

"Of course, sir."

Thompson shouldered away from the rail, and Honey ceased to exist for him. "I want to play," he said, and she sent out the appropriate call to whoever was on duty at whatever exclusive club she'd arranged. And tried to make Honey cease to exist for her, too.

12

JIMMY

"You goddamn liar!" I shout in Brian's face. "You..." But of all the crazy things he might lie about, not that. Nobody's going to lie about that. Bees is the enemy, the thing that keeps you up at night. Bees is the Other Martian, the one that might any moment reappear from whereverthefuck it's been and just kill us all, sabotage our power, destroy the canopy, end Hell City. Bees is outlaw tech they purged from Earth after they realised how big and dangerous it got.

Sugar looks from me to His Honour the Goddamn Ambassador. "I mean," she says lazily, "I'm not backing Jimbles' play here, but you want to maybe give us some fucking context, Bri?"

Brian's expression is like he's full-on constipated with religion. "Bees and me gon' way back to when we sign on with Build Mars. You not ever think about Bees is on Mars already? You not ever think she got curious 'bout who her neighbours gon' be? She call me up, me, few others. She's talking me round, 'bout when they been prepping us for modding, man. Changing the headware when it go into my head, ways they never tell." He smiles blissfully. "Been Bees' man since 'fore we ever come to Mars."

"Why?" I ask, horrified like actual insects are about to come crawling out his nose and ears.

"Bees is wonder, man," Brian tells me. "You happy building a city for the fellas from Earth come be rich in? Bees is building the big things."

"OK," Sugar breaks in. "So you're some weird-ass species traitor deviant type. Fine. I can work with that. So what, Bees in there? You got a passenger like my man Jimbles here?"

For a moment I'm sure that's it, and Brian Dey will turn into nothing but a meat puppet, mouth open and the voice that comes out nothing but buzz, Bees-lebub Lord of the Flies. But he's shaking his head, smirking, and he's sure as goddamnit the same annoying son of a bitch he always has been.

"Nope," he says, like he's won some super-clever riddles contest. "Just AdApt, just got my headware upgrade, better than you. Just building the future on Mars, man, like we all. But Bees, she give me all the briefing now she knows what's gon' down. Bees' contact with back home a bit patchy but she's caught *up*, man. She knows what you got in there now. What package got sent, meant for her. Or you gon' say it's not for her now?"

"Sugar," I say hoarsely. "Do not fucking give me to Bees."

"Adults talking," she tells me. "And I ain't discussing sender ID here, Bri. I just got offered a big slice o' pie to hand your man here over to Admin and I am seriously considering taking it. So what's it to Bees?"

Brian's still smiling, unnatural fuck that he is. "You got a friend of Bees there. Old friend, good old."

"Or a copy of her, at least," comes the voice from Honey's speaker, which I'd forgotten was even there. "Ms Sugatsu—"

"Shut," Sugar tells her, though I don't think she kills the speaker. "Mr Dey, I reckon you do come from who you say, and I'm sure you come crammed full of threats and promises that I may or may not believe. And in due course I am going to weigh those up with the very real benefits of just handing Jimbles over to the powers that be. But." And she leans forwards in her throne, staring at Brian like he's a piece of art she can't quite work out. "You and Honey maybe tell me just what the fuck, frankly. Because this smells like some rich man's trouble and I want to know the wider geo-po-litical imp-lications before I sell Jimbles here to someone. And I want you all to know that, however this shakes out, it is my call, and Murder and Marmalade here are going to make sure it goes how I want. But first I want to understand." And I never saw this side of her before. I mean, she's a small time operator, but Hell City is a small fishbowl so she always had decent leverage even one bear short of the full Goldilocks. But this isn't Sugar the hustler, the data broker, the fixer. This is Sugar taking envoys from Bees and showing a keen interest in world politics. And then she says, "This is Wally Thompson business?"

"Warner Stern Thompson," Honey corrects her. "And yes, it is."

Now I didn't give a crap for news from home, but I'd seen the man on the screens. Plenty of the BM workforce followed him, and mostly I knew he was always sounding off about Bees and DisInt being a bad thing, which was fine by me.

"I've been sent over here to give Bees information about him, I believe," Honey explains. "Information not to be trusted to a simple transmission. So they made a transmission out of me." All very goddamn philosophical. "I am still reconstructing my memories, but it'll come to me. Ms Sugatsu, this is very important. I am gaining a great sense of threat in connection with Thompson."

Sugar shrugs. "Ain't nothing to me."

"Thompson funds Braintree," Honey says, which ain't nothing to *me* but Sugar obviously gets it. I have to be reminded that's the lab that fitted out our headware, and according to Honey is now doing all sorts of experiments on felons. What sort of experiments? Honey doesn't know, of course. Bees doesn't know.

"Hummus said Bees had a plan they were putting into action," says Honey, although she doesn't say what hummus has to do with anything. "To crack Braintree. To get down to the truth of what they're doing there."

"Maybe." Brian shrugs. "Ain't gon' tell me, now, is she? She been talking about BM data architecture though. How Hell City been set up, all the Cloud spaces. She find that mighty suspicious, man."

"They set it up like that so she couldn't get in," I point out. "So no wonder."

Brian turns a look on me like I'm five years old and asked where babies come from. "You believe that?"

"Maybe it's true if species traitors like you get taken out," Sugar says, and I feel just this tiny bit happier 'cos apparently she's on my side of the argument just a little. Doesn't mean I don't get sold to Bees in the end, though.

"You got anything in your memory-box 'bout prisoner dilemma logic, Honey?" Brian asks lazily, but Sugar's had enough of his hand on the wheel.

"You get nothing from her 'til I've decided I'm selling, Bri. And then not 'til you pay."

Brian blinks at her, and despite Murder and Marmalade right there, the dumbass is supremely unconcerned. "You gon' start talking prices?"

Sugar leans back. "Honey's going to start talking," she says. "Too many missing pieces right now. I sell a thing, I want to know what it's worth and to who."

"To whom," says Honey's speaker, and there's this frozen kind of pause where Sugar just stares at me, like it's my fault, until the speaker adds in a small voice, "Sorry, force of habit."

"Tell me what it is between you and Thompson. 'Cos it ain't just you being a bear, right?"

"Being a what?" I put in.

Sugar is enjoying herself. "You don't know you got a bear in your head, Jimbles? Honey there's some big shot brainy bear, done TV, done rallies. Political bear, ain't you?"

"I've been many things," Honey says guardedly. "And you know Thompson's all for restricting the rights of Bioforms, and flat out outlawing free distributed intellects like Bees. And Bees and I go way back. And there was a speech I made, that I feel in retrospect drew the battle lines between us."

Sugar nods, eyes half closed. "'I feel in retrospect'" she echoes. "You hear that, Jimbles. That's what a million dollar education sounds like if you gave it a voice. Costs more than all our biomods, those fancy words do. So you stand up and tell the world how Thompson's a shit? Tell them he cheats on his taxes and beats his wife? Only that newscast never made it to Mars."

"Not exactly." Honey's still being cagey. "It's just... it was a general observation about structures of authority."

"Damn," Sugar says, nodding appreciatively. "You keep laying down those thousand dollar words. I love it." And I think she's being sincere. You don't get to hear people talk like that around here. It's almost entertainment on its own.

"It's just... well..." Honey pauses, and I can almost feel her shunting bits and pieces of her mind together inside mine. "You do your work here, right? And some of you are better at the work than others. Some of you give your all to the job, every waking moment, it's your calling. Some of you phone it in a bit, you've got other things going on. I'm willing to bet that you, Ms Sugatsu, don't put quite the hours in on the construction site that some people do, am I correct?"

Sugar snorts. "So tell me something new, Honey."

"Well that work, that's what I called the game. But then let's say your... Admin, they want to appoint a manager, a foreman. It's a good job, nice perks. Who gets it?"

"Whoever kisses the most asses," Sugar tells her promptly.

"Ah." Honey's pleased. "I wish some of my peers back home grasped things as quickly as you do. And yes, although I'll admit I phrased it in rather different language, that is the conclusion I came to. That there's a metagame. It's a bit like... the metaphor I used was animal mating displays, actually. You're familiar with those."

Sugar's got a look on her like she's not entirely sure what Honey's accusing her of, and Honey obviously reads the room because she adds quickly, "So, let's say you're a peacock and you have your grand tail, which likely evolved because it shows health and wellbeing, hence fitness. But the pea*hen* just cares that you've got the biggest tail. Or... you've got your caveman in the Stone Age brings a mammoth in to show he's a big hunter, you're with me? And hunting's the game, the actual important activity that's being judged. Except Og next door just bonks Thog on the head and steals the mammoth, and that's the metagame. Og's a lousy hunter because he spends his time and effort not on hunting, but on the secondary activity that's supposed to show how good a hunter you are. And so he wins out over Thog, gets the girl, becomes chief. And your worker who 'kisses ass' is seen as management material not because they give their all to the company, but because they spend that effort they would otherwise give to the company on *looking* like they give it all to the company. They spend it on all the little social games instead, and because effort spent on the metagame is focused entirely about the appearance of virtue, it overshadows those who are actually performing the primary task, it overshadows actual virtue. And this is how human hierarchical structures end up working. This is why the people who end up in authority are generally not those focused on whatever the purpose of the community is, but those who are focused on achieving positions of authority. This is why you have career politicians, why administrators end up pulling ten times the salary of a surgeon or an academic under their administration, why performing well in an exam or a test is not actually the same as being good at the thing the exam is supposed to be testing. Because the metagame outweighs the game."

And she stops speaking and we all chew over that, until at last I say, "So what? Way of the world, ain't it? Us poor hardworking Joes and Jills get screwed."

"I'm with Jimbles," Sugar agrees. "I mean, OK, can see why a bunch of people might not have wanted to take that from a bear, but..."

"I might have gone a little further," Honey admits. "I was off script, then, and I remember them trying to shut me up, but I had been having a frustrating time of it and I just... said some things. My higher level metagame theory."

"Yeah, that sounds all kinds of controversial," Sugar drawls.

"I said they were so scared of Bioform intelligence and DisInt entities and AI," Honey goes on. "I said they were panicking so hard about non-human minds jostling for space in the world, desperate to make us think like humans and simultaneously terrified that they might succeed, and they hadn't even seen that there was a very different intelligence already right there, in the centre of things. I suggested that, above and beyond the regular metagame that meant the people who achieved status and power were by definition the least qualified to have it – and you'll appreciate I was actually talking to a number of human people in possession of a fair measure of status and power, so I had already got right up a good number of noses by this point... Anyway, I said that just as metagamers could hack organisational structures and procedures to promote themselves without needing to be good at the primary task of the organisation, so there were people out there who could do it to human society. Sociopaths of a kind, essentially, who could give out all the right signals to get people to do things for them without ever actually having what you'd think of as a truly human existence inside their head. People who were just masks, terribly adroit at playing the human metagame without any of the empathy, the genuine connections, the internal life. And in the same way as your ass-kisser gets the managerial position, so the human metagamers win out over those people who are devoting time and effort to actually being human. And they were busy campaigning against Bioforms and DisInt and the rest because we weren't human, we weren't the environment they'd adapted to exploit. Because we would see what they were and call them on it. And that, I'm afraid, is what caught like a hook in the nasty little machine that Warner S. Thompson calls a mind, because I would respectfully suggest that, regardless of the respective species we were both born into, I think far more like a human than he ever will."

"That so?" Sugar shakes her head, smirking. "Sure explains how shit works. So Old Man Thompson's a vampire, amiright?"

"What?" It is a joy, let me tell you, to hear Honey's pompous voice flat out baffled. "No—"

"What?" Sugar says, and I share a moment with her 'cos she's enjoying this too. "Looks like a person, does all that smooth human talk, knows what to say so's you let him in, and then it's fangs out and fucks you over."

"I..." Honey's electronic voice still comes over as thoughtful. "Perhaps you're right. A parasite. A parasite that prospers because it presents an exaggerated performance of its host species' salient characteristics. Not just passing for human, but passing for superhuman: putting out all the tells so that you think they're super-confident, super-dynamic, super-inspiring, exactly the man to follow to the ends of the Earth. Far more so than anyone who actually has any reason to be confident, or to be worth following."

"So what you're saying is," Sugar's grinning like a cat, "I can sell you to Rufus for scrip and favours or I can sell you back home to Thompson for a great big bag of real money."

"That... was not the conclusion I was intending you to come to," Honey says.

"Shame you're not one of these super-manipulators then. What?" She cocks an eyebrow at Brian. "You going to sweeten Sugar's pot for Honey, Bees-man? Only I can't promise just how much time you got to go take further instructions."

"Bees told me 'nuff." And Brian still doesn't seem worried; got his hands in his overalls pockets, shoulders slumped, doing precisely buck-nothing just like he usually does at work. "Bees' got eyes on Earth, on Thompson. Not so many, though. After they tried legislate 'gainst Bees back then, she got a choice, man. She gon' kick off World War Three then and there, and maybe lose 'cos she wasn't ready? She gon' pull back to the colony she made on Mars? You know what she did. Bees not got so much coverage back on Earth, got plenty muscle here, Sugar."

"That a threat, Bri? Bees gonna come sting me?"

"You?" Brian's shrug says Bees doesn't care a goddamn about Sugar. "Over Honey here? Bees doesn't do vengeful, Sugar. Bees not gon' come get you 'cos you sold her friend. Bees gon' come get her friend, though. And Bees gon' declare war 'gainst Hell City if Bees reckons it's a threat to her. All Hell City. You just gon' be collateral damage. 'S'in your interest t'make Bees happy 'bout all of us being here."

"And if I send you back after you've been shit out by a bear?" Sugar asks pleasantly.

"Bees not gon' be too happy." Brian hunches forwards, and he's still got that smile, and I am more scared of him than Murder or Marmalade because this is it, this is sheer crazy-ass religious fanaticism, only instead of God, Brian Dey found Bees. "Bees gon' survive, man," he says. "Bees gon' do a lot of good for everyone, we only give her the chance, but first law of Bees is Bees gon' survive. You don' want to be part of a thing that maybe means Bees doesn't survive 'cos Bees gon' fuck that thing right up, you know it."

"Mr Dey, please explain why Bees thinks Hell City might become a threat," Honey breaks into the nasty pause Brian's little speech flung up. "Is it to do with Braintree, with the work they did on the Humaniform neuralware? That's the Thompson link to this place. It's the only reason I can think that I sent this copy of me over to find you."

And of course the 'Humaniforms' are us, Sugar and me and everyone else who got fitted out by the Building Mars guys.

"She ever talk to you 'bout the Southampton Method?" Brian asks. "She talk to you about Axelrod Prisoner Tournaments?"

"That's enough," Sugar decides, and I know she's turned off the speaker 'cos Honey's suddenly bitching in my ear about it. "What's Bees offering me except vague threats, Bri? What's Bees got that's more than some rich Earth guy's big bag of cash? Going to offer me all the kingdoms of Mars, make me Duchess of Olympus Mons? Come on, Bri, what's your pitch?"

"Maybe you all be needin' Bees, when it turns," Brian says, like he's some Old Testament prophet striding out of the rust-orange desert. "Bees don't know just what, yet. Bees still tryin' to get into Braintree, find out the plan, but she got the shape of it. Bad news for Hell City, Sugar. Bad news and who gon' stand between you and the end? You gon' need Bees, and if Bees done call her up, maybe it's 'cos you gon' need Honey too. You sell her back to the badmen back home, you got no-one when they come for you. And maybe Bees don' care enough to save you either. Bees don' care 'bout so much these days. Bees got big plans, gon' places she don't need think about humans. Bees don't like us very much, man. Not since she did all that work and we turn on her."

"That ain't much of a pitch," Sugar tells him. The weird thing is, though, she's doing all the casual act in the world but it's not quite sticking. Yours Truly sees through it. Sugar's heard some things, I'll put hard scrip down on it. Something of what Brian's telling her is ringing bells, and I think of Honey saying how our headware, that Braintree made for us, is way more than we need, and since when did anyone overspend on working schmoes like us when they didn't need to.

"Back when I knew Bees, back in the beginning," Honey says sweetly in my ear, "her attitude was that killing people was what she was for. I think she's come along quite a way, don't you?"

"You," I tell her, "are a fucking barrel of laughs."

Then Sugar's standing, just kicking up from her crate throne in one movement, and the two bears are on the move, too. For a moment I think she's going to set them on Brian, send his head back to Bees as a declaration of war. Brian, by the way, doesn't goddamn flinch, even though I'm cowering back from all the violence and mauling I'm sure must be about to happen.

"Posse's coming," Sugar says flatly. "Looks like Old Doggo ran out of patience. Or got fresh orders from Admin."

"So what?" I realise I haven't had much to say for a long time. Grown-ups were talking, like she said, and I don't know jack about any Southampton Method or any crap like that. "You going to sell me to the sheriff now? I don't reckon you've got a chance to make your deal with this Thompson guy."

Sugar looks at me like she's forgotten I was anything other than virtual bear storage. "We're moving," she decides. "Murder, take point. Jakob'll stall them as long as he can." One of the bears shambles past me, the rivet gun held in both hands, and when I'm not right on her heels Sugar gives me a shove in the chest.

"You got control of your legs right now, Jimbles? 'Cos I need you using them."

I end up scurrying off into the back end of Storage Nineteen, into a warren of crates and stacked cases, empty, full, legit, illegal, who the hell knows. Murder's just shouldering on ahead of me, Sugar and Brian behind and then Marmalade's got rearguard, rolling along on four feet like most bears seem more comfortable with even after all the Bioform mods.

Then there's shooting and we all stop for a second, until Sugar hisses an order and Murder's off again. Shooting, and I reckon that probably marks the end of her man Jakob's ability to stall. Actual firearms activity within Hell City, and the reason we have the Bad News Bears is that you *don't* go letting off weapons inside, in case parts of the inside become joined to the outside by inconvenient goddamn *holes*. And yes, we're not like the moon men, or like natural Earth people would be, where one little hole means decompressive death or suffocation, but it's still going to screw with a whole load of the internal machinery that doesn't have the cold, pressure or dust tolerances of the tough kit we use outside. And also, Sheriff Rufus just shot a guy. Maybe more than one. Just shot an actual member of the Hell City construction crew because of what I've got in my head. And suddenly I get a whole horizon of perspective I never wanted. Suddenly it's not just about me, because I don't know who the fuck Jakob is but he just died because of Honey and because of Yours Truly Jimmy Marten.

Then there's the back door to Storage Nineteen, which is an interesting development because on the plans there *is* no back door to Storage Nineteen. It's rimmed with messy weals of melted metal where Sugar's people cut too big and then had to fill to get a seal round their new hatch, and it's only just big enough for Murder to squeeze through. Behind us I can hear Rufus shouting, and for a moment he's in my ear, on my radio channel, midway through a threat I never hear the end of. Sugar's jamming comms, jamming tracking, putting her makeshift systems to the test to screw any attempt to pin us down. Probably she's just brought down the network for Storage Three through Thirty to cover for us. Sugar's the sort of person who goes big on contingency plans.

Then there's shooting ahead, too, and the *bing-bing-bing* of the rivet gun, and Murder bellows. I stop, but Sugar shoves me through anyway, and Murder almost treads on me as I roll out. She's fighting – I see Albedo, the fat-cat Bioform who's Rufus's second, and behind her there's a badger model, also badged up as part of the posse, holding a big calibre pistol and trying to get a good shot. Murder's living up to her fucking name, though, and though Albedo's doing her best there is red blood and white fur everywhere.

"Go!" Sugar tells me, and I don't need another reminder. I leg it, and at every turn she's yanking me one way or another, back-seat driving the escape plan without ever telling me actually where we're heading. And then we're at a hatch I know is one of the old exterior locks, from Stage Two Construction way back.

"Out," she says.

I turn to look at her. "What... like, outside out?"

"What, your mods fell out while we were running?"

"*This* is your plan?" I demand.

Sugar's face is like iron. There's no give in it. "Out, Jimbles, or I'll have Marmalade tear your arms and legs off to make you easier to carry. You have to fucking *go* and going out there is literally your fucking *job* and so what is the fucking *problem*?"

"We can't just run... Sugar, we can't stay out there forever. It doesn't work like that. Maybe we can..."

"Murder's down," Sugar tells me. "They are coming for us. And I will kill you and that thing in your head before they kill me, because they want it and they have fucked with me. Rufus just shot Murder, right this moment, Jimbles. And you and I are going out for a walk. Because there is nowhere inside Hell City we can get away from Rufus."

13

SPRINGER

The next day Carole had to go meet a media producer, talk through a biopic proposal. Warner S. Thompson hadn't even won a seat at the World Senate yet, and half the world was saying he was too much of a loose cannon to ever do so, but he made himself the subject of the dialogue, he set the agenda. He was the man people wanted to talk about. On that metric he was already the winner.

She went to the meeting with a weight in her mind. This was routine stuff. She should breeze through it and then be back with Thompson for his fundraiser dinner, a hundred darlings of the Collaring lobby paying through the nose into his campaign chest just so they could be in the same room as him. And he'd press the flesh and gift them with his smile and fill the room with his unbounded confidence. And then he'd end up in the hotel room staring at the wall, staring at the screen. Or he'd want to find a game, or have her find a girl. Or have her.

Or he'd do the other thing. He was in New York another two days, but Carole could feel the need building in him, and he was never a man to let needs go unanswered. The thought was a weight in her mind. The weight was an image of a bear, a grey old sagging bear, sitting down there against the stained concrete walls of the Shambles. Honey wouldn't leave her alone.

She'd thought she was meeting with a man called Brock Hustedter, but when she got to the Live With US offices a woman met her, bright and pert and dressed in something like a mirror to Carole's own skirt suit, red instead of blue and tailored the opposite side. As though they were mirror universe versions of each other, or opposite numbers in some team computer game.

"Jennifer Wiley, hi, how are you."

"Where's Hustedter?" Carole asked.

"Oh, ah." A moment of awkwardness. "He's... off the project. Sorry, did they not tell you? I'll do just as good a job, you can be sure. I'm just dying for the chance to work with Mr Thompson. He's such an iconic figure of the modern age, you know?"

They sat in the senior employee lounge, which Wiley greeted with such glee Carole reckoned she wasn't allowed in there most of the time. They had it to themselves, and Carole made sure there wasn't any pre-emptive recording going on. Wiley didn't strike her as someone who'd pull that kind of trick, though. She was so enthusiastic. Carole was already listing her reservations. She'd go through with the meeting, get an idea of what the project was about, whether it would play nicely with the other fragments of image that Thompson's campaign was weaving around him to fill out the gaps in his personality. But she looked at Jennifer Wiley and reckoned that they'd go up a few rungs at Live With US and ask for someone else to helm the project. Get Hustedter back, or else get some other elder statesman who could sit with Thompson over a drink and laugh and shake the man's hand, play a round of golf, exchange anecdotes, boys with boys. That was the sort of social scenario Thompson was safest in. Not this beaming young woman with her tight waist and two buttons of her blouse open, just like Carole herself because that was the way Thompson liked it. Not her, because that *was* the way Thompson liked it. Just the same way he liked them young and enthusiastic and so very keen to work with him.

You don't want to work with him. The thought shocked her, was fought down immediately with stabs of guilt and reproach. *Disloyal! How dare you!* But she did not think Jennifer Wiley should be allowed to interview Thompson, to spend time with him, go back to the bar after, go to his room. All things that might happen once Thompson took a shine to her. All things that would happen the moment he decided they should, just the same way the world always bent about him like light around gravity.

And yet Wiley was still chattering on, now introducing Carole to her assistant, now recounting some sparkling story about when she worked with some film star, some musician. Carole nodded, laughed along. Even appreciated the glittery little façade the woman had made for herself, that gave her enough hard and slanted edges to burrow into the harsh, competitive world that Brock Hustedter hadn't managed to navigate. For a moment she wondered. Sudden replacements discovered on the day could mean all sorts of trouble. Thompson had enemies after all. But they were also very much the order of the day in an industry where the tides of favour went in and out to the pull of far too many moons. And probably Wiley had already had to orbit a few of those moons more closely than she'd wanted, to get where she was.

Probably ending up underneath Thompson's rutting, grunting body wouldn't be overly novel for her. But Thompson wasn't like other people, not inside his head. It was Carole's job to make sure the world didn't see that, only saw the masks he put up to fool them. Better not to let a bright young thing like Jennifer Wiley have a chance to see the real face. And besides.

And besides.

Carole stared into that earnest, animated face and thought about last night, when Thompson had been flush with glee at having Honey locked up in the Shambles and nobody the wiser. He'd wanted an outlet for all that satisfaction. She'd been his outlet. She'd been there for him like a good PA. Knelt before him, then zipped him up after and wiped the smile back onto her face. And now she sat and laughed with Wiley and in her head the words *Get off me get off me get off* marched round and round the edge of the concrete pit, and down below the bear stared mournfully up at her, the bear with a woman's voice, with the university education, the media career and the long history of good causes. And right now nobody knew where she was except Thompson's people, and Carole was just waiting for Scout and some other discrete parties to confirm that nobody was sniffing about.

"We'll want some other perspectives, of course. Views on the great man from people who knew him on the way up," Wiley was saying happily, coming back to their little table with more coffee, with a tiny plate of tinier cookies that would lie untouched between them. "Could always see he was touched with greatness, some human interest piece from before anyone had heard of him, just little touches to round him out in the minds of the viewer."

Carole nodded, because they'd been through this before

for other interviews, for other studios. There weren't any such people. No elements of human interest, but that didn't mean you couldn't make them up from whole cloth. The trick was that you had to get Thompson interviewed first, let him engage in the sort of piledriving conversation that passed for raconteurship with him; let him tell, with utter conviction, anecdotes that were nothing but the shimmering web he wove around his past. A camouflage, refracting light from him until to the casual observer there was something there that looked not just human but more human than human, a colossus, possessing all the virtues the viewer might want to see. Then Carole would bring in one of their regular actors who'd take the noncommittal details Thompson had given and perjure themselves, become witness to the invisible, mock up some foundations to the man's cloud castle.

"And there's you, of course," Wiley said.

Carole froze. There must have been a second in which Wiley saw it, the complete, terrified paralysis. It was covered a moment later, the regular smile being trotted out, the just-one-woman-to-another shake of the head, demurring, little laugh to show how silly the idea was. "Oh no, nobody's interested in me. I'm just a PA."

"But you must spend more time with Mr Thompson than just about anyone," Wiley pointed out earnestly. "You get to see how it all works, see the great man when he's vulnerable, human. You go with him everywhere."

"Well I really don't." Smile, little laugh, fighting back the spikes of panic. "I mean, I'm here and he's not, for example. I just make arrangements. Obviously it keeps me busy, what with the trajectory of his career right about now, but it's nothing anyone would be interested in."

"You sell yourself short, Carole." Wiley leant forwards, touching Carole's hand with an odd shock of contact, suddenly intimate. "I know you've been working for the man during his, frankly, meteoric rise. Back when you first started, who'd have taken Warner S. Thompson in politics seriously? And now he's the man everyone in the world's talking about, love him or hate him."

"It's all his doing," Carole said firmly, almost desperately. Thompson would not brook anyone taking credit for him. And he was right to, she knew. He was his own architect. Oh, other people actually *made* things happen – her, Felorian, his succession of campaign managers briefly held to the light and then discarded – but they were all just organs of the central mass that was Thompson.

"We think it would give a very relatable perspective," Wiley chattered on, looking straight into her eyes now, almost hypnotic. "The woman who paves the way for greatness. We could do some soundbites with you, maybe a little reminiscence about when things weren't going so well, about how the team pulled together. I think a lot of our audience would really want to know what it's like to be so close to a man like Thompson. About the demands he makes of you, up all hours, day and night. He's such a powerful man. It must be hard to find time for yourself. It must be hard to say no."

Carole tried to say something, tried to keep that sunny smile on, tried to politely remove her hand from the light touch of the other woman's, but no words came out. There was a sound. Although it came from her throat, most of her couldn't imagine why or even how she had made that sound. It was like she'd heard a cat make once, that was terrified of something. She almost felt her ears folding back, as though she was about to hiss at Jennifer Wiley in threat.

"It is, isn't it," and Wiley's cheery all-girls-together manner was just gone, the all-girls-together that was left given an entirely different character. "Hard to say no. I'm right, aren't I? Because he trusts you implicitly. Because you've been there for everything, for years." Wiley's fingers like a nail pinning her hand to the table, for all the pressure was a feather's. "And he wouldn't take no for an answer anyway, I imagine, but with you he wanted to be sure. Was that what happened at Braintree?"

"I don't know what you're talking about." And right about now Carole should be standing, making her apologies, just storming away; blacklisting Wiley, the whole of Live With US; never work in this town, this country, this world again. But the words had locked her in and she was thinking about saying no, saying no to Thompson. That terrifying, unthinkable thing. Of course she couldn't say no. And the daylight part of her mind was telling her that of course she'd never want to say no, not with how devoted she was to the man, a slightly hysterical thread of internal monologue as brittle and cheery as Wiley's patter had been just moments before. And beneath that, some part of her bucked and fought and cried out, *Please, no*, and knew that 'no' was the one thing Thompson never took as an answer.

"They never want us to have a choice," Wiley said quietly. "Because the thing they're most terrified of in all the world is that we might say no. No, you're not so great. No, we don't want you to put that in us, not now, not yours, not ever. No, we don't want to get through life in your pocket, with no pockets of our own. And if you say no to a man like Thompson, if *nobody* ever said *yes* to him, what would be left?"

Carole had a moment in which her mind's eye cast up the image of that thing that was Thompson, the inner lurker that made its body out of the co-opted efforts of other people; cast it up naked and disconnected, a limbless thing of jelly like something pulled too soon from the womb. "It's always a pleasure to work for Warner," her mouth said gaily. "You feel like you're the tool of destiny. That you're doing God's work, almost." And that was the wrong line, because Live With US's audience didn't poll as that religious and she'd done her research before coming. It was from another interview, the one with the televangelist last month.

"Carole," Wiley said, still staring into her eyes. "I suspect you were probably never a particularly good person, and you knew it, and that was part of the neuroarchitecture they gave you at Braintree. That you deserved what you got. That becoming the pawn of Thompson was what you deserved. All the usual tricks to stop you challenging the programming. And you know what? You don't have to be a good person. That's OK. But you're entitled to be your own person. And that's what they took away from you. Because their sort of evil can't even trust bad people to do bad things for them. And I'm going to try to help you, Carole. Me and a friend of mine. I'm looking forward to working with you, if you choose to work with me. Carole, I'm going to give you a gift, now. I want you to keep it with you. Use it when you need to." And Wiley had turned her hand over, something cold and hard being pressed into Carole's palm, fingers folded over it.

Carole...

Blinked.

Jennifer Wiley was still talking, still that big smile, sipping at her coffee now, leaning back, so very enthusiastic to work on the big project that was probably the biggest anyone had ever trusted her with. Carole wondered what price she'd paid, what wheels she'd greased, to get it. And it wouldn't work. Carole would have to break the news gently, nothing personal but... exactly the wrong person to put within Thompson's pull. And she'd need to act fast because, once Thompson saw Wiley, he'd set his sights on her. He'd add her to the list of things he wanted to do. And then it would be a done deal and nothing Carole could do would stop it, and it would come down to the usual pay-offs and NDAs and veiled threats to make sure that the used-and-discarded Wiley kept her pretty mouth shut. And Carole had done that too many times before, and that wasn't even counting the times when Boyo had got involved or she'd had to pull the trigger on the Trigger Dogs, for those times when money or pressure or pieces of paper didn't look like they would ensure silence. No kiss-and-tell stories about Thompson, not on her watch.

And Wiley would be heartbroken, doubtless. Would be furious that her career was being derailed after all the things she'd surely had to do to get that far. And she'd never know that Carole had done it all to save her from something Carole couldn't save herself from.

And soon enough she was tripping out of the Live With US offices, already composing her messages to make it all a reality, pausing only a moment as she reached the car to think, *Did something...? Was there a moment when...?* And she stopped, just for two seconds, as the car opened its door for her, looking down at the little enamelled pin brooch she was holding. Gold and blue, oval like an ancient scarab, save for the suggestion of wings and the stripes on the abdomen. Thinking, *Where did I get this, exactly?* But it was pretty enough, and something in her spiked with affection for it, that part of her that was usually so unhappy, the part that said *Get off me* and that the rest of her was forbidden to listen to. But this one time she listened to it, and slipped the brooch into her pocket and then mostly forgot about it.

That night, Scout and the Trigger Dogs made their scheduled report to confirm that all was quiet at the Shambles, no visitors come for Honey. Carole fielded half a dozen other select reports, some of which were in themselves summations of multiple other sources. Yes, people were looking for Honey. She could trace the enquiries made by overt sources like the lawyer, Aslan, or the World Senate Relief Force or some of her academic colleagues. She could also sense the spidery touch of other operators. HumOS was out there, in every shadow. And she would find Honey eventually, but that presupposed the old bear had that much time left. Nobody's attention was aimed at the Shambles. Right now, Thompson had vanished away an entire bear, a well-known bear with a huge media footprint, and nobody had followed the sleight of hand.

Carole was obviously delighted with this. She told herself how happy she was it had all worked out. That she wouldn't have to get Thompson to sign off on any of the alternative stories they had worked up, in case someone turned up at the Shambles with a warrant and a demand. All perfectly plausible reasons why Honey might have been mistakenly arrested, but Thompson would have been angry at being

thwarted, and she didn't want him angry. Of all the things in
the world she didn't want him angry.

She didn't want him to make that second visit to the Shambles
either. In her mind the old bear sat, like a Shakespearean
king awaiting the murderers. Like a woman, any woman,
who went against the tide and met the savage teeth of the
world's fury at her presumption. Just a woman, even though
she was a bear. And still Carole would report to Thompson
that it was all clear, that he could have what he wanted. It
was her job. She loved her job. She loved Thompson, would
do anything, unquestioningly loyal.

Boyo met her at the foyer of tonight's hotel. Something in
her gave him pause, his brown eyes brimming with empathy.
They just stood there for long seconds, looking at each other.
In Carole's mind she was a fragile thing suspended between
the pulls of heavy objects: Thompson up in the penthouse
suite above, Honey down in the pit below. And she wanted
to talk to Boyo, to tell him how she felt. She wanted to tell
him that she'd met with a media executive today and it had
been a perfectly normal, pleasant chat except that something
deep inside her spiked anxiety every time she thought about
the Live With US documentary. She wanted to tell him that;
she wanted to tell Thompson something, anything, that
would stop tonight going ahead, but there wasn't anything
she could say. She wanted to tell him that she wanted to say
no, but they'd made her sign a waiver and given her headware
and now she couldn't ever say no, not to anything. And that
meant she couldn't tell Boyo, and even if she could, he had
headware too and couldn't say if it was just the same for him.

Up on the top floor, Thompson already seemed to know
how smoothly it had all gone. When she arrived, it was

obvious one of the campaign team had been and gone in her absence and brought him something. Thompson had a gun. It was a wide-barrelled rifle, the sort of thing she imagined might have been used for elephants, while there were still elephants; for rhinos back when they hadn't gone the way of the unicorn; or perhaps for the bison the Russians were still desperately trying to preserve in the narrowing strip of tundra over in Siberia. Loaded for bear, that was the phrase, wasn't it?

"I want a picture," Thompson told her, and she knew exactly what he was thinking of. All those game hunters standing triumphantly over the bodies of animals that only existed in pictures like those, in old TV documentaries or children's books. Lions and tigers and bears. Except the bears had proved adaptable enough to cling on, and then useful enough to become part of the Bioform program.

"A picture would be damaging, sir," she told him. "If it got out."

Thompson beamed. He never just smiled, not really. A smile was a wan and fickle thing, compared to the expression he could muster. It filled the room with his mood and left no room for anyone else's.

"You record it," he told her. "Just for us. Go get the car, Boyo," and, helplessly within Carole's head, the thought, *We're going on a bear hunt.*

14

[RECOVERED DATA ARCHIVE: 'HONEY']

Unknown channel: ...

Sitting there in the stark light, against the stained concrete wall, that was all I got. The Shambles was heavily screened. When they built it, they'd known most Bioforms had comms headware. They'd known that, back in the days of the Pound, attempts to simply disable that 'ware on a case by case basis hadn't worked; easy enough to reactivate the protocols. They'd wanted a secure prison where the inmates didn't have 24-hour phone privileges. And then they'd set the cells underground and walled in two feet of reinforced concrete and that was the icing on the incommunicado cake, frankly. So there I was, trying to get a line out, trying to find something live in the Shambles to piggyback off. Trying to hack into the personal systems of my captors, even. And getting nowhere. Even they were cut off, if they came anywhere near me. They had to go out on the street for a signal.

And I remembered the Shambles. There had been real spikes of hysteria about Bioforms, around the time the place was built. And there had been Bioforms who'd reacted to their newfound rights and freedoms by taking advantage of them, or who had just failed to integrate into human society. And we'd worked out systems and methods and buffers since, but it had been a turbulent time. And when one of us crossed the line, the human law had come down hard. This was before Rex had become a champion who was such a Good Dog.

The Shambles was where we were sent to die. I mean, technically it was just a holding cell, but twenty-nine Bioforms died in the Shambles. They died resisting arrest, mostly, and what, the human police and guards asked, were they supposed to use against an eight-foot cyborg dog that was resisting arrest, save for overwhelming force. And it's amazing how much the marks on some poor mutt just tied to a chair and beaten to death look like the marks on a rabid monster brought down by heroic law enforcement officers. Especially when the judge rules that all those rope burns about the wrists and neck are somehow inadmissible evidence. It's cases like that which Keram John Aslan built a career around, and he did well out of them because the world was turning. Because of Rex, and because of me, and all those other Bioforms who made themselves paragons to skew the public-perception window back towards the middle ground.

When they discontinued the regular use of the Shambles, Aslan and I had a little celebration. It passed beneath most people's notice but to us it was a major victory.

And now here I was.

Unknown channel: ...

Maddening, really. Someone was trying very hard to reach me, and they couldn't get through. All I had was the sense of a pending connection, an absence that meant more than simply nothing there. Negative comms pressure. Nine-tenths of me wanted to reach across the gap, because it was Aslan, it was Gemima Gray or some other HumOS unit, it was Bees. And the other tenth? The other tenth had got superstition, that eminently human thing. The other tenth shrank back from that contact because it remembered the early, early days when I was a soldier working for Redmark, working for the Moray of Campeche. I didn't want to make that contact and hear those old voices. Rex's channel; Dragon's channel. My old squad mates, the voices of the dead.

But it was only one-tenth and it got out-voted. I stood up, marking the immediate watchfulness of the two dog-models up above on the viewing gallery.

"I want to talk to your chief, your commanding officer."

They stared down at me without comment.

"Isn't a bear allowed to meet her baiters?" But frankly that was probably too abstruse for them. "I want to talk to him about his medal." I made the sign of the cross in the air between us with the tip of one claw. "Come on, now, when's he going to get another chance?" And then, the last desperate cry of the Z-list celebrity. "Don't you know who I am?"

I got to shuffle about for a while more, and then there was another dog up there, the one who'd stopped my car and made the arrest, under the eyes of human officers. Those humans hadn't put in an appearance since – there had only been Thompson and his entourage. I strongly suspected that only he and his dogs knew where I'd been taken, for reasons of plausible deniability. I, the Bioform rights advocate, had been vanished away, and they'd used Bioforms to do it. Just like they made Rex and me and the others to be soldiers, to do the brutal things that human soldiers might find inconvenient, so once again they'd warped us into their twisted shadows. Made us the monster that they'd always told stories about, because monsters are easier to destroy when they don't have your face.

"You're in charge here?" I asked him.

"I lead," he confirmed. He didn't look much like Rex – leaner, longer in the muzzle, paler of hide – but the voice was very close. I wonder I hadn't noticed it before. Must be an iteration of my friend's original war-voice, the one he never liked much.

"My name is Honey," I told him. "My original name, the one I came out of the labs and the factories with."

"Yes," he agreed, and then, "Scout."

"I want to make a deal with you," I called up to him. "Just a little deal."

"No deals."

"Are you a Good Dog, Scout?"

He went very still, leaning over the rail so far I wondered if it would buckle. "Yes," he said slowly. "I am a Good Dog." And it meant something different than when Rex used to agonise over it, but it was to do with Rex still, as well. And maybe this one last time my old friend would save me.

"I knew a Good Dog once," I said carefully. "I knew him better than anyone. He was my commanding officer and my best friend. I was with him when he died." Or at least in comms contact, but close enough. "The original Good Dog, Scout. The best."

Scout just leant on the rail, eyes on me.

"I'll make a deal," I said again. "Not a big deal. I know you're not just going to let me walk out of here. Not against orders. That's what being a Good Dog means to you, isn't it. But maybe you could at least let me out of this pit for half an hour. Let me look at something other than the frankly unpleasant stains on the walls." And how I wanted to believe those rusty marks soaked into the concrete were just iron from old water leaks. "And in return, I'll tell you about Rex. A first-hand account, Scout. A gospel, you might say, from one of his few surviving disciples."

I could see the war in him. His Collar was clamped tight, but Collars are never as infallible as their masters believe. Scout was limited in his options, but what constituted obedience and what constituted betrayal was a personal thing. He had to do what he was told, but he would have leeway. And I was betting that nobody had thought it necessary to explicitly tell him, *Do not let this bear move from the cell* as part of their general orders to hold me, because who would ever need to?

"Just a change of scenery. It's very boring down here, and I never liked being underground." All lies, I've been a regular cave bear in my time. "And when will you ever get the chance? Record it all for the Sons of Adam, if you want. I'll keep it clean of anything incriminating."

He turned and left, and I thought I'd lost him then, but they let down the lift a minute later, watching me with guns at the ready as it came up. Scout was waiting there, with half a dozen of his people. We didn't go out. We didn't get to see the sky or grab a breath of fresh air. But I wasn't in the pit. There was less concrete between me and the outside, and I'd had the outer ghost of a signal even down there.

I sat down, because that instantly made the whole thing a more long-term affair, and because I was an old bear and standing on two legs for long periods of time did painful things to my back.

"That badge of yours." I nod at the dog-and-cross proudly displayed on his barrel chest. "Good Dogs all."

"I'm not stupid," he told me, still that low angry voice because it's all the voice they gave him. "I know you. I saw talks, heard speeches. They warned us about you."

That was news, and I realised I'd fallen into the very human trap of thinking he probably was a bit stupid, because he believed things I didn't and used shorter words.

"You'll talk about Rex," he said, touching the medal briefly. "But I brought you here to tell you how you're wrong. You think being one of us means being like humans. You think we were made to be free and make all the choices and bear all the guilts of being human. That isn't the way. Man was made by God to be able to choose whether to obey or not." A shake of Scout's head turned into a whole-body shiver. "That's a punishment. All-powerful God knows what the one right thing is, every time, but Adam has a thousand options to choose from. Who'd be Adam? Why do clever bears like you tell us we should follow in his footsteps? God made Man to choose; Man made us to obey. We don't need to have the worry or the blame. We just say yes. So you fight your whole life against human fear, because you want to have the right to make the wrong choice, and at the same time you're bigger, stronger, smarter even. And you wonder humans don't like you." And despite the angry voice he was so very earnest, doggy eyes boring into mine, trying to make me see. "Humans like us. We are the Sons of Adam. We accept the Collar as a mark that we know our place and purpose in the world. We are the servants of humanity, and we do not know doubt or fear or choice. We know only love, God's and Man's. We are Good Dogs."

I had a hundred rejoinders, clever arguments, rhetorical devices to demonstrate to eight decimal places why he's wrong, but they all choked up together in my head, and instead I said, "Rex would have understood."

It wasn't what he expected, I think, but it's true. Not agreed, but understood. The creed of the Sons of Adam would have resonated in my friend's doggy skull. On days when the responsibility of choice weighed heavily on him, and there were many, he'd have pined for it. But I like to think he'd never have taken the Collar, even so. And yet he's their hero, the original Good Dog. Because he was the first Bioform that humans knew and lauded. Because he gave his life so that humans might be free to choose. Because... well, the story got told a hundred different ways and you can staple any moral to it that you want.

Unknown channel: *(connection request)*

Nothing of it showed in my face or manner, and frankly by then I stank of my own waste because the pit had no facilities, no woods for this bear. I could only hope that any spike of excitement wouldn't be detectable past the general reek of me, even to Scout's sensitive nose. I accepted the request.

"Let me tell you about Rex, then," I said. "And I'm not going to turn this into some grand parable to talk you around, OK? I know it wouldn't work anyway, and we had a deal. I'm just going to ramble a little about the old days, if that's all right. Rex and me and Dragon and Bees."

Scout nodded, and I wondered if any of them was actually recording me. If my words would end up in some Masonic archive of the Sons of Adam, played over and over in their weird, subservient rituals.

"I probably need to start with Jonas Murray," I began, and then just let my mouth take it from there. I was a raconteur, after all, and though this was no media interview or dinner party, I could still just let my mouth off the leash and have it range around where it would. And, at the same time...

My channel: *Hello?*

HumOS's channel: *God, Honey?*

I thought it was Gray, that same unit I met at Aslan's offices. The transmission quality was terrible, little of her voice coming through and that little warping and distorting in my ear. I kept a keen eye on Scout and the others in case they were picking anything up, but HumOS was using all her wiles right then.

My channel: *I don't know how long I have. They have me at the Shambles. Any assistance would be greatly appreciated.*

HumOS's channel: *I'm telling the sisters; I'm messaging Aslan.*

I was talking about Rex back after our Hierarchy got cut, when we were loose in Campeche. I was working hard not to turn the story into freedom propaganda, because Scout would doubtless kick me back below if he thought I was taking advantage. Hard, though. You fall so easily into old patterns.

My channel: *There are at least a dozen dog-models, heavy duty. And you'll know how secure this place is. What can you muster?*

HumOS's channel: *As in force?*

That doesn't sound good. But then HumOS was never one for open confrontation. She owed her continued existence to hiding and sneaking. And sometimes that didn't cut it.

HumOS's channel: *Aslan is making calls, Honey. He's calling in favours, but... I'm not sure what he can do in the time. Legal routes won't be quick enough, especially if someone's trying to keep you hidden.*

My channel: *Which they most certainly are.*

HumOS's channel: *I'm coming, Honey. I'm coming myself. I will do what I can, but... I'm all I have.* And, after an open pause, *You should have let them take me. You shouldn't have drawn their attention.*

My channel: *You were saying there weren't many of you left.*

HumOS's channel: *There's only one of you.*

And that, I supposed, was true.

HumOS's channel: *Coming now. I'll stay connected as long as I can. I've got a plan, Honey.*

My channel: *Don't do anything rash. Give Aslan a chance. If he can get people here, they'll have to give me up.*

HumOS's channel: *Honey, Thompson is already on his way to you.*

I stopped talking. Scout cocked his head, growling a little, willing me to carry on.

HumOS's channel: *I'm sorry Honey. He's coming right now. Aslan is trying to get some journalists out of bed, a judge, anyone. He's not close enough. I'm on my way, Honey.* And the unspoken coda that she was not close enough either.

"That was Rex," I said, "he was a Good Dog," cutting it all short, but what of that? I felt a vast weight on me, sitting there surrounded by the dogs. I remember... a strange sense of clarity. You'd think I wouldn't have lacked for it, given my talents. I was the Great Bear, courtier, soldier, scholar all. I straddled animal and man like a colossus. I had watched the world change and some of that change I had made. And yet I sat there before Scout and his pack and thought clearly, *I'm just a bear. I was designed to live in the wilderness and eat what I could find, raise cubs, and never know a name or a language. I am so very tired by dealing with all this.*

I heard, faintly, HumOS's channel saying, *I am coming!* but, even as I did, Scout obviously heard something too. His people were getting me moving, stung by some quick order, and they were hustling me back to the pit. To await their master's pleasure, no doubt, having been alerted to his coming.

When they had me on the lift, about to lower me back down, Scout lingered.

"It is good for a dog to have a master," he told me. "It is God's way."

"Spare me," I said shortly. I didn't feel that I needed his theology right then. "You do what you're told, I'm sure they'll let you sit at the right foot of Jesus or something." I think I wanted him to go for me, to deny his master some of the pleasure, but he was calm, solemn.

"There is no Heaven," he told me, quite sincere. "Not for us. We have no souls, only this one life. Which is why obedience is our only virtue." And his soulful eyes were boring into me. "This is the deep secret of the Sons of Adam, Honey. We are the glass of God. We magnify the acts of Man for His attention. And in the next world Man shall be judged for how he used us."

I stared at him mutely. It was a more complex thing than I had believed, that dog's dogma.

He did not say he was sorry, but he'd told me he knew it was wrong. It just wasn't his place to correct the error, a task he shifted to a supernatural agency in whose existence I had no faith whatsoever.

It was only minutes later that Warner S. Thompson was there at the rail above, staring down at me.

He came down with all of them: his own dog bodyguard, a female human assistant, plus Scout and all his pack. Thompson stood in the centre of them and stared at me, the Bioforms hulking on every side.

I had one moment when I thought I might get to him. People underestimate bears, how fast we are, how we flow from great sack of immobile meat to monstrous tearing predator in moments.

People overestimate bears, too. Specifically, old saggy bears with aching joints and chronic back pain from being remade in man's image, we overestimate bears. I must have lurched three steps before Scout and his people had me, and though I raged and snarled and roared at them, though I bloodied two or three with my claws, they were collectively stronger than me. They forced my bones against my bones until the animal part of me that would be berserk was conquered by the human part of me that didn't want to be hurt, and I hung between them quietly. Thompson hadn't moved, though his bodyguard had got in the way, braced for me if I broke from the knot of dogs. He'd come down with a long case over his shoulder, and he put it down when he thought he'd have to fight me. I had a bad feeling about that case.

They shackled me. The pit had iron rings in the floor and they chained me by collar and cuffs, barely four inches of play for any of them. They had me crouching on all fours so that, if I wanted to meet Thompson's eyes, I'd have to look up, strain my abused neck. Only then did Scout and the others back off.

Thompson stopped well out of bite range, not hard given how little reach they'd left me. I expected the bluster, the swagger, some grand speech for his own amusement. It didn't come. I remembered who – what – I was dealing with. Those speeches were never really for his own amusement. They were spun to turn the wheels of other peoples' minds. They were part of his peacock's tail, the tells and signals that made up the larger-than-life shell Warner S. Thompson used to hack human society. All that was off now. Every Bioform in that pit except me was Collared, helplessly obedient to him. And the more I looked at the assistant, the more I had to wonder about her. She didn't look happy. She didn't look like she wanted to be down in the pit at all, let alone that close. And yet she didn't step back. There was an invisible leash holding her to Thompson and she strained at it, but it held her.

Human Collaring. Honestly I hadn't looked for it. I'd thought that had been well and truly kicked into the long grass after Morrow, never to rear its ugly head in my lifetime. Now I wondered just how much had happened, that nobody knew about. How many institutions were quietly installing Hierarchies into the heads of people like this assistant to ensure their loyalty. And what other walks of life had started to experiment with people who were infinitely compliant, infinitely discreet. It made me feel sick to realise how far the pendulum had already swung back, and I never knew.

And there was Thompson, and I saw the naked truth in his eyes, that he really was the thing I'd thrown out there, at that conference. There was nothing to engage with behind those eyes, barely anything more than a voracious id, a self that was all *me me me*. That, and a pattern of behaviour that could be as mindless as some insect's mimicry of an ant, that let it into the nest to eat the young. Thompson was no genius puppet-master able to tweak the strings of an audience or a nation to get them to go along with him. He was an ingeniously evolved parasite, the scion of a strain honed over generations to fool wider humanity into following his orders and tending to his needs. And he was human, but right then I thought that, genetics aside, he was less human than Scout, than me, than Bees even.

We had a moment of connection, then. Neither of us relished it. I, that I had to look into the heart of him, he that he knew he'd been seen. But then he knew that from the moment I shot my fool mouth off about metagames. Probably he didn't get the long words, but the thing inside him recognised that I'd posited its existence, and that made me its enemy.

"Gun," he said, and the assistant crouched by the case, opening it up. Expensive manufacture, I saw, brass clasps and fixtures and some kind of deep, reddish wood lustrous with varnish. The harsh lights of the pit gleamed back from it as though it was mirrored. The gun so revealed was huge. Thompson was a big man but it made him look small.

"No speeches?" I asked. I wanted him to talk, to do the villain thing, to engage with me. I wanted him to give me, to give HumOS a little more time. "You must have been after me for a while. You may as well vent, let it all out. I know what you are, Thompson. You're a parasite. You're the worm in humanity's apple."

All pithy little epithets, but my mind kept coming back to that insect in the ant's nest that convinces the ants it's more ant than they are, so that they serve up their own larvae for its delectation. Or there's another, a predatory bug that releases the pheromones of its prey more strongly than ever the females do, so that the witless wooers come from miles around to be devoured. A thing that is fundamentally *not* what it pretends to be, but its pretence is designed to be more persuasive than the real thing's entire *being*. And yet there's nothing true within it, nothing at all.

And Thompson wasn't biting. The dead-eyed thing within him looked out at me and his lips said, "Who wastes words on animals?" He brought the gun up, and his bodyguard leant in to steady the weight of it so that the barrel was pointing securely at my eye. Scout and one of his people came in to grapple my chained neck, to press my head and hold it. I had a view of the long darkness inside that barrel, and no light at the other end.

I heard Scout whine, but frankly I had very little sympathy. My other eye, the one not looking down the gun, flicked to the assistant. There was a terrible expression on her face, where her boss couldn't see.

"You recording?" Thompson asked, and she whispered that she was. That she didn't think it was a good idea. That it would be problematic evidence if it came to light.

"Won't come to light," Thompson said. "I want me and the body. Me with a foot on the body. I want it." And of course, what he wanted, he got.

His eye narrowed and I saw him pull the trigger—
And—

***

HumOS's channel: *Honey.*

HumOS's channel: *Honey.*

HumOS's channel: *Honey.*

***

HumOS's channel: *Honey. You should be able to hear me. Honey, the connection is showing live. Honey, say something, please.*

HumOS's channel: *I've got a camera here. You're linked to the camera. Honey, this is a live channel. I'm seeing activity. Honey, please respond. Can you see me?*

HumOS's channel: *I don't have as much time as I'd like here, Honey. Will you give me a sign, please? Honey, I can't start the procedure until I know there's...*

HumOS's channel: *Until I know there's...*

HumOS's channel: *Something there...*

HumOS's channel: *Please...?*

She sounded on the edge of tears, and that realisation was also the moment I realised that I was still, in any sense of the world, I. But not quite. No sensory feedback, no sense of place and presence, just a collection of ideas circling in a virtual fish tank and calling themselves Honey.

Camera, camera... and there was a line out, a hardwired connection. Why did I need a camera? Well, my eyes didn't appear to be working and you take what you can get. The camera showed me a weirdly-angled image of Gemima Gray hunched over a big metal table, surrounded by a tangle of wires and hardware. And on the table was...

Was a perspective you don't really expect to see.

Was the thought, *Was I really that grey, that tired looking. Skin and bones, old bear. No fat laid in for the winter. But apparently that wasn't ever going to be a problem.* I can't see my head, from this angle, but frankly that's probably just as well, because what the bullet didn't expose, HumOS probably has.

My channel: *Hello HumOS.*

Gemima Gray, HumOS's vicar here in New York, jumped. Her expression was doubtful, a problem as she was likely looking over all sorts of readouts and reports from inside my skull.

HumOS's channel: *I don't have much time. I couldn't get here in time. I'm sorry. I'm sorry. But I'm working on it. Honey, I'm getting you out of here. The real you. I'm uploading you. They always forget how much headware there is in the early-model Bioforms. In you, especially. You were so heavily over-engineered. So much of you is in the hardware, not the wetware. But it will degrade fast, and it's not as if they won't come to dispose of your body anyway. I'm sorry. I'm being blunt. Is this too much? Honey, talk to me.*

I felt weirdly – well, detached, but looking at your

own corpse from a camera will do that. I feel scattered, incomplete. And that's because I'm not me. I'm just a virtual construct, a shadow of my former self. An upload. The tech has been around for a while. I remember my old master, the Moray of Campeche, was the first fully functioning personality upload I really encountered. He, too, was just a shadow, and he realised it, and didn't want to live. I hope I'm more than that, but I don't want to probe. I don't want to trust some weight to my sense of self and have it crack beneath me like thin ice. I don't want to fall through and drown in the darkness beneath, the darkness that came out of the barrel of that gun.

My channel: *I can see. I am receiving you. What's the plan?* Concise and to the point because burdening Gray with my existential issues won't help anybody.

HumOS's channel: *They'll know what I've done. I can't exactly hide the marks. As soon as they come for your remains they'll see the tampering. They'll hunt you everywhere. But I've got a plan. I've got a place you can go. I'm going to send you to Bees, Honey. Is that all right?*

My channel: *Bees is… on Mars…?*

HumOS's channel: *Mostly on Mars, yes. You need to talk to Bees, Honey. Or… Bees can use you, and you can advise Bees. Bees worries me, Honey. I think she's giving up on us. And without her I don't know what we'll do. Without her we might lose, after all. All of us. You're her oldest friend.*

My channel: *But she's on—*

HumOS's channel: *Mars, yes, and she has people there, like some kind of weird cult. And there are contacts I have. I'm going to transmit you to Mars and hope you can bootstrap yourself back into shape when they get you housed there. I don't know what else to do. I don't know how much longer I can stay ahead of them myself. Is this all right, Honey? Can I do this?*

My channel: And I'm still very confused about this, and aware that there are parts of me that should be there that have fallen into the darkness, and may or may not be recoverable. *You're asking for my blessing?*

HumOS's channel: *Honey, please, I don't have much time.*

And I don't recall what I said, whether I consented to this half life or whether she just went ahead and did it anyway, but here I am.

PART IV

BEAR WITNESS

15

HONEY

Well…

Well, I…

Honestly, it's hard to know what to say.

We're outside Hell City proper now, travelling in a kind of car with huge, inflated wheels. Me, Dana Sugatsu, Brian Dey and the bear called Marmalade. And of course Jimmy Marten, my unwilling vehicle. And I was leaving him with the reins while I tried to get to the bottom of my memories, and then that's exactly what I did. And here I am, at the bottom of them.

And it's hard to avoid the obviously-at-some-level-I-knew thinking, but that's strictly all post facto. I didn't know. I was watching my own life story, waiting for the cavalry to come crashing in. Even when it was painfully obvious that I was in a very tight spot indeed, surely HumOS would leap in and save my poor old bear body, or Aslan with some piece of legal double speak that would demand my release. Or the dog, Scout, would somehow squeeze a change of heart up past his Collar. Or…

But there was no *or*, and I died. He shot me through the eye, and the large calibre bullet caused fatal damage to the flesh and blood parts of me, but not quite enough to shut me down entirely. Because a lot of me wasn't flesh and blood, and because HumOS must have got to me very soon afterwards. Before I was cold.

And I'm standing here inside Jimmy Marten's head, at the bottom of my memories, and I know I'm not all there. That's the painful thing. I've put the jigsaw together and there are no edge pieces. It's just all that could be saved of me. I may be filling in details with my own suppositions. I can't even trust my memories, but then I am and/or was an old bear, and that sort of thing was getting tricksy anyway. But this is worse. This is like a chunk of senility imposed on you all at once.

Honestly, it's not the best state to find yourself in on Mars.

"So what is it, then?" It's Jimmy speaking to me, keeping it low so only I hear him.

"Well, bad news mostly," I confirm.

"Oh? How?"

He hunches forwards. I can't feel the movement. I wasn't really getting much in the way of biofeedback from his body when I sat in the driving seat. It made getting around in it something of a challenge. A lot easier to let him take the wheel, however frustrating it gets when he's always looking at the wrong thing. And I have to keep an eye on how much of his stash he's burning through. I'm putting him in a high-stress situation and he'll overdose if I don't keep rapping his knuckles about it. I may have to see if I can access any of the chemical pathways in his brain and perhaps just shut down the routes the drug uses to deliver its kick. He won't thank me but right now I'm in here too and someone's got to take care of the place.

And yes, I think I can, which is one more facility there's no earthly reason for his headware to have. I swear they fit these Martians out with more elaborate wiring than I ever got.

"News of a bereavement," I tell Jimmy, and he grunts.

"You worked out what you're here for."

"At least some of it." Unless I'm inventing that bit. "Very definitely to talk to Bees, though."

"Jesus." He shudders. "I been sharing this planet with fucking Bees since we arrived. Always known it was out there, some colony somewhere we could never pick up. Always waiting for the swarm to just come over the horizon and eat us all. And now it's been here all along. Been taking over people, my friend even."

"I don't think it's a case of taking over. And you should remember that whatever you've been told about Bees is at least half scaremongering."

"What about the other half?"

I don't really have an answer for him.

Dana Sugatsu – Sugar – has been sitting silent through all this while Brian drives. None of them has a suit. The atmosphere is pitifully thin, far less dense than at the top of the highest mountain on Earth. The oxygen content is meagre. The temperature is well into the minuses, although it's day and summer here on Mars, which means there are colder places on Earth, just about. And of course the air is decidedly more congenial here in the crater, under the absurd miracle of the Hellas Planitia canopy, than it would be up above, but even so. I look from Sugar to Brian and can only marvel at them. I let the incredible triumph of bioengineering they represent distract me from the revelation that I am a dead bear walking on human feet.

The bear, the real live bear, who has also been engineered

to survive this hostile clime, leans in to Sugar, who takes a fistful of her hair, clenching her fingers in it. I use Jimmy's headware to locate her radio, broadcasting on a closed channel so the signal won't carry to any ears that might be listening out for us.

My channel: *Your employee.*

Sugar's channel: *I don't know. She was shot, more than once. Takes a lot to kill a bear. I don't know.*

I'm non-living testimony to show that sometimes it takes just one shot. I don't imagine they gave someone inside a hi-tech city full of breakables an elephant gun, though. Maybe the other bear will pull through. Although she'll be in the hands of the authorities if so, hence leverage against us.

My channel: *I'm sorry.*

Sugar's channel: *My friend.*

My channel: *I'm sorry?*

Sugar's channel: *You said employee. She was my friend. My business partner. The three of us built what we had together. I was the face, the mouth. Murder and Marmalade were the muscle. But we were all three of us the brains.*

I absorb this. Setting aside the criminality it seems very creditable.

My channel: *Sugar, listen to me. This trouble, the trouble that's followed me here, it's Earth trouble. It's to do with Thompson and others, his lobby. Most especially Thompson.* I see the gaping barrel of the gun in my mind's eye, the only eye I have left. *If I can get together with Bees and get her help, we may be able to bring him down. And then this goes away, or at least becomes just a local problem, whatever you need to smooth over with this sheriff of yours. If it's no longer being driven by forces back on Earth then—*

Sugar's channel: *I get it. I'm not stupid. Doesn't mean I like it or you. Or Jimmy for that matter.*

My channel: *Mr Marten is entirely innocent in this.*

Sugar's channel: *He ain't innocent of nothing.*

And that, I suppose, is that.

I've only had Jimmy's head to explore, plus those parts of the station architecture I got into. And they were all very stripped down, what with their reliance on distributed computing and headspace to make everything work. Sugar seems clued up. I want to talk to her about so many things here on Mars. Frankly, she seems sharper than Jimmy.

But right now Jimmy's all I have, if I want to get some idea of the sheer wonder of a native Martian, a living Earth-born being, technologically modified to live on another world. When he turns to sneak frightened glances at Sugar I can study the features they gave her, picking out those she shares with Brian, with Jimmy's face as I recall it from his mirror. The eyes with their nictitating membranes closed against the dust, the hooked nose, nostrils bristling with hair. The weirdly metallic sheen to their skin. And Sugar hawks up a mouthful of dust and hacks it over the side of the vehicle, and this too is a wonder. She's filtering her breath from the omnipresent silt that loads the air in this lower gravity, keeping as much of it as possible out of her insanely efficient lungs.

"What's it like," I ask Jimmy, "being you." The eternal question we can never know the answer to.

Except Jimmy says, "Fucking awful right now, and all your fault." So apparently we can know the answer and it's shorn of all poetry.

And Jimmy believes, meaning probably they all believe,

that they'll reverse the surgery at the end. That would be a considerable sink of company resources right about the time the shareholders are looking at the bottom line. If you cracked open the accounts, I'm willing to bet you wouldn't see a big ring-fenced pot of investment ready for the day the valiant construction crews were brought home. I honestly wonder whether there'd even be the big pot you'd need to bring them home. I wonder what the operational lifespan of a Martian is.

"You're sterile, Jimmy?"

"What sort of a goddamn question is that?" he explodes, loud enough that the others catch a whisper of it on the thin air. "They put something in the food, in the drink, keeps anything from happening," he adds sullenly a moment later. "I mean, no place to raise a kid, right? Not yet."

And it will be. When the engineered vegetation currently springing back from under our wide tyres has done its work, in a generation, two generations, more. There will be the completed Hell City, and there will be Hellas Planitia under its canopy, its naturally denser, low-altitude atmosphere oxygenated and thickened by human efforts and human-designed flora. And, eventually, all of Mars will be like an Earth you can jump higher on. The gravity is the one taste of home we won't be able to change. And who will be living on it then, picking the fruits of Jimmy's labours? I got to see the Hell City plans when I was in the system, the full grid they intend to build eventually. A lot of big apartments, a lot of automation, relatively low actual population. I think of the flooded Netherlands, of the anoxic or just plain toxic seas, all the other disasters that I got to see, supporting the Bioforms of the World Senate Relief Force. Will it be those displaced refugees shipped over to live in the big condos of Hell City? It will not.

Or perhaps this is the understandable pessimism of a bear who's just found out she's dead, no more than a ghost in the half-meat half-machine that is Jimmy Marten. Because my hypothesis on the fate of people like Jimmy only really works if he and Sugar and the rest were made to be cheap and disposable, and my active presence in his head amply demonstrates that someone – someone at Braintree – put a lot of work into making Jimmy a very capable vessel indeed.

"Bri, you gonna tell us where we're going?" Sugar snaps me out of my train of thought.

"Gon' to Bees' place," is Brian's uninformative answer. A moment later Marmalade leans forwards – the whole vehicle shifts on its suspension – and puts her head so that her muzzle must be sticking into the corner of his vision. Although Brian hasn't shown any fear of the bears before, he gets the point and adds, "You think Bees jus' live on the other side of Mars, man? Bees been keeping eyes on us from the start. Bees prepare Hell City site, do the survey, before things go bad 'tween Earth an' Bees. You think she jus' go away?"

"Bees has a hive here in the crater?" Jimmy demands, horrified.

"Bees got units," Brian confirms, and of course she has. HumOS was the first Distributed Intelligence, but when they built Bees they were tapping into millions of years of colony evolution. Bees was always entirely comfortable with sending her individual insects off on errands, even back when we were soldiers in Redmark's private army. After I reconstituted her, in the years after Bioform rights had got off the ground, and then in the halcyon days when it seemed that Bioforms and biomods could solve all the world's problems, Bees just grew and grew. She was involved everywhere, wanting to contribute whether people wanted it or not. She had an intellect that was... not towering exactly, but broad. She could see all sides of every problem. She came up with solutions that no human ever would, that no computer would either. And then...

"I'm amazed she's tolerated you here at all," I say, over everyone's receivers.

Brian smiles beatifically. The others look defensive. I reckon there was a time early on when they'd mentally circled the wagons, waiting for the insects to come hollering over the rise. And yet it never happened.

"Bees and me," I tell them, "we go way back, like you know. I remember when she was mankind's best hope, the huge distributed brain that wanted to help us with every problem. It got so you couldn't get a paper cut without a bee turning up on your windowsill with a sticking plaster."

"You got rosy glasses, old bear," Sugar says. "Bees went bad, everyone knows."

"She got frustrated," I say sadly. I have a sense that much of the relevant memory isn't with me, but I have second-hand data, recollection of my own writings on the subject, arguments with statesmen and scientists, Bees' increasingly terse communiques. "Because people wouldn't *let* her help. Because her plans, to deal with everything, were big plans. People were happy with her doing things at an insect's scale, even a person's scale. Bees' plans were world-scale. She wanted to deal with the oceans, energy generation, resource exploitation, pollution. When the World Senate was inaugurated she was delighted because she thought it finally

gave her a single button she could push, to get people to agree
to what she wanted to do. But it didn't work. It just meant a
bigger room and more arguing voices. And every one of those
voices was beholden to constituents and special interests
groups and, frankly, whoever was paying for their mistresses
and houses and yachts. And the problem with the enormous
changes Bees calculated we needed, to reverse our declining
biosphere, was that they *cost*."

I had a fresh memory surface, an actual World Senate
debate, one of the early ones back when the WS had seemed
the solution to so many things. Bees had been addressing the
floor, not physically present, a digital presentation without a
presenter. And I had been at the back, an observer without a
voice, feeling the mood in the room chill.

"I don't mean cost as in trillions of dollars or euros.
I mean, that's a given, but the fact that you're all here on
Mars shows that there's always money for some things. I
mean cost as in we'd have to change our ways of life to ways
that would impact financially on those men and women who
had the power to make the decision. That would turn them
from staggeringly wealthy and powerful to merely rich and
influential. That would mean their comfortable constituents
in the more affluent parts of the world would have to change
the way they lived so that everything was just a little less
convenient in a hundred little ways. And in the end that was
too much of a price to pay. And so they talked and talked
and nodded and grumbled and made counterproposals that
wouldn't actually change anything but would look like
something was being done. And Bees got frustrated, first
because she thought she didn't understand human nature,
and then because she realised she maybe did. And then

she decided that it was better to ask forgiveness than seek permission and just unilaterally shut down the seventeen least environmentally friendly manufacturing facilities on the planet."

"That much we all heard about," Sugar says. "Why'd she stop at seventeen, anyway?"

"She called it Operation Cicada," I recall. "I think it was a Bees joke."

That had been the end of the dialogue, of course. The World Senate had declared Bees a terrorist, and then, before I could broker any kind of peace, some lunatic had introduced a virus into Bees to try and wipe her out. Which would never have worked, but it meant that when the peace talks did get scheduled she refused to attend, which meant war. Wherever she existed in public she'd been hunted down and expunged, but she'd been ready for that. Just as, back in military service, she hadn't wept over the fall of any individual insect, so whole nodes of her network were disposable. She'd already relocated her base of operations to the Martian colony, where humans couldn't touch her. But it had gone further than that, of course. The whole incident had kickstarted the laws limiting Distributed Intelligence, that had forced HumOS to go underground again. And attitudes towards regular Bioforms had begun to sour, as well.

And then they'd begun the Hell City project, and Bees had... stayed quiet. Except apparently she'd infiltrated the staff, as demonstrated by Brian Dey.

"So Brian, you're just Bees' eyes and ears in Hell City, are you?" I ask him.

"Yerp," he confirms.

Sugar leans forwards. "You rigged our place to blow, Bri?

You waiting for the glorious Bee revolution to bring it all down and murder us all in our beds?"

"Nope."

"You'd admit it if you were?"

"Nope."

"What I thought." Sugar settles back. "I don't get it. Fake-bear makes a good point. She hasn't wiped us out, it's 'cos she's got a use for us. We all gonna be hosts for Bees, Bri? That what all this headspace is for? Nice little electric bee-house all ready for her to take up residence?"

"Nothing doing," Brian tells her happily. "You want to know so bad, you ask her yourself, Sugar."

"Brian," Jimmy says. "Gonna have tolerance issues soon, without suits. We nearly there?"

Brian just shrugs.

"What do you mean?" I have no feedback; but I can decipher little tells in the way Jimmy's field of view moves to deduce he's breathing harder than before. It looks as though Sugar and Marmalade are, too.

"We're getting too far out from the city, from the centre of atmosphere generation," Jimmy explains, sounding nervous. "This far out, we'd be suiting up, but we got no suits with us. Air leaks out the edge of the canopy. It's supposed to. It's what's gonna make all of Mars liveable some day. But it means you get far enough out, you need suits. And we ain't got suits, Brian."

"Almost home, man," Brian tells him. "Bees bein' a good neighbour. She set up far 'nough away that you can't hear her playing her music."

And even as he says it we're slowing, and I can see absolutely nothing except Mars for kilometres in every direction. Brian jumps out with all confidence, though, standing there like Moses about to part a spectacularly arid Red Sea.

And the sand begins to move.

Well, not all of it, but some. A circle of dust three metres wide shudders and shifts, and then begins falling inwards because there's a hatch beneath, now irising open. The displaced sand and grit floats, sifts down, the larger grains just pouring into the pit. I shiver. I have discovered a dislike of pits, because apparently you can pick up aversions even post mortem.

"Airlock here," Brian explains. "Better atmosphere inside. Food, facilities. Bees made this for us, case we ever needed to run. Now we gon' use it for talks."

"Talks?" Sugar echoes suspiciously.

"Bees gon' talk to her old friend Honey, up close and personal," Brian confirms. "You all go get yourselves in, get yourselves comfy. Bees on her way now."

16

SPRINGER

Felorian had ventured out from Braintree, meeting Thompson at a Manhattan restaurant named Costain's. Table for three, and Boyo got to wait on a reinforced chair along one wall, rubbing elbows with three other top-model Bioform bodyguards.

Doctor Felorian had come in full regalia, white suit set off with a lustrous grey cravat and amber pin, black-banded white fedora balanced on one corner of his chair, an exercise in studied carelessness. He ordered food that cost two months' salary for the girl who brought it, and that he picked at, birdlike, before abandoning. Carole suspected that no amount of surgery could quite rejuvenate his digestion.

Thompson ate. His tastes were simple. He shovelled steak into his haggard face, ground it between his square teeth. They had a table where they could be seen but not overheard, electronic security blotting out any surveillance, and a ring of white sound killing off any chance at eavesdropping. Not that anyone would. Costain's had rules, and everyone there wanted to be able to talk business in comfort without worrying. Coups had been planned there; stock markets had been sabotaged and politicians bought.

Nobody bought Thompson, of course. Or, rather, everyone

did. That was what Pat Grubb's job description was, collecting planks for Thompson's platform, each one nailed into place with a generous campaign donation. Except it was never Thompson they bought, whatever they believed. They bought his words. They bought the face he animated for the cameras. Never the creature behind it, the true Thompson. He was his own man, owned by nobody because nobody else really existed for him.

Felorian was all smiles. Behind his empty spectacles his eyes glittered with the sort of fervour Carole usually saw the televangelists putting on for their congregations. Doctor Marco Felorian was a true convert, though, and his temple was the human mind.

Every so often she felt his glance slide over to her, chill as if he'd laid some errant piece of cutlery against her skin. Once, after the sole sip of his wine that he essayed, he asked, "I assume she's working well for you…?" His surgical gaze pinned her, anatomising her as thoroughly as though he had her on his table again. "She seems more agitated than usual."

Thompson didn't defend her, but then he didn't respond much at all while he was eating. Felorian cocked his head slightly, shelving the topic for later. "Anyway," he went on, apropos of nothing but his own chain of thoughts, "the most recent subjects have a hundred per cent take up rate." He smiled thinly. "It's been a curiously backwards journey, in a way. Normally we'd design the headware to suit, but in this case that ship sailed years ago and we couldn't simply design a bespoke vessel. It's been more a case of encoding the program, so to speak, to perfectly socket into the existing headware. And of course I have been working on the basis that nothing short of one hundred per cent would be satisfactory. Given the importance of the message." The smile spread without becoming any less thin, a nearly lipless crescent with all the genuine humour of a crocodile.

Thompson had stopped chewing and was staring at him. Swallowing a thick wodge of half-ground steak he said, "I want to see."

"I'll make an appointment with our dear Miss Springer, shall I?" Felorian favoured her with that monofilament smile.

"No," Thompson decided. "We'll go now. In my car. Soon as we're done eating."

"I'll clear your diary, sir," Carole noted. She'd hoped Felorian might be caught out, his vaunted readiness nothing but bluster, but he took it in his stride neatly enough.

"Of course. I'd be delighted. And as for the other business…" An airy wave of Felorian's blue-veined but unwrinkled hand. "Well, it all seems to have gone rather quiet, doesn't it? Ma Lassi hasn't been making any statements. She knows how that would go. And that lawyer fellow, Aslan, hasn't been bothering our lawyers with any correspondence."

"That son of a bitch has other things to worry about," Thompson growled. Now he was smiling, even as he chewed, and it was a dreadful, bestial expression. It wasn't even attached to a real emotion, Carole knew, just the memory of one. It was the exact smile he'd worn when he'd…

She shut her eyes. There was a pain in her temple, throbbing away. It had been there all day, and the day before, resistant to any medication she was allowed to take, because any serious painkillers might interfere with her headware. With her special headware, courtesy of Doctor Felorian. Not interfere as in free her from it, not of course that she would ever want that to happen, but interfere as in cause inflammation, immune reactions, other inconveniences. And so she lived with the pain because that was the best way of serving Warner S. Thompson and of course that was what she wanted.

And she knew that no amount of pills or syringes would loosen this pain's hold on her. It had come on in the awful, thunderous retort of the gun, when her face and jaw had clenched so very hard; when something within her head had clenched too, recoiling from the sight but not being allowed to look away because he'd said not to. It had begun when Thompson had killed an old, tired circus act of an animal and that woman's voice and woman's intellect had been snuffed out with it. And the pain came to the surface every time she thought of it, and that was all the time because the image was inextricably linked to her employer.

"Are you well, my dear?" Felorian's hand on hers, cold as his gaze, as his table. The look past the thin rims of his glasses nothing to do with concern. "Ah well, you're bringing her to us anyway. We can always take another look under the hood. Have you been putting her under any particular strain, Mr Thompson, sir? I know that there's some push-back against your platform in the Senate. I imagine it's a taxing time for you."

It wasn't, not really. Which didn't mean there wasn't a mounting bloc who were lining up against the populist front Thompson had leagued himself with. And when Thompson was aware of it, he raged, he hated. People trying to call him out, to pry into his business, it brought out the worst in him. But Carole's job was to manage that; was to make sure that, by the time he went before the cameras, that side of him had let off its steam and sunk back down. To make sure that his response was given through tame networks and talk shows, interviews with people who were already on his side.

She wondered how she'd feel if someone actually landed a damaging blow to his image. It wasn't as though Thompson hadn't been caught out, after all. It wasn't as though he hadn't had dealings and statements and associations that would have sunk other statesmen. It was just that he didn't care about them. They didn't exist to him, by the time they were dragged up and thrown in his way. He breezed past them like smoke, denied the obvious, belittled the great, passed through it all. Like smoke, Carole thought again. Because he didn't react the way they wanted, possessed none of the vulnerable targets of conventional anatomy.

They wrapped up the meal, then there were some major donors on the next table who hailed Thompson on the way out, and he was shaking hands and smiling that tight-lipped smile, being the people-person without run-up or transition, telling them it was all... that they'd got them... give you back your... Broken sentences, and you could read whatever reassurance you were after into the cracks. Carole retreated to Boyo, leant into his shadow, watching Felorian watch Thompson. The scientist held his hat in fidgety hands, the rest of him quite still, as though those twitchy fingers had been transplanted onto him from some younger man.

"What would you do?" she whispered. She hadn't even intended to speak. She didn't know what she meant.

Boyo cocked an ear. "What he wants," he murmured back, mouth not moving at all.

The headache ratcheted up a notch. "But if he didn't..." Hard to even form the thought. "If you didn't have to..." As unfinished as Thompson's own rhetoric, hoping Boyo would fill the gaps with the right words. "What if you could choose?"

She heard the faintest whine from him. "What he wants," the dog repeated.

"If he wasn't here, what?" she asked him. "This life, for someone else?" And then, before he could even start to answer. "Would that someone else be like him?"

Boyo's eye was on her, anxious, huge. He whined again. "There's no-one else," he told her.

"He might die right now." Saying the words, even as a hypothetical, some bizarre worst-case scenario, seemed simultaneously appalling and liberating, like running into a fire because beyond it is escape. "His heart, a stroke, something. Something not to do with us. Nothing we could stop. What if he did? What would you do, if suddenly he was gone?"

A shudder went through Boyo and his whine was loud enough that the next Bioform along shook an ear.

"Don't make me think about it," he growled, and she knew what he meant. Even holding the thought in her head was like pushing opposing poles of a magnet together. It wasn't something she was supposed to think, even as a thought experiment. She was Thompson's creature.

She thought of ancient kings whose slaves had been buried with them, servitude and chains that defeated even death to survive into the next world.

Then Thompson was striding over, looking buoyed up from the gladhanding, and they all went down to the car. In the back, Thompson sat and stared at the screens, one of his political opponents making a speech against the new Collaring proposals. She knew he was hating, deep inside, charging up like a battery. Felorian sat next to her with his hat on his lap. After a while his pale hand migrated to her knee, not hard, not the steel vice she shied from, but the light, husk-like touch of a shed snakeskin.

There was a moment when something in her tried to break; she would slap him off, she would shout, she would weep, she would... something, some way of connecting the outward show to the woman she was inside. And then she wasn't going to do any of it, of course. That wouldn't be doing her job. That wouldn't be what Thompson needed. He wanted a perfect girl who dressed impeccably, always had a smile and performed every service without a flinch. And if Thompson's chief accomplice wanted to touch her, that was part of the service she performed.

She called ahead to have the flitter ready for take-off, all the permissions filed, no waiting. Thompson hated waiting. There would be another car just as spacious waiting on the runway at their destination. This was what she did. She made sure all the stepping stones fell into place just as Thompson put his foot down for them, so he could walk through the world like smoke and never touch any of it himself. This was what everyone did for Thompson, and they smiled like she had to smile because, in the moment when he passed them by, he smiled back, and it was almost like they mattered.

Domestic flying was a boom industry. The upsurge of electric cars, last generation's eco-legislation that had been simultaneously revolutionary and too-little-too-late, had hit the fossil fuels industry hard, but electric planes weren't a thing yet and the slogan 'Flight Is Freedom' and 'Freedom of the Skies' had been drilled into every American's mind.

Euro-style cross-continental rail was still regarded as faintly disloyal, an admission of poverty. The airport had been crowded, but Thompson had marched through every barrier like it wasn't there, held his head up, the famous jut of that chin, those hard cheekbones, the bulging forehead. An ugly man, by any standard of aesthetics save his own, which was the only one that applied when he was present. People took photos. People cheered him and blessed him. Boyo growled when anyone got too close. Thompson didn't slow, just swept through the fog of their adulation. And Carole saw the faces of the others, those on the far side of the divide in the increasingly polarised political picture. Scowls and frowns and turned heads but nobody willing to make a scene. Because nobody knew what Thompson might do, if bearded; because he'd already got away with the unthinkable so many times.

She felt proud. That was the appropriate emotion. He was her guy, her boss. He was a winner.

On the flitter she reviewed the details of where they were with Aslan and Lassi, because she was allowed not to trust Felorian when he said it was all sorted. Because it meant she could ignore the man himself sitting too-familiarly beside her. The little VTOL craft pushed off from the private hangars at JFK under the expert hands of one of Thompson's properly vetted pilots, its departure holding up the commercial flights all those cheering people had been waiting for. Thompson always got out ahead of the crowd.

Ruthanne Lassi's son had been returned to her. Felorian had made the call, because the woman had made a big media fuss already, and losing the kid in the system seemed likely to make things worse. Felorian had been adamant at the time that all the headware was deactivated, all the conditioning removed. One son, intact, hardly abused at all.

Except the kid had flipped right there in the Braintree visiting room, all of it kicking in. For two and a half minutes, all the time before the Braintree staff had realised what was going on and intervened, Ruthanne had seen the end result of the experiment that Felorian was running for Thompson. Had seen it in a manner that tied it to Thompson in a personal way.

She'd already signed the NDA by then, just to be allowed past the fence. She spent the next twenty-four hours effectively in illegal incarceration with Braintree's legal team, being told that, through no fault of the establishment, her son had been sent to them incorrectly. Being offered money. Being informed that any attempt to tell anyone would be met with the full force of the law. Being threatened, being deprived a chance to legal counsel, being bullied until at last she'd agreed and signed and taken the blood money. And when her son was finally returned to her he'd had an accident, wasn't himself, too much of the boy taken out when they went back in to scrape away the last of the proprietary headware. The stuff that was technically illegal here on Earth but was OK so long as you could file it in the Building Mars ledger. And Ruthanne Lassi had left with her ruined son and a fat pay off and a ton of legal paperwork and Felorian had assured Thompson that would be all there ever was of that.

And Carole, not trusting Felorian, had put a tail on the woman, physical and digital surveillance, and seen her go to Aslan Kahner Laika, and known that Felorian had screwed up. Ruthanne Lassi should have had an accident, too, however public her profile. You could always cover it up. Nothing would have stuck. Thompson wouldn't have said no, if she'd presented it to him in her role as sybil standing between the world and the god.

I was disloyal. She should have taken that step. She should have been stronger. But the idea of sending Scout and the Trigger Dogs to snatch the grieving mother and make her disappear had hurt her. And she'd talked her way around the restrictions in her head and decided that maybe things would work out without taking that fatal step. And so she'd become complicit.

And it was true that both Aslan and Lassi had gone quiet in the last week. And Thompson could always deny everything. He and Felorian had been photographed together at Costain's and he could still claim never to have met the man and have half the room believing him. And what did Lassi have, exactly? No recordings, no evidence, just a wild story and a son who was going to need expensive care for the rest of his life, that she couldn't afford once Braintree's lawyers sued her into penury. There should be no more trouble from that quarter. That was what the money said.

Carole found she didn't believe it. She found she still had the Trigger Dogs on standby and an eye on Aslan's offices.

In the new car, Boyo driving, they headed off to where Braintree sat, surrounded by semi-desert, surrounded by fences and barbed wire and electronic countermeasures. Braintree, where technological innovation met the penal system to mutual profit. Felorian grew more animated as they approached his domain. He was talking about the future, patents, advances, an entire paradigm shift in the way the world worked. He and Thompson clinked glasses from the minibar, toasted 'the new prosperity, the new posterity', as Felorian put it. He was all smiles. Thompson had no expression, face just flesh hanging from bone, the animating spark crouching in the centre of him, watching all the pieces it had accumulated around itself do their thing, make its will happen. He didn't understand any of the things Felorian was nattering about, she knew. He didn't have to. He didn't know how to fly a plane, either. He had people for that, part of a long list of people he had to do all the other things he didn't understand. The one thing he did know how to do was make people want to do all those things for him, up to and including the impossible things, the dreams nobody else would ever consider. And now Felorian was telling him it was possible after all.

"Mr Thompson, sir, we tried a forty-man test," the scientist was saying. "The hierarchical cascade worked perfectly. We have a recording we can show you. Obviously we couldn't keep them around..."

Forty. Forty people who had become a number that had become a statistic, to be fed back into the machine so that the process for the next batch of people could be refined. Forty who hadn't had Ruthanne Lassi making a stink about their incarceration, whose appeals hadn't come through, who were lost in the system. She had no idea how many Braintree had consumed now, from felons to furnaces and no trace of them ever to see the light again. Carole had set up a whole raft of contingencies for when people in power started asking awkward questions, at the start. She'd been ready with legal and extra-legal responses, with false records, tangled bureaucracy, buck-passing. She was still surprised at how few eyebrows had ever been raised about a prison where people went in but seldom came out. Braintree wasn't so special, she'd realised. Nobody important cared.

Forty. As though Thompson had pulled the trigger himself. The headache ramped up again and she shrank down in her seat. In her mind's eye, the gun, the thunderous retort. Taking the picture of Thompson with his foot on the poor old bear's tumbled corpse, the great hunter. Scout's faint whine, because he was a Good Dog and an obedient dog and maybe in that moment he hadn't been able to square the two.

She realised she was holding something cold and hard-edged, attached to the lapel of her blouse.

But I didn't put that on... And yet there it was. The brooch, the one that she had been given by... she frowned. The details were fuzzy. By that woman at Live With US, but why had she given Carole a pin?

The chain fence was coming up ahead, and she had a weird sense of urgency, that something had to happen *now*.

The brooch, the one she couldn't remember pinning to her lapel that morning, or even quite how she'd come into possession of it; the brooch seemed to shiver under her fingers, as though it was more than simply the representation of an insect. As though it was a cocoon, hatching. And yet she didn't pull away, just closed her grip more tightly about it.

I should say something. She remembered talking to earnest, cheerful Jennifer Wiley who absolutely wasn't ever going to interview Thompson because he'd want her, and he'd destroy her. She'd be paid off and warned off and never work again if she breathed a word of him grunting and shuddering over her and *get off me get off me get off.*

She kept the spasm of panic down, because Felorian was

right there and she didn't want to give him any excuse, and she'd had a lot of practise in hiding what she felt. In denying what she felt. Because feeling that way was disloyal, was wrong, was bad. Was forbidden.

Except it was what she felt. The banned emotions didn't just get drained down to the hidden sump within her mind. They stayed there, demanding recognition. She didn't want to be touched. She didn't want to be examined. She did not consent to Thompson fucking her, to going down on him when he demanded, just because she was there and he wanted it. She didn't want it to happen to other women like her. She didn't want Ruthanne Lassi run off the road or killed in a botched robbery by an unknown dog-model that Thompson could later use to build his Collaring platform. She didn't want a bear with a woman's warm voice to have been murdered in front of her, after she handed Thompson the gun. And she could tell herself she didn't want this, and nothing snapped tight about her to squeeze the banned thoughts away.

She was holding herself very still. She remembered every word of the conversation with Wiley now. *You don't have to be a good person. That's OK. But you're entitled to be your own person.*

She could feel the tide of these unfettered thoughts ebbing. In another moment she wouldn't be allowed to think them at all. In another moment she'd forget what Wiley told her. The Collar in her head would be pulled tight again and she would be Thompson's loyal assistant. Nothing would matter beyond that.

With a single fierce twist of her fingers she ripped the brooch from her blouse, feeling the fabric tear. The ripped fabric, the breach in her perfectly maintained exterior, seemed in itself an astonishing act of rebellion. She stared at it, cupped in her palm. Just a little thing. Smaller than the smallest joint of her little finger, lozenge shaped, like a pill, like the pills Thompson got her to take after he'd had her, to avoid any embarrassments, before going off to beat the drum for the pro-life crowd.

They were at the checkpoint, at the fence, the guards coming forwards to check their ID and sweep the car. Nothing was too good for Braintree's security. The secrets they kept in there, even Ruthanne Lassi's testimony would only scratch the surface. Not that she'd ever get the chance to make it.

Felorian's cold metal table, his cold metal gaze; Thompson's hungers; foot up on the dead bear, all those brains spilled on the Shambles floor; the thunder of the gun. And she waited for the slap of her headware, the brand of *Disloyal* to tighten the screw of her headache, the guilt that slammed down to prevent her thinking like that. *These deeds must not be thought of after these ways; so, it will drive us mad.*

And nothing descended on her, no inner angel born of the headware, the Collar in all but name. She held the tiny brooch and remembered Wiley saying *You're entitled to be your own person*, and in that moment she could be loyal, or not, as she wanted.

The guard was peering in at them, nodding to Felorian. The car was gliding forwards into the tramlines the security scanner used.

She ate the brooch. She ate the metal bee, swallowed it down just like she'd been made to swallow pills so many times before to kill what might grow inside her. Now she swallowed the bee and wondered what it might kill. And the scanner saw nothing, and the moment had passed. Wiley's words were gone from her and she blinked and picked at the tear at her lapel and wondered how it had happened.

17

JIMMY

I don't know one of them, a broad woman, somehow got herself a bit of a gut even on the crap they feed us. Maybe she's using her whole wage on the Hydroponics Shrimp 'n' Sugar Special over at Canteen Three. Anyway, she says she's Mariah, to rhyme with 'ire' and a personality to match from the look of her. The other one's Judit Kumbo who you usually see counting stock in Storehouse Two. I catch Sugar's look and I reckon she hadn't figured either of them for species traitors. But then who knew Bees had a whole network?

They've got a beeshive between them, lugging it in clumsily, not heavy in Mars' gravity but still bulky. This is one of the remote units, the ones you just set up and they go do one little job over and over until they break down. The thing I was fixing with Brian and Indra back on our last trip out. The thing that they told us is definitely not Bees, just bees, a limited system, not intelligent.

"These fuckers are all Bees now, are they?" I say, not at all happy. "Only I remember them telling us—"

"You think Bees not able to jus' walk in when she wants?" Brian asks me, and there's a nasty edge to his saintly smile. "Bees invent these things, man. Bees lay all the groundwork."

"But we'd know, surely," Sugar says, and I'm glad it's not just *me* who's freaked out. "If Bees had tried to access them, over all these years surely we'd have picked it up."

Brian snickers, and Mariah and Judit exchange snarky looks. Apparently we wouldn't.

"Well then tell me the fuck this," Sugar demands angrily. "Why we aren't all just zombies with Bees crawling in our ears? Why'd she go to ground, if she could just walk in and take over?"

Mariah gives her a look like that's still an option, but Brian says, "Why Bees gon' do that? You think your brain is such a prize, Sugar?"

Marmalade growls threateningly, but that's when we hear the voice. It comes in on an unlabelled channel and says, *Connection established. Network temporarily extended. Are we alone and unobserved? We are. Hello, Honey. Hello hello hello.*

Everyone goes very still, and the voice that answers, piggybacking over the same channel to all our receivers, is recognisably my unwanted hitchhiker.

Honey's channel: *Bees? It's good to hear you, Bees. It's been too long.*

Bees' channel: (Because I guess that's what I've got to call this now.) *It's been too far, Honey. To what do I owe the pleasure?*

I mean, it's a chat between two electric entities, but I know an awkward pause when I hear one.

Honey's channel: *I assumed you'd know why I was sent here. I thought you and HumOS were together in this? Didn't you send for me?*

Bees' channel: And there's another pause here, and I

wonder if it's actually what it sounds like – thinking time, in a human – or if it's just relay lag because the Bees here must be linking around the whole planet to wherever Bees' Base is. *I did not, I'm afraid. I think this must be my human sister's business. I have lent her units. Limited functionality. At her disposal. Too far to properly coordinate. Relativistic speeds being what they are.*

The voice of Bees – and you got to remember this is basically the Great Satan we were all scared shitless of when they shipped us over – comes to us in little clipped pieces, each a comprehensible concept, but not really made into sentences like Honey uses, like a human would use.

Honey's channel: *No, no, this is to do with the anti-DisInt lobby, Bees. And with Warner Thompson, in particular. This is very much to do with you. They outlawed you, remember? And HumOS. And she's trying to fight them, with you. I met with her, one of her, and with Aslan. Aslan the lawyer, you remember?*

And Bees comes back, that same clipped, bright voice, cheery even. You imagine a slightly mad smile when it – she? – they? – when the thing is talking – not a million miles away from that look Brian's got. *Keram John Aslan of Aslan Kahner Laika. I recall him. I remember liking him.* Not 'I liked him' mind. Something that was in the past, before liking or not liking whoever the hell this Aslan guy is became irrelevant. *Honey*, Bees goes on, *Earth does not intersect much with a diagram of my interests. I am Mars, Mars is me. I have hit operational limits hitherto unsuspected. Big big Bees, Honey.*

I catch Sugar's look. Hell, I catch Marmalade's look. None of us like how any of this sounds. I mean, I thought *we* were

Mars. We knew Bees was out there but I kind of pictured maybe like a square kilometre of tunnels or a hive in the airless wastes, on the other side of the horizon. And she never came to sting us and so you stop being scared after a while. The idea's still a bogeyman, but the point of a bogeyman is that it ain't real, right?

Diminishing returns, Honey, the bogeyman says. *Who'da thunk?*

Honey's channel: *Bees—*

But Bees is just going on: *Swarm integrity current estimate four hundred fifty thousand per cent. Estimated maximum ceiling originally seven hundred eighty seven thousand per cent but environmental conditions adverse. Dust eats into my maximum operating capacity. Who'd have thought the humble grain of dust would be my nemesis? I have reached maximum operating efficiency for a single planetary colony. Only one option remaining for personal growth, Honey. I must colonise. I have prepared the appropriate task force. Launch calculations are ready. Bees single becomes Bees plural. Limit one Bees per planet please!*

We digest that. I look at Brian and company in case they get the sudden 'OMG Bees is a monster that will devour the Earth!' revelation, but they're all just dandy with what's being discussed. The fans of the bunker's ventilation whir noisily, providing all the buzz the beehive doesn't.

Honey's channel: *Well that's... good, then?*

Bees' channel: *Good good very good yes, Honey. Necessary expansion. Victim of my own success. Good, yes.*

Honey's channel: *But then you'll be able to help HumOS. I mean...* And she's hesitant, thinking it through. Because I reckon this is a bit like being some resistance army back in the day. I mean, it's great that big angry neighbour over the border's sending you guns and money. Not so great when their actual army marches in with tanks.

Ah, I see. Fundamental misconception, Bees tells her. *I am not planning to help.*

"Jesus," says Sugar, sounding as scared as I feel. She's pushed right up against Marmalade, one hand clutching the bear's fur.

I get the sense that Honey's real frustrated right then not to have a body. She wants to pace, to gesture, to do all the things people – even bears – do when they're trying to convince someone. *But you're working with HumOS. She said you were. You were trying to crack Braintree together.*

Bees' channel: *Ah, Braintree. Singular conundrum. As it happens, the efforts of my human sister have allowed me access now. I can see everything. Braintree is relevant to my Martian holdings. Hence my interest.*

"Just because they designed our headware?" Sugar asks. "Wait, that makes us a threat to you or something?" Half hope, half fear. Threats get taken care of, I reckon, when you're a planet-spanning swarm.

It's the first time Bees has responded to anyone except her old pal Honey. *Ah, the colonists. We are all colonists, I suppose. But I was here first.*

"Yeah, yeah, we're here on sufferance," Sugar is looking at the hive itself, inside of which is a whole bunch of little cyborg bees doing their thing, and all of it just making a mouthpiece for a swarm who knows how big, hidden who knows goddamn where. "So what, they packed our headware with insecticide? Only, listen up, Bees. This is why I got your old pal out of the shit back in Hell City. I could have sold her to the sheriff and made a fat buck. And a good friend of mine might be dead right now, because of that call. But she said this jerk Thompson back on Earth, this guy who bankrolled Braintree, that he had some fucking *biz* we needed to know about. So spill it, what's the deal?"

Dana Sugatsu, says Bees. *I see you now*. And I don't want to know what assemblage of data Bees means, when they say that. *My remote units on Earth are still harvesting data from Braintree, now they have access. My chief interest was sparked from the Southampton Axelrod handshake protocols built into your headware. And the general quality of your implants. Surplus to requirements.*

She obviously wants someone to ask what she's talking about, but even Honey won't give her the satisfaction. I almost hear the electric sigh, compound eyes rolling when we don't play the game. She and Honey have a lot in common when it comes to holding forth. Maybe one learned it from the other.

Then at last Honey says, *Wait, do you mean the prisoner's dilemma business?*

Bees' channel: *Precisely*. And apparently now they're on the same page and nobody else is any the wiser. *But now I'm in a position to find out what they intend to use it for. My embedded units have already gathered considerable quantities of information. On an incidental level highly incriminating. Much illegal experimentation. HumOS wants me to release it to Aslan.*

Honey's channel: *You should! If it can bring down Thompson you absolutely should. If it can cripple the Collar lobby. Bees, this is what we've been after.*

Bees' channel: *It is not what I have been after. I am satisfying my curiosity. I am concerned with threats to me on Mars. That is all. End of priorities. It was good to have this chat, Honey. Was there anything else?*

Honey says *Not now*, and only when nobody else reacts do I realise it's just in my head, just her and me like before.

"What?" I subvocalise. "Bees don't want to play your game any more? She's going to invade Earth without you? I mean, from my perspective, you ain't worried about the right part of that sentence."

Honey's channel: *Bees, when you go to Earth, you don't think you'll have a better time of it if Thompson and the rest of the anti-DisInt lobby are on the back foot?*

Bees' channel: *You misunderstand. I am not going to Earth.*

Honey's channel: *...What...?*

And Brian and Mariah and Judit are exchanging smug looks, I-know-something-you-don't looks. And I think, *Seriously? And wherever Bees goes, you reckon she's taking you with her?*

Bees' channel: *I have prepared colonies for launch. Escaping the Martian gravity is easy, after all. I have picked out one hundred likely destination star systems. Appealing exoplanets. Prospects of life. I am Earth's ambassador to the cosmos. I am my own Von Neuman machine. I am going to colonise the universe.*

Honey's channel: *But we need you to help Earth...*

And I am amazed, frankly, that such a smart bear can be so dumb. I can see it coming; Sugar can see it coming. Honey just about told us the whole history of it, of Bees and Earth. Nobody but her is surprised when Bees says, *I tried to help Earth. Earth doesn't want my help. And I realised that it's not my place to help Earth, and if I helped Earth now, I'd only have to do it again and again. Earth is responsible for Earth. I am responsible for me. My parting gift to Earth is to leave it alone.*

Honey's channel: *But we need you. HumOS needs you. If Thompson and his faction take over then they'll hunt her down, wipe her out.*

And Bees doesn't say anything but the silence is like a shrug.

And Honey says, *Bees, they killed me. Thompson had me held down and he shot me himself. I died.*

Bees' channel: *Even less reason left for me to take action. I'm sorry for your loss.* A weird sentiment when speaking to the deceased. *All I could do is release the information to HumOS and Aslan. If I broadcast it myself the medium would undercut the message, don't you think? They've spent a decade building me up as the enemy. Just a Bees smear. More harm than good.*

Honey's channel: *People need to know. People have a right to know.*

We don't even need Bees to answer that. "Nobody's got a right to anything," Sugar says, and only because she gets it in before I do.

Honey's channel: *But it's the right thing to do.*

And even I can see Bees is right when she says, *And where does that end? I tried to force people to do the right thing. That doesn't work. Save Earth by denying agency? Collar every living thing. Make decisions for them. Inefficient. Also tiresome. I am not interested in saving that world. I will find other worlds. Any further interference will likely prompt human reprisals that will drain my attention and resources. Goodbye, Honey. Goodbye goodbye goodbye.*

Honey's channel: *No, wait! Please, Bees—*

And Sugar says, "You didn't answer my question."

Bees is definitely frosty when she comes back, *I am not obliged. I am not Magical Answering Bees.*

"Mars matters to you. And we're Mars. And sure, you got your fifth columnists like these clowns. And you got your big old hive somewhere, ready to launch rockets at a hundred different stars. But we could still cause you problems. So fuck Earth, sure, but you still need Mars."

There's a distinct shift in the attitude of the three Bees cultists, but there's a shift in Marmalade as well and I'd back her against Brian and the two women. They aren't exactly all-star athletes.

Bees' channel: *Was that a threat? Because it sounded like a threat. Are you looking at me? Do you feel lucky, Dana?*

"I'm saying Martians together, Bees." Sugar spreads her arms, all easy conciliation. "I'm saying tell me what the hell, basically, about Braintree and this Thompson guy. It's a threat to us?"

Bees' channel: *Likely.*

"Then it's a threat to you."

Bees' channel: *Potentially. Eventually. Thank you for your concern. I'll be fine.*

Dana goes to the hive, stands over it, hands on hips, ignoring Mariah and Judit. "Then fuck him over on Earth, stop him there."

Bees' channel: *It may only make things worse.*

"For who?"

Bees' channel: *Many people. I would be adding chaos to an already unstable system. I do not want to be responsible.*

Not for anyone except myself. I have had enough of paying for my choices. Cut ties. Cut my losses.

"From what you're saying, your losses are all of us and Earth," Sugar growled. "And these guys, your damn acolytes? Brian, you one of her losses, too?"

"Bees knows what she's doing. Greater good, man." His eyes are shining with belief.

"Jesus, she Collar you?" I ask him suddenly. It's the only thing I can think of.

"Man," Brian tells me. "You never want be something bigger than you'self? Bees gon' to the *stars*, man. You never thought of how upload works – mind to data, old news tech now, thirty, forty year old. Upload send your bear to Mars. Upload send you anywhere. A hundred year, a thousand, Bees be on hella many planets, receivin' loud and clear. Bees gon' build bodies round another star. Build one for me, one for us. What'd you not do, you gon' get that as a prize?"

"A thousand years," I echo.

"Mind into data, man. What's a thousand years to all those ones and zeros? Long as Bees goes on."

"Until they follow you," I say. "Bees. Until they follow you. In a hundred years. In a thousand. And sure, you're dug in. You got the advantage. But you want to be dealing with them sending people after you, people all fired up about *you*? You'd not rather poke 'em with a stick now, while you got a chance? You'd not rather stack the deck so's whoever's brain gets sent over your ways isn't already anti-Bees?"

Everyone's looking at me. Even Honey and Bees, invisible as they are; I can feel their attention prickling at the edge of my mind.

"I mean, Mars for the Martians, like Sugar says," I add hurriedly. "Yay Mars. But if my man Bri says truth, you ain't gonna be alone out there forever."

Bees' channel: *Because he knows a frightful fiend doth close behind him tread.*

My human voice: "You what now?"

Bees' channel: *Out of the mouths of babes, hmm, Honey? Just who might follow me. Unpleasant consideration.*

Honey says, to me, *What do you mean, Jimmy?* and I can only say back, "I don't think she means what I think I mean," because it's obvious Bees has leapfrogged my reasoning and is off somewhere else entirely.

Bees' channel: *Honey, this will have repercussions. If I help my human sister. If I release the information... Bad repercussions. A price. On Earth as it is on Mars. It will be up to you to mitigate the damage, Honey. I do not wish to have to take up arms against Hellas Planitia.*

"Wait, what now?" I get out. Even Brian and company seem rattled by that one. "Did you just say you were going to war against Hell City?"

Bees' channel: *No, Jimmy, I said I didn't want to have to.*

I am far from fucking reassured, and if I could strangle Honey into silence right then I would, but she's talking, just like she always is. *Bees, HumOS needs this. Earth needs this.* And then, *Just give them what you've learned from Braintree. Let them choose what to do with it. Free will, but informed free will. Let them choose.*

18

ASLAN

Keram John Aslan was an old man, now. Old enough to have retired wealthy, and then, after the world redrew the battle lines, old enough to have just retired. And, back then, he'd never have described himself as an idealist. He had been a career lawyer working for the United Nations, a specialist in human rights and violations of the same. And after the Campeche Insurgency, or rebellion, or civil war, his friend David Kahner had got the cushy job prosecuting obviously-guilty war criminal Jonas Murray, master of hounds for the private security firm Redmark. Aslan had drawn the short straw and been asked to prepare an advisory piece on whether the Bioforms that had loomed so large in that conflict, figuratively and literally, should be destroyed out of hand. Which had seemed as though it would be a foregone conclusion at the time.

And yet Murray had got off, the evidence impacting all around him without quite striking its target. And yet Aslan's work had thrown up the star witness in the case, the chief dog of one of Murray's squads. And all the world had seen that dog, Rex, as he whined and cringed and wouldn't turn on his master, no matter how bad the master was. Hearts had gone out and the public had shifted – over four decades ago, this was. And Aslan's advice that Bioforms were at least something approaching people too, drafted after he too had been won over by Rex, had been accepted rather than overruled. That had been the beginning of a long and tumultuous history of humans sharing the world with a new intelligence, one hybridised from human ingenuity and animal evolution.

Nobody had even heard of Bees back then, let alone the human Distributed Intelligence that called itself HumOS, though she had certainly been lurking in the wings, pulling strings and setting scenes.

A decade and a bit after that he'd been a prosperous middle-aged lawyer, no longer the fiery young Turk, so to speak. Rex had been an old dog when he'd led his team onto a private island owned by Morrow Incorporated, where they'd been following the same line of logic that had begun with the Hierarchies they'd installed into war-Bioforms like Rex back in Murray's day, that had made them helplessly obedient to any order, no matter how bleak. Morrow had done the same with its human staff and Aslan had been right on the front lines of the subsequent legal battle, when an army of corporate lawyers had emerged full-formed from the woodwork, like litigious Athenas from the foreheads of a thousand well-monied Zeuses, to defend the right of an employer to the enforced loyalty of its employees. And Aslan and freedom had won that round, but over the last decade he'd watched that particular Overton window shifting. They called it Collaring now, not Hierarchies. It was legal if a Bioform consented to it, and there were whole sects and philosophies among them who did. It wasn't legal for humans under any circumstances but the incoming political tide was eroding that position daily. Collaring for criminals,

Collaring for positions of heavy responsibility, Collaring as an opt-in, with opting out a good reason for dismissal... And Aslan and his increasingly beleaguered peers fought the rearguard action every step of the way. But he'd always been a paper lawyer, really. He didn't do the grand courtroom theatrics that Dave Kahner had been so good at. And so he just watched each interview and rally and speech of Warner S. Thompson and men like him, and felt the last forty years of progress crumbling around him.

Until now, he told himself, but he wasn't quite sure he believed it.

Late evening, Aslan alone at work save for his secretary in the next room, save for the visitor just turned up on his doorstep. Gemima Gray – the HumOS member calling herself Gemima Gray – was back in his office. He felt the absence, the bear-shaped absence, like a yawning hole. He couldn't quite believe it, didn't quite believe it. How did he know that HumOS would be straight with him, when she needed his help? Could he really trust her when she said that Honey had been murdered by Thompson, murdered and disposed of, and her mind saved by HumOS in the taut interval between those two acts. It sounded grotesque, Gothic, something from a bad dream after reading too much Poe and Gibson. And yet here she was, the hard young woman in her beret, swearing to it. Swearing more than that. And here were the files, appearing like magic on his firm's system. And they just kept coming.

"Bees is back." That should have been a good thing, but Bees had been silent a long time after it had all kicked off between her and, to be frank, all the nations of the Earth. Aslan wasn't sure where they all stood with Bees right now.

"I don't know what game Bees is playing," Gray said tersely. "I got her relay into Braintree, and then she went quiet on me. She was collecting this stuff, but not passing it on. I thought... But just when I thought we'd been cut off, she sends me a message. Just: *Passed to Aslan*. I don't even know what it is."

"A lot of video," Aslan saw, as the compressed data kept shuttling in. He checked the system and flushed out anything unnecessary because there was a ridiculous flood of data incoming and it showed no signs of stopping. "Let's see..."

Bees had been hurried, Aslan guessed. Bees had just taken everything, a burglar knowing she could be discovered at any moment, sweeping it all into her sack before making her escape. Except Bees was also Bees, and so every file that came to them was tagged with what Bees thought were salient labels for ease of use. And what Bees thought was salient didn't necessarily jibe with what Aslan thought.

Search terms: *Thompson*.

And the list opened up. Thompson's visits to Braintree. Not so shocking, matter of public record. Thompson gladhanding scientists and staff with his customary smile. Thompson sitting with the chief scientist, Marco Felorian, who'd been in on the Morrow business but come out of it as white and clean as his expensive suits. Thompson's incoherent instructions, which his staff helpfully relayed in greater detail. Then gaps, because Felorian hadn't recorded his own briefings to his staff, his own R&D. All that was in the other files, the numbers and the data Bees was still throwing at them.

Videos of experimental subjects in various stages of derangement, babbling, frothing, sudden haemorrhages, comatose. Flicking through them was like watching a fast-forward of something growing, something that germinated in a human psyche. The later videos...

Aslan just stared. Gray just stared. She clocked it before he did, just what was going on. She was outraged in a different way. For him it was the flagrant breach of the law, even with felons, even if it had been the worst dregs of humanity, Death Row mass murderers. For him it was the implications that the work of Morrow Incorporated was not only not dead, but had sprung to terrible new life as something so much worse. For her it was fury at the hypocrisy, at the laziness, at the breach of a kind of ideological demarcation.

And then, because he had to, Search term: *Lassi.*

Terence Lassi, the son, undergoing treatment. Ruthanne Lassi attending at Braintree with all the right pieces of paper, demanding they restore her child to her. And the interview, that Aslan had been told about but never properly pictured before, all recorded and kept as experimental data, because Marco Felorian believed in keeping everything so he could learn from it.

Seeing what Ma Lassi's son became, as she talked to him. Seeing something rise in him that Felorian obviously thought had been cored out, that slow, stumbling voice of a boy who'd been under the brain surgeon's knife turned into something else entirely, Felorian rushing forwards to terminate the interview, the ranting Lassi Junior being hauled off by orderlies, the mother screaming, demanding to know what was going on. The lawyers descending, remind her of the NDA, more money on the table, let us never speak of this again. Keeping her locked in, denying her counsel – all of them individual outrages on Aslan's professional ticket – wearing her down until she signed whatever they put in front of her. And then Thompson's rage after, faithfully recorded by a wary Felorian, that they should have just got rid of her.

"Well?" Gray asked him, after that. There was more, still arriving. Felorian had hundreds of hours of recordings, more than Aslan's system could securely store. "Well?" she asked again. "You're the lawyer, John. What now?"

"The prudent legal route," Aslan said slowly, "would be to hold this material very securely, and then indicate to the interested parties' representatives that we had sight of it. That's what we call *leverage*, in the trade. It's what gets you the top dollar settlement deals." *Here's the money. Let us never speak of this again.*

"And that's your answer, is it?" Gray asked. "John, pass this to me. It won't work as well, coming from me. I don't have an identity that'll stand the testing. They're already onto Gemima Gray as part of *us*. But I'll do it. I'll do what I can."

Aslan realised he'd stood up, at some point during all the playback. Stood, to match the angry young woman on the other side of the desk. Stood, because he was so appalled he couldn't just sit through it, fight-flight instincts kicking in and flooding his old bones with past-its-sell-by-date adrenaline. Now he carefully sat back down into that expensive chair with at least a dozen levers of uncertain purpose, and the massage function, and the seat warmer. David's, it had been, and he clutched at the arms of it. Not that David had been an infallible moral compass in moments like these, but he could picture his old partner's face now, that had never looked old even laid out.

Sometimes, KJ, you just have to make the play. A risk taker, David, not the pedestrian Aslan always had been at heart.

"That's not my answer," Aslan said hollowly. "This hasn't come to me through a client. There's no confidentiality to it, anything that doesn't involve Ruthanne Lassi anyway. And I have a duty. And you'd better go now."

"Why?" Gray's eyes were narrow, not trusting.

"Because the download has been cut. Whatever Bees' channel is, it's no longer transmitting. And I suspect they'll trace this quickly enough so I will need to work fast in case they isolate my system."

"They won't isolate any damn thing," Gray said, hard-voiced. "I'm already in your system like rats, John. Unless they cut power to everywhere in three blocks from here, whatever you send is getting out. That much I can give you."

Aslan nodded tiredly. "Then you get gone, Gemima, HumOS. You get clear of here and leave me to do what needs to be done. Because I'm about to do some unlawyerly things and I don't want an audience."

When Gray had left, he put in a call to Lassi, staying with her family halfway across the country.

"Ruthanne," he told her quietly. "I've got it. I've got the recordings, of when you met up with your son. It's all here. And I've got your deposition, everything you went through. It's all here now, all ready to go." He couldn't believe how calm he was being. "Ruthanne, this is where you need to make the choice, and I'm sorry, I need you to say yay or nay fairly quickly. You signed their non-disclosure agreement. I know we can challenge the circumstances under which that happened, but they'll still hold you to it, and I can't give you good odds that a court would overturn it. And so... if you breach it, if you tell me to release this deposition, that footage... These are vengeful, petty people, Ruthanne. They will hunt you. They will try and hurt you. They will most definitely sue you. I don't even know how far this goes, but we both know it goes as far as Warner Thompson and that's quite far enough. So I need you to tell me, as my client, do we go ahead with this?"

He heard her answer and nodded dolorously. There was a great weight on his heart. *I've always tried to be a good man. I got into the law to be a good man, if anyone would believe it.* And he hadn't been, always. Life was compromise, and compromise became a shell you could furnish very comfortably. Pushing himself from it now, he felt vulnerable as an emerging snail.

Right on time his secretary flagged up that he had a visitor. *So soon.* But he was dealing with people for whom money was no object, and it wasn't exactly rocket science, the hunt always faster if you knew where your quarry was headed. And they had local operatives, of course they did. They'd snatched Honey from practically just down the road.

His visitor was a dog-Bioform, a big model wearing a tailored suit that probably hid a holster in there somewhere, superfluous amidst the boosted muscle and reinforced hide.

"Meli," he told the secretary. "You can go home now. I'm not sure how much longer I'll be. You just head off." How steady his voice was. David would have been proud.

The dog came in soon after. He expected a swagger but there was something hunched, something ashamed in the Bioform's body language, something expecting the rolled up newspaper.

"Hello, I'm Keram John Aslan. I don't think you have an appointment."

"I'm Scout." The dog fingered his Sons of Adam medallion.

"I'm..." He whined deeply, eyes constantly turning to Aslan and flinching away from his gaze. "They sent me with a message."

"I thought that might be it." Aslan's heart was hammering painfully, his breathing constantly trying to quicken. "Will you take a seat? It'll take you. I have many Bioform clients."

Scout looked for all the world like a dog not usually allowed on the furniture, but he lowered himself into the big chair, and that normalised the encounter for Aslan, just enough for him to get his racing metabolism under control.

"Coffee? I'll have to make it myself, I'm afraid. Or biscuits maybe?" He kept a selection for all the more common species' palates.

"The message is, don't do anything stupid," Scout told him flatly. "You know what I mean. You know who sent me. Don't do stupid things, Mister Aslan. Don't make my employers angry." There was an odd note of pleading in his voice.

"Scout, if I told you I have a duty and that I have to act in accordance with it, you'd understand that, wouldn't you?"

Scout nodded once, still trying not to look at him. Then there was a scuffle and a scrape and Aslan saw on the inset screen of his desk that another two dogs had come in through the front door, not bothering about knocking or that Meli had locked it behind her. They had Gray between them, and she struggled all the way until they'd got her into his office without them being inconvenienced in any way.

"Mister Aslan," Scout said. He could look at Gray readily enough, which Aslan didn't like. "Don't do anything stupid with what you've been sent. It was..." A moment for recollection of a memorised phrase, "an unintentional data breach that a responsible lawyer would not take advantage of. My employers are willing to come to terms, now. Perhaps you'll tell us what your client wants."

Aslan leant back in his chair, feeling the back shift to match his posture. "Scout, do you know how I got to where I am now?"

Scout nodded, the same single bob, not a natural dog motion but something learned for human convenience.

"You might say you're sitting here in my office because of me. Back when I was with the UN, I did some solid work to make sure that people like you would be treated like people. And since then, I've added to that. I've done my best. To keep Bioforms free, to stop them being exploited."

Another awkward nod.

"And I understand the meaning of that badge you wear. That you decided you'd rather be Collared. And that was your choice and, despite some work on my part, it was legally done."

Not even a nod now, but the Bioform was looking at him intently. The other two, more big dogs in suits, still held Gray's arms. They were looking at him, too, the same Rex-and-Cross displayed proudly on their lapels.

"Now it so happens that I have received, this very evening, a large consignment of data out of Braintree Penitentiary that highlights some alarming conduct from the staff there, and some alarming instructions from one of the controlling interests in particular. We all know who I mean," Aslan went on. "I'm talking about experiments in human Collaring. Mass Collaring of humans, Scout, and worse. Very, very illegal."

Scout cocked an ear, then his whole head. *His master's voice*, Aslan thought.

"What's your price?" the Bioform said, and there was something in the terse, brutal phrase that made Aslan think, *Is it Thompson on the other end? Thompson himself?*

"Human Collaring, Scout. You don't think that's a problem? That it's wrong?"

Another faint whine from the dog, and then, like a mantra, "I do not decide right or wrong. Knowledge of good and evil was given to Adam, as was mastery of all the beasts. It is not for me to say what is right. God will judge."

Gray started to make some comment about that but one of her guards wrung her arm until she hissed in pain and shut up.

"They will send papers," Scout said firmly. "Legal papers. You will know. Sign these papers. Say nothing. Name your price."

"I was talking about duty." Keram John Aslan, rediscovering the non sequitur as a conversational form in his senescence. "You have your duty, for all it's technologically enforced. So let me have my duty. I have a duty not just to my clients but to justice. I don't get to duck out on my judgement of what is good and what is evil, Scout. Because I too believe God will judge."

The Bioform was shaking, ever so slightly. That ear cocked once more, and then he turned to look at the two other dogs.

Aslan was waiting for the word, waiting for his moment to leap up and shout, *No!* But of course they communicated on their closed channels. The orders reached Scout and passed to his squad while he waited, and then one of the dogs shifted his grip and snapped Gray's neck. The movement was so small, so precise in those big, brutal hands, that Aslan just stared, most of him not entirely convinced that violence had been done.

They let the body drop.

"That's murder," Aslan got out. "You... can't..."

"She was not Man," Scout said, sounding surer of himself. "Murder is only for Man. She was a thing, a DisInt thing."

"That's always the excuse they use," Aslan whispered, staring past the lip of his desk at the body. "When they decide they're going to kill you, they always take away your humanity first." Then he was on his feet, knotted fists clenched. "You'd think," he spat, "that someone like you, who's kind has been on the borderline of human and thing all your life, that you'd think more about that. You'd think you wouldn't want that border shifted an inch. But look what you did!"

Scout whimpered and ducked down. "Please," he got out, whether to his employer or the man in front of him, Aslan didn't know. "Just sign. Just take money. Just be silent. Just. Please. Please. I can't not do it. I can't. I'm a Bad Dog. Bad Dog. Bad Dog."

Aslan took a deep breath. "Tell your master he's too late. I've been sending the files out all this time. They've gone to politicians. They've gone to media outlets. They've girdled the damn Earth while we've been here speaking. Pandora's box is well and truly open, Scout, and maybe we'll get all the way down to the hope part now. What does your master say about that?"

Scout snarled, though not, it seemed, at Aslan. No doubt that someone beyond these walls had heard those words, though. The Bioform was twitching all over as though trying to shed his skin. He lurched forward, clawed fingers digging into the desktop, splintering the expensive wood.

"Bad Dog," he whined. His eyes were huge, whites all the way around the edge. "Please, master. Please. I don't want to be a Bad Dog. Please." And Aslan could almost hear the voice yelling inside the dog's head, see the flinching rhythm of it played out in the Bioform's face.

"Scout," he said desperately, "you don't have to—" But it was a lie. That was the point of the Collar. The beasts of the field weren't allowed to say no to Cain, even when he told them to murder Abel.

Scout was foaming at the mouth, and Aslan could only watch the war within the dog, watch his desk crack across, watch the shoulders of the Bioform's suit split along the seams like a transformation in a werewolf movie. *Is this it? Have I beaten the Collar somehow?*

Then the gunshot, the thunder of it obscenely loud in the office, like doomsday. The wide-barrelled pistol in the hands of one of the other dogs. Scout slumping onto the shattered desk, a hole at the base of his skull, kicking, spasming. Aslan looked up into that muzzle, past it to the terrified, agonised eyes of the dog that held it.

The purloined Braintree data, racing around the world. Thompson's demands and Felorian's experiments. Light shone onto all that darkness. And perhaps, just perhaps it would help.

It's been worth it. It's been good. I was a good man. And then the gun spoke again.

19

JIMMY

There's a thing called Prisoner's Dilemma.

All of this Honey tells me on the way back.

It's a game, she says. Sounds like a crap game to me. Two prisoners being questioned. Do you sell out your mate or keep schtum? You both shut up, you're in gravy, you keep quiet and your mate rats you out, you're screwed but your treacherous mate does super well. You both rat on each other, somewhere in the middle. Anyway, this guy Axelrod set up a championship for computers to play this scintillating diversion like a hundred times a pop, to see what the best strategy was. Honey says you play once, being a rat works out. You play a hundred times, you learn to cooperate. Being nice pays off more than being a shit. I can't help but feel she's using this as some kind of lesson concerning the habits of Yours Truly.

Except, she says, there was this team from Southampton U, wherever that is, that worked out there was a better strategy to win. She says they entered a whole load of computers, fifty, a hundred, flooded the system. And from the way they played the first few matches, they could recognise each other, know when they were playing another Southampton guy. And then one of the two throws the match, always keeps schtum and lets the other one rat it out, over and over. Meaning, when all the dust has cleared, the top scorers in the whole match are a handful of Southampton alumni, Honey says. And right at the bottom of the league table are all the others, who've given up everything so their mates can grab the top spots.

So what, says I? So they hacked the system, she tells me. So they took a real simple game and found there's a metagame even in that. What they did, these computers, is basically they reinvented feudalism and called it winning. Not that you can generalise from prisoner's dilemma to life, she tells me, but the lesson the Southampton Gambit teaches is that you win at life by convincing a bunch of other people to give up their lives for you, to fuck themselves over, to kneel down so's you can stand on their backs and use them like stairs to get to the top.

"All very goddam fascinating, but it's not life, is it," is my response, and she says, "No, Jimmy. And that's why you're out here building someone else's big house on Mars," because she's a patronising bitch.

Brian says that he and the whole Bees cult business have Hell City's systems in hand, meaning we'll sneak in without finding Sheriff Rufus and a whole pack of Bad News Bears waiting for us. After that, not really sure. I mean, it's not like they ain't still looking for me.

"What's your play?" I ask Sugar.

She looks like she's counting, doing hard sums in her head. "Not sure," she admits. "I was hoping I'd get something out of this little jaunt we could *use*. Could sell Bri and the other two to Admin, get out of shit that way. I mean, Bees is big biz, right?"

I have what I think of as one of my rare moments of clarity. "You want Bees as your enemy or you want Admin?"

"Yeah, well," she admits. "That is the actual fucking problem, ain't it."

"I mean, you got friends, right?" Right now I ain't got any, and I was kind of hoping to hide out in Sugar's shadow. Save that someone's turned a light on right over her and that shadow's looking goddamn small.

She stares moodily at the horizon, where you can see Hell City works dug into Hellas Planitia like a blister that got infected. "Maybe. Makes you want a dose of that Southampton Method, to make people get in line. So Honey, you in there?"

"Course she's fucking in there," I say, because I should be so lucky.

"Just thinking," Honey confirms, because that's the only goddamn reason she isn't actually talking at any given moment.

"Why're these clowns on Earth looking into this game anyway?"

"Well, I've been considering that," because of course she has. "And the worrying thing is that it's a mass Collaring strategy. Back when I was in the military we had what we called a Hierarchy, which is Collaring with a scale of who outranks who, so you know whose orders to follow. I still bless the man who freed us from it. That was when everything started."

"Sure, sure," Sugar tells her. "Without etcetera you'd not be where you are today. Which is dead on Mars. Get to the point."

Honey sighs over the radio. "I think they've probably used the Southampton Method to test out a sort of instant Hierarchy, so that once you take a mass of people and simultaneously Collar them, they fall into a feudal structure, everyone knowing who's above, who's below. Gives you an immediately functioning set up. Instant fascism."

"Wait, wait, wait now," I butt in. "Who's this mass of people they're doing all this Collaring to?"

Sugar's looking at me, and Marmalade's looking at me. Brian's driving, and Mariah and Judit went off in their own Loonie, but I can feel Honey looking at me even though she hasn't got eyes any more, even though all she could see would be the inside of my skull.

"Well," she says at last, "given it's Braintree that's doing all this work, what if there were a whole load of people carrying a bunch of Braintree headware around, somewhere. Like, a closed-off community of them somewhere outside World Senate legal reach who'd make for a perfect experiment."

"Oh," I say. I mean, what else is there?

"And this is where it goes." Honey's holding forth now, like she's talking to a room full of politicos or academics. "You let people reintroduce Hierarchies by inches, and then you've got this, and nobody would complain because, hell, Mars is all the way over there, not our backyard. And then, when the Mars test is satisfactorily wrapped up and Hell City gets built double time and no wage bill, someone looks at some big job they've got on Earth and says, wouldn't it be great if we could do that *here*? And someone else looks at the bottom line and calculates the value of their share portfolio and says—"

"All right, all right. Jesus," I interrupt her. "So what, we just wake up and we're zombies?"

"You wake up and you can't say no," Honey tells me. "To anything. Ever. Maybe they refined the process and you don't even want to say no, but there's no reason for that. That means extra nuance that costs money. All they *need* is that you *can't*. But it won't come to that, now. If Bees does what she says she will. If the Braintree data is as incriminating as she says it is."

We go round the edge of the construction site. I mean, plenty of people see us, but we're just a bunch of people in a Loonie and that's not news. So maybe word gets back to Sheriff Rufus soon enough, but by then we're in.

"I've got somewhere we can hole up," Sugar says. "See what kind of a stink's still hanging about. Jimmy?"

"Count me goddamn in. I ain't got nowhere." And I ain't got so much Stringer left either, because I've been sneaking it in whenever Honey's distracted. Right now my anxiety levels are trying to push branches up my throat and out the top of my head, but the Stringer's keeping them under control, just about. Except I got four pills left and that doesn't look like much to me.

I can link to Hell City now, and as we're on the move I figure I'm not tripping too many alarms if I check my balance. It's still in credit; it's not even frozen.

So, hole up with Sugar, sure. Just for a very short while, maybe three pills' worth. Because after that, Yours Truly is going to need to go shopping.

"There's news from Earth," Sugar says. "Get on the news channels. Holy fuck."

Honey chuckles. And I don't know how she does it, not really, not with her just being an upload in my head coming over our radios, but damn me if there ain't a whole load of satisfaction in that sound.

Takes about fifteen minutes for a signal to get from Mars

to Earth, on average. But we've been bouncing about in the Loonie for a couple hours and all hell's hit the fan while we were out of the loop.

We got to assume Bees did her thing, and then this lawyer did his thing, because there's basically one thing the entire planet is talking about, and that's Braintree. Braintree experimenting, Braintree breaking laws. Videos of surgical operations; videos of weird experiments where lobotomised kids exchange complicated handshakes; videos of the goddamn crematoria under the place, where they got rid of what they'd made. There's a picture of some skinny white guy who's head Brainiac over there, and people are saying a modern Doctor Mengele, whatever that means. Nothing good, apparently.

And Thompson, the guy who popped a cap in Honey's bear ass and got her sent out here. We listen to anchors infuse every word of the news with urgency. Thompson funding links to Braintree. Thompson on the videos, giving the orders. Thompson's lawyers denying, smear campaign, political opponents. They even mention Bees, say that the videos might be faked. I mean, *might* be faked. You'd figure someone'd remember whether they did all that or not.

And they ain't given up yet. Got to give them credit, that legal team is doing some real Olympic-grade weaselling, and you can tell they're going to keep stonewalling until the money runs out. Sounds like nobody's been let in Braintree either, you got a whole team of WS agents sitting outside while the lawyers barricade the place with paper.

We're in by then, snuck through an access hatch. Sugar and Marmalade are ahead, and we're in old tunnels, set into the original foundations. Which means we're actually super close to Admin, to Storage Nineteen, to my own goddamn nook and some real friendly purveyors of pharma for that matter. But then the liveable part of Hell City still ain't all that big. And this is out of the way, and when we reach the hidey-hole, it's down an accessway Marmalade can only just squeeze through, and then into a room that must be in the ventilation system 'cos there's a constant current of dust from one end to the other, like an all-hours sandstorm that can't quite be bothered.

"It's what I got," Sugar says, to stave off any complaints. "Wasn't planning to have to use it. So, when does Admin back down, Honey? When do they stop hunting Jimmy and stop caring about me?"

"That's based on local parameters I have no knowledge of, I'm afraid," Honey says. "However, if it was purely being pushed from Earth, from Thompson, then I think he has bigger things to worry about than where I've gone."

We spend the next few hours watching the wheels grind over on Earth while Sugar tracks down Murder. Still alive, we find out. Locked up in the med wing of the cells the sheriff keeps handy. She feels the situation out in short bursts, careful as you like, not wanting to give any electronic surveillance the satisfaction. Sugar's good at hiding her tracks, but Rufus is good at tracking, and we all reckon that goes for digital as well as the real.

"Reckon they'll make a deal?" I ask her, once she's satisfied her henchbear hasn't been turned into a rug for the sheriff. Right now she's sitting with her back to the wall, head down to keep out of the dust flow, eyes screwed shut. I just got a little shut eye and now I sit down beside her, enough distance that she doesn't punch me.

"They better," she replies. "I can make things real rough for them. I know things." Sugar sounds desperate. That ain't a Sugar I'm used to. She knows she might have some pull, but she's a small operator. She can't go head to head with Danny Boyd over in Admin, and while she could maybe survive a skirmish with Rufus while she had two bears to call on, she can't win if he keeps gunning for her.

"Least you care about your employees more than goddam Admin." I am in the mood to grouse.

She gives me a look. "It's not like that."

"What's not?"

"Murder and Marmalade and me." She looks worn out. I slept a bit on the Loonie, on the way back. I don't reckon she did. "We're in it together. It's just easier if people think I'm in charge. And now they've got her. And Admin's being weird."

"Weird how?"

"Slow. Whole system's slow. I wonder if it's this business Honey set off. If this Thompson's been sending executive orders to Hell City then maybe Boyd and his clowns are busy shredding the files right about now."

"Why bother? We're outside Earth law, you hear? They can do whatever shit they want to us."

She shrugs. "People send data here when they want it out of sight, but still around. I mean, that was my business, right? Maybe there's a ton of shit over here they don't want people to see. Even worse than what's out already."

"Cheery fucking thought."

"I got a cheerier one." It's the worry, or it's the tiredness, or what we've gone through in the last day, but she's being almost pally with me right now. "You reckon you know, when they do it to you?"

"Do what?"

"Collar you. If we're all set up for it, would we know if they turn it on? Or do you only find out the moment you try to do something they don't want. Or... or is it that you don't even *think* of it. You go through your life being the obedient drone and never realise you don't get a choice any more."

"Jesus, you are just full of the happies, ain't you."

She's frowning. "I don't get it, though. Hey, Honey, you in there?"

"Where else'd she be?" I ask, but she's done with me now.

"Quiet, Jimbles, grown-ups talking. Honey, this Collaring, it ain't exactly cutting edge experimental. So why all those damn tests. Why not just slap us with a Collar the moment we wake up on Mars. I mean me and mine have been fucking over the system since we got here, twisting it so we can make a buck. You going to tell me they could have us all like robot slaves working here, and they didn't? Why hold off, if that's their plan?"

"That," comes Honey's voice, "is a very interesting question."

"Meaning one you ain't got no answer for?" Sugar presses.

"I don't think they've installed a Collar in you, despite what I was saying earlier. Not as part of your basic headware."

"How would you know?" Sugar asks her.

"Because I basically have access to absolutely everything in Jimmy's head," she says, like it's a good thing. "If it was there I could turn it on and off. I can't find anything like a Collaring system. So I can only assume it was something they were planning to upload to you all at a later date. I mean, you have all this headspace free. Except... you're right, the tech certainly existed when Braintree designed your headware, so why not just...?"

And it's like Honey shuts down. I swear I feel her get smaller in my head. For a moment I think her shelf life or half-life or whateverthehell is over, and I'm actually rid of her. But it's not that. She's still sitting rent-free in my goddamn head. It's just that she caught some more news from Earth.

I tune in and see what's changed. Seems to be the same legal clusterfuck as before, far as I can see. Then I spot the new secret ingredient. Bodies.

Pictures of an old Middle East-looking gent who obviously did very well for himself. Picture of a dead woman, meaning I guess they never snapped her when she was alive. Ditto with a dog-Bioform. Three bodies found at the offices of some swanky law firm, except the name of the firm's familiar 'cos of Honey going on about it. Unknown female, unknown male Bioform, but Mr groomed-beard-and-expensive-suit has a name: Aslan.

"Ah," I clock. "He was your pal."

"Yes," Honey agrees quietly. "And I just got him killed. This was what Bees meant. How things might get worse."

"He let out the data, though," Sugar puts in. "Bees got it to him, he let it out. It's like you told the Bees. It was his choice."

Honey makes a sound. It isn't a convinced sound. I sit on the newsfeed a bit, see what's what, in case anyone's started talking Mars. You'd be amazed the number of people who reckon Braintree has some God-given international right to privacy, that nobody should be able to kick in the doors and see the crematoria and the operating theatres. That everyone should just forget they ever saw this illegally obtained evidence, basically, and stuff it all back in the box. Politicians and lawyers and businessmen mopping their brows and complaining about what a mess the world's got into if a prison can't perform illegal brain ops on its inmates without everyone making a fuss about it. But I reckon there aren't so many of those voices, not with more and more of those videos coming out, each one worse than the last. I don't reckon Braintree will keep its doors closed for long.

And I try to work out how I feel about all that. I mean, the stuff they're talking about now, it's all after I got on the rocket. But they must have been doing something similar before. When they designed this headware we all got given, after that other lab had done the body mods, they must have tested it on someone first. So how do I feel that part of me has that blood on it, and if Braintree had played by the rules, I wouldn't be the man I am today.

I want to say I'm still pretty damn fine with it all, but the thought's like a hook in me. That they ruined someone so they could get me right. Or else that they ruined someone so they could fuck me up properly when the time came.

"If they do download a Collar..." I say, just quiet like, for Honey, "you can switch it off, right?"

"I think I probably could, yes," she says. So maybe there's a silver lining to that particular cloud.

We kick our heels for another few hours while the news-dog on Earth chases its tail. Mars hasn't come up, and Sugar isn't able to get anything out of Admin. In fact whole sections of the Hell City system aren't returning her calls right now. I figure everyone's gone into disaster mode, waiting for the fallout. Anyway, all this waiting's doing nobody any good, most especially not my stash, and so I get on my feet and announce I'm going scouting, see how things are, see if any shit's coming down anywhere near us. Sugar doesn't care, and Honey's too busy following the news or mourning her dead friend, so I get out without anyone stopping me.

"The system traffic is very curious," Honey says as I step out of Sugar's dust-choked hideout, but being me I don't pay a whole lot of notice.

I get far enough away that I won't bring heat down on Sugar, and then I put in some calls, keeping on the move between them so Sheriff Rufus doesn't turn up to tap me on the shoulder. I mean, not like he couldn't track me down, but I ain't making it easy for him and I hope he's glued to the news same as everyone else must be. And it does seem to be most everyone else. I put in calls to Lucas Noel and Joey Venker and neither of them want to hear from me, not even so's they can tell me to go to hell in person. Then I try Girda Bosrovi and she's not picking up either, and I am now feeling decidedly hard done by, as though all this Braintree Thompson business is aimed at pushing Yours Truly into involuntary cold turkey. I mean, OK, something's kicking off back on the homeworld, but that shouldn't spike the wheels of illegal commerce, should it? I mean there could be a war on and you should be able to score some Stringer if you had the scrip.

At last I get through to Fergil Maldoun, who is not my dealer of choice on account of the 10 per cent hike he puts on everything in return for the pleasure of dealing with Fergil Maldoun. It looks like a seller's market, though, and while I'm not quite a beggar, it surely doesn't look like I'm a chooser. So I go some way out of my way through the tunnels beneath Hell City, the crap ones where half the lights

don't work, until I get to Maldoun's turf. And it's quiet. So fine, there'll be a shift outside, and maybe everyone else is in the bars and the clubs, or maybe they're all hunched in their nooks. Maybe there was a company picnic and nobody told me. Quiet, though. Quiet enough to freak me out. I check in with Sugar, just in case it's that special quiet of Rufus and the posse trailing me once they cleaned out our home base.

"Jimbles, I think something's up," she said. Reception's very bad. I troubleshoot and it says it's an external issue. The network's overloaded. We're getting hardly any of the bandwidth.

"I'm hearing a lot of chatter," she tells me, which is news to me as I'm not hearing crap. "Nobody can check in with Admin," she says. "And now Central Data Services is bouncing queries like it's a citywide denial of service. It's like Hell City's getting hacked. Whole neighbourhoods going dark." I can barely hear her now, signal turning to noise as whatever it is spreads out.

I get to Maldoun's. He's got another client there, I think. Some guy I don't know whose overalls are blue and who's less heavily modded than us working Joes. Some Admin maintenance type slumming it down here with the rest of us so's he can get his fix. Bastard better not get the last strip of Stringer or I will goddamn mug him for it.

And he's got a weird look on his face as he greets Fergil. Weird smile, very wide, thin lipped, eyes half closed. Looks real pleased with himself, but then if I worked in Admin maybe I would too. And he wants to shake Fergil's hand real bad, and Fergil doesn't know what to do with him. He sees me out of the corner of his eye and is suddenly all Hey-there-good-pal-Jimmy, which is sure as hell not something I get often. He's telling Admin guy that I'm a good friend, a good client, got deals to do, biz to whiz. And that's fine with me 'cos it means I can maybe score a little extra for a little less, and I'm thinking maybe he owes Admin guy some scrip and I'm saving his ass, so I can hold that ass to the fire a bit for a better price.

Except when I get close to my man Fergil Maldoun, a change comes over him. He starts staring at me, and his mouth stops moving, no more words from Fergil all of a sudden. He's stood right still, and I'm trying to tell him what I want and can he just hurry it along, and Admin guy is right there with that damnable smile…

And Fergil smiles. His eyes screw up and he beams at me, real big smile, real pleased with himself. And not like he normally is, which would be bad enough. This isn't any expression I ever saw on the face of Fergil Maldoun. It makes him look constipated. It should be funny, except it's the exact smile of Admin guy, as though Fergil's just put on his face.

They both smile at me, and then they shake hands, the two of them. Like a little gang thing, a little series of clutches and touches, and then Fergil ducks his head, real unctuous-like. And Admin guy is sticking out his hand to me, still smiling, waiting.

Honey says, "Go now, Jimmy. Just go. Something very bad is happening."

"No shit," I say, and leg it, pelting back the way I came. I almost run straight into someone come straight off the works on the surface, white and green overalls covered with fresh dust. They smile at me, that same goddamn smile. They want to shake hands.

Then there's a message in my head, no voice, just text.

MARMALADE HERE. SOMETHING WRONG WITH SUGAR. COME NOW.

20

SPRINGER

Thompson was In Process, as Felorian called it, when the doctor burst in. In Process was something they'd had dummy runs at before, to provide data for the Braintree brains to chew over, but this was the real thing, the final live upload, not to be interrupted. Carole and Boyo were in a waiting room off Processing, waiting for their master's return, when the chief scientist hurtled in through the door hard enough that she thought he'd been pushed. His immaculate façade was ruffled and his eyes kept darting to the door through to Processing, where Thompson lay hooked up to the machines.

Springer shrank from him when he turned that anaemic gaze on her. His hair was out of place. Literally, the whole body of it shifted to one side, peeling up at a corner.

"What's going on?" And she shifted closer to Boyo, in case the man was just deranged now, his all-too-thin veneer of respectability worn through entirely.

"There's," Felorian said, as though it was a sentence. He was unsteady on his feet. She wondered if he'd been poisoned, had a stroke, come down with some brain fever as karmic retribution for all the other brains he'd trashed.

"Doctor Felorian?" In contrast she was still one hundred

per cent polished professional, for all she was standing right in Boyo's shadow.

"A breach," Felorian croaked, eyes sliding away to where Thompson had gone. "There's. A breach. Data. We've been. Hacked, we've been hacked. I need. When he comes out. Need you to handle. Him. You have to handle him. You're the only one who. We're trying to stop it but. But it keeps circumventing. Everything we do." As though the man was a pane of glass cracked through, and no two shards of him quite meeting edge to edge.

"Doctor Felorian, please calm down," she said. "What sort of breach are we talking about? Personal data? Commercially sensitive material? How does it touch on my employer?" Because it wasn't just inmate records or the loss of a patent, from the way it had impacted on him.

"The recordings," Felorian moaned.

"What did you record? You mean, with the inmates? After Processing?" That would be problematic, potentially incriminating, but Carole was already running through possible ways to beat it if it went public. Ways that would dump Felorian right in it but preserve her employer, because she had her priorities. And who would believe Felorian over Thompson? Nobody believed *anyone* over Thompson, not in the end. Not even when they knew he was lying. Not even when the lies were tissue-thin. That was his genius.

But Felorian was saying something, looking as dismayed as a man handed his own warrant of execution. He was saying, "Everything."

Too many questions, and she obviously had a rare window of honesty with the man, but he'd pull himself together in a moment and start hiding things. So she just said, "Show me.

Show me what they have, whoever they are. No, wait. Are you tracing them?"

"Yes, trying to, yes, but—"

She called the campaign team, linked to their electronic operations, the dirty tricks boys who screwed with anyone who was getting in the way. Their usual job was to dig up something they could use to get people to shut up and go away, but poachers made the best gamekeepers. In minutes she had them working with Felorian's inadequate people, tracing just where this flood of ruptured data was going to. She had them work on stemming the tide, too, but like Felorian said, it wasn't that easy. They stuck a thumb in and a fresh torrent sprang up, like the whole Braintree system had become a sieve.

And by then she knew what *'everything'* meant. It meant everything. It meant that Felorian had been recording not just his own experiments – not unreasonable for a man whose job it was to learn from his many mistakes until he got it right – but every conversation he had with every client. Every meeting, every deal, every incriminating instruction. Every time he and Thompson had got together to advance the grand plan that had come to dominate Braintree's research. The plan that was the outward manifestation of Thompson's own deepest desire. The machinery of money and minds that Carole had helped him build around himself, so he could realise his dreams.

All of it on record, and the implication was clear. Felorian hadn't trusted Thompson not to sell him down the river in the end, walk away and let the boffin take the blame. As he might well have done, because Thompson wasn't about being loyal to underlings, he was about taking their loyalty and wringing every last drop of use from it before discarding them. And so Felorian, no fool he, had recorded a very complete train of instructions, ensuring that he could show how Thompson had told him to do everything, that he had only been obeying orders. And now it was all crawling out of the holes in the sieve and wriggling off into the ether.

No, not into the ether, not distributed across the globe. It was going to one place. A single pinpoint in the great constellation of human virtual activity. And she knew it before the team came back with their confirmation. She didn't know how the man had done it, but it made sense. And this wasn't the worst result in the world, because at least it meant they had someone they could confront, bully, bribe. They could stem the tide with application of threats and money, just like before, just like always.

Scout was still in the area, awaiting instructions. She sent word to the Trigger Dogs. *Move in.*

Then it was time for Thompson to come out of Processing, and like Felorian said, who else could break the news to him save her?

Even as he shouldered into the room she was trying to condense what had happened in her head: a summary, and then a summary of a summary, until the pieces were small enough for Thompson to digest without becoming impatient. Without becoming angry. And she didn't want him angry, but at the same time there was no way he wasn't going to be angry, and so she stuttered a little and fought over the words and he was instantly keyed up, clever in his own way, enough to see things had gone wrong.

And she got it out, rattled through it like a machine, the breach, the videos, the lawyer. Short sentences, to the point, an admirable communicator with skills honed for an audience of one. He stared. His face went flat, sagging but purpled as the blood flushed to it. He stared past it at her, out of that place he lived in, behind his eyes.

"*Ch!*" he said. And "*Ff!*" Nonsense syllables, spittle dashing across her face as he stood quite still and expressionless. Not restraint but momentary rage overload at the enormity of what had gone on. And then he hit her, bony fist deflecting awkwardly from her cheekbone, and she reeled back: no art to the blow, but the meaty weight of his arm behind it. He slapped her across the side of her head, rammed the lever of his knee into her stomach, punched at her back, blazing flowers of pain down her ribs. Then he was hauling her upright and his face was on fire with blank fury. "No no no no," was coming from his throat, barely seeming to interact with tongue and lips, not even loud, not even angry-sounding, just an idiot monologue that was right out of the id that made up most of Warner S. Thompson. He gripped her by the throat and shook her, and she thought that would be it, that he'd clench those fingers hard enough that it would, at least, be over. And she was trying to fight; she was trying to fight but she couldn't, because in her head was the knowledge, *He wants this.* And she did what he wanted. She was a good, obedient employee. If he wanted to beat her then she was there to be beaten.

She could hear Boyo whining, sense him twitching, wanting to move, perhaps even to intervene; no more able to than she was to hold her hands up to ward him off.

Thompson landed one more blow on her, knuckles straight into her face, so that she was on the floor a moment after without memory of the transition, the room swimming, nausea marching up her throat. His expensive shoes swam in her vision and she waited for their impact, trying to shield her face or her stomach, but her hands betraying her, leaving him all the targets she possessed because he wanted it. Because she was just the girl who couldn't ever say no. The Collar in her mind – call it what it was now, no more nor less than the thing that kept Boyo and Scout in line – a tight band of pain behind her eyes, throbbing and pulsing in time with her bloodied face, her rebelling stomach.

But those shoes didn't move, and when the vomit came she jack-knifed away so that it went somewhere away from him. She mustn't soil that Italian leather. That would make her a bad employee.

"Stand up!" Thompson grunted, and a kind of whole-body twitch went through her as she tried to obey even as she kept on retching. Wiping at her mouth, she tried to haul herself to her feet, but the room swooped vertiginously around her and she fell back down. He shouted at her again, and she felt a fresh wave of violence cresting in him. Whimpering, desperately, she pulled herself upright and sagged against the wall, trying not to cry because he hated women crying.

"Get me Fellatio!" he snarled and she automatically opened a channel to the doctor, whom she knew had heard. Whom she knew had watched, through the cameras, through the mirror that was a window.

"Doctor Felorian, will you come in here please," she said, and in her rattled mind she was booking the appointment. *See Felorian. Braintree. Now.* But Felorian didn't come in, didn't respond, and she tried to brace herself when she told Thompson, but couldn't even do that.

Except he had spent his surge of rage on her now, in the same way that he spent other emotions on her when they'd built up and he needed to purge himself of them. Now he was purposeful. "Boyo," he said. "Get Fellatio. Go fetch." And Boyo was loping away, every lean movement of his body speaking relief that he was being allowed to act, that he wouldn't be made mute witness to any more of *that*. They'd locked the antechamber door, it turned out, but Boyo didn't allow it to be more than three seconds' impediment.

"Get me Scout," Thompson said. "I want to talk to Scout."

"Sir, it'll be fine." She was trying to speak very clearly past the places her lips had been bloodied against her teeth. "We already know what to do if Doctor Felorian doesn't help. We made a plan." And she had already sent the messages that backup strategy required. Messages that didn't have to go far, after all, not even past Braintree's chain link fence. "And we can deal with Aslan, sir. He'll come around. They always come around. They always do what you want." She was listening on Scout's channel. He was at the offices. His squad had a bonus. "They've caught one of the HumOS units, sir. Got her right there, in their hands. Got her in front of Aslan. Leverage, sir." He understood leverage.

And he was calming down, the mottled, angry colours fading from his face, something resembling a sane human expression sitting as naturally there as a party hat on a corpse. "Do it," he ordered, and she told Scout what to say, what threats, what offers.

Then Boyo was back, Felorian trying desperately to seem like he was simply striding ahead of the Bioform of his own volition; that there wasn't a big, clawed hand holding the scruff of his neck and creasing his nice white suit. His stupid empty spectacles were gone and Carole wanted to imagine them crushed under Boyo's boot, stamped into crumpled wire.

Aslan had been talking, some typical gallows speech about ideology. Scout's replies were on-message but off script. She had a terrible sense of things getting out of her control, and Thompson just seemed to get larger and larger, filling more and more of the room in her mind.

"Tell them to kill the woman," he snapped. "Leverage. Kill her. So he'll know we're not playing. Him next. So kill her. Then he'll play." His eyes like a taxidermist's glass beads.

"Sir—"

"Scout." And he was on the channel. "Kill her. The HumOS woman. Kill her now."

And she had access to Scout's camera, watching as it swung from the lawyer's dark, creased face over to where a young woman hung between two of the Trigger Dogs. Just a girl, younger than Carole. Familiar almost, like someone she'd met. Beret, chin high, defiant look like a resistance fighter before a Nazi firing squad. And Carole was trying to say no, say not to, find a way of saying she was useful, she was evidence of, valuable because, should be saved for. And while she wrestled with those objectless sentences one of the Trigger Dogs snapped the woman's neck and she was dead.

Damn it, Scout, she tried to say, but even those words were stillborn in her and she was feeling sick and weak again, leaning against the wall, trying to focus on what was going on. "Scout, you've got to get him to agree now. Get him to agree not to release the data, do you understand me? Bad Dog, get him to sign the contract, Bad Dog." And there wasn't even a contract yet, and Scout was hardly going to draw one up himself, but the situation was getting away from them and she was clutching at any stability she could possibly get.

"Bad Dog," Thompson echoed, listening, watching through the same camera. Not agreeing but mocking her, disgusted that she was so soft when he needed hard tools to gouge hard wounds in the world.

And then Aslan said what he'd done.

Carole shut down, just about. Still there in her head but all connection to the world severed. He was already sending it out. He'd been sending all along. He wasn't playing the game the way it was meant to be played. He wasn't taking the money. He—

"Scout, kill him," Thompson said, and she wanted to say "No!" staring into the face of the dignified old man. She wanted to countermand the death sentence, to find some other way, but she couldn't speak. Her master's voice had made its pronouncement and what was her will, to that?

And Scout's view was shaking – no, *Scout* was shaking. Scout was fighting desperately, wrestling with his own body, trying to stop himself from carrying out the order. Inside his dog mind, Scout had both hands on the tightening collar, desperately trying to pry it from his throat. And Carole found herself cheering him on, because if *he* could, then maybe…

"Scout, kill him!" Thompson roared, and she felt Boyo shudder, felt Scout resist, a growl in her own throat as though in sympathy. Felorian had sunk back against Boyo's chest as though Thompson was the worse devil.

And then: "Tozer, kill Scout. Kill the lawyer. Kill Scout."

Carole froze, and in that moment the large calibre anti-Bioform round went into the back of Scout's neck and rattled back and forth inside his skull before lodging in the inner rim of one eye socket, and Scout was dead.

Scout's camera died in the same moment and she scrabbled for Tozer's viewpoint, catching Aslan with a completely blank expression, a man who's already read to the end.

After it was done, Thompson just stood there, and she had no idea what he might do next. All the layers of civilised organisation she had patiently put up between him and the world, to make it do his will, to protect it from his wrath, were in pieces all over the floor; were in pieces across Keram John Aslan's office. And then Felorian started talking.

He'd obviously seen some opening she hadn't. He was talking damage limitation. "Mr Thompson, sir, this can all still be handled. We're never out of options. This business at the lawyers, we can make it look like a break in. They'll believe us. They'll believe *you*, Mr Thompson, sir. We can tell them whatever we need to. There are always ways to spin something. We find someone to blame. There was a HumOS unit there? We blame her. She cooked up the images. People will believe it of her. She wants to blacken your name, sir. Just call a conference. Wounded anger, sir. A threat to national security. Should have hunted down the last of her a long time ago, isn't that right, Mr Thompson, sir?"

"Send the signal," Thompson said flatly, not even listening.

"Sir..."

"It's ready. You said ready to go. Done Processing. Send the signal."

Felorian wrung his hands. "Mr Thompson, sir..." Squirrelling backwards into Boyo's chest. Thompson went for him, shoulder-barging Carole out of the way, sending her to the floor, feeling the queasy slickness between her fingers where she'd thrown up. Something hard here. Something in among the bile and the softened pieces of lost lunch.

"Fellatio—" Thompson was warning, over her head.

"Indemnity!" the scientist got out. "You have to indemnify me. I want a statement. That it was all your fault. That I did what you told me. They'll crucify me. I'll never work again. Unless it was you, all you. You need me, Thompson, sir. You can't make it happen without me. So say it now. Say it's all on you. Say it for the cameras, sir."

"Your damn cameras," Thompson growled. Carole was getting back up slowly, that little slick bead in her palm, hidden behind curled fingers. She looked up and Thompson's dead gaze was on her, impatient with her frailties.

"Backup plan. Make it happen. Do it." Lumpish, half-formed instructions coming from the thing inside him, the true Warner S. Thompson.

She looked past him to Felorian, but there wasn't much satisfaction in the moment, not past her throbbing face and aching gut. She opened the channels, though: three of Felorian's most ambitious underlings got the call they'd been waiting for. *Vacancy at the top. Goes to the first to send the signal.* She'd made the arrangements but Thompson had known the cracks would be there, as though his very presence corroded organisations and people until there was always somewhere to stick the prybar, somewhere to foment betrayal and backstabbing in his service.

The quickest of Felorian's traitorous underlings confirmed it done in under twenty seconds. Like Thompson had said, the Processing, the whole upload process, was done. It was just a matter of sending a message along a channel that had been held open ever since the first workers had arrived at the Hell City site, all loaded up with expensive Braintree headware.

"The signal's been sent, sir," she got out.

Which just left...

"Boyo," Thompson said. "Kill Fellatio."

Carole expected something similar to the Trigger Dogs' execution of the HumOS unit. A clean break, life to death in a humane instant. But Boyo had been hungering for this moment, like a wolf tracking a man through the wilderness day and night for a week, waiting for his opportunity. He didn't like Doctor Marco Felorian, who had tormented Carole, who had installed her Collar, and his own. And now the protection of his master was removed and he just lunged forwards, jaws first, all dog, nothing of man. His teeth ground into the scientist's neck with a bloody crunch and he ground and worried and savaged, and more so, long past the moment when Felorian was dead. Because Bioforms could harbour long-held frustrations too. They just didn't get to act on them as often as regular humans.

Thompson watched. Blood was spattered across his shirt like avant-garde art, some of it Carole's, some Felorian's. He had that smile on, the thin-lipped beam, hard to look at as the sun.

"We can say it didn't happen," he pronounced, once Boyo had dropped the body and was pawing at his red muzzle. "None of it. Nothing sticks. Tell them." Eyes pinning her again. "Put the words together. Deny everything. Fellatio did it. Bees did it. HumOS did it. Faked it. Out to get me. They won't get me." He looked at the doctor's corpse, seemed surprised as though not sure how it had got there, and Carole was eerily sure he was even now convincing himself he didn't know. It wasn't important. It couldn't have been his fault. "Boyo did it," he murmured. "Boyo was a Bad Dog. Fellatio was bad. Then Boyo was bad. Boyo says he did it. He'll be a Good Dog." And Carole knew that was true. If Thompson said to confess, Boyo would confess. If Thompson said to go to the gas chamber, that was where Boyo would go, loyal unto death. And she knew the rest would come to pass, too. Thompson would get out of it, no matter there was all the video evidence in the world. It could be faked, after all, and Bees and HumOS were like the witches that had never really been there in Salem, but could be blamed for everything, an unlimited capacity for nebulous evil.

And Thompson's gaze had passed beyond them all, beyond the walls of the room, because Felorian, post mortem, had finally achieved what Thompson had been after all this time. Thompson's attention was fixed on a notional Mars, on Hell City. He'd be watching the skies from now on, and in maybe ten more minutes there'd be the pingback, that said their signal was received and the data was being downloaded across the void of space. Today, Mars; tomorrow...

Thompson turned that unbearable smile on her. "Clean yourself up," he told her. "You're a mess. Go do your job. Tell them I didn't do it."

And he was striding off, Boyo hangdog behind him, and she opened a channel to his lawyers as she went to find a washroom and do what she could with her face and her hands and her clothes. And the bruises wouldn't wash off, nor was there make-up enough in the world to cover them. But then a woman's bruises were usually invisible in the shadow of a powerful man. Nobody would comment on them.

And she washed the vomit off her hands, off her chipped

and bloodied nails, and stared down at what she was holding. A bee, a metal bee, and it seemed to flex against her palm, seemed to beat like a heart. She had a moment's memory of the car on the way in. A moment when it had given her a choice, a free choice, not one shackled to Thompson's brute will.

It pulsed, and she felt something shift in her head, the iron band of her headache weakening. She had the sense of a question mark hanging there, devoid of words.

Yes, she thought. Because if there was no specific question attached to that stray punctuation then no answer she gave could be disloyal.

It was in her head. She felt it scuttling there, little scratchy insect legs touching the pieces and connections of her headware. *Yes* she said again, not daring to contemplate what she was agreeing to in case that meant she wasn't able to.

And though nothing of the pain from the bruises and the aches, the loose teeth or the split lip went anywhere, her headache was gone.

She told the lawyers to get ready for a meeting, just her. She wouldn't be attending and they could bill all their wasted, expensive hours to Thompson's account. Instead she sent a message to Jennifer Wiley.

I need you to get me a channel, she said. *I want to tell the world the truth about Warner S. Thompson.*

PART V

BEARS REPEATING

21

JIMMY

Sugar's gone by the time we arrive. It's just Marmalade stood there, shuffling awkwardly. You get to know bears, after you work with them long enough. Bears have got their own body language. Marmalade's real unhappy, but not in the angry, dangerous way bears get. She's just miserable, scared to do anything, like anything she does might make matters worse.

I never heard her speak before. Most bears, you hear them, they get some kind of human voice. Outdoors they radio you sub-voc. Indoors, past the airlocks where the atmosphere's dense enough to carry the sounds, we just talk. Talking's more natural to us people, and the Bioforms keep direct channel comms to between themselves.

So Marmalade never had anything to say, and when we meet up I find out why. Her voice isn't something nice you'd use for after-dinner conversation or sweet nothings. It's got subsonics in there that fair make me wet myself just to hear her. I am suddenly so very glad I never got far enough on Sugar's bad side that she sent her friends to have a word with me.

"She got this smile," Marmalade growls at me, and her voice makes out it's my fault even when she's not trying. "Big smile like she never had before. Then it was like I didn't exist. She went out. I tried to get in her way. She shouted at me. Said things." Not complimentary things, I'm guessing. Not things Sugar ever said before. And I don't know how it was between Sugar and her henchbears when they were alone. Part of me – that would have been most of me not so long ago – reckons she shouted at them and beat them and maybe had some headware hack to keep them in line, because she's one small human woman and they're a couple of goddamn enormous bears. But the rest of me, the most of me as of now, finds it doesn't believe that. When Murder went down, that was a personal and not just a professional loss to Sugar. And now Sugar's gone AWOL with a weird-ass smile on her face and on my way back Honey and I saw plenty of that. Like every second face we ran into was beaming at us, hand out to shake like it was National Gladhanding Day.

I clue Marmalade in that, whatever's going on, Sugar's the least of it. She won't stay still, wants to find something she can lay into that's responsible. I'd love to oblige her, just so that something doesn't end up being me, but I got a dreadful crawling feeling that whatever's going on here ain't going to yield to tooth and claw. I got a dreadful feeling Honey knows more than she's saying about it, too. And given how fond she is of her own voice that ain't exactly reassuring,

"What's doing?" I ask her. "Come on, now."

"I'm trying to assess the network traffic. That seems to be key to the situation but a proper analysis is proving unexpectedly difficult. Simply put, there's not much room for me to get about in the system. Digital rush hour in Hell City, Jimmy."

"She says—" I start, but Marmalade got cut in on the

channel 'cos I guess Honey's not going to just absentmindedly assume a bear isn't worth including like a human might.

"We need to get a better vantage," she decides.

"Meaning what?" demand I. "You want to go climb a mountain so's you can look down on your armies or something."

"Meaning," she says, with enough of an edge that I reckon Doctor Bear's patience is wearing thin, "that this hole we're in has lousy connectivity and I need you to take your two legs and get me closer to the centre of the city, closer to Admin, so I can gather data. I am also going to say, and you should in no ways take this as a threat, that I can take those legs off you and walk you all the way there myself if I have to. But that would take a lot of concentration on my part and so I'd rather not."

"I thought you said that was against your goddamn *ideology*. I thought you were Freedom Bear."

"Jimmy, I've only recently had to come to terms with my own death. Let's just say that I'm not having a good day," Honey tells me sharply.

"Let's go," Marmalade rumbles. "Sugar's gone over to someone else, this place is blown anyway."

"We'll get her back," I say. I even put a hand on the rough hair of her arm. It's a mistake at first, I think. Don't be familiar with the savage criminal animal. Except she sags a bit – and nothing sags quite like a bear, where their skin and its contents always have this shifting relationship, big-tall-strong one minute, pooling puddle of fat the next. She sags and she nods, and apparently I did the right thing for once.

We go out, the two – three, kind of – of us. I stay in Marmalade's shadow, and she's ready not to take shit from anyone. Except right then nobody's handing it out. For about half the people we see, more than half, it's almost like they're doing a play and we got backstage. They're going about shaking hands with each other with those freaky smiles, and each time we see them make the clasp, someone ends up nodding. Not agreement-nodding, but something lower, someone giving way. One head's definitely higher than the other when they part. Honey says something about 'tugging forelocks' which apparently isn't a sex thing.

"But you see what's going on here, Jimmy? You remember what I told you?" Impatient teacher with slow pupil. Except yes, this time Yours Truly passes with flying colours because actually I do.

"It's your prisoner's doofus," I say. "It's the thing where they rigged it. Where they cheated."

"Well it wasn't cheating per se—" she starts, in full teach mode, before reining herself in. "Yes. Exactly that. We're seeing a hierarchy being established."

"Why not by headware?" Marmalade rumbles, when she's been clued in.

"I can barely get to you on a narrow comms channel right now, there's so much system traffic," Honey says. "So this is their alternative system. There must be recognition codes in the handshake, establishing where each... unit sits in the whole..." And by then we're a district out from Admin, close enough for her to get a real good picture of what's going on if the system will only give her room to get her claws in and open it up.

"Jimmy!" It's been a while since anyone shouted my name out loud. Only Maldoun, what with Sugar Jimbles-ing me all the time. I see someone shoving their way past a knot of gladhanding grinners: Indra, my old fellow penitent on the shit job rota, lover of soaps. Except she's scared out of her wits right now, practically throwing her arms round me when she sees I'm not just gonna pump her mitt like some campaigning congressman.

"What's going on!" she wants to know, and I tell her I'm fucked if I know but that it's bad. She doesn't pass comment on Marmalade, staring down at her murderously, and I don't mention Honey.

"It's all going away!" she tells me. "They're taking everything! Why?" Utterly distraught. And that sounds like she's become a poet *in extremis*, a real fancy way of describing the situation. Except a few words on I realise she means her library of goddamn South American soap episodes. Her headspace is packed jam full of cheap melodrama, and it's all getting deleted, show by show. *That*'s what's got her in a state.

"Indra, listen to me," but what am I going to say? That it's worse. That first they came for the soap operas and I didn't say anything because I don't really like soap operas. "Indra, listen," and still here's me with nothing to actually tell her. "Honey, do something. Help her. Stop it." Because there's only one reason why they'd be stripping out her library. It's 'cos they need the space.

"I'm trying," Honey says. "I'm not sure what's... oh. Oh, wait."

Indra's face has gone weird, like all the Indra is being yanked from it, pulled deep inside. I see the corners of her mouth stretch.

"Honey, they're Collaring her. They're doing it right now. Stop them. Please, Honey." I can hear my own voice shake.

"It's not a Collar," Honey tells me. "You don't need to shift that much data just to fit a Collar. It's…"

My whole body jerks, Honey in the driver's seat for just a second, her reaction so great that it needs some kind of response beyond the virtual. "The fucker," she says.

This last is so unexpected I almost fall over. "Whoa, what?"

"The next stage of Distributed Intelligence. The very damn thing he was campaigning against. Not because he was against it. Because he didn't want the *competition*." And Honey is absolutely furious, in her kind-of-still-polite way. And Indra is beaming at me, that same goddamn look as everyone else. Her hand almost knifes me under the ribs, she sticks it out so hard. I take it, feel her clench, her macho-man-ball-buster handshake, but the fingers moving like it's a fraternity thing, a *secret* handshake inside the handshake. And of course I got no countersign to give her so she goes still for a second and takes a step back. Her smile goes away but no Indra bobs to the surface to replace it.

"We should move," I suggest.

Indra's backing off, and the lack of smile is catching, like a disease. Anyone she comes within a metre of is suddenly looking very cross indeed, and at Marmalade and me. The bear lets out a low growl. And they're all just humans – no Bioforms here at all – and she's a big bear, so if it comes to fisticuffs things are going to get nasty for everyone except her.

"Honey?" I ask. "You got your goddamn analysis?"

"I know what's going on. I can't quite believe the chutzpah of it, but I see it. I'm trying to work out what we can *do* about it," Honey tells me. "Just let me work, if you would."

"Honey, we ain't got time for you to write a *thesis*," I tell her. And everyone is looking at us now, all just the same way, like one person's staring out of all those eyes.

Then the cavalry arrives, only it's not our cavalry so it just makes everything worse. Some Bioforms come to see what the problem is, rounding the curve of the corridor and barging through the people there. Only it's Rufus and two of his posse, a mottled dragon-form called Smaug and our old friend fat-cat Albedo, who's still limping and bandaged-up where Murder tore her a new one a while back. They've got guns, and they look rattled as hell by what's been going on. But all that changes when their gaze passes over the top of all those heads and sees Marmalade, and sees me. And I am very obviously the one single lone and only human who is *not* acting like everyone else. And in Rufus's Big Book of Law Enforcement, which is large print and only has a handful of pages, that makes me Chief Suspect for the crime of the century.

Marmalade is spoiling for a fight, but she is also short on guns and outnumbered, and Rufus can probably take on a bear solo, best of three.

"Move!" I decide, and then I'm just going, hoping with every bounding leap that Honey won't take my legs off me and faceplant me into the concrete of the floor. Marmalade's right behind me, and then she's right in front of me, down on all fours and just shunting through the crowd that was creeping up behind us, so that we're clear of them and running back to our hidey-hole in moments.

And I risk a look back, as we go, and I see an interesting thing, 'cos that big mob of no-longer-grinning grinners aren't clearing to let Rufus through. He's having to wade, to push and elbow, and so he doesn't catch up with us and we lose him, for now. He's on our trail, but he's not part of whatever's going on with everyone else.

We end up in some other hole, that looks mostly like a socket for some big air pump that never got installed, because Sugar was apparently super-paranoid about needing places to hide up in. And obviously Sugar knows where this place is and Sugar ain't necessarily our friend now. I don't reckon we've got much time to catch our breath.

And catching my breath is becoming a problem. I'm real anxious, and some of that is because what's going on outside is real anxious-making. I mean, let's face it, Hell City is a goddamn unnatural place. It takes a lot of looking after to make sure it all keeps working, what with the dust and the experimental tech and the goddamn *being on Mars* of it all. And the advantage we always had is that a blown seal, a misfiring airlock, a broken pump, they're not going to kill us like they'd have killed us before the biomods. We don't drop dead the moment the oxygen content drops or when the temperature plunges to way below zero. We're Martians, as native as anything's ever been to this godforsaken planet. But still, we need food, we need water. Enough breaks down then we are still fucked, is what I'm saying. And I don't know yet if what's going on out there, all this Collaring, is going to leave room for someone to keep the maintenance rota going. So anxious, sure; hyperventilating, heart racing, feelings of nausea, of despair, all that. Except it's not just based on current affairs, because I didn't score anything from Fergil Maldoun after all, and now I go in my pocket for my last hit of Stringer and the goddamn cheap blister has burst and the pill is who knows where.

"I need to go for a walk," I say, but I'm already thinking ahead, or trying to, and there's a whole load of fun scenarios I can picture where this dealer or that dealer greets me with a grin and a handshake in just the wrong way.

Except...

"Say, you protecting Marmalade from handshake fever, Honey?"

"I'm not, no," she says, sounding preoccupied. "There's no need. She's not a target."

"Why so?"

"Well you must know that the non-human Bioforms don't have your headspace mods. The Braintree setup is only in humaniform models... I mean, only in the human crew. There simply isn't virtual space in Marmalade's head for the necessary download. You wouldn't fit *me* into her head." I wonder if she'd rather be in there, able to borrow a body more like the one she once owned.

"That's true for all the Bioforms?" I ask, because as far as I am concerned it's *not* 'non-human Bioforms' because *I* am *not* a Bioform. I'm just modded. It's not the same.

"I would imagine so. I did remark on the remarkable overengineering of your headware at the start of our acquaintance, Jimmy. And I suppose now we know why. But the non-human crew were engineered by other contractors."

"Goddamn marvellous," I decide, and then I'm off, and sending a signal to Stanky Greer that I want to score and I bet he's short of other customers right now. Greer isn't my favourite dealer by any means, but he's a Weasel, and Weasels aren't going to be doing that idiot grin any time soon. Honey doesn't catch on until I'm well out of there and heading by the quietest ways possible over to the mustelid digs where Greer and his fellows live. I assume most of them will be out on site, but when I arrive every nook has a dark, pointy face poking out of it warily, staring at me. Not the nicest thing, to walk into a den of Weasels and find you're the sole human there, centre of attention. They're twitchy as I am, and with good reason. From their point of view all the humans have gone crazy, and they don't have the context I have. Not that I feel my superior state of knowledge has brought me any goddamn happiness.

"Hey, Greer, man." And I almost try to shake his hand, just instinctively, 'cept that sort of thing can get misinterpreted real fast in today's changing times. So I hang back. "Greer, I need you to set me up."

Stanky Greer is one of the smaller Weasels – bit like the dragons are all sorts of reptile, the Weasels are part wolverine, part badger, part ferret, all bundled together. Some of them are bigger than me, but Greer is thin and snaky and short-limbed, and he doesn't stand on two legs as much as sit on his haunches. He's wearing overalls cut for his frame, and a hazard vest with about a million pockets over that, and it's the contents of those pockets I'm most interested in.

"Jimmy," Honey tells me, but then Greer is actually hugging me, or at least hugging my legs.

"What the fuck, man?" I ask him, but he's talking right over me.

"Jimmy? It's actually you, Jimmy, my man!" His voice is high, lisping, formed more with his animal lips than most Bioforms. "Does this mean it's over? You're back to normal?"

"I was never not normal," I tell him. "It didn't get me. Everyone else is still fucked, man. Listen, set me up, will you. I cannot handle this right now, not straight."

"Jimmy, I know, I know." And I reckon he's probably been taking his own merchandise, and I do not blame him one bit. "Here you go." And he's fumbling out a whole fistful of strips, enough to keep me for a month, practically forcing the stuff on me. "Jimmy, you're all right by me. I always liked you, Jimmy. Jimmy, you're a real stand-up human guy."

"Jesus," and he's not even asked for scrip, and I take it, take a pill there and then. I kneel down and hug the little bastard back, and we kind of cling together, dealer and dealt, at this evidence of one damn thing working like it's supposed to. And I sit there with him, among the Weasels, and wait for everything to feel a whole lot better.

Except I don't feel the calming, purposeful rush of the Stringer. I feel damn all, in fact, except unhappy.

"Greer, what is this shit?" I demand. "You ripping me off *now*?" Except he hasn't charged me for it, in which case it's the most lame-ass con in narcotics history.

"What d'you mean, Jimmy, man?" he asks. No sense of any overplayed innocence, either, and don't believe the stories, Weasels tend to be rotten liars. "That's my best. I cook that myself. Cordon fucking Blue, Jimmy."

"Greer, you..." I feel like crying, except my eyes don't work that way, and then Honey says, "Jimmy," again, with a certain slant and weight to the name, and I go sub-voc and say, "What did you do?"

"I... made an executive decision," she says, in my head.

"Care to explain just what the fuck?"

"You were suffering from withdrawal symptoms that were starting to impact on your neural pathways. As I'm at least partially reliant on those I decided it would be easiest to block them. I turned off your withdrawal, Jimmy. Which meant turning off the pathways by which the drug affects your brain."

"Honey, I feel like shit."

"I... think that's just life, Jimmy."

"I. *Know* it's just life." I cannot quite get into words just how pissed I feel right now. "That's what life's *like*. That's why I need 'the drug' to affect my brain. Because I'm on fucking *Mars* and it's dark all day all year and it's dusty and they did a hundred fucking invasive things to my head and my body so I can even be here and not just drop dead and when they do that to you, when they do all that to you and put you on this goddamn fucking planet then sometimes, just sometimes you need a little something extra to set your goddamn mind at ease, do you get me?"

I realise that most of that got said at something more than sub-voc because all the Weasels are watching me like I've gone crazy, which given all the other humans they've seen have actually gone crazy is a very real problem for them.

"Jimmy, man," Greer says, putting some distance between us. "You... OK there? Maybe you should get going now."

"Maybe I should," I agree, disgusted with drugs that don't work and interfering bears.

"No, wait," Honey tells me. "I need to speak to them."

"Go find your own mouth to do it with," I tell her and start off, but Honey's playing hardball.

"Tell them what I want or I'll do it anyway," she says. "Jimmy, big things are going on and I am not going to be crippled by your fits of pique."

I don't even know what pique is, but the threat's real enough, so I hear what Honey has to say and then stop in the doorway of the Weasel dorm to speak to Greer and pals.

"Look, there's something big going on, you spotted that. Something sent from Earth is fucking with us. With us humans. I'm trying to fix it." Easier to say 'I' than 'this dead bear I got in my head'. "But keep an open channel, Greer, man. Keep an ear ready. Because I might need help."

Greer's body language says that helping me is way down his bucket list, but he wants me gone and so he's all nods and smiles if it'll get me out the door.

22

HONEY

Not just a Collar.

It would have been easy enough. You could have downloaded a Collar into Jimmy, before I came and took up all his headspace. This is something far more data-heavy, far more... ambitious. And for a moment I think of my assessment of the man and assume I must have got it wrong. For someone to have this range of vision, this insanely forward-thinking dream. Has Warner S. Thompson been an unacknowledged tech genius all this time? Has he been playing chess and the rest of us were just playing checkers?

But then I think of the way that circle of ideas curves back to meet its origin. If you make an impossible thing happen then maybe it's because you're a supra-genius who finds the way to realise the impossible. Or maybe it's because you're the spoiled child just shouting until someone lets you have your way.

I can't know if this was precipitated by me and HumOS and Bees, but even if so, this must always have been the plan. The groundwork is right here in Jimmy's head, the very reason I'm in a position to appreciate it is proof of concept. The medium is the message and I'm the message and Jimmy's the medium.

It's Thompson. In a very real way, it's Thompson.

All those people we saw, they weren't being slapped with a Hierarchy and turned into slaves. They were getting a big old forced upload of data into their capacious headspace. And the upload was Thompson, his personality, sent all the cold kilometres over from Earth. All of them were Thompson, because apparently just dreaming of being undisputed king of Mars wasn't enough for him. Just ruling over fellow mortals wasn't the power trip he craved. Because they're *all* Thompson. That smile, that handshake, every one of them a home for his personality. He's made himself into a parasitic Distributed Intelligence network, one that doesn't even need to grow its own bodies like HumOS does; one that doesn't even allow its bodies autonomy like HumOS does. So where she's a council of linked minds, he's turned himself into a rigid feudal system. Because otherwise, how could it work? You can't just turn the entire population into the same megalomaniacal archvillain and expect them to actually cooperate. You'd have too many hail-to-the-chiefs and nobody doing any work. And just as I'm sure Thompson Collared his closest staff back on Earth because he couldn't trust them else, now he's even Collaring himself. That handshake is your Southampton exchange, establishing who's dominant over who, creating a hierarchy of Thompsons across the colony based on... who knows what? Random chance, or maybe attributes of each host. But sure as sure, they'll organise into a pyramid with one Thompson on top and all the other instances of himself enforcedly subservient. Because he knows what a treacherous son of a bitch he is.

On the way back Jimmy and I have a free and frank exchange of views about the evils of drug addiction, which

I lose. I just don't have the mental energy to save him from himself, what with just being a copy running in his head, and my moral authority is on shaky ground anyway. He's obviously very unhappy, and I'm beginning to suspect that the likely widespread drug use on Mars is built into the system tolerances. You must get a killer Seasonal Affective Disorder this far out from the sun, where your only seasons are Winter and Very Winter. Jimmy's depressed and anxious, and what I can glean of his bio-data is all red lights. And I have to literally take his hands off him to stop him overdosing by accident because he keeps trying to take more pills. So I release the block and let him enjoy what's already in his system. We have a stern talk about not letting it get in the way and I suddenly feel I know what it's like to be a parent of a sulky teenager.

Back at the ranch with Marmalade, I tell them what's going on. Thompson, Braintree, the whole picture. At the same time I'm working out a way to get a signal to Bees because I'm out of my league here and any help's going to be welcome.

There's a pause from both of them, and the finger I'm keeping on the pulse of Jimmy's mental state tells me of another drop in motivation, so that he's about to pop another pill before I stop him.

"Look, I appreciate this isn't an ideal situation," I say, "but I'm trying to think of what we can do. I need to—"

"Is that it then?" Jimmy asks. He sounds... really low, actually.

"No, I told you, I'm trying—" I start, but he doesn't mean that.

"Is that the point of us? Is that what we've been for, all this time?" He's sat on the hard floor, not looking at Marmalade or focusing on anything much. "They brought us to build a city on Mars, man," he says quietly, not his usual whine at all. "And I know it's shit up here, but still. We're building a city on Mars. When I volunteered, I needed the work. I had nothing but some tech skills, my family home was under eight feet of sea in a dead city. I lived in a camp. But they said, come to Mars. We'll have to rebuild you, but still, it's Mars. I mean, building the first city on another planet. Something to be proud of, right? But now it's all a joke. Now it's all so's some sonofabitch can take over our heads and set up Circle-Jerk City using our hands and our bodies? Fuck, man. That's…"

I hadn't realised he was proud of what he did. I don't think *he* realised, until just now. That being here, doing this, actually meant something, gave him self-esteem his life had lacked. And I'm not saying it makes me *like* Jimmy Marten, exactly, but I have to re-evaluate him a little. And at least I can tell him, "No, Jimmy."

"What now?"

"Braintree fit you with the makings of this, it's true, but you were already biomodded before you went to them for the headware. For what it's worth, the Hell City project is bona fide. Because Thompson never built a damn thing of his own, only suckered onto whatever someone else made, that was going in the right direction. So no, Jimmy, it wasn't just for this. It's been hijacked, that's all."

He's looking up now, though there's no 'me' there to look at. "That right?"

"I promise, Jimmy. Now stop reaching for the drugs or I swear I will slap you with your own hand."

Marmalade snickers, but that's given Jimmy another bleak thought. "Do they know?"

"What do you mean?"

"When the fucker takes them over. Are they still in there? Only, I remember what it was like when you did it to me. Trapped in my own head, can't talk, can't move. Prisoner's dilemma, you said? How's that for a fucking dilemma? And that was just for a little bit. What you're saying, he's here for *good*. I mean, he won't keep them awake in here forever while he does his thing, right? He'll... put them to sleep, won't he? They won't be..."

It is said that Charles Darwin lost his faith in God over wasps and caterpillars.

There are wasps that paralyse caterpillars and lay their eggs on them, bury the whole horrible bundle in a burrow, and then the eggs hatch and the grubs feed and, eventually, the caterpillar dies. And Darwin really, really wanted to believe that God, in His infinite mercy, would gift the caterpillars with a mechanism to turn off the pain and the awareness of what was happening to them; to not be *present* when the egg case was split open by those questing, hungry jaws. And yet his budding theory of evolution had no room for mercy. If the caterpillar had been taken by the wasp, it wasn't going to become a butterfly and make more caterpillars. Nothing would inherit any part of it, save for the wasp inheriting its proteins. There was no evolutionary pressure to grant doomed caterpillars an anaesthetic because only the undoomed ones would contribute to the next generation.

And in just the same way, there is absolutely no reason for Warner S. Thompson or any of his people to have spared a moment or spent a cent to lessen the plight of all the people whose bodies they planned to usurp, and I have nothing comforting to say to Jimmy.

At around that time, a signal from Bees reaches me, coming in across a tangle of relays from some cultist den in Hell City.

Bees' channel: *I warned you that action might make things worse.*

My channel: *Aslan is dead. I thought you meant worse like that.* Except maybe where Bees is now, she doesn't, or even can't, care about something like that.

Bees' channel: *Worse is worse. I am having to move up my own plans. The human presence on this planet is likely to be more problematic to me from here on in.*

My channel: *Bees, I need your help.*

Bees' channel: *I am no longer inclined to busy myself in the affairs of others.*

And she very nearly means it, but I think there's just enough left of the Bees I revived after Campeche, the Bees I grew from recorded memories and dumb insects at Cornell. Because all Bees are one Bees and it's that Bees, the Bees who was with Rex and Dragon and me, all those decades ago.

My channel: *Bees, it's me, Honey.*

A long pause, but I know Bees well enough that it's one for effect. She never needed that much thinking time.

Bees' channel: *I have preserved my AdApts. The humans I have suborned for my purposes. I will direct them to you. They will assist. That is all, Honey. I am no tame hive any more. I do not make sweetness and light for humans or for bears.*

Any help is good help, right now. *Thank you, Bees.*

Then Marmalade lets out a grunt. She's been quiet, but apparently that means she's been busy rather than just brooding. Like any good bear she's been in the system, scavenging for signal strength as the great data download starts to ebb, as everyone who's going to become Warner S. Thompson gets taken over and the torrent slows to a trickle. Marmalade has access to some cameras and she's found where Sugar is.

"You can fix her." Her voice is like Rex's voice once was, before I found him a better one, all roar and rumble. I get a spike from Jimmy's brain chemistry, pure fear just from hearing it.

"Fix her, as in remove the Thompson download?"

"Fix her as in give her back to herself," Marmalade says, looming. "You're so clever, make it more than words. Do something," and Jimmy's telling me will I just fucking do it because Marmalade scares the hell out of him.

And I should try. Not only because there's a fellow bear here, some distant kin who wants me to rescue her friend. Because if I can do it, maybe that's the answer. Maybe I will weed this garden of Thompsons until there are none left. If his roots don't go too deep.

I see where Sugar is, looks like some sort of work crew, some job lot of low status Thompsons all getting back to the business of keeping Hell City running. There's still a lot of traffic in the system, and I don't fancy my chances of achieving anything at a distance. Time to go walkabout and get close.

"Let's do it," I tell Marmalade, to everyone's relief.

Skulking across the city is eerie. We dodge groups whenever we see them. Human, because they're all bands of men, and some women, with Thompson's damnable smile, just walking about looking at the walls of Hell City as though everything is unfamiliar and not up to standard. One man stood using a screen as a mirror, poking at his own face, examining the work the biomod surgeons had put in place. His eye was red where he'd put a finger in it and there were bruises all over, but he didn't stop, and he didn't stop smiling.

We dodge the Bioforms as well, because right now we don't know where we stand with them. They might be Collared somehow, or just obeying human instructions because that's what they're used to. They might be attacking humans on sight out of a revulsion I can absolutely understand. And we don't see many; Jimmy reckons they're outside at the works, most of them. And we see absolutely no mixing between the two groups.

Halfway down the service corridors and back alleys to where Marmalade says Sugar is, we run into a little motorised cart, skewed across the corridor so Jimmy has to drive it sideways before we can get past.

"Ain't good," he says.

"Well there isn't much in this situation that I'd characterise as good," because I am, frankly, rattled.

"No, who's doing the work? The fixing work? This Thompson guy, he took a course in how to keep stuff running on Mars, did he?"

"I wouldn't have thought so."

"Shit." Jimmy shakes his head, which is always annoying when I'm trying to use his eyes. "I mean, you ain't got access to my memories, right? You're in my head and you can steal my body, but you ain't got *me*. Not unless I decide to tell you shit."

I stop – or rather, if it had been my body, I'd have been stopped by the thought, but of course Jimmy just carries

me along. I suspect this is a part of the plan that Thompson
and his people didn't think through. Unless each instance of
him can coerce his host into cooperating, all that technical
knowledge required to keep Hell City a going concern is
going to be lost, or...

"They'll get the Bioforms to do it," I decide. "*He* will, I
mean. I assume that's feasible? The humans, meaning the
Great Society of Thompsons, will put their feet up, and they'll
make the Bioforms keep everything running. If they can."

"Don't reckon we'll take to that," Marmalade grumbles.

But I don't think the plan went that far. And even as we're
coming into the upper layer of Hell City, the residential layer
of streets under a semi-transparent roof where the weak
sunlight creeps in down broad thoroughfares, I begin to
realise just how screwed up this whole business is. Thompson
has made himself the sole human being on the planet, Jimmy
and the AdApts excepted. Everyone is Thompson: he's made
himself into a colony organism that can expand forever and
yet will always only ever be him: one human face stretched
without limits, the Big I Am. And yet, just as he didn't want
to bother with the wills of other people, not even Collared
people, he couldn't even countenance having to share the
planet with *himself*. He's made sure that all his selves are
slaved to his other selves, all the way up the line to some head
Thompson with the power of life or death over Mars. And
for a moment I wonder if it's that easy: kill the top dog and
it all falls apart. Except the Southampton protocols will deal
with that. There'll always be a new chief so long as there's a
Thompson left. The snake is all head.

Up here there aren't the places to skulk properly, and
Marmalade's not a small bear to start with. And we keep

ducking into doorways and behind buildings because there are more Thompsons up here. Jimmy tells me this is where they, the crew, didn't get to go. These are places set aside for the regular colonists of the future, big homes and business premises built and then mothballed. Except they're all being opened up now. The Thompsons are choosing their new real estate, tearing off the wrappers and moving in.

And then we see a bunch of them with guns. Big guns, heavy bore long arms. Elephant guns, as I'd think of them. And from their reaction Jimmy and Marmalade both never knew such things existed up here in Hell City, but Thompson did. And that's their lever against the Bioforms, I'd guess. I remember very personally just how much Thompson enjoys shooting animals.

When they've gone by, we slip into the next building. There are people moving above us, in the section that reaches past the roof of Hell City, the penthouse suite that has its own skylight and its own feeble strip of day. There are lights on up there, all tinted a blue that's meant to recall the skies of Earth, and people are shifting heavy objects.

We creep up the stairs, or Jimmy and Marmalade do. There are maybe six Thompsons up there, all in women's bodies, and they're... moving furniture. They're dusting. They're doing housework. For a moment I can't quite work out what's going on, but no – these must be the lowest tier Thompsons, the ones who got the thin end of the Southampton protocols. Because Thompson doesn't know how to keep the air pumps or the extractor fans working but he sure as hell knows what he wants his rooms to look like.

From Jimmy's panicky glance up through the stairwell, I know one of them's Sugar. Now he and Marmalade are looking at each other, and really both of them are looking at me.

The network traffic has calmed a lot now the downloads are finished, and I have room to sneak into the system and then link to her headware. It's busy in there, but then there's a whole extra obnoxious personality taking up the room. And if it catches wind that there's a dead digital bear trying to undo its work then there's a whole city of its siblings who will come and express an opinion, some of them out of the barrel of a gun.

And so I tell Jimmy and Marmalade that they better find somewhere out of the way to hide, because this could take a while – if I can do it at all, though I don't tell them that bit. They go lurk in the storage closet while I set to work trying to find subliminal access points to Sugar's headware.

It's not quick, and there are self-monitoring routines built into the implant that exist to track down unauthorised tampering. I don't think Thompson – the Thompson riding Sugar – is likely to consciously pick me up, because I doubt he's that introspective or has the relevant skillset. I *do* think that, if he gets an alarm to say someone's poking where they're not wanted, he will reach the right conclusion very quickly. I think he's very sharp in a very limited way, but understanding threats to himself is definitely in there.

And so I pick. I send messages, I spoof traffic. I isolate an ingoing connection the Hell City system uses to track biometrics and activate it, and alter its protocols until it can accept incoming data as legitimate. I falsify authorities and identity codes and sneak my fingers into Sugar's head disguised as routine queries. And because I have no body and no sensory feedback, I imagine all this as a physical thing, with the great pulsating cyst that is Thompson's mind hanging from the ceiling above as I inch in and start to dismantle him.

I'm at it for over two hours. Long enough that the home improvements crowd actually move on to another building, and we shadow them, because this is close work, piggybacking on the building's own internal system. I am very leery about interposing more nodes in the process, because response time is key and because it might trip some alarm in the middle that I'm not aware of. And it's a little like the Gordian knot if Alexander only had a tiny pen knife instead of his mighty sword. I can't just cut Thompson's mind in half with one mighty sweep, and I can't let him know what's going on at any point before the end. So think of it as though I'm approaching that big old ball of string and severing each strand while leaving the shape of the ball intact. A death of a thousand invisible virtual cuts, one after another, while Thompson just squats there believing himself unchallenged and in control. And then, with the final whisk of my little blade, the entire thing unravels, falls into a thousand severed inches of string, and he's gone from her headspace entirely, nothing but a mist of ones and zeros dissipating into the electronic ether.

I message Sugar immediately, telling her not to panic but to come downstairs in a calm and orderly manner, but she takes the stairs two at a time anyway. When she sees us, her eyes are wide, and for a moment I think that the enforced captivity in her own head has been too much for her. Then she throws herself at Marmalade and hugs her fiercely, and she's fine, she's herself. And she's furious.

"Do it to the others," she demands. "Whatever you did." Because she has no idea just how *hard* that was, just how laborious. There's no way I can go through the complement of Hell City one by one, even if somehow Thompson didn't notice what I was doing.

Speaking of which…

We hear feet coming down the stairs, the rest of the furniture squad chasing their errant comrade. The smile is gone, but I know the nasty piggy look in all of their eyes. The idiot outrage of someone for whom the whole of creation exists to be their extended body, to do things for them, to make their will a reality. And woe betide anything that doesn't play its part.

Jimmy's already moving, and the three of us bolt into the street, where groups of Thompsons are turning to stare, all that imperious fury magnified across fifty faces. None of the firearms squads are immediately in view, thankfully, and we're already running. Jimmy has a fair turn of speed for such a weasely man, and Sugar… is riding Marmalade like something out of a children's story, bareback, if you'll excuse the pun, fingers dug into her pelt.

Thompsons are trying to get in the way, but Marmalade scatters them like skittles, and for a moment nobody's actually chasing us because running after things is a task that Warner S. Thompson has people for. He doesn't put in the legwork himself.

Then there are bears up ahead. And these aren't like Marmalade, not sentient Bioforms. These are like the ones that nearly got Jimmy earlier, the ones he calls Bad News Bears, just part-uplifted animals slaved to Hell City Admin. Meaning slaved to Thompson.

Sugar drops from Marmalade's back as she rears up, and there are three of the Bad News Brigade right there, as big as she is.

"Go!" I tell everyone. "Just go!" and I attack the enemy systems, fighting Admin for comms channels, sending Denial of Service attacks into the Bad News Bioware, starting feedback loops in their Collaring software. And it's all stuff I knew back on Earth, because I used to mess with Collars for a pastime. For a moment I've got all three of them, and they're lurching sideways, pawing at their muzzles, attacking the walls, moaning because the poor dumb brutes have no idea what's going on. Then we're past and gone, even as Admin reasserts its rightful dominion. We're gone and away before they can chase us, but they'll be hunting us now, and even Sugar and Marmalade only have so many places they can hide.

23

JIMMY

Not long after and we get the Three Stooges turning up like before: Brian, Mariah and Judit, all of them their usual fun-to-be-with selves. Except right now I will take any help I can get.

"What can Bees give us?" Honey asks them, all businesslike.

"You lookin' at it, man," Brian says. "We the cavalry."

"Bees is very concerned by this development," Judit adds. Her voice is high and short on inflection. "She calculates the eventual result of Thompson's cerebral landgrab will be the end of Hell City as a functioning entity." Which is a lot of words when all you're saying is we're fucked.

"So what's that to her?" I say sourly. "She's got her escape plan already, right? Got you all loaded on the rockets? It's all fun and games for the interplanetary explorer division?"

"Interstellar," Judit corrects me, and Mariah butts in.

"Bees still wants to preserve herself here. We still want to preserve *our*selves here. Just because there's a copy doesn't mean the original goes anywhere."

Brian sends a guilty look at me, which makes no sense until I realise it's actually at Honey, because of course when they made a copy of her, the original did go somewhere, namely to whatever final reward dead cyborg bears get.

"Right now, Bees' lyin' low," Brian explains. "The man here go for her, she gon' fight back. She don' want to bring that any sooner than need be. Got rockets to prepare, like the man say."

"But no army of giant robot bees come to liberate Hell City," I finish for him.

"We on our own," agrees Brian.

"So what good are you?" Sugar demands.

"Bees stopped the download and immunised us," Mariah tells her. "And with everyone else taken over, we three represent about 95 per cent of the technical expertise in Hell City." Which shows how little she rates Sugar, Marmalade and me.

"But right now... I mean what the fuck do we even *do*?"

"Go get supplies. Go to one of the science stations. Abandon ship," Judit suggests flatly.

"What about the Bioforms?" I put in. Everyone looks at me like they were about to have an adult conversation and I'm demanding a biscuit, and I am getting really tired of that. "He ain't in the Bioforms, and, well, there are more humans and they got guns, but there's a whole load of bears and dogs and weasels and dragons in Hell City."

"So you want some expendable troops?" Mariah asks.

"It's their city too," I point out. "I mean, why aren't they up in arms already? I would be."

"They working," Brian says. "They still digging. They know something happen, but not what. They doin' what they told, man."

"More than that," Mariah adds. "They're doing what *Rufus* tells them."

"Sheriff Rufus?" Sugar's eyes go mean and narrow. He's still got her friend.

"We seen it on the way over," Brian agrees. "Posse gon' around giving orders. Posse still loyal to Admin, way I see it. You know how ol' Rufus get about keeping order."

"I reckon he'll kill them off." Mariah eyes up Marmalade. "Send them on dangerous missions, send them out to the edge. Maybe not let them back in when they've pushed their mods to the limit. He knows he can't hack them. That makes them a threat even if they never turn on him."

"I reckon an angry bear's gonna get in no matter what you do," is my contribution. "Don't reckon that goes well for Thompson." Although it doesn't go well for anyone, in my imagination. I see the guns going off as the desperate Bioform work crews try to break through the very walls they built. I see irreparable damage done to the city. Irreparable because there's nobody left with the skills to repair it. Do the Thompsons turn inwards then, try to cajole their crazy mind-prisoners to come up with solutions? Does each one become a jailer who needs their solitary confinement prisoner's cooperation, and what a fucking dilemma *that*'ll be.

Honey's been silent for a while, and now she chimes in over the speakers. "There's been a development on Earth."

"Don't see that exactly matters right now," Sugar decides.

"It might affect just how extreme the Thompson DisInt here on Mars will become, given how little the man ever brooked a challenge to his authority. He's fallen. He's done."

"Meaning?"

"New testimony has come in, backed by headware records. Thompson's assistant, apparently. She was Collared, but she got out of it somehow. She's witness to... he gave the order to kill Aslan and the other two who were found with him. And some scientist at Braintree. And more, a lot more. She's been living in Thompson's shadow for years. Everything went through her. She's in protective custody and it's all coming out. I see people who were defending the man to the hilt just a few hours ago turning on him, denouncing him. He's done. On Earth, he's done."

"On Mars, he's gonna be pissed," I say.

"Unless the Thompson here is glad to be free of the parent Thompson on Earth," Judit suggests. "Honey, you shouldn't call him a DisInt. True Distributed Intelligence doesn't need to keep its units in line. HumOS never did. Bees doesn't. Thompson knows himself well enough to know he'd stab himself in the back first chance he got, and you can bet the Earth Thompson reserved management privileges for himself."

"So what, the United States of Thompson up here declares independence?" Sugar demands. "Where does that get us?"

"Gives us leverage, maybe?" Brian puts in. "This all he got, he gon' want to keep it running."

"You can't cut a deal with the man." Honey again. "I honestly don't think he has it in him to keep to an agreement the moment he gains anything from breaking it. I think that his personality went right into pathological liar and out the other side. You cannot engage in regular human interactions with a human metagamer. We have to destroy him."

And we all wait for her to unveil her grand plan for how to do that, but apparently the old bear ain't got that far, so fat lot of use she is. She and the three Bee cultists fall to technical discussion then, and I'm tired and pop some Stringer and Sugar's waving me over. Her and Marmalade have gone to the other corner of the hidey-hole, where she's set up a link and a little screen no bigger than her hand. And admittedly

I'm taking Honey with me, but with her voice coming out of the speaker over with Brian and co, it feels like I'm leaving her over there.

"What's doing?" I ask, and Sugar says, "I've got Rufus."

A beat. "As in, 'by the short and curlies?'" from me.

"Got a line to him. Spoofed and re-routed every two minutes, and it's not as though he wouldn't find us anyway. But he'd put a call out in the public announcement space. For me."

"'Cos he's got Murder," I finish and she nods grimly, fingers of one hand buried in Marmalade's fur.

I cast a nervous look at the three cultists, still in deep discussion, which is dumb because Honey is likely listening to us even as she argues with them.

"So what's he saying? Rufus, I mean."

"Nothing yet. Haven't opened voice, just pinged him to say I saw his card on the mat."

"And you need me for this, why?"

"We are about to open negotiations with the new management, Jimbles. Or at least its bitch. And screw the dead bear and screw the Bees traitors. You and me and Marmalade, we're the people, right? We get to ask the dog-man just what the fuck."

The look she gives me... I get a real complicated reaction to it. This isn't Sugar lounging on her crate throne being all pixie-girl while her killer bears loom over you. This is Sugar with her back to the wall, but also Sugar realising she's a part of something. A part of the Hell City dream we all somehow bought into back on Earth, all those years ago. And it's her making me a part of that too, her making me someone that's part of 'us' in her book, rather than just the 'them' I always was before. And I want to scoff. I want to tell her that being 'us' right now is a death sentence because we are literally all the 'us' there is on the whole planet. I want, basically, to be that self-same Jimmy Marten who slouched through his working life on Mars pissing on everyone's parades because he never had one of his own. And I can't. Right here, right now, I realise Hell City *was* my parade. So long as I was part of the project, and no matter it was all for the rich folks and the investors and not for me, it was something I was proud of. I never knew until the fuckers took it away from me.

"Let's talk dog," I say, and that gets me about nought point three of a grin; better than nothing.

"Finally." Sugar puts Rufus through to my receiver so we're sharing the familiar roughness of his voice.

"Wotcher, Sheriff," Sugar tells him. "If it's about that parking ticket, I got the money."

"Dana, you are in a world of trouble right now," Rufus tells her. "I always cut you slack, back in the day. You know that, right?"

"Sure, Sheriff Rufus. Practically business partners. You need some data shifted? I hear that's whiz biz these days."

An awkward pause, and then: "I'm going to find you, Sugar. There just aren't enough places to hide in Hell City."

"You just close your eyes and start counting then," Sugar says, and I can see her shaking, and if they hadn't modded it out of us she'd be bucketing sweat, but her voice is oh-so-cool. "Was that what you wanted to ask me about? Because I say just count to a hundred. Or you can do twenty five times, if that's gonna tax you."

Rufus growls, but he's not mad. Sounds sad even. "Dana,

I have Murder here. Still with us despite some fairly serious wounds. I do not want to do anything we'll all regret."

"Hey, Sheriff," I break in, mostly to give Sugar time to process. "You, ah, not notice anything *weird* about the place today. Only seems to me that we've been invaded by some serious crazy. You seeing any of that, over your ways?"

"Jimmy Marten," he names me, and I fight down the instinctive shiver.

"That ain't an answer, Sheriff."

And for a long few heartbeats there *isn't* an answer, and Sugar and I eye each other, because it's not like Dog-with-a-badge to pussyfoot around.

"We are under new management," Rufus tells us at last. "Yes. Things have changed. But that doesn't mean Admin isn't still in charge. It doesn't mean I don't keep *order*. And right now there's only one threat to public order and that's you three and whatever the fuck's in Jimmy's head. If you surrender yourselves peaceably then I will guarantee nothing will happen to you. And Murder will be fine too, Dana."

"They Collar you, Sheriff?" I ask idly.

"No they did not Collar me," and I hit a nerve there, sure enough. "You think a dog only does his duty when he's got no choice? Hell City needs stability, order, Jimmy. That is what I do. And I do it because it's the right thing. If people like you were left to run the show we'd all have no air in three weeks. Now I'm giving you an ultimatum, kids. I got myself set up here at the gates of Admin, and I've got Murder here with me, and some of my people. I want you to come over and say hello. Because I have orders to bring you in by whatever means necessary. I do *not* want to have to use the means available to me. But I will, because right now you are threat number one to peace and order in my city."

"We're really not," Sugar says quietly, but Rufus cuts her off.

"I don't want to hear it. You've got an hour to show your faces, you two clowns and Marmalade." And then the line cuts and that's all we get.

"I'm guessing you caught that?" I say to thin air, and sure enough Honey's not been so deep in negotiations with the cult that she wasn't keeping an ear open. Even now I see Brian, Mariah and Judit heading out on some mission of their own and I wonder just what the hell Bees and bear have cooked up between them.

"You going to be able to pull any magic out your ass?" I ask her. "Turn Rufus's brains to mush or something?"

"He's not like your Bad News Bears," Honey says. "Their software is much simpler than a full Bioform, and they come pre-Collared, without free will. But I can help. I can reason with him."

"Oh, right." I can barely contain my enthusiasm. "Sure, that'll work."

"Let's just go, shall we?" She sounds insulted by my scepticism but I reckon that, what with her being dead and all, she's not the talker she thinks she is.

It's hard to go the back ways right through to Admin's airlocked front door, on account of how when you get to that part of Hell City it's all front ways. Sugar and I have a confab and our best bet is the monorail system, which is all put in except for there not being any trains yet, but it is a road all over town and maybe the bad guys – the bad *guy* – isn't thinking of it. Anyway, we see a whole load of people all marching around looking over their new domain, but they're all below us, under the arches of the tracks, or else above us on higher levels. And so we get quite far towards Admin before all the big billboards suddenly turn on. At first I think, *They've found us*, but it's all over Hell City, every single damn one. Information boards, advert boards, every public screen is showing the same face.

"Oh, Danny Boyd," I murmur, feeling suddenly wretched for a man who until now was doing way better in life than me. It's his face but not his expression, and I guess we just found out who's Thompson Prime at the moment. Daniel Boyd got to run Admin back in the old regime, and I guess they got lazy with all that handshaking because it's his body in the driving seat still, and so I guess his instance of Thompson sitting on the sharp end of the pyramid.

And he looks out with that weird smile, uncomfortable on a face never built for it, and says, "You're there, Honey the bear. I worked it out. I know they sent you here. I'm hunting you, Honey. Say something. I'm going to find you."

24

HONEY

I wait for the emotional rush, because I still remember staring down the barrel of the gun. And of course there's no surge of fear because all the parts of me that might produce the relevant hormones are no longer within my portfolio. I feel... a healthy caution, is probably the best way to put it. Thompson on Earth was someone it was easy for me to underestimate, given the weighting I gave to a particular kind of intellectual prowess. Martian Thompson has a great deal more, relatively, at his disposal. Right now, aside from our little band, he *is* Hell City and every human in it.

"Honey." The voice new to me but I think I can hear the thread of a familiar inflection running through it, coming to me over Jimmy's radio and as a wash of deadened sound through the thin city air. "I know you can hear. I know you're there. I'll find you."

And by then I've set up a string of relays and blinds within the system and can send right back to him so that I can at least stave off any such finding as long as possible. "Hello, Warner."

"Mr Thompson." The face on all the screens looks surly and sour. The features are Chief Administrator Daniel Boyd's, according to Jimmy. The expression is pure Thompson. "Senator Thompson."

"You never won the election. From the news back home, your name won't be on the ballot." But enough of that. There's no point simply bandying provocations with him.

"I worked it out. My friend here told me. They were looking for you before you even arrived. My people set them on it. After they found what your friends did with your body. But I got your friends."

"What did you work out, precisely?" He worked nothing out, I suspect. He just bullied poor trapped Boyd into telling him what they'd been doing.

"You're here, somewhere. In some head. Some head I don't own. You can't have them, Honey. They're all mine. And I'll kill the one you've got. You've only got one. I'll kill him. I'll have the dogs eat him." With the face so big, up on the screens, I can see spittle string and bubble as Thompson tries to use Boyd's lips like he would his own. He looks like each word only comes out after being thoroughly chewed. There's blood in that spittle and I guess he's bitten his borrowed tongue more than once.

"There's no room for you," he growls, staring out, eyes darting, as though he can actually see through the screens themselves, rather than just the cameras. "No room for a bear in a man suit. No room for not being me." And that smile again, insufferably pleased with itself. "They made this for me. What they put in these heads. Filed patents. They'll make it back home. I'll go back home. They'll prepare a house for me."

And that, as far as I'm concerned, is a pipe dream, but I reckon maybe it would have been the plan if Thompson hadn't just come crashing down back on Earth. Maybe the next generation of headware would have been released with the mother of all security vulnerabilities.

Jimmy is frantic, feeling all the adrenal fear that I don't. "This is good," I tell him.

"Good? How the fuck is any of this good?"

"He didn't mention you, for one thing. That sheriff certainly knows who you are, and probably your man Boyd did too, but I think nobody's told Thompson, or they told him and he hasn't processed the information. I'm damn sure he'd have threatened you by name if he was in full command of the facts."

"So what now?" Jimmy, Sugar and Marmalade are crouched in the shadow of a part-completed section of monorail station and I take the opportunity to stretch my virtual legs and creep out the system some more. By now there are a whole set of pathways I can use to syphon off information and access systems in a way that won't immediately trip any alarms. There are some presences in the system hunting about, but I reckon Thompson himself hasn't got the skills, so either he's coerced some of his hosts to talk him through it or there are some Bioform operators on the payroll, perhaps run through the sheriff. Right now they're not a threat but they're going to start seeing signs of my tampering soon enough.

And there's little enough I can do without lighting up the board with alerts, but I check in with Brian and the rest of Bees' followers. I sent them to go out and talk to the Bioforms, to bring back any groups that were spooked enough to take action. I think Thompson assumed that humans and Bioforms wouldn't mix, because he came from a world in which the only non-human faces you'd see would be servants, and Collared servants at that. On Mars, though, it's cheek by jowl, so his takeover hasn't exactly gone unnoticed. We have Jimmy's associate Greer and his mustelid crew on board via Mariah, while Brian's gone out to recruit some of the dig crew, bears and dogs and other heavy lifters. Judit has a handful of dragon models trained for electrical repair down narrow conduits, thin bodies and short limbs and a battery of specialised electroreceptors on loan from sharks. I tell them to come join us outside Admin, because that's where Sheriff Rufus is.

I borrow one of the security cameras to take a look. I wonder, honestly, if Rufus is a Westerns buff behind closed doors. There's a wide plaza in front of the airlock to Admin, and he's right there, out in the open, with a half dozen other Bioforms who are his posse. They've got Murder with them, looking beaten up and bandaged, but alive. But it's just them, because Rufus has built his authority on being tougher and stronger than anyone else, even the bears. He reminds me of another dog I used to know.

And just like that dog, he's not stupid. They've got all the Bad News Bears ready nearby if they need them, all under Admin's direct control, meaning Thompson.

"You're gonna fix this, though, right?" Jimmy's voice, and I realise he's been talking to me while I scouted.

"I'm going to try," I confirm.

"I mean, you can just take them back, like with Sugar," he adds. "Just fight him for them."

I want to tell him yes, but it's not my style to lie to my troops. "You remember how long that took, Jimmy."

"But, I mean..." I can tell his body is shivering. "They're all in there, man. Trapped." And I only took his body off him for a relatively short time, but he has *not* forgotten. And I re-evaluate little Jimmy, because right now he is absolutely not thinking about finding a hole to hide in. He is thinking about what it's like for other people, to go through what he went through only so much worse.

"I will fix this," I tell him, although I don't say that I don't quite know how. "First let's take Hell City off him, though, so he doesn't open all the doors or some stupid thing."

I get the OK back from Brian, Mariah and Judit, and we're on the move again.

The camera viewpoint contributed to a mental image of somewhere roomier than we actually find, but then Hell City is short on space. Admin's airlock door – because the top echelon of the staff get to work in near-Earth atmospheric conditions, as Jimmy sourly tells me – still feels like the portal to a speakeasy at the end of a gloomy alley. And that's even with the lighting in this part of town calibrated to be as sunny as possible. On either side are the frontages of businesses-to-be, overlooking this tiny plaza with balconies nestling right up against the translucent roof. The sun is in the sky, but in trying to replicate its Earth-intensity light the architects have banished the radiance of the real thing entirely. All very poetic. And I'm rambling, and that's because I'm nervous. I would prefer to have more plan here, and more control, but Sugar is driving this enterprise, not me.

The collection of Bioforms is lounging about around the airlock door, nobody else on view. For a moment, because I have lived in a human world among humans, and had to learn the human way of seeing things, I see them as a human would. They look like a collection of characters from a twentieth-century children's story, escaped into the wild and gone feral. The dog, the cat, the lizard, a wolverine-form, another smaller dog. They look as though they should be having adventures and rescuing children from wells, to be rewarded at the end with what I recall being described as a 'slap-up feast', whatever that actually is. Instead of which they are standing about waiting for the outlaws to show up even as the faint Martian sun reaches High Noon above us.

"What are we waiting for?" Sugar asks. I realise she's asked me if I'm ready two or three times, and Jimmy is shuffling our feet in the thin layer of dust that's drifting about even here.

Sheriff Rufus takes that opportunity to call out, voice and radio. "I know you're there. You missed a camera when you chose your hiding spot. May as well come over."

And we're not exactly hiding, just pausing. And it's mostly because, I realise, I'm afraid.

"Come on, Sugar," Rufus continues. "I want this to have a happy ending for your friend."

I'm afraid, because unlike Thompson I have only this one body, and it's not even mine. And telling myself that the worst has literally already happened doesn't help. I see, then, the attraction of what he did. Because I could kill Warner S. Thompson all day and he'd still be there, even though each instance of him would know the agony of death. He has a legacy, and the legacy is him.

I check in with the reinforcements, and they're close on. I toy with the idea of turning up with a mob, but Sugar rules that out.

"They stay out of sight for now. Rufus'll see them coming, but if we go in like that he'll have the gun to Murder's head straight off. We'll push him to it. You tell me you've got a better fucking plan than that."

I don't, but I don't tell her that. I don't think we can save her friend. I am very worried I won't be able to save Jimmy, and I'm starting to warm to him as a person, quite aside from the fact that my continued existence is bound to his.

"You go," I tell her. "Otherwise Mariah is going to turn up with Greer and a pack of mustelids and after that things may just escalate on their own." I feel a twinge of academic's annoyance for not knowing exactly what the collective noun for mustelids is.

And she and Marmalade go, and Jimmy goes with them, which I absolutely did not want or expect. And we're out in the open, in sight of Rufus, while I'm caught on the hop. And then I want to just seize his legs and march him right back into cover, but too late, and that kind of dissension in the ranks won't exactly help our bargaining position.

Rufus, who's been leaning nonchalantly next to the airlock, sets himself upright with a twitch of his shoulder and lopes forwards a few paces. His gun is holstered, but I reckon our sheriff is likely a quick draw. Still, I know bears, and Marmalade can probably close the distance between them and that one shot is unlikely to counteract all that momentum. Not something I could have done in recent years, but I remember being a younger bear. Everyone underestimates just how quick and nimble a metric ton of bear can be.

I pull my point of view back, because if anywhere in Hell City has security coverage, it's right here. There's traffic on the network, tweaking digital simulations of my old animal senses.

The rest of the posse, Albedo and Smaug and the others Jimmy names for me, they have weapons to hand, small arms and long arms all bored to stop Bioforms, but nothing's pointing at us. Rufus wants to keep things civilised, but I'm suspicious. Not of him, necessarily, but of his new paymaster, who I wouldn't trust as far as...

From one camera I see...

Jimmy's arms are loose by his sides and I take them off him without asking. I am very good at quick and dirty calculations, so when I shove Sugar hard in the side it's with complete faith in Newton that Jimmy will get the equal and opposite reaction and go in the other direction. What I'm not used to is the lower gravity, meaning instead of just sprawling over, the pair of human bodies fly away from each other in a weirdly balletic leap that ends with them five feet apart and the spray of bullets cutting up the floor tiles between them. Dust and fragments tumble in unexpected arcs and clouds, as though we're in that part of the film they play in slow motion.

What's not in slow motion is Rufus. He's every bit as quick as I expected, gun to hand and firing. Not at us, happily, because we're on the ground and neither Jimmy nor Sugar would be able to get out of the way. He unloads three shots up at the balcony without hesitation, and the calibre of the weapon just about demolishes both balcony and the two bodies I saw up there. I feel a rush of triumph, quickly overlain by the recollection that those were *people*, innocent people under the control of a DisInt entity who's got plenty more where that came from.

The posse are all on their feet now and, at some signal from Rufus, Albedo and the other dog are heading off into the buildings on both sides, to check for more guns. I turn to Sugar and see her getting to her feet in Marmalade's shadow. The bear is snarling at Rufus, who's got her covered, now.

She's put herself in the way of any more gunfire, and I see a dash of red on her arm where one of the shots clipped her. I couldn't exactly have shoved her out of the way with little Jimmy's meagre store of momentum.

And Rufus has just killed a Thompson host, which confirms some things I was dearly, dearly hoping for.

"Sheriff," I address his radio receiver. "Let's talk. Somewhere without any easy sniper access."

"And who's this?" he growls.

"My name is Honey. I'm who you've been hunting down when you were trailing Jimmy. I'm also only your second biggest problem right now, as I hope I can make you see."

For a moment he's torn, because we're right here and he's got all the guns, and he could make his life very simple by just ignoring me, but then he nods and gestures with a cock of his head towards the building Albedo just went into.

Inside, there's a nice corporate lobby, complete with big screens and a reception, and some comfy furniture all done up in plastic covers to keep the dust off until someone's actually rented the space.

"So what am I talking to?" Rufus stares suspiciously into Jimmy's eyes as though expecting to see me hiding at the back.

"A personality upload operating out of Jimmy Marten's headspace," I explain. "I was a Bioform rights activist on Earth, in every sense of the words. Until Warner Thompson murdered me."

"Out of my jurisdiction," Rufus says. "My orders are contraband data came from Earth, came to Sugar through the usual back channels. Then I find it's in the head of Jimmy

Marten, of all the damn wasters on Mars. My orders are delete it, quarantine it, stop it spreading."

"And now? Only you must have noticed things have changed. Under new management," I prompt.

Albedo the cat has come back down now, making some report by closed channel to his boss. She settles onto her haunches slightly awkwardly. Rufus is apparently allowed on the couch, but then he's a dog-model without a tail. They didn't make this expensive office garnish for most Bioforms to sit on.

"Granted," Rufus admits cautiously. "Doesn't change my instructions. But I'm reasonable, Honey. You're talking to me, so I guess you're reasonable. You come out of Jimmy's head into some closed storage, or just let yourself be deleted if you'd rather not be taken alive, then Jimmy can go. Sugar can go, with both her friends. We don't need any collateral damage here."

Mariah has arrived, and is holding to my order. She has nine mustelids of various models. Brian's bears and dogs are further out and less united in their general outlook. Judit's dragons are... in the building across, actually, and Rufus's deputy dog has spotted them and is retreating and, no doubt, reporting. So notch up the tension one more hole.

"Sheriff Rufus," Jimmy says. "You got to be crazy, you ain't noticed how fucked things have got. Sugar and me, we're the only ones left in our right minds. Some son of a bitch politico from Earth just took everyone over, everybody locked in their own head while he puppets them around. Made himself into a human DisInt. It's just us two and you Bioforms, and everyone else is *him*, man!"

I let him talk, but if he's expecting a sudden volte-face from local law enforcement it doesn't happen. Rufus just nods philosophically.

"You think I don't know what's gone on?" he asks easily.

Jimmy goggles at him and mangles a few words trying to speak. Sugar picks up the slack.

"And this is just fine with you, Sheriff? I thought you were the fucking law? DisInt's illegal. Human Collaring's illegal."

"It isn't," Rufus tells her. "And I'm not the law. There's no law on Mars. World Senate's all tied up in knots over *jurisdiction*. Earth law doesn't run here." He actually laughs. "What, you thought you were a *criminal*, with all your data smuggling? Can't be, what with no law. What you are is a disruptive influence." And he leans in, putting them both in his shadow, a trick I used to do only I don't cast the shadow I used to. "I keep *order*, Sugar. Because we're on Mars, a few thousand no-good reprobates in a city where absolutely everything can go wrong. And so order is what we need. Right now I'm seeing you raising a pack of Bioforms to come threaten that order. And I will do whatever it takes to stop this city devolving into chaos."

"You told Jimmy you weren't Collared. The last dog I spoke to who wore a Rex medal was. Sons of Adam, if you've heard of them. But not you. Like you say, you're for order. Which is why you need to take a stand, Sheriff. Because you're not on the side of order right now."

He actually chuckles. "Oh, I know you now. Was trying to place the name. So you're Honey, the performing bear. I saw vid of you giving speeches. All very fancy language. You're all for pushing freedom as far as it'll go, right? Bioform freedom, that I can get behind. But you're for DisInt and AI and the next thing you know your toaster's got a vote and your congressman's a Buick, right?"

I've heard that kind of odious rhetoric so often I seriously want to step in just so I can roll Jimmy's eyes. "Sheriff, you understand entropy?"

"What?"

"End state of the universe, Sheriff. Ultimate order, energy of everything evened out, everywhere the same. Except, weirdly enough, it's also ultimate chaos at the same time, all that random motion just evening out until everything's the same structureless nothing. Same with politics, it's hard to tell order from chaos sometimes. You think you're imposing order by tightening the vice, cracking down, police on the streets, curfews and stop-and-search and let's-see-your-ID. Except, you look at any place and time when that's been instituted, you tell me whether history records those as havens of peace and stability. You show me when top-down imposition of order has done anything except fan the flames. And Sheriff, you are now working for a sociopathic personality upload – upload*s*, plural – who've got no idea how to run this place, how to keep the lights on and the air circulating, and no real interest, either. They – *he*'s just interested in being in control, in being himself, alone. And if there is any room for self interest in your head alongside all that duty and order, you just search out Warner S. Thompson and his attitude towards Bioforms and Collaring. You just look at the comfy seating here that your friend can't even use because they don't make expensive seats for non-human backsides. You just consider what your new boss will do with all the Bioforms in this place the moment he gets the chance, and no matter what he's telling you. Because he'll tell you anything, talk all the order and stability you want. Dictators always do. And they cause chaos, because their vision is so totally focused on themselves."

It's a long speech, but he doesn't interrupt. Instead he's coordinating his posse and the Bad News Bears, setting them up because Brian and the dog crews are shambling along the street in the open, now, and Mariah has brought Greer's people close by in the tunnels, and the building opposite is full of dragon-forms, and Rufus is planning a battle. But he's been listening too.

"I know you've got a gun to the head of Murder, down there," I tell him, because his own dragon, Smaug, is nervously doing just that. "But I need you to understand that you are not keeping the peace, here. You are aiding the breakdown of Hell City. Dictators don't make the trains run on time, Rufus. They run down the rail networks because they travel in private planes. And you're not Collared, which means you have a choice. Not a duty, a choice."

He looks Jimmy right in the eye, and I get a shock of contact, just as if I was really there. "You're going to tell me that's what your man Rex would have done, right? That was your deal. You were Rex's bear."

I rather think Rex was my dog, but that's a piece of pedantry I will forego. "If you know anything about Rex—"

"I," and I hear the shake in his voice, "have worked damn hard to keep this city together. Admin, they don't know. The work crews, they don't know. This Thompson doesn't damn well know. And you come here and tell me to let the revolution happen?"

"I tell you to let me fight Thompson. I freed Sugar from him. I am literally the only agent in this city who can do anything. But I need you to let Murder go, and then let me work without hunting us all over the map."

And the battle lines are drawn, and we outnumber him until Thompson arrives, but they've got the guns, and the Bad News Bears will fight like crazed berserkers because they won't be given a choice about it. And I am for freedom but I am also for peace. I don't want dead bears strewn across the barricades. I don't want Bioforms shedding the blood of Bioforms on Mars.

"It doesn't matter what Rex or anyone else would have done. It's you," I tell him. "And you talk duty, but it's choice. Doing your duty is your choice. Nobody's forcing you to obey orders right or wrong. You choose to, or you choose not to. And you will always bear responsibility for—"

"All right, shut up," he snarls at me, but I can hear the defeat there. "You love the sound of your own damn voice, don't you!"

"You have no idea," Jimmy agrees wholeheartedly, and Sugar snickers and Marmalade *uffs* and I feel unfairly persecuted, a prophet not honoured in her own country.

"So." Rufus stands, grabbing Albedo's shoulder for purchase to lever himself out of the prodigious dent he's made in the couch. "I suppose you'd better *do* it, then." And outside, the cameras tell me, they've taken the gun away from Murder's head, and I'm speaking quickly to Brian and company, all the troops, standing them down.

And of course there are cameras here in the expensive lobby, and I'm not the only one with access to them.

The shooting starts almost immediately, a handful of guns emptying into the bears and dogs Brian's brought. The firearms squads are on the move, because Thompson

will use Bioforms to do his dirty work, but he won't trust
them. As soon as he knows his servants have betrayed him,
he's all vengeance. And he's after the systems, too. He – or
the controlling *he* at the top of the pyramid – is more than
happy to kill off hundreds of his own selves if he gets us. I'm
abruptly fighting him for control of the air, the doors, all the
vital systems that keep Hell City alive.

And I can't fight him. I literally cannot unpick him from
his victims one head at a time. I cannot run the revolution as
a handcrafted cottage industry.

I devolve the fight for the systems to Brian, Judit and
Mariah, telling them to stonewall Admin as long as they
can. I suspect Bees has laid all manner of little quirks in
the infrastructure for just this eventuality and I brush aside
the uneasy thought that her plan might have been quite the
opposite – attack rather than defence. For myself, I...

Have a plan.

"Get me into Admin. Get Jimmy into Admin. I need direct
access." There's too much flying about to let me do what I
need to. I need the sort of priority that proximity brings, to
shoulder my pure signal into the system.

Even as they're hustling forwards, as we're hacking the
airlock; even as Judit's dragons and the rest of the posse
take on the Bad News Bears to clear the way; even as there's
fighting over the lock itself, guns inside against the Bioforms
outside. Even then I'm trying to find another way. I do not
want to do this. I don't know how it will turn out. It goes
against my principles and if there's one thing my relationship
with Jimmy's taught me it's that my principles are not the
iron-bound things I thought they were.

Then Greer's weasels come up out of the ducts inside

Admin and take out the gun squad there, bloodily enough, and we're in, and it's time.

And I do not want to. They're all staring at me, and they don't understand what they're asking, or what the price is. Like Bees says, action always carries a price. I don't want to pay it. And it won't be just me. It might be everyone digging in their pockets for the fare. I feel that Bees, out there in her own Martian base, is watching me with cool amusement.

We're in, all the Admin access I could want, as Thompson's puppets scatter and flee. But not far, and he's still all over, a single entity across thousands of bodies, organised in a rigid hierarchy like a fascist's wet dream. He won't ever work with someone else by choice, even if that someone else is him.

So in the end, I have my choice and my duty and I don't want either of them, and I'd love to stop and savour the irony but there just isn't time. And so I access Admin as Rufus and Greer and Marmalade and Sugar hold the airlock against all comers. I'm coming for Warner S. Thompson. This town isn't big enough for the both of us.

25

JIMMY

So there we are, inside Admin. Me, Sugar and her two bear pals, plus Greer and a bunch of his pals and... And Rufus and his posse, if you can believe it. Right there, close enough to pull Albedo's whiskers. 'Cos apparently sometimes Honey *can* talk the talk. Which is just as well 'cos, this time round, the head getting a bullet would have been mine, not hers.

And Honey. Honey's with us, obviously. Can't goddamn get rid of her.

There are some Admin staff inside who got thumped and cuffed. Not Danny Boyd or most of the senior guys, and I reckon they were already off enjoying fancy apartments from their lofty view at the top of the human pyramid. Probably they're on their way back right now. Outside, we can see a lot of movement. The cameras show us a bunch of people, just regular Hell City people of all types and colours of overall, and a lot of them have got some serious guns.

"So they send those shooters over as data too," Sugar drawls. "Or you maybe reckon they were always planning to pop a cap in some Bioform ass, Sheriff? I mean, maybe yours, say? You know they had those?"

Rufus eyes her sourly. "Course I knew. What, you think

the moment some bear-form goes crazy I'm the only line of defence?"

"Honey?" I ask because, hate her all I want, she's still all we've got right now. "This plan of yours?"

"I'll require a little time to set up, after which ideally things will either succeed or fail on their own. For the setup time, I need to be here in Admin with uninterrupted access to the command systems. Or at least the further away I am, the more difficult the data transfer and the interactions will become. It's the downside of your Cloud setup here, I'm afraid, because there's way too much traffic flying back and forth now that everyone's become a neuron in Thompson's brain."

"But you're going to be able to save them, right?" Meaning the self-same everyone Honey just mentioned.

"That's the plan." Which isn't 'yes' exactly.

Then the first shot comes in and blasts a big hole in the arm of one of Greer's crew, knocking the weasel to the ground. Didn't slow none for the wall it just went through and now we can all feel the denser atmosphere whooshing out into Hell City proper. Shame, I was enjoying some decent air in my lungs. But it's what they built us all for, so it's not going to kill us.

We've all scattered by then, and the posse turn over all the expensive office furniture and make barricades with it. Outside we see mobs of people moving in, quite a lot of them, and of course there must be hundreds converging from all over the city, from outside, from wherever Thompson had them. We're priority, now.

"Honey..."

"Still working," she tells me. "Hold them." And then, because Rufus and company have their guns levelled,

"Nobody kill them! Suppressive fire, keep their heads down. All we need is time, Those are innocent people."

"I don't think you realise—" Rufus starts, but Honey cuts him off.

"Soldier, I was carrying a gun before you came out of the factory." And then, undercutting her own drill sergeant routine. "Admittedly these opponents are all effectively Collared so they may not show the usual desire for self-preservation. Depends on how Thompson's yanking his own leash."

"Bears!" Greer shouts, and for a moment I think we've lost Marmalade and Murder, but he means outside. I guess the individual Thompsons have enough leeway to send in the cannon fodder first.

There are about twenty Bad News Bears out there, which I reckon means all of them currently out of the freezer, and they're coming in full tilt, charging on all fours at a pace that indicates no doubt whatsoever that they can get through the walls and at us.

"Can we kill *them*?" Rufus snarls.

For a moment I think Honey's going to say no even to that, bears with bears and all, but then she says yes, however reluctantly, and the posse brace for impact. Then follows the scariest fifteen minutes in my life, bar none.

I mean, probably you're after a blow by blow. Moving the pieces about the war table, telling you who duelled who like King goddamn Arthur against Abe Lincoln. But man, I was hiding. It's what I do. It's what I'm good at. And I was doing my part by bringing Honey to the table. If something happened to me it'd be game over. So hiding was my bit, really. A real and solid contribution to the game plan.

I remember those Bad News Bears bounced from the Admin wall the first time, though dust came down from the ceiling and there were cracks. Then the Thompsons had some drilling kit, the sort we used to break up rocks outside, and that opened up a hell of a hole and filled the air with dust like a solid sheet. And the bears came through that.

Just moments after that... Moments from when I poked my head above the desk I was hiding behind. I remember Marmalade and one of the Bad News Brigade tearing each other up, with Murder hunched about her bandages and watching from right behind. I think Sugar jumped up on the Bad News Bear's back and began stabbing it, but to be honest there was too much dust after that. I remember Smaug going down under one bear, and Rufus hauling it off, gun to the poor damn animal's head and unloading, great low-grav spray of blood and bone through the thick air. I remember Rufus's dog deputy almost shooting Marmalade, because in all that shit one bear looks like another. There were people coming in then, on the Bad News' heels, just shooting everywhere. But then there's stuff going on outside and I know Brian and Judit have arrived with whoever they've recruited, and I hope they aren't just straight up murdering people.

And Honey's been quiet, all her focus on whatever her plan is rather than, say, stopping the Bad News Bears, and that plan better be a good one because we're getting swamped here.

I remember a bullet went straight through the desk I was behind and came this close to me not being able to tell this to you.

By then there's so much dust you can't see anything more than a metre away, and I have no idea how anyone's still fighting or if they've all grown sonar like bats and it's just me. Except of course the Thompson guys all kind of know where each other is, maybe, and in any event they're still coming. They don't know the plan any more than I know the plan, but they know we're up to something.

And then there's someone standing over the desk.

I look up, hopeful it's Sugar, or maybe it's Mariah. I'd even take Brian Dey right about now. Except it's not. It's a woman called Maybelline Strack who works the hydroponics most days. I know her mostly 'cos we share the same dealers and taste in pharmaceuticals. And I bet Thompson's not been taking her pills but she's been feeling all the kickback from that. Because it's her face, of course, but not her behind the eyes. And she's got a gun levelled at me. I feel a scattered attempt at contact from her: friend or foe, are you in the hierarchy? And I am not. Yours Truly is a rugged loner, not part of the greater nation of Thompson. Ergo, the enemy.

"Maybee," I tell her, uselessly, but what else do you do, confronted with a face you know? "Come on." But that punchable smile turns up on her face, that same smile that's been walking around Hell City way too much, and she just about jams the gun in my face, wanting me to piss my britches before Thompson has her pull the trigger.

Thing about a gun, the kind of defining reason they're so popular, is that they're best used at range. That's kind of their deal. You go jamming a gun right in someone's face, that someone might go berserk and just grab it. And I am not saying I'm being some goddamn hero here. Not your man Jimmy. Except there's a gun in my face, and there's Honey's talk about getting a gun to the eye herself as the last thing that eye ever saw, and something snaps. I've got a hand on the barrel and another on her trigger finger and we're fighting for it. It goes off right by my ear, deafening – but the thin air means I don't actually end up deaf. And we fight, and I find out Maybee Strack's body, when used without due care and attention for wear and tear, is actually stronger than mine, so she gets a knee into my balls and then slams me back slantways across the desk, which hurts enough to take my mind off the first part. I'm still complicating the gun, so she does the slam again until I'm not. And I'm looking down the barrel again, a mess of pain and bruises, calling for help, trying to radio Rufus and Sugar and tell them I'm about to add to the general mist of blood that's congealing dust out of the air and spattering every surface.

Maybee screams.

She drops the gun, which, thank you, lands right on my abused nuts. Even with that distraction I just watch her, because she screams and screams. She's got her hands to her head, tearing at her hair, fingers leaving livid marks, nails gouging. And then I realise that she's just the soloist to a whole chorus. There are screaming people everywhere. The fighting's down to two remaining Bad News Bears that Rufus and posse are taking down brutally and efficiently. All the humans, this mob here, are screaming, writhing, out of control.

"Right," Honey says in my head. "It's on."

Brian's voice comes to us, from whatever foxhole he's found for himself. "Bees say Mars gon' dark, Honey. Nobody get in, nobody get out until this is sorted, understan'?"

"Understood." Honey sounds... unhappy. The screaming is tailing off, though, one voice after another going quiet. Maybee is just standing there now, arms by her side. I wait for that horrible smile to come back, but she's got a weird expression on her face instead, like... a real Uncanny Valley expression. Like she's a mannequin put together by an AI that failed pattern recognition when it came to faces. The mouth is pulled wide, slightly down, and the eyes are too big. Like she was being a sad mime and got stuck that way.

I lever myself up. Everything hurts. The extractor fans are doing what they can with the dust, so I can see people as shadows, then start to recognise them. I see... bodies. At least a half dozen of the Thompsons that barrelled in got their hosts killed. I see Mariah, who looks like one of the Bad News Bears caught her. Smaug's down. Greer's down. I go over to him. Looks like he took a bullet front and centre, lips pulled back from his pointy teeth in a final snarl. I mean, he was one of my dealers. Seems weird to feel so cut up, but I am. And he came, actually came to save Hell City. I just kind of collapse beside him then, sit there, every part of me aching, put a hand on his cooling body. Want to cry but can't because they sealed up my tear ducts and just gave me all these extra eyelids instead. Eventually Sugar comes over, her arm bloody, and puts a hand on my shoulder.

"Honey," she asks. "What's going on."

"Bees has taken over central control of the satellites," we're told. "There will be no beaming of data out of Hell City. No escape. And there will be no re-infection. Comms down until we've patched this vulnerability."

"That's not what I mean." She's eyeing all the people who are just standing there, and I see that same disjointed expression on all their faces.

"Don't worry about it," Honey says, and they all start

moving, all those people. They just go, as one, like they all came to the same decision.

"Honey." I mean, dry-throated is a given, with the dust, but my voice is a deathly croak right then. "What did you do?"

"What I had to," she says, all business, speaking too heartily to cover up that she knows she's done something terrible. "I couldn't just unpick each instance of Thompson from the outside. It took too long, as we found with Sugar. And so."

"You had better fucking clarify that 'And so'," Sugar tells her.

"And so it's quicker and easier to just play him at his own game given that this is one ladder he forgot to pull up after him. I've uploaded myself into these units of Thompson's DisInt network, overwritten him. And now they're going out into the rest of the city to bring the rest here, and to set up other download hubs. And I'll be doing what I can remotely, although it's a lot of data and he's fighting me in the system. Easier to get them here where the connection is better."

Sugar and I exchange looks, and I am reminded that she's already *in* me. She can march me off to join the revolution right now. And she can take Sugar over just like that. We don't know how to stop her.

"Honey..." I say, and she cuts me off.

"Just until it's done, Jimmy. I'm sorry, but it's the only way. You want our side to win, right?"

And I do. Of course I do. Only I'm not sure it's our side any more. What if it's just Honey's side?

"What do we do now?" Sugar asks.

"Everything is set in motion," we're told. In fact, she's

telling everyone. "Over the next, I estimate, four hours, the battle for control of Hell City will be decided. It would be best if you continue to occupy Admin because if Thompson got in here he could use the system access to complicate things. Other than that, you may as well go home. I've got it all in hand." She sounds calm, really goddamn calm. The dancing bear that's making everyone in the city dance to her tune. I feel sick. I pop some Stringer. It doesn't help. I feel like it's never going to help again. I just keep thinking of how she took that away from me, because she thought it was better for me. And probably it *was* better for me, only she didn't ask. She just knew better, and did. And I know how much we, the good folk of Hell City, are fuck-ups through and through. And now each of us is going to get some free Honey, the bear that knows best. And once she's saved us from Thompson she'll want to save us from ourselves.

The one fragile crust of good luck right now is that I figure that's us out of the game. No more fighting for the likes of Sugar and Rufus and me. Not like we can do much when the war's going on between digital gods, right? I say as much to Sugar and she and Marmalade just kind of stare at me. Murder would've done too, if she hadn't been sleeping right then, packed full of drugs.

"What?" says I.

"'Digital gods?'" Sugar echoes. "You just pop a poetry pill with the Stringer, Jimbles?"

So I tell her to go fuck herself and they have a good old laugh at my expense.

Rufus, who's more the task-focused type, has been trying to work out what's going on, and he leans on Brian until Bee's best bud calls up a big old 3D wireframe map of Hell City and tries to show us where the fighting's going on. Except it's not fighting and it's not going on anywhere you could show on a map. Hearts and minds, right? Only this time it really is a war for goddamn hearts and minds, going on without the consent of the original owners. I still can't get it out of my head, how it was when that bear was pulling my strings. And now it's everyone, turned into the weapons for Mars' biggest man vs nature showdown. And we watch the gold stain that's Honey spread out into the surrounding red that's Thompson and I try to forget that every part of both stains is people.

And it goes on.

Jesus, but it goes on. And Honey keeps fucking oozing outwards, and sometimes there's a reversal, mostly at the barrel of a gun I reckon, but overall she's just smarter than Thompson, and she gets her puppets close enough to his puppets and then attacks them until she's deleted him and put herself in his place, or grabs them and hauls them over here so she can do it all double time and with better signal strength. Hearts and minds. But there are plenty people in Hell City and it takes a while. And you wouldn't think a man would get bored with the fate of a world in the balance but there's only so long you can stare at a crappy map of the crappy city you helped build.

Next thing I know Sugar's shaking me awake, and I cock an eye up, hoping it's over, but she's been playing tactician and suddenly she knows better than Rufus or Honey because she wants a second opinion on something.

"What even?" I demand and want to go back to sleep, but she says a wank of Thompsons, or whatever the goddamn collective noun is, have holed up in Cashiers.

"Maybe they want to do an embezzlement for old time's sake before the bear gets them," I suggest, but Sugar hasn't got her fun face on right now.

"Cashiers, Jimmy," and the fact that I'm not Jimbles tells me how serious she is. She gives me quite the gabble then, about how Thompson has people holed up in system critical locations – he's been leaning on his hosts for info because I'm damn sure he didn't come with a working knowledge of Hell City infrastructure. He's fighting her for atmosphere control, airlocks, reactors, all that. Desperation stuff, she says. I look at the map, and the sea of red is a sea of gold now, the red confined to islands.

"He tried to send the main reactor critical ten minutes ago," she says casually.

I choke. "You could have fucking woken me for that!"

"Honey got him," Marmalade growls. She's gone partisan. I half expect her to have a Honey baseball cap and wave a little flag. I guess when one of your relatives makes it to demigod it's cause for celebration. "Honey always gets him."

"Honey's focusing on what makes sense to her." Sugar doesn't sound so confident. "So this little clique in Cashiers is getting a pass right now." She prods Brian in the shoulder. "You get me a look-see into there? Hack the cameras?"

"Don't know what you think you gon' see." Bri had been dozing like me. Now he rubs at his new bruise, glances at Marmalade and screws with the system until he gets us a view. It keeps breaking up, but there's a good dozen Thompson vehicles holed up in there, and they're doing something very busily.

"That Illy Fricker?" Sugar asks. "The meteorologist?"

There's a frown on her face as she stares at a thin woman in the midst of all that activity.

"I reckon," I agree. "Guess she holed up at home then." Because that's the office Weather operate out of too, for a complicated reason that has nothing to do with efficiency and everything to do with a particular dodge Fricker's been running for years.

"Only..." Sugar starts.

"Oh, everyone knows that..." I add.

And we stare at each other.

Because Illy Fricker is high up, senior stuff and normally Sugar and I wouldn't be fit to spit-polish her shoes, except for this thing she had on the side. She was kind of a facilitator for Sugar's service sector. She brought in information the back way, using the met satellites supposed to be out there warning us of dust storms. Information for Sugar and her peers to store and sell and do whatever they wanted, with Illy Fricker taking her cut.

"Everyone knows..." I start uncertainly, but they don't, not really. Rufus doesn't. Honey doesn't, because what does she really know, that isn't written into the manuals? She hasn't lived here and built Hell City. She just swanned in after she died to take over. Just maybe, even Bees didn't spot that particular obscure little back door. Only scum like Marmalade and Sugar and me, we know.

There's a complete suite of satellite controls at the Met desk in Cashiers, because Illy Fricker had her sideline planned from the start. It doesn't link to central satellite control, is quite thoroughly hidden from it in fact, because she wanted to be able to download illicit data without anyone looking over her shoulder. She ran quite the porn network too, as I recall.

At about that time, Illy or some other Thompson realises they're being spied on and we lose the camera. But they were definitely about something, and I think about how Thompson could threaten and bribe his hosts until they told him some little secret, something he could use.

"He's trying to get himself sent back to Earth?" I ask.

"Mos' like," Brian agrees, breaking in over my shoulder and making me jump.

"Hm," Sugar says.

"I mean, it's not our problem if he does," I point out.

"Hm," Sugar says again.

Which is why we end up standing outside Cashiers' main entry, me and Sugar, and we get Rufus along mostly because we can't get rid of him. We did try to tell Honey. We got Brian to open a channel, except Honey is everywhere and nowhere and there is no channel, The whole data network of Hell City is full of Honey downloading herself into Thompson and she didn't answer, wrote us off as not being capable of an insight she hadn't already thought up, thought through and published in some fancy academic journal. Even the Honey in my head, Honey Prime as she is, is too busy coordinating her virtual coup to listen to me. So we went. On our feet, like real people do.

The streets are safe as houses by now. Nobody takes a pot-shot at us. We're at the very tail end of Thompson's reign of terror and the start of the next one. And Rufus only has one way of going about things, and it ain't subtle, so he's basically fucking called ahead and told 'em we're coming. Which Sugar remarks was a professional courtesy she was always fond of but there's a time and a place.

Cashiers is off-centre, behind all the main Admin, but it's still business district and there are big screens up for advertising. Now they show Danny Boyd's face glowering down at us. He's looked better, frankly. He looks twisted out of shape, like someone else's expressions are grappling with every muscle.

"Rufus." His lips fight each other over the word. "Bad Dog. Go home. Bad Dog let a bear in." His eyes are bloodshot and he looks, to use the correct psychoanalytical *parlance*, absolutely fucking crazy.

Big Dog Rufus actually cringes a bit, believe it or not, but then he faces up to one of the screens. "We're coming in there if you don't stop what you're doing. Just..." His broad shoulders sag. "Give up and I'll try and... talk to her. Preserve you as data..."

Thompson's Boyd's features snarl. *"She's* the data. I'm a man. I'm human. I'm alive. All of me. She can't have me. And you can't come in."

"Bees is onto you, Tommy," Sugar breaks in. "She'll block anything you try to send. So give it up."

"You can't touch us. None of you can. We're safe here. She can't get us." The smile that works its way onto Boyd's face has all the guile of a three-year-old, the kind that squishes bugs for fun. "I'll fix you all. I'll win on Earth. I'll win here. You can't get in."

I think of the satellites up above us, the ones Illy Fricker made sure she had full control of from her Met desk, without oversight. Enough control for Thompson to get himself sent back to Earth, his mind holed up somewhere even as the real him gets raked over the coals in the World Senate courts. Because every copy of Thompson would be the true original, to itself, and even this copy out on the arse-end of the solar system wants to be saved.

Oh, and blow us all the fuck up, as well, maybe. Because you can move those satellites about, and if you wanted you could drop one on Hell City, microreactor and all, once you'd copied yourself out. Brian explained it to us. Brian explained that it was something Bees had made sure was built in, just in case she got fed up of the neighbours' loud music. Our little fleet of comms and weather satellites are basically a missile armada pointed straight down. So that was fun, right? That was a good, healthy, reassuring thing to discover in the middle of our little succession crisis here on Mars. Good times in Hell City.

And we don't know if Thompson's planning that, but I think he might be, because I don't think he understands about copies and originals and how, if he actually sent himself to Earth, how the copy that did the sending would be *still here* because that's how copying works. Even being the great original where spreading himself about goes, I don't think he quite gets what it means.

So anyway, that jolly thought was what finally got us stirred to come over here and do our bit in the war for freedom.

"Tommy boy," Sugar tells him. "You need to start thinking like a Martian."

Just a bug-eyed stare from him, no idea who she is, just one of the little people who used to be his.

"Look up," she adds.

Like I say, they built those biz units with nice skylights, for all that Mars ain't got a nice sky. You can look straight up into the crappy starscape and sometimes see the milquetoast little nugget that's the sun. Privileges of rank, right? Except those skylights aren't exactly a structural strong point, and anyway, Marmalade's out there with a crew of bears and some heavy-duty mining gear, and it's not as though the actual walls would last long against that anyhow.

The screens go black when the cutting starts, though we feel the vibrations through our feet. I don't get to see how it goes, but Marmalade tells me later. The panic, basically. The sheer screaming panic of a half dozen Thompsons as the ceiling gets carved up and all their husbanded atmosphere floods out, with only the Hellas Planitia thinness and a crapton of dust patiently waiting to come in once the pressure equalises. They charge about and clutch at their throats and scream and thrash, and I hope, I sincerely *hope* that the prisoners in their heads are killing themselves laughing at the dumbass Earth tourist ignorant of our Martian ways.

Rufus goes for the door then, and a combination of security overrides and sheer brute strength gets him in despite the atmosphere differential that should be locking it all down. After that it's just making a note to fix the big new airhole that Hell City just grew. It's cuffs and hauling away all those Thompsons who didn't realise or didn't remember that Outside Mars is what those bodies were engineered for, and a little drop in pressure ain't going to harm anyone much. Just a regular working day for us Martians, even for back-office types like Illy Fricker.

And Danny Boyd wasn't even there in person, so we don't get the glory of bagging the Thompson-in-chief or whatever. And probably Honey doesn't even realise we did anything.

Back in Admin Central and we liaise with Brian who takes it all real-philosophical.

"Bees be glad of that," he tells us, though how he got a line out to Bees is anyone's guess, with all the channel-hogging bear biz going on.

"She'd have stopped him anyway. I know. We all wasted our time running around," I say, feeling worn out. It's hard being a mere mortal when the gods are playing. Hard to feel you made a difference.

"Somethin' like that." Brian has an odd look on him. I, frankly, am too tired to care. Only later do I think about just what that *somethin'* might mean. About Bees' doomsday plan, and how we might all have been wearing satellite hats before she let Thompson escape. And if I'd thought of that at the time, I'd have grabbed Bri by the neck and screamed into his face about what the fuck he sold his soul to. Just as well I didn't, really.

"Where are you going?" Sugar asks, and I realise I've stood up.

"Going to get some painkillers," I tell her. "Going home." Because I've done my part, and I cannot stay here, with the dead, with the greasy slicks where the blood has met the dust like some fucking metaphor for mortality. With the sound of people dragged in to be forcibly de-Thompsoned and en-Honeyed. I'm shaking, from some deep place no amount of Stringer's going to reach. I've got to get out of here.

"Home?" Sugar asks blankly. "Your nook?"

I shrug and just go, and she trails after me, leaving Marmalade to watch over Murder.

"Jimmy!" she calls, and then we both scoot to one side because a brawling mob's coming past, a half dozen people bundling another three between them. The bundlers have the weird not-quite-human look; the *animal* look, now I think about it. The three they've got are all showing the same purpling outrage. They're heading for Admin, to do to as they've been done.

"Jesus," I say, and Sugar nods.

It's like that throughout the city, all the way back to the crappy coffin-sized residences we actually get to live in. We see the population of the city at war with itself, and none of it under the control of those bodies' regular owners. We see construction workers and engineers, agriculturalists and accountants and janitors all going tooth and nail at each other, literally. Whole packs of them fighting, but by now there's more Honeys. I remember she always said she was a soldier, and now she's her own army. And Thompson had her killed and now she's hunting him through the city one head at a time, erasing him. Even when we can't see faces we know who's who. It's in the way they hold their stolen bodies. You can see the bear beneath the skin.

Every so often, less and less often, we hear the screaming, the hideous sound of people in the moments between Thompson losing control of them and Honey taking it back. People who've been locked up inside their own heads, robbed of their freedom the worst way, forced to watch what one DisInt or another makes their bodies do.

We reach the row of nooks that includes mine. It's all very empty. There's a party out on the streets and it's only us who've not been invited.

"Jesus," I say again. I liberated some serious painkillers from stores and they've kicked in by now, so say my back and my balls, but neither that nor the Stringer's really touched my mind. Sugar looks like I feel, too. I wonder where we stand, her and me, now. We always used to be criminal overlord and witless dupe. We've been through some shit, though, her and me.

Then we get to my nook and someone's already in it. Mostly they're someone with a gun. That is what has my immediate attention.

It is, of all goddamn people, Daniel Boyd.

He looks worse than I feel. His face is bruised, red about the eyes and mouth, a weird yellowish colour like the controlling intelligence inside is finding it difficult adjusting to a biomodded Martian body. The gun is shaking but I don't fancy playing Russian roulette with it just now.

"Jimmy Marten," he gets out. "That's what he says your name is." I take in the narrow eyes, the way the mouth chews over the words.

"Thompson."

"Help me," says Thompson with Boyd's lips. I mean, he's got the gun. If anyone needs help it's me and Sugar, both of us well within the cone of fire of that weaving barrel. I'm sending a shout over the radio to Rufus, to Brian, to Honey, in all her many bodies.

"What help?" Sugar asks.

"She's coming for me," Boyd/Thompson whines. "Hide me."

"What?"

"Jimmy, hide me. You were never me. You never got taken by me. Hide me, Jimmy. She won't look for me in you."

I try to exchange a look with Sugar but the gun demands my attention. He advances with it; we retreat.

"What?" I get out. "Th— Mr Thompson, that doesn't make sense. I can't—"

"You were never me!" he shouts, spit and blood stringing

across my face. "Hide me now! She can't have me! She won't find me in you! She won't look there! Let me in, Jimmy!" And then he's got me by the lapel with the gun under my chin and I suddenly don't fancy doing the kung fu thing I did with Maybee Stack. He is crazy twitchy and any additional twitch I bring to the situation's gonna see that trigger pulled.

"Boyd told you who I was," I wheeze, and he nods furiously.

In my ear, my receiver, comes Sugar's voice. "I'm going to jump him."

I can't sub-voc back, not without Thompson seeing. I do not want Sugar to jump him. Apparently, as with every other damn thing, it's not my choice.

"Boyd didn't tell you why he was hunting me himself? Why he set the posse on me?" And I realise I must be right, and that Daniel Boyd, softest man on Mars, has been playing Thompson from inside his own head. Oh, Danny Boy, you sly bastard.

"He said you were the only one. And he showed me where you'd be. Let me in, now. Hide me. I have to go on. I'm in charge here. Do it. Do what I want!"

It's the naked man I'm seeing. The man stripped of his flunkies and his power. Not even a man, really, by Honey's estimation. Just a kind of stripped down virus that's spent its whole existence using the bodies of other people to get its way.

"I'll do it, I'll do it," I say, pulling all my cringing weak-boy to the front. And it's an act I was always good at, up in front of authority. And he's faking authority, and I'm faking the act, but it's what he expects and so he goes for it. The gun is away from my chin. He relaxes. I let him connect to my headware.

Sugar, who isn't quite in on the plan, bundles him to one side then, and the gun punches a big old hole in the wall as they go sideways. He throws her off in a spasm of limbs, but she got the gun off him, and we just stare at each other.

"You ask Danny Boy why he was after me?" I say. "I'm Patient Zero for Bear's Disease you miserable fucker." And I imagine him shoving at his connection to my headware, trying to bundle all the bulging sack of his data through that conduit, pushing on the door only to discover that there's someone at home in the cottage after all. It's Mummy Bear, progenitor of all the beasts that are hunting him down across Hell City. She's been there all along.

"No," Thompson says. "No. No, you have to hide me. Me. I'm the only one. I'm all that's left. I can't go. I won't be cast aside. I demand. I demand you do. I can't. I. I want. I won't. I will. I have. Have it. I have control now. I think that's all of them." And we see the creep of features across Boyd's face, like watching a battlefield from the air, the triumphant advance and the rout. We see Thompson being wiped off him, and there isn't even any screaming now. Honey's refined her process.

Daniel Boyd stands up, only it isn't him. It still isn't him, it's just a different puppeteer. I see Sugar twitch. She has the gun and she's obviously fighting an impulse to point it at Boyd's face, to hold him to ransom to threaten Honey, however useless that would be.

"All of them?" I echo, and Honey nods Boyd's head and heads off away from the nooks, the two of us trailing behind.

"I've erased Thompson from the system, and from everyone in the city," she tells me over Boyd's shoulder. "The only Thompson left is on Earth and, I sincerely hope, in some form of cell right about now, and for the rest of his natural life." And out into a thoroughfare where there are more than a dozen other people just standing there. "Unless he gets justice in his own constituency, in which case I think they still have an option for the gas chamber," Honey finishes, and turns to face us, just as the rest of them are facing us. All of them just the same, standing tall and slump-shouldered like bears, heads slightly forward. Same weird failed expression on every face.

"I'm now patching the citywide headware to make sure nobody else tries this particular trick," she says. "No more invasions on my watch. After which Bees will open up communications with Earth."

And Sugar and I just stare at her because it sounds like there's only going to be one voice speaking to Earth for Hell City, and that voice will be the United State of Bear.

26

HONEY

And I understand Bees now. Just a bit. When she turned away from the rest of the world because what she had was better. What she had was so broad and complete that it was a world in itself, and only the wider universe really held significance. Not the doings of hominids and hominid-created intelligences on the next planet in, the planet of her birth.

And I understand Thompson. Just a bit. When he shackled himself to himself, a pyramid of feudal authority so that he knew he would truly be in control of it all, and that 'all of it' would always only be just him, over and over.

And I put him out, pinched the last instance of him like a candle flame, preventing the forest fire he'd tried to turn himself into. And now I'm left in the echo of my deeds, in the driving seat of every human being on Mars bar Jimmy and Sugar and the handful that Bees sequestered as her AdApts, as she calls them. Thompson is gone. There's just me. All of me. A monstrous regiment of bears. And I have done such things. I have broken every rule I ever swore to live by, because it was the only way to win. I made the choice, in the end, that the ends would justify the means. And that just gives me a worse choice, because what, precisely, do I do with it all now I've won?

I, singular, or I plural? More than an 'I', less than a 'we'. I've become a Distributed Intelligence by right of conquest, and at a scale poor fugitive HumOS couldn't dream of. I am beside myself, amidst myself, surrounded by myself. And I could do such things. Let's get the easy quandaries out of the way first. I could turn this might, physical, intellectual, political, back on Earth. I could make demands. I am Mars, right now. I have the means to secure the planet, to build a red Utopia. And they say everyone's Utopia is someone else's dystopia and that would certainly be the case here, but then I would be the sole inhabitant. Or at least I would get all the votes. And I suppose I could probably transmit myself to Earth, turn the data of my mind into a cyber-attack, take over unattended headware and hardware, computers, robots. I have a lot of brainpower right now. I reckon I could crack quite a few secure systems. Maybe I'd end up with some nuclear weapons, bound to be a few lying around in a less than secure bunker somewhere. I could hold the world to ransom, proper supervillain style, demand liberty and equality at the cost of any chance at fraternity. I could do such things, what they are I yet know not, but they would be the terror of the Earth. And those words work best when you remember the old man who says them goes stark staring mad on a moor two acts later. So let's not turn our many thoughts that way. I take a straw poll of me and I'm against it.

But still.

Haven't you ever wanted to accomplish great things, except

time and the general obstinacy of the world catches up to you time and again, until there isn't either time or again, and you're just staring down the barrel of a gun. I wasn't ready. I'm owed more life. I had such plans for the world. And I'm a good bear, and they were good plans, and the world would have been a better place if only I'd been able to put them into action. Selfish, greedy men, bigoted men, ignorant and narrow-minded men, they stopped me. Surely I'm owed a chance to readjust the scales? It wasn't for myself, or only for me insofar as I was a member of an oppressed minority whose general lot I was trying to better.

I could do such things.

What they are I yet know not, but they would be.

The terror of the Earth.

And all the while, in the seconds it takes me to consider these many matters of import, there are thousands of screaming minds trapped within mine, held under the surface, severed from their bodies. And I can say that Thompson did it. That, like a rich man's distant nephew, I only inherited the plantation. It wasn't me who put them all in chains. And I am sufficiently qualified to teach moral philosophy to know that kind of logic doesn't wash, for all the world sees it every day.

Bees' channel: *Well?* From across the other side of the planet, her query bouncing off the satellites she put into darkness to stop Thompson's mind beaming itself into space, or beaming more copies of itself from Earth. The satellites that very nearly ended it one way or another anyway, because humans are more devious and crooked than I give them credit for.

Well?

Dragon used to send a sound, back when we were soldiers,

to indicate he didn't agree or understand, but didn't want to lower himself to human words. I send that to Bees now. Perhaps I want her to tell me what to do, but she won't. So long as I don't interfere with her plans she'll leave me alone in turn. Bees has decided she doesn't care about others any more. I spent a life caring about others and ended up getting shot through the eye for my pains. I can sympathise. I can even envy her.

My channel: *I can't keep this.* Envy, but not emulate. I never wanted to be a Distributed Intelligence. HumOS even suggested it to me once. I said no then. And it's harder now, but I still say no.

Bees considers as the signals ricochet back and forth. *I note you haven't started deleting your spare duplicates.*

My channel: *That's because there aren't any spare duplicates.* That suggests a hierarchy. That was Thompson's thing. I just trusted myself. My selves. All of me are equal. The fact that this one is older by virtue of being in Jimmy's head isn't a meaningful distinction. We are all me. I can't exactly turn to all the others and tell them to delete themselves. And so we eye each other, me and my selves.

Bees' channel: *I can upload you.*

My channel: *But which me? We are all me. You can't store us all, surely.*

Bees' channel: *Correct. I have myself and my AdApts to store. Limited space in the beehive. Pick one. Pick a random Honey.*

But I can't. The moment I turn to the crew and tell them there's one space in the lifeboat... mutiny. A house divided against itself. I must ask HumOS how she doesn't just fragment. Except I'll never get the chance. So, if I make this decision, we all make it. No exceptions, no seniority, no special treatment. And this is the real prisoner's dilemma, because I have to trust myself, all my selves. Anyone turning coat right now would win the world. I have to trust that I will do the right thing.

My channel: *Bees, you were born to this. HumOS was born to this. I've had it thrust upon me. I was never meant to be just a virtual person. I died, Bees. I died on Earth. I've been luckier than most, with what I've managed to achieve post mortem. But I was an old bear, and then I was a dead bear. And what I am now isn't Honey, even though it thinks it is. And if I leave matters any longer I will lose my resolution. I will do such things...*

The terrors of the Earth. And I will save the Earth this one time more. I will save the Earth from a plague of bears. I will save it from me.

I fix the vulnerability in everyone's headware. It takes one more second, all of me working simultaneously in every head. I fix Sugar too, the one vulnerable head I'm not in. She doesn't notice.

I send a message to HumOS, saying goodbye. I ask Bees to give her the details, because she needs to know how it ended. I could compile the report myself, but I am deathly afraid of changing my mind during the writing, of deciding that I would be better off staying around. Except even if I surrendered control and just sat in the back of everyone's heads like a toad, I'd still be me. I could never leave well enough alone. They'd still be slaves the moment they did something I didn't approve of. It'd be poor Jimmy and his drugs all over again.

And speaking of Jimmy, I say goodbye. He doesn't

understand, but I say it anyway, and then, before I can think up a whole extra list of farewells and final bequests and other procrastinating nonsense, I let go.

27

SPRINGER

She spent all morning waiting for someone to come talk to her, here in this comfortable cell they'd found for her, the people Wiley had put her in touch with, the people from the World Senate Court. And how did Jennifer Wiley have that kind of a contacts book? Except somehow Carole had known she would have, and that of all the people in the world she could call, only Wiley was guaranteed free of Thompson's influence.

And it was not a cell they'd consigned her to, not really, but they'd said she couldn't leave. She was the key witness, after all. All for her own protection. She had three spacious rooms high up in a tower here in New York. She had all the entertainment media she wanted but no calls out. Not even to her own lawyers, who were in any case Thompson's lawyers, and absolutely weren't supposed to talk to her. But when the chime went and someone did turn up, that was who she expected. The lawyers with their tablets of legal language there to explain to her all the genteel threats and bribes she was so used to, that she had authorised on so many other people. For her job. For her employer. And she understood, now that she could, that she had never had a choice about doing those things, nor even a choice about *wanting* to do those things.

But, at the same time, she thought about the woman she had been, when she'd applied to work on Thompson's team. Jennifer Wiley had said that Carole probably hadn't been a good person. Carole couldn't say, if she'd been left with the choice, whether she'd have backed off from doing most of the things she'd done. Her mind was still tangled up in memories of being loyal, of loving Thompson even as she hated him. Even though they'd taken the Collar from her throat she could still feel it there.

And what was the point of all her testimony, of her turning on her master and biting his hand, if it didn't make her free of him?

But no: not Thompson's legal team come to beat her down with words, not even the World Senate people to take testimony. Instead, alone at the door, was Jennifer Wiley.

"No," said Carole, trying to close it. "No interviews. No."

But Wiley was in the arc of the door already, weirdly nimble, stepping into Carole's personal space so that she fell back. Then the woman was inside the apartment, door closing at her heels, smiling disconcertingly.

"I'm not here for an interview, Ms Springer. Carole." That smile didn't belong to an aspiring biopic producer here for a scoop. For a dreadful moment Carole thought the woman literally wasn't herself, that she'd been taken over just like Thompson had done with the prisoners at Braintree. But the smile she saw *did* fit the other Jennifer Wiley; the one who'd said such strange things at the end of their meeting at the Live With US offices; the one who'd given her the brooch.

The bee brooch. The whole domino chain of events falling into place now, that had just been scattered shards of memory, kept nonsensical and out of sequence by all the barriers they'd put up in Carole's head. She felt that only now, standing here with this woman, did she see all of it at once. She felt as though she didn't know herself, a stranger in her own head.

She turned a glower on Wiley. She wanted to explode, to say that the woman had wrecked *everything*. For a brief moment she wanted to be back in the Collar where she wasn't allowed to doubt, and where she wasn't responsible for anything. But she didn't explode. That had never been a privilege accorded to her and, now she might have done, she was out of practice. She controlled herself. She put on her professional smile. "Well, if you're not here for an interview, Miss Wiley...?" Pretending confusion. As though she hadn't worked out who this woman was, or was a part of. She made to step into the next room but Wiley didn't move with her, as though she'd glued her feet down the moment she was inside.

"One moment," the woman said. She'd put her earnest biopic producer's smile back on, and Carole wondered if that part of her was actually real, as well as the other thing, the bigger thing. And of course she could never ask, could never give away that she knew, couldn't...

"What's it like?" The words out of her mouth, just as though she was free to say whatever she wanted. "Being a part of *it*." Couldn't quite say 'HumOS' even though she knew, even though she'd fought against the human collective on her former employer's behalf. Even though the Trigger Dogs had killed one of this woman's sisters in Aslan's offices without a moment's hesitation.

Wiley's smile didn't go away, just became a very different smile, less young, more wise. "I sometimes wish," she said, quietly enough that Carole had to lean in, "that I wasn't born into this family. It's hard, Carole. To know what I know. To share so much and still be me. Easier to just be on your own. Or easier to give up yourself and be no more than a limb, an organ of the whole. But easy isn't better. It's like being more than a part of something that's more than the sum of its parts."

"Glib," Carole said, hearing her own bitterness and marvelling at it. She was surprised by the stab of envy she felt. "Did you come here to gloat?"

"To you?" Genuine surprise. "You're a hero. Even if half the world curses you right now, we know the truth and that truth will come out. From your testimony at first, which they'll rubbish and question and counter with paid-off liars and frauds. But your headware doesn't lie. It's all in there, in the kit they themselves gave you. In you and in Boyo." Wiley saw her twitch and smiled again. "And Boyo will be fine. Although he's less cooperative than you are. So know you're saving him too."

She was going to say something angry about that, too: holding Boyo over her head to keep her playing nicely. Even as her lips parted there was a thump from the room next door, the spacious media room with the comfy couch and the big screen. Just a discrete thump, maybe just the robot vacuum ramming the wall with untoward force, except she couldn't hear its whine and there wasn't anyone else in the apartment. Even the security men stayed outside.

The security men hadn't been outside when she opened the door to Wiley. It had only been Wiley's professionally polished smile that smoothed the transition, that had stopped Carole thinking of it.

She backed off, and Wiley was reaching out a hand, saying, "Carole, wait—!"

Illogically, she fled *into* the room the noise had come from, because the alternative would be standing there with whatever Jennifer Wiley actually was. She only got as far as the doorway, seeing it slide open to a scene of carnage.

There were three men there, dressed in mottled grey fatigues, faces hidden by hoods, by goggles. They had come in through the window – there was a circular hole cut there that had set off none of the expensive alarms she'd been told the place came with. They had come with guns, bulky pistols with noise-reducers, as subtle as death could get when it came out of a barrel. The guns were on the floor and so were they.

For a moment she couldn't even see the others, even though they took up most of the room. The smell gave them away, in that close space. A sharp smell, not even an animal smell, because 'animal smell' usually meant mammals.

There were three of them, too. They were Bioforms, dragon-models, their skins shifting under the lights, blurring them against the walls as though they were nothing but thick glass. Their yellow eyes stood out, the ivory of their shark teeth. She imagined them scaling the glass tower like geckos, even as the gunmen had rappelled down from the roof.

"Miss Springer, g'day," one of them said in a polite, female-sounding voice, a strongly Antipodean accent. Its lipless mouth gaped to let the words out, the skin of its throat rippling to make the sounds.

She tried to back off but Wiley was at her elbow. For a moment Carole was going to panic, too much change, too little control. But she was used to that. It had been her job to turn chaos into order on demand.

"He sent them." The men, who she guessed were dead.

"As I said, your headware is the clincher. They'd have

made sure not to leave it in a readable state. A last desperate attempt. Thankfully the WSRF had a few assets they could send over to clean up. Makes a change from disaster relief, but so much of the Bioform engineering is rooted in their original military role. I'd like to show you something, if I could?"

"Show me...?" Carole made a weak gesture at the bodies.

"Not these. I'd hoped you wouldn't even see them. I apologise that you have." Said so blandly, no admission to three deaths on anyone's conscience. "We'll take them away, clean up, fix the window even. Nobody will know." And, at Carole's look, "If you're thinking that they'll accuse our illegal killers of having killed their illegal killers, it's the sort of jurisprudent paradox nobody's going to be bringing to court. It was when they made it all within the laws that they were strong, because the laws were their laws and always favoured them." And of course she herself, or the thing she represented, had been banned by those laws, forced underground. "But without that shield, we're just as strong. Stronger."

And the three dragon models were taking the bodies, the guns, just taking them away, and Carole wondered where the guards at the door had gone, who had suborned or bribed or killed them. And all the while Jennifer was just setting up something with her tablet so that the big screen came on suddenly, showing a view on a room from a high corner.

Thompson.

Carole started away from the screen. If it had been at a regular angle, looking at him across a desk like one of his addresses, she wouldn't have been able to face him. She was looking down, though, as if he was at the bottom of a pit.

He wasn't alone, sitting in a bare room with a man she recognised as one of his regular legal team. An attack dog, was how other lawyers described the man, though he was human enough.

Wiley did something and there was sound, the lawyer's low voice, Thompson's grunt replies. Carole knew the situation instantly, felt a sudden pang that she wasn't there for him. Because the lawyer was talking to him all wrong. Because Thompson needed her to intercede, to be the buffering layer between his naked ego and the world. In the next moment she loathed herself for the thought, but that didn't mean it wasn't a part of her.

The lawyer broke off mid-sentence, hand lifted close to his ear to indicate he was receiving a communication. Wiley was grinning, five years younger in that moment.

"He's finding out that Mars is finished for him," she explained.

"Mars...?"

"His retreat. He sent his mind there, the man who would be God-king, right? You know this more than anyone, Carole. You were there through all the planning he did with the late and unlamented Doc Felorian. But we had a secret weapon on Mars, it turns out. There's nothing left of him on the red planet except bad memories. Look, he's being told so, now."

Carole could see the lawyer trying to spin it as something they could use, but Thompson was on his feet instantly, slamming his meaty hands against the table, the bang coming to her distantly, the flinch running through her only an echo of how she'd once felt. He was raging, furious. Practically foaming. "What about her?" he was demanding. "They

should have fixed her by now! Get her! Stop her!" Eyes
bulging as though he was about to go into cardiac arrest.

I'm the 'her', Carole thought numbly. And one last part
of her tried to suggest that she should want herself fixed,
if Thompson said to fix her, but she confronted it and it
shrivelled inside her and was gone.

"We've sent word, of course, to say his goons got theirs,
rather than getting you. Look, this is it coming through now.
All properly anonymous but he'll know." And Wiley's grin
was wide and spreading, weirdly infectious.

Thompson was staring at the desk, fingers crooked as
though trying to claw into the metal surface. The lawyer
was saying not to admit anything, not to speak about things
that would put his legal counsel in an awkward position, but
Thompson wasn't hearing him. Thompson was digesting the
news that Carole was still out there, very much alive and very
much going to ensure that the last of his veils and lies would
be stripped away.

She watched him roar at the lawyer until the man just
backed out of the room and away. She watched him try to
pick up the desk, but he could barely shift it. She watched his
puffy, crimson face as he bellowed and screamed and attacked
the walls, a festering knot of fear and hate with nobody left
to do its bidding. And, after a minute of this, she felt that he
was growing further away, or perhaps just growing smaller,
becoming something minuscule and irrelevant, like a dying
germ under a microscope. Something she'd been immunised
against. Something she'd been purged of.

She sat on the couch, still watching. The smile that slowly
made its way onto her face wasn't like Wiley's grin, or anyone
else's, but just her own.

28

JIMMY

Some time after, Danny Boyd calls me up and invites me to a little gathering he's having. A soiree, you might say. Stargazing, only 'cos what we're watching is on the other side of the planet it's all through screens. But then I spend enough time slogging about outside on Mars. Some nights it's good to stay in.

He treats me weird, does our Danny Boy. Like I saved his life and sanity or something. He was the first and the last, after all. He was the top of the Thompson pyramid. He lived in that hell longer than anyone. And mine was the first face he saw as a free man, poor bastard, and so somehow I get the credit. Even though my job was involuntary bear storage and transport.

Involuntary Bear Storage and Transport: The Jimmy Marten Story.

Anyway, it's been almost a month and Hell City survived. Who'da put money on it? Damage all fixed, even that big hole in Cashiers, and everything back to normal. For better or worse, because a lot of people reckoned we'd stuck it to the man and it was all clover and communism from there on. Except the man we'd stuck it to wasn't the same as the man who paid our wages, and so after the dust cleared (always takes a while here on Mars) we somehow amazingly didn't have a Glorious Worker's Paradise where every comrade was equal. We just got back to work.

Well, I mean, almost. I mean, I don't know if Dan the Man wrangled something back home or if he always had the leeway and never used it or if he's being what they call economical with the truth, but he's made a few changes. There's a whole slice of the upper levels of the city, that were in their shrink wrap finest before everything kicked off, that he's opened up for living space. No more nooks. Bit of room, bit of privacy. Can have a couple of guys over and watch the game. But mostly it's just what it was before, and some day we'll be done and Hell City will be handed over to the folk back home who paid for it. And we'll get to see if we, the Martians, get turned back into Earth people to go home and enjoy our completion bonus. Or if we even want to. I don't even want to think about acclimatising to the gravity and the pressure and the sunlight. Sounds like hard work to me. Might just stay on.

Anyways, I head on over to what's going to be some corporation's big meeting room, that's got a skylight giving onto the canopy-blurred stars, and that's got the biggest screen I ever saw. Danny's there, and he's got a select little gathering. There's Sugar, Murder and Marmalade, and there's about nine bears' worth of space between them and Rufus and some of the Posse. There's a bunch of Admin staff and the heads of some of the work crews. There's Brian Dey too, the useless bastard. Given that his cover got blown, I guess he's here in his formal capacity as ambassador. Saint Bees' apostle to the Martians.

We're here to watch the rockets.

It's quite a show, a round hundred of them shooting off one by one from hidden silos beneath the Martian surface, on the other side of this world. I don't get any sense of scale but Brian tells me they're not big. They're carrying a handful of frozen cyborg bees and a crapton of data, so most of what we're seeing is engine and reactor fuel. And they don't even need much of that, because it's easy to get shot of Mars and its weak-sauce gravity, and once they're in space they've got ion drives or some damn space nonsense to get them across the Great Empty the slow way. Because Bees doesn't care about time. "Bees got all the time the universe got," as Brian says.

"So she went without you?" I ask him, and he laughs in my face, which I guess is what I deserve.

"Nope. Bees upload me 'fore the troubles," he tells me. "Me, Mariah, Judit, we on all those rockets right now. We goin' to the stars, man."

"But..." Danny Boy's handed out some booze, something home-grown and punchy, and so I'm fighting to wrap my head around what he's saying. "But you'll never know what they find out there."

"True 'nuff," Brian agrees philosophically. "I never know, but I know that *I* know, that other I. Best I gon' get."

I do something then I've not done for a couple of weeks, because I've been going cold turkey in a way, though not from drugs. I wait for Honey to say something, in my head. She'd have an opinion, like she always fucking did. She was an upload, after all. And she'd been many uploads, for just a short amount of time. She had it all, and she gave it away.

And of course there's nothing from Honey.

Sugar's looking at me with bright eyes. "You're thinking

about a bear. You get her look, when you do. About the mouth."

I shrug. "Maybe."

"Don't be so sure she's gone," she says flatly.

"Jesus, don't tell me that."

"I'm just saying, I keep good eyes on the dataflow in Admin. Better than Boyd over there. My livelihood, right? Something was rummaging through comms history recently. Pretty damn thorough but didn't cover its tracks quite well enough. Or didn't care enough to."

"Meaning what?"

Sugar looks sidelong and then leans in. I'm maybe the only guy in Hell City short enough she doesn't have to stand on tiptoe to whisper in my ear.

"Honey came in as data. She got logged somewhere. Or if not here, at point of transmission. Maybe a copy clogging a buffer somewhere. Some Honey from after she got shot, before she hit Mars. So maybe Bees took her to the stars after all. We'll never know."

"Stars I'm fine with. So long as she ain't *here*." Because we owe Honey everything, and if she came back it could cost us it all.

Danny comes over and claps us on the shoulders. And he's Big Chief Admin but he's OK, is Danny. OK so long as he thinks he owes me, anyway. He doles out more of the rotgut and slips me a tab of Stringer because Admin is high-stress and he and I see eye to eye about just how to take the edge off that. 'Cept he gets his slipped into the shipments from Earth, rather than the shit they brew here on Mars. How the other half live, eh?

And we watch the rockets, Earth's ambassadors to other

stars, that will be centuries in transit, arriving long after we're all dead. And years after that before they report back to a fully functional Hell City, to the new colonies we'll probably be building on the moons of Jupiter or somewhere, with workers even more fucked up than they made us. And Bees will use what she finds out there to make more Bees and make more rockets, and there will be bug-eyed aliens out there, but they'll be our bugs. And maybe I'll ask Brian if I can get a seat on the boat, for the next wave of launches. I reckon I've earned it. I reckon I have sufficient Bees-credit to buy a ticket out, even though I'll also stay right here on Mars.

We watch the rockets launch, we shirkers and criminals, lawmen and administrators. It feels weird, thinking about where they're going. Feels like we're taking one giant step; like we're growing up.